Advance praise for
RED LILY

". . . a masterfully written, whimsical spy thriller set in Paris just before the Cold War fizzles and the Berlin Wall crumbles . . . . With its firm grasp of the period and punchy, believable dialogue, *Red Lily* is an irresistible offering . . . . **Highly recommended** for fans of Mick Herron's *Slow Horses* and Linwood Barclay's *Never Saw It Coming.*"
— *BlueInk Reviews* **(starred review)**

". . . an intoxicating blend of espionage, family intrigue, and historical reflection . . . . Graham weaves a story that is both thrilling and deeply human. . . . One of the novel's greatest strengths is its protagonist, Lily—a woman whose past is as layered and complex as the secrets she has spent a lifetime guarding. Though she fits into the tradition of the wily older female sleuth, à la Miss Marple or Jessica Fletcher, Lily's story is uniquely her own . . . . This is historical suspense at its finest."
— *Los Angeles Book Review*

"... Graham does a remarkable job of building suspense throughout her novel ... a striking balance of excitement, humor, and sincerity, perfect for anyone seeking a lively, twisty adventure."
— *Kirkus Reviews*

**Praise for
Janice Graham's novels**

FIREBIRD

A *New York Times* and international bestseller

"*Firebird* is the debut of a major writer. A tender and beautifully written adult love story."
—**Mary Higgins Clark**

"What a page-turner! Not only believable and compelling, but well-written enough to satisfy fans of the likes of Alice Hoffman and Barbara Kingsolver."
— **Eileen Goudge, author of *Garden of Lies***

"Graham is an astute chronicler of sentiment and motive ... (her) dexterous storytelling pulls at the heartstrings."
— *Publishers Weekly*

THE TAILOR'S DAUGHTER

"Graham is always and abundantly a good time . . . the sheer generosity of her invention, and her unfailing ability to create believable characters of every ilk, from the tepid to the grotesque, are nothing short of stunning."
— ***Kirkus Reviews***

"A stunning novel about a complicated and beguiling young woman . . . [with] moments of almost unbearable yearning, truth, and beauty."— **Luanne Rice, author of *Last Night***

ROMANCING MISS BRONTË
(Written as Juliet Gael)

"A moving view of a literary giant and the emotion that fueled her work." — ***Booklist***

"A must-read for Brontë aficionados and anyone interested in the lives and concerns of Victorian women."
— ***Kirkus***

Also by Janice Graham

NOVELS

Firebird
Sarah's Window
Safe Harbour
The Tailor's Daughter

Romancing Miss Brontë
(Written as Juliet Gael)

FEATURE FILM SCREENWRITING CREDITS

Until September (MGM)

Red Lily is a work of fiction. Names, characters, places, and incidents are the product of the author's imagination or are used fictitiously, and any resemblance to actual persons, living or dead, business establishments, events, or locales is entirely coincidental.

Copyright © 2025 by Janice Graham

All rights reserved. No part of this text may be reproduced, scanned, or transmitted in any form without written permission of the copyright owner except for the use of quotations in a book review.

First edition 2025
Cover and interior design by Claire Brown
Published by Vendome Books
ISBN: 979-8-9921747-0-0 (eBook)
ISBN: 979-8-9921747-2-4 (paperback)
ISBN 979-8-9921747-1-7 (hardcover)

www.janicegraham.com

*For my dear friend, Jan Ryon
And in memory of Les Ryon*

RED LILY

JANICE GRAHAM

PROLOGUE

DEATH ON THE RUE TONTON
PARIS 1989

Paris languished in the August heat, the streets deserted except for the usual tourists and a few remaining Parisians plodding slowly along their routine paths. Pet owners dragged unhappy dogs to the corner and back indoors, where fans whirred behind shuttered windows until night fell and a breeze cooled things down. In the evening, when the holdouts on the upper floors watered the flowers in their window boxes, the cool water dripped onto the hot pavement, where it lay in warm puddles and was gone by morning.

The Rue Tonton, even more deserted than most streets, given its obscurity (it figured on only the most detailed maps of the 6th *arrondissement*), snoozed away like a tightly packed herd of sheep in the sweltering sun. It was certainly not the best time and place for a medical emergency, seeing that ambulance drivers and doctors were all on holiday at the beach, but whoever plans that sort of thing? Having lived on the street since time immemorial, the old lady was undoubtedly thinking if she could just make it home and out of the killer heat, the malaise would pass. Sadly, she got as far as the antique store, only a few steps from the entrance to her apartment building, let out a faint cry and fell to her knees, toppling an Empire chair and a gilded Italian frame that the antique dealer had set out on the sidewalk to attract business, such as it was. There was no little irony in the fact that the only one who heard her cry and came rushing to her side was the antique dealer himself, who, only days before, had publicly vowed in a very loud voice to smoke her out of her home with his newly installed pizza oven, the exhaust of which happened to be the most recent bone of contention between the two. His acrimonious relationship with the woman on the third floor sometimes took on the flavor of an old married couple who could neither live with or without each other—an opinion, or you might say piece of propaganda, put forth by the owner of the Russian bookstore across the street.

Vladimir watched the scene from the shop window, suspicion lurking in his pinpricked blue eyes. With few to no customers, he spent a lot of time at the window fabricating things to be suspicious about.

"He's finally done it," he murmured to the young salesclerk at his elbow.

"Done what?"

"Murdered her."

The girl, a student of Slavic studies at the Sorbonne, pressed closer to the window. "It looks to me like he's trying to help."

"It's a ruse," Vladimir said with a grimness that carried a

note of glee. "How convenient he happened to be open today, so he could pretend to come to her rescue."

It was true that no one took the antique store very seriously, since the only hours the dealer kept were his own, which were a mystery to everyone, himself included. He was forever accumulating more antiques and rarely sold a thing. With his dense crown of silver hair concealing a missing ear, and his powerful rolling stride, the fellow resembled a hulking mad scientist. He was a contradiction in terms, a sociable hermit who opened his shop only when the mood seized him. On his more affable days he might sit down at the battered Pleyel piano at the back of his store and perform a lightly improvised Erik Satie for no one in particular, and when he was deep in his cups, he'd invite a customer to pull up a chair and entertain them with tales of his misadventures, which, if not exactly illegal, certainly implied a thorough contempt for the law.

"Do you think she's dead? She isn't moving."

Vladimir shrugged.

"Should we call an ambulance?"

"We mustn't get involved," he warned in a low voice.

"But how could he have murdered her? He was inside when she collapsed."

"There are ways," he replied with a hint of a smirk.

They watched as the antique dealer gathered the woman into his arms and carried her inside.

"Wow," the girl said. "He's strong."

"I tell you, he murdered her."

"You're so paranoid."

"How do you think he lost that ear?"

There were all sorts of rumors to answer that—most of

them floated by the antique dealer himself, all of them very colorful.

"You're always saying they used to be lovers," the girl said.

"All the more reason for murder."

They were distracted by a phone call from a customer inquiring about a very particular translation of Maxim Gorky's novel *Mother*, which had to be looked up in the catalog and then ordered, and by the time they had finished the business, an ambulance had already pulled up in the street and a sheet-shrouded body was being maneuvered into the back on a stretcher. The burly antique dealer looked on with a childish helplessness, then, after a few words with the medics, he quickly moved the Empire chair inside, drew down the rattling metal shutter over the storefront, fastened the lock and climbed into the back of the ambulance.

"I can't believe it," the girl declared in astonishment. "She died. Just like that. How awful."

"The deed has been done," Vladimir said with finality. "Now get back to work."

Vladimir went home a few hours later, leaving the girl to lock up. The incident had left her shaken. As a student of Russian literature, she was familiar with dark, nihilistic stories and tortured characters, but this was the first time anyone had died right under her nose. As she crossed the street on her way home, she noticed the lady's sunglasses lying on the sidewalk. She thought she should retrieve them and return them to the antique dealer, but what would be the point of that? The woman certainly wouldn't be coming back for them. With a long glance she took in the narrow street. Not a soul stirred; the bakery on the corner was shuttered, the café terrace of Le Petit Verlaine deserted. A fan whirred in one of the apartments overhead. A sudden movement caught her eye when a man sporting a white clerical collar stepped out of the café at the corner, took a swift look around and then retreated back inside again. Finally, at a loss as to what to do with the sunglasses, which were very stylish, she slipped them on. If she were in a Russian novel, she knew this moment would have great significance, but for the life of her she couldn't think what it might be.

CHAPTER 1

ORLANDO, FLORIDA
SEVERAL DAYS LATER

The news of my aunt's death had come as quite a shock. Mainly because I believed her to be already dead. My parents had only ever spoken of her in the past tense, like a mishap one has almost managed to forget, but not entirely.

I was telling Mimi about it as we sat on a park bench in the hot Florida sun, gazing out over Epcot's World Showcase Lagoon. She sipped a Coke while I explained that I had been summoned to Paris to attend the funeral of an aunt I had never met and who had bequeathed to me some small piece of property.

"She is rich?"

"I don't believe so."

I withdrew from my briefcase the envelope addressed to me, *Mister Carl Box*, Esq., and showed the contents to Mimi. There was a letter in English that sounded as if it had been composed in the previous century, with a closing entreating me "to accept my civilities the most honorable," signed by someone with *notaire* below his name. Folded inside was a plane ticket.

"It's for the day after tomorrow."

"Première classe? Mon dieu."

I could feel my father rising up from his grave. He strongly disapproved of wastefulness.

"It just strikes me as so unreasonable. Expecting me to fly off on a moment's notice."

Truth be told, I had a week's vacation coming up for which I had no plans. I was perfectly content to stick around and explore Disney World's new attractions. Maybe entice Mimi to meet me some evening at the Biergarten. Besides, the letter had been so oddly worded that I couldn't figure out exactly what I was to inherit. Surely my presence was not required.

"Don't you want to go?" she asked.

"I don't see why I need to," I said. "These things can be handled perfectly well over the telephone."

Saddling me with a piece of property in a foreign land seemed like a bit of mischief on my aunt's part. My father would have said it was typical of the sort of trouble she caused. For all I knew, I could be inheriting legal disputes and debts.

"Do you not want to see Paris?"

"I can see Paris just fine from where I am. Look, there's the Eiffel Tower. And there's the Seine."

"It's a lagoon."

"And China is just a short stroll away."

"That is a faux China."

This was the sort of argument I warmed to. "Ah, Mimi, there is faux, and then there is—" I gestured with the envelope in my hand "—*this*. Just look at the Morocco Pavilion. I dare anyone to call that faux."

My father and I had had a long and very successful working relationship with the Walt Disney Company in California, but Epcot Center's World Showcase in Orlando was in a league of its own. I'd already told Mimi the story of how King Hassan II had sent his best artisans all the way from Morocco to design the mosaics for the pavilion. The company never ceased to impress me with their extraordinary attention to detail and devotion to authenticity. For a man in my profession, details were everything.

I adjusted my sunglasses and gestured again, this time to the west. "And Italy is only a few minutes away, just past Japan and the United States."

"Monsieur Box, you really must get on more in the world."

"It's 'get out,' Mimi," I offered gently. I wouldn't hurt her feelings for the world, but she insisted I correct her English. "Not 'get on.'"

"English is very difficult."

"You've made tremendous progress. I'm very proud of you."

She pressed the ticket back into my hand.

"You must to go, Monsieur Box. How is it possible to throw up a chance like this?"

I tried not to smile. "I think you mean 'throw away.'"

She frowned. She was a very conscientious student. "Yes, I am sorry, throw *away*."

I could feel a rivulet of sweat run down my back. It wasn't even noon and the temperature was pushing one hundred degrees. "Is it hot in Paris in August?"

"The weather in Paris is very..." She hesitated; I could see her struggling with all those syllables. "Unpredictable."

"Could I wear my shorts?"

"I think for Paris your pants is better. Or a jean."

I was going to correct her again but I didn't want to be too heavy-handed—I was afraid she might lose heart. She was over here on a yearlong visa, one of hundreds of college students from their native countries employed as cultural ambassadors by the Epcot World Showcase. She was sharply critical of our use of air-conditioning, which she found excessive, and our fondness for supersized portions, but she loved the diversity of the experience, meeting people from all over the world. That had been the point I was trying to make. I didn't see why I needed to travel when I worked here.

I unwrapped a stick of chewing gum and popped it in my mouth. I was trying to cut down, but my nerves were winning out.

"Do you have a passport?" she asked.

"I do. The problem is, I don't know what to do with Billy. Would you take him for me?"

There weren't many people I'd trust to take care of Billy, not after the trauma he'd been through. Mimi had witnessed the horrifying incident, she was the one who had held me by the ankles as I hung over the edge of the bank and fished the stray pup out of the Epcot lagoon just in time to save his life, but not in time to save his back legs. The alligator kept those, long digested by now. It had been a bonding experience for the three of us.

"Oh, Monsieur Box," she said, "we can't have the pets in the dormitory. I'm very sorry."

She insisted on calling me Monsieur Box, which made me feel much older than my mere thirty-four years, which I suppose is old to a twenty-one-year-old. I think if she had ever once called me Carl, I might have asked her to have dinner with me. Instead we just met up from time to time, for a cappuccino in Italy or a beer at an English pub, or sometimes, like today, on a Paris park bench overlooking the shimmering waters of the lagoon that had lost a little of its romance after I'd seen what terrors lurked in its depths. Mimi, who worked in the boulangerie at the France Pavilion, always brought croissants, or a *pain au chocolat*, which I used to call a chocolate croissant until I learned better, or, like today, a sandwich on a crusty baguette. And she always asked about Billy.

"I couldn't bear to leave him in a kennel. I'm afraid he wouldn't get the care he needs."

"But you can take Billy with you."

There was a flake of bread clinging to her bottom lip. She licked it off with the tip of her tongue and then brushed over her mouth with the tips of her fingers. The gesture must have lasted all of two seconds, but it was enough to make me lose my train of thought.

"Uh, yes . . . oh, no, I couldn't do that."

"But you must. He will be going home. Imagine how happy he will be."

Billy, we had discovered, spoke French—or rather that was the language he responded to. I thought he might be French Canadian. Mimi, who was the expert, insisted he was from France.

"Would they let me take him on the plane?"

"Air France? *Mais bien sûr.*" There was an air of Gallic triumph in the way she said it, lifting her chin and pursing her lips, which I found very endearing. She looked just like Leslie

Caron in *Gigi* playing opposite that sly old charmer Maurice Chevalier. "Dogs are welcome everywhere in France. In the restaurants, in the shops, even at the Métro if you carry him in a bag."

"Even dogs like Billy?"

This time she gave one of those shrugs the Brasserie's chef was famous for, along with his *soupe à l'oignon*. I felt myself weakening. If anyone could persuade me, it was Mimi.

"Ah, Billy will be the star," she said. "You will see. Everybody will love our Billy."

I wished he was *our* Billy, but as far as I could make out, he was just mine.

CHAPTER 2

Three days later I stood in the lounge of a small and very luxurious Paris hotel where the *notaire* had reserved a room for me, with Billy under my arm, wondering what my father would say about such extravagance. Despite the assurance by the front desk that the bill would be handled by another party, I couldn't help but wonder if I would somehow end up paying for it. My aunt, I had learned when I checked in earlier that morning, had been well known here, although I could not imagine how and in what capacity she had frequented such a place. It was like walking into a Visconti film set in the 1800s, an old-world drama shot in Technicolor, all lush, plush, tasseled and draped in fire brick red, honeyed light bouncing off crystal tumblers, walls hung with historical mementos, and a sea of books that seemed to be trying to make a point. I heard the tinkling sound of cocktails being mixed somewhere in the background, although it was early in the afternoon, and the only guests seemed to be a few solitary businessmen in suits working quietly in secluded corners.

My worries about Billy had been completely unfounded—he

had been accommodated without so much as the bat of an eye. I had decided to introduce him as my companion dog, hoping I wouldn't be required to declare some incapacity since it was obvious Billy was the incapacitated one, and I'd been ready to argue my case, but none of this was necessary. The bellhop even showed up at my door a few minutes later with food and water dishes and a plush dark cyan-blue dog bed, along with a map showing directions to a small treed square just a block away, where I could walk him. The reception also volunteered the names and phone numbers of several dog-walkers who could tend to Billy while I was out. Their attentiveness relieved my conscience. I had learned thrift from a sternly frugal father who had not become wealthy by throwing away money on lavish hotels, but Billy clearly had no such reservations. When I placed his bed on the floor near the window, he wagged his feather of a tail, dragged himself across the room and curled up on the plush pillow, then turned his eyes up to me with such contentment, I began to think that Mimi was right. He had come home. For all I know, Billy had once belonged to an aristocrat. But I digress.

    I had intended to take a short nap but slept straight through my alarm, and it was midafternoon by the time I went down to the lounge, where I ordered coffee to clear my head so I could decide my next move. I had called the *notaire* upon arrival and left a message asking to meet in the afternoon to discuss my aunt's will. My call had still not been returned, but when the waiter brought my coffee, he slipped me a sealed envelope that had just been left for me at the front desk. Inside was an address, a door code and three keys attached to a miniature Eiffel Tower keyring. Not a word of explanation. I presumed this had come from the *notaire*, but when I went to the reception and dialed his office, once again I got an answering machine. This time, I passed the receiver to the desk clerk and asked him to translate the voice recording for me.

"The *cabinet* is closed for the month of August, sir. They will reopen on the eleventh of September."

I hung up and took another look at the envelope. There was no return address, only my name and that of the hotel, handwritten, hastily from what I could tell.

"Who delivered this?"

"It was a courier, sir," he said, and added, perhaps because I looked as if I might run after him, "I believe he came by motorcycle."

I figured this must be the address of the property, and that I was to visit the place unattended. I heaved a deep sigh of frustration followed by a yawn. It was nearly past four in the afternoon, and I was only beginning to wake up. Why had they gone to such expense to get me over here and then not bothered to meet me?

All this laxity made me very nervous, and I found myself fishing a stick of gum out of my pocket while scolding my dead aunt for such sloppy estate planning. I was beginning to get an idea of why my father, who had been a meticulous planner all his life, might have wished to shield us from her influence. There had been just the three of us—Dad, Mom and me—and with the exception of a few hiccups, life and death had proceeded along a sound and orderly path. Taxes had been filed, mortgages paid off, investments placed with just the right degree of risk versus reward. They had become parents at a late age, and their deaths, within two years of each other, had left me with a comfortable sum of money and loneliness to match.

I offered the bellboy a reasonable tip and showed him how to attach Billy's wheels, then I set off for the address on the note, which the desk clerk assured me was only a few blocks from the hotel.

I walked briskly, hoping to give the impression that I knew where I was going. I've never liked to draw attention to myself, and I felt ridiculously exposed in my brand-new Nikes and fresh white polo shirt, when everyone I'd seen from the taxi on the way in from the airport looked wilted and resigned, which I suppose was the only way to look in a big city in August. The only person I passed, an elderly lady in a faded purple bucket hat lugging a large plastic jug of liquid laundry detergent, seemed not in the least interested in me, neither did a skinny young man pacing in front of a doorway and smoking nervously.

The weather had changed and now ghost white clouds moved slowly across the slate roofs, casting a blinding silvery light on the face of the buildings lining the street, all uniform and yet distinct from one another. The air smelled of rain, and I realized I hadn't brought an umbrella. I don't think I even owned one.

The directions were simple enough to follow, and along the way I kept returning to the question that had been worrying me from the first, which was why my aunt had named me benefactor in her will. Surely she had a favorite charity, or a church that would have gladly taken possession of her worldly goods. I certainly didn't need them. The fact that she even knew how to reach me I found curious. My father had always discouraged any questions about her. I had never actually seen a photograph of her until after my father's death, when my mother dug out an old photo album and nervously, as if he were still standing over her shoulder, pointed her out in a black-and-white photo of the three of them taken at the end of the war, my father proud in his naval uniform and my mother in a breezy floral dress with her head resting on his shoulder. Next to them stood my aunt in loose trousers like they wore in the late forties, her hair in a bandanna much like the old posters I'd seen of Rosie the Riveter. Tall, rail thin, hands on hips and legs planted apart, looking tough and bellicose except for the smile that dazzled. She must have been a teenager at the end of the war, but I could easily imagine her on the assembly line building a B-17 or operating a turret lathe. I had been surprised to discover she was beautiful.

The Rue Tonton stretched quiet and treeless from a café on the corner to the end of the block where it intersected with another quiet, treeless street. I passed a few shuttered shops and found number twenty-one, an entrance built for carriages in a previous century, tall and arched with a heavy wooden door that clicked open when I coded in the number. I could just make out an elevator at the back of a long, dark entry hall, a cagelike contraption retrofitted into the stairwell. Prudently, I opted for the stairs.

A sense of the surreal had gripped me upon my arrival at the airport, but the nap and brisk walk had put me right again. I found myself humming as I climbed the stairs, and smiling for no reason whatsoever. This happened to me often—cheerfulness seemed to cling to me in the same way that unshakable depression hung like a cloud over others. I often wondered if something might be wrong with me—even during the difficult years with my parents' illnesses and deaths, and then my divorce, there had been moments when life seemed to me just plain beautiful. The giddiness seized me most often when I was alone, when no one was watching me, that's when I would give myself over to completely irrational behavior. I sang, I shuffled and spun—not quite John Travolta, more like a shadow of Fred Astaire. I could be insufferably good-natured at times. And so here I was climbing a dim, stuffy stairwell, humming "The Look of Love" and wondering what I would find.

The building inside wore an air of dusty neglect; the stair carpet had been worn threadbare in places, and on one of the recessed window ledges mid-flight between the floors stood a withered potted plant that no one had thought to throw away, perhaps because it had become useful as an ashtray—someone had even gone so far as to design a heart with cigarette butts in the dry soil. On the next window ledge there was an empty plastic bottle with the rim cut off—left for watering the plant on the floor below, I imagined, and now a depository for little bits of paper trash. I expected my aunt's apartment would be the same. Derelict and with the untidiness one comes to expect from old age. Nevertheless, the building appeared to be situated in a prime location, which should make the property easy to sell. I had already determined I would set the price low.

My aunt's apartment was on the third floor. There were three keys on the ring and two locks on the door. The problem was that none of the keys fit either lock. I was fumbling through yet another attempt when suddenly there were loud clicks from the inside and the door was swung open by a very large and impressively tall gray-haired African lady cradling a cereal bowl in one hand. A TV played in the background, and the look on her face made me think I'd interrupted her favorite soap opera.

I stuttered a greeting. "Hello, uh . . ." I smiled congenially and she glared right back. "Uh, bonjour," I repeated, thinking I should make some effort to speak the language.

"I'm . . . is . . . is my aunt home?"

Well, of course she wasn't. It's only that I was taken by surprise. I hadn't expected to find the apartment occupied, and I didn't know how to introduce myself. I wished I'd learned the word for *nephew*.

Finally I blurted out, "I'm Carl Box."

Her brow furrowed. Never had I seen consternation so severe.

I pulled the note from my pocket, unfolded it and showed her the address, *21 Rue Tonton, 3rd floor*. Then I dangled the little green Eiffel Tower key ring in front of her.

"My aunt . . . Mrs. Box. Lillian . . ."

Now her puzzlement turned into a fierce scowl.

"Lillian Box." I pointed a finger at my chest. "I'm her nephew."

The astonishment this elicited made me think we were getting somewhere. I gave her my best engaging smile.

"Her nephew." I poked my chest again.

In a lightning quick movement, the woman snatched the keys from my hand and slammed the door in my face. Before I had a chance to react, I heard the sound of locks latching on the inside.

I stared bewildered at the door. Would she come back?

Was she going to make a call and confirm my story? I waited a moment and then knocked on the door.

"Excuse me... ma'am, miss, madame. There must be some misunderstanding. Please . . . open the door." When I didn't get a reply, I began to pound loudly. Maybe if I made a racket someone would come to my rescue to sort all this out. No doors opened. No one appeared. The building, like the city, appeared to be deserted.

I stood for the longest time wondering what had just happened. What was I to do? Call the police? What would I say to them?

Rather than make an even bigger fool of myself, I decided to return to the hotel and ask for their help. Perhaps they could make some calls. Track the courier who had delivered the message. Clearly, I'd been given the wrong address.

But if it was the wrong address, why on earth had she snatched the keys? And if it was the right address, who was in the apartment?

CHAPTER 3

Back at my hotel I was assisted by the uniformed concierge, a mannerly gentleman who listened to my story, took a look at the note, and then, with a kindliness I hadn't expected, asked me, "You took the stairs?"

"Yes."

"You did not take the elevator."

"No."

"How many floors did you walk up?"

"To the third floor."

"Forgive me, sir, I mean to say, 'flight of stairs,' is that not the correct term?"

"Well, then two."

He smiled sympathetically. "We count floors differently. We start with the ground floor, the next is the first floor. That would be the second floor to you."

"So I had the wrong floor."

"I'm afraid you did, sir."

"But then why . . . ?"

I didn't bother to finish the question. It was all too absurd for words.

I thanked the concierge and headed back to my room, where I found Billy curled on his Prussian blue bed near the window, staring up at me with his head on his front paws and his gray flag of a tail wagging merrily, daring me to utter a word of complaint.

I could tell he would have much preferred to stay in bed, but I needed a drink and something to eat. So I picked him up and together we set off for the café I had passed on the way to my aunt's place, which I remembered as having a large pleasantly shaded terrace and plenty of empty tables. Despite the absence of customers, we waited for what seemed like a long while before the waiter made an appearance; he redeemed himself, however, by returning with a dish of water for Billy along with my glass of burgundy. It was Billy's soft whine that alerted me to the large white dog lurking in the doorway. Mimi had explained that I might run into one of these *chiens du patron*, the café owner's dog, which I assumed to be the case since he didn't seem to be too bothered by strangers on his turf. After straining his big head in our direction and giving us a thorough sniff inspection, he turned back inside in a manner I could only describe as haughty.

I directed my comment to Billy under the table. "We've been snubbed."

Billy couldn't have cared less. Ears up, posed jauntily on what was left of his backside, his nose read the air as if it were a gossip column. He could tell me who had been here before us, their gender, where they'd come from, what they'd had to eat and drink, how long ago they'd left. I envied him his perspicacity. I had foolishly jetted off to Paris at my deceased aunt's bidding—half-cocked, as my father would have said, assuming I would find answers to the most simple questions: What had I inherited and how could I dispose of it as quickly and painlessly as possible? But then, how could I have possibly imagined such a fiasco? Now what was I to do? Wait two weeks until the lawyer returned from vacation? Out of the question. This was a riddle I had to solve.

Even as a child I was obsessed with solving problems. Sometimes when my father had misplaced one of the tools in his workshop, he'd call me down to the basement to help him find it. He knew I wouldn't give up, no matter how long it took—even if Mother was calling down the stairs that dinner was growing cold. I think sometimes he'd hide something just to give me the satisfaction of finding it. I remembered how relieved he'd been the time I found his square hole drill bit. By then his memory was slipping.

Recalling those moments opened up a fresh wave of nostalgia. I still missed my parents very much. Ours had been a safe and happy home. Finding myself alone in a foreign city made me miss them all the more.

I'd brought along a postcard from the hotel, and I had just finished addressing a few lines to Mimi when I heard a man's voice asking me in English if he might borrow my pen. I turned around to see a middle-aged priest in a clerical collar sitting at a back table fanning himself with a folded newspaper.

"I say, you must think it very impertinent of me," he said. "I'd ask the waiter but he might not be back for some time. He's watching the football game, you see. European Championship. I noticed you had a pen—but only if you've finished."

"Please, be my guest," I said as I offered the pen to him, and before I knew it he'd draped his black jacket over the chair next to mine and settled at the adjoining table with his empty teacup and the newspaper folded back to frame the crossword puzzle.

"Very kind of you," he said as he took the pen with an apologetic smile and quickly filled in his answer before returning it to me.

"Please," I said. "Keep it."

"Are you quite sure?"

"Absolutely."

For a moment he appeared to struggle between returning to his crossword puzzle and engaging me in polite conversation. Finally, with a resigned sigh he removed his spectacles and massaged the bridge of his nose. He had a long, lean, austere face, the sort I associated with certain English types, and the pouches beneath his eyes gave him a melancholy appearance. It was a face that invited confessions. *I am no stranger to suffering*, it said.

"Do you do puzzles?" he asked me.

"Not that sort."

"I didn't use to. Not until I found myself with so much time on my hands."

He slipped his reading glasses into a shirt pocket, then reached into his jacket to pull out a wristwatch that was missing the band, and checked the hour.

"Nearly six. Good," he said with relief.

Looking around, he caught the waiter's eye.

"Ah, there's the fellow," he said, waving him over. "Can I offer you a drink? I've trained them to make a decent gin and tonic. You have to pay a little more but it's worth it."

I looked down at my empty glass, wondering if I had ordered red wine out of deference to some silly cliché.

"I'll take the same," I said. "And could I see the menu?"

"Try the steak and fries," the priest counseled. "You can't go wrong there."

I took his advice, mainly because I was hungry and thought a steak and fries could be whipped up even if the chef was watching the game.

A cheer went up from inside the café, and the waiter hurried back inside.

My companion was squinting at the logo on the pen I'd given him. "Your hotel?"

"Yes."

He nodded. "Not the best time of year to visit Paris, is it?"

"I'm afraid I didn't have a choice."

"So you're not on vacation?"

"My aunt died." I said it with the ease of a man unloading his woes to a total stranger he would never see again. "She lived just up the street."

"I'm very sorry," he said. "My sincere condolences." There was real empathy in his voice. Perhaps it was his spiritual training, or maybe he had chosen the priesthood because he was compassionate by nature. "Were you close to her?"

"I didn't think I was." I noticed how he kept darting surreptitious glances at the street. "Are you waiting for someone?" I asked.

My question startled him. "Why, yes, I am. In a way. Does it show?"

The sudden sharpness in his voice made me think I'd

upset him.

"Forgive me, I didn't mean to pry."

"Not at all, my good man, not at all. I'm waiting for my wife."

"Oh, so you're not Catholic."

"Catholic? Good heavens, no. Church of England." He pocketed my pen and said, "I thought I saw you earlier this afternoon."

"Yes, you may have."

He nodded thoughtfully.

"I'm Father Henry, by the way. Henry Huggins."

"Carl Box," I said, offering my hand to shake.

We slipped into a discussion of the French, whom he professed to dislike for any number of reasons, the most serious being that he could never find a cricket match on TV.

"Perhaps I should try your hotel. They might have more channels."

"I'm sure they have vacancies."

"I meant to say earlier, with regards to your aunt, God rest her soul, if you should need any spiritual guidance while you're in Paris, here's where I'm staying."

He pulled out the pen I'd given him and jotted down a phone number in the margin of his newspaper, tore it off and gave it to me.

"How long will you be in Paris?" I asked.

"Quite some time, I imagine."

"Your wife's a shopper, is she?"

The smile he gave me was a slow, sad one. He struck me as a doting type, perhaps even a little spineless, the type that would give his wife a credit card and watch helplessly as she ran up bills he couldn't pay. "She does indeed like to shop around."

My steak and fries came, and out of courtesy he let me eat, turning his attention to the occasional passerby, which he would follow with his woeful gaze while making casual observations about the city. He told me he'd accompanied his wife on more shopping trips to Paris than he cared to remember, and he pretty much knew his way around. He'd spent a lot of hours sitting in cafés with the *Daily Telegraph* and crossword puzzles.

"My wife used to be very fond of the antique store about halfway down the street here," he offered. "Although I believe it's closed now. There seems to have been an incident involving someone from the neighborhood."

I nodded, only half listening. I'd already wolfed down the steak and was finishing off the last of my crispy fries.

"Where did you say your aunt lived?" he asked.

I folded my napkin and leaned back with a sigh of satisfaction. Evening was approaching, the air was cooling, and I'd just finished a really good meal. Perhaps a dessert? A chocolate mousse would be nice. Life was beginning to feel manageable.

"My aunt? Number twenty-one."

His brows folded into a frown. "What a coincidence. That's where the lady was found."

"What lady?"

"Why, the woman who collapsed on the street. Right in front of the antique shop. I believe it was the antique dealer who found her." He turned to me in horror. "Good heavens, it wasn't your aunt—"

"It could have been. I don't know the details."

"She died? Are you quite sure?"

"My aunt? I hope so. That's the only reason I'm here."

I immediately regretted my choice of words. But for a second there, he had me doubting myself. As if he knew more than I did.

"I didn't mean it to sound like that," I apologized. "It's just that—well, I didn't know her at all. But everything has landed in my lap for some reason, and I'm not sure what I'm doing. I'm not much of a traveler, you see."

I let it rest there, although he seemed perfectly content to listen. He was the listening sort.

After a moment of silence, he said, "If I can be of any assistance, you have my phone number." He raised a hand to signal for the waiter. "Now, if I might make a suggestion. The chocolate mousse here is excellent."

I left Huggins nursing a cognac at the café and took Billy to the nearby square to let him nose around the trees. Then I tucked him back under my arm and set off for an evening stroll. A few blocks away I found just the thing I needed, or so I thought—a lively pedestrian street lined with sidewalk cafés and restaurants filled with people my own age jammed elbow to elbow, smoking, drinking, laughing, talking. It sprang up like a brightly lit carnival in the midst of a dark and silent sea. Where they had all come from I had no idea—even the rumble of noise seemed to be contained by design. I hesitated on the corner, struck by the foreignness of what I was witnessing, then finally stepped into the stream right behind a couple draped amorously over each other. The fact that I had a dog under my arm instead of a date didn't merit so much as a glance. There was just too much else to look at. I passed a trio of older Spanish guitarists strumming away savagely, trying to draw attention to themselves and not doing a very good job of it, and at another café a swarthy-looking man hawking long-stemmed red roses was weaving among the tables. I scanned the crowded terraces for an empty table, but for some reason, the idea of sitting down among them felt terrifying. They all seemed to belong here, to have sprouted from the cobblestones preprogrammed with their mannerisms and rituals. While I felt cut off and alien. A stranger in a frightfully indifferent world where everything had been stripped of its meaning, its connectivity. The moment had the same surreal quality I'd experienced upon arrival, and I felt a sudden longing for home, for the familiar faux streets of Epcot's French or Italian pavilion, for the park bench where Mimi and I met to eat ice cream, where there were no unsolved mysteries. I turned around and headed back to my hotel. Overwrought in crimson as it was, Visconti's palace held out the only promise of safety in this alien land.

A phone call had come while I was out, informing me of my aunt's funeral service tomorrow morning at 10:00 a.m. at the Crematorium of Père Lachaise Cemetery.

Back in my room, I filled Billy's dish from the plastic bag of kibble I'd packed in my suitcase; then I ordered a scotch from room service, turned up the air-conditioning and turned on the TV. The call about my aunt's funeral had eased my anxiety somewhat. I still didn't know who was leaving me these messages, but at least someone knew I was here. Someone somewhere had a playbook, albeit a faulty one. I scrolled through the sports channels looking for something, anything American—baseball, NASCAR, preseason football. All I could find was tennis and soccer. I even found a cricket match. Poor Huggins. I was beginning to feel bad about abandoning him so abruptly. It wasn't his fault. He was a lonely husband waiting for a wife he couldn't afford and looking for companionship. If anyone understood his predicament, it was me.

CHAPTER 4

The temperature had plummeted overnight and the morning air had the crispness of early autumn. I had reserved a taxi to get me to the cemetery well in advance, and I arrived with a good half hour to spare. At the entrance, I had a difficult time explaining myself to a guardian who kept insisting I buy a map of the resting places of famous people, until he understood that I had come for a burial. I bought the map anyway, as a sort of souvenir of the moment, and then followed the signs to the crematorium. The map came in handy since I was stopped by a number of tourists along the way who asked if they could have a look at it. Most of them were hunting for Jim Morrison's grave, although I did have one request for Sarah Bernhardt and another for Chopin. I myself was curious to see Oscar Wilde's grave, now that I knew he had died in the hotel where I was staying. It seems it had been a dingy, filthy place back then. I think he would have approved of the new decor.

I was not, however, prepared for the tall cylindrical smokestacks rising from behind the dome of what looked like a small Byzantine church. I suppose it was naive of me, but the sight of those tall brick towers gave me a bit of a chill. I had watched my parents being lowered into the earth, but I had walked away with the impression that they were both tucked in well for the eternal night; the thought of listening to furnaces roar for the time it would take to render my aunt to ashes was another thing entirely. I had no idea how long these things took, but if I had to wait around, at least I had my map. There were any number of dead souls I could visit while waiting for my aunt's remains.

Inside the crematorium I was approached by a solemn gentleman who also had a difficult time understanding me and thought I wanted to see their selection of urns. Eventually we got it straightened out, and he escorted me to a sleek desk where a young English-speaking woman in a trim navy dress consulted a folder and then escorted me to a small wood-paneled room with wooden pews facing a lectern. The room was empty and coldly impersonal—not a single flower arrangement had been sent, and for the time being I was the only mourner. I'd brought along a bouquet of white lilies and daisies, and the young woman thoughtfully offered to lay them on the flower stand opposite the lectern. There was another stand reserved for the urn—that too was empty. I took a seat in the front pew and waited.

The private war between my father and my aunt had always been a mystery. From obscure hints he'd dropped over the years I got the impression that she had embroiled him in some very shady activities; it might have been gambling debts, or bad investments, or extravagant living, or any number of immoral and illegal behaviors, but the exact nature of her transgressions actually had never been stated, which made her all the more mysterious. Occasionally, when I had done something to displease my father, he'd say with horror, "If you're not careful, you're going to turn out like your aunt Lillian." I still haven't quite recovered from the trauma of that threat. I rarely asked about her, and if she did come up in conversation, my father referred to her simply as that VBP, a Very Bad Person. My mother's silence on the matter was profound.

As the minutes passed I began to think it odd that no one else had appeared. Even if she had been thoroughly unlikable and had made nothing but enemies, surely someone would have found it in their heart to attend the service. I found it hard to imagine a person so odious that they inspired not even a little pity. I wished I'd bought a larger bouquet.

I was brought back to the moment by the sound of quick footsteps and urgent whispering at the rear. I turned around to see the receptionist hurrying toward me.

She said there had been a change; unfortunately, there would be no service. However, if I would please follow her outside. She seemed intent on appearing unflappable, clutching her folder tightly to her chest as she led me at a brisk clip back down the hall to the front entrance, although I could see she was as bewildered as I.

At the bottom of the long imposing staircase stood a man of considerable stature wearing a motorcycle helmet and a rumpled grimy jumpsuit that looked as if he'd just emerged from under the hood of a car. When I appeared, he withdrew an urn from a bag, flew up the stairs two by two, flipped up his visor and thrust the urn into my hands while bellowing something incomprehensible at me; then he galloped back down, hopped onto his motorcycle and roared away.

I turned to the receptionist, who appeared as shocked as I was. "What did he say?"

"He said, 'Here she is.'"

She couldn't take her eyes off the urn in my hands—it had the appearance of an antique Greek funeral vase painted with rows of dancing women and snakes slithering down the handles. A small envelope was unceremoniously Scotch-taped to the lid.

"That's all he said?"

She looked a little embarrassed and only nodded her head. I would have sworn I'd heard him mutter the word *imbecile*, but she must have censored that part.

"So, it's already done? I mean, the cremation."

She said something that I took to mean yes, although she didn't look convinced.

"Do you want your flowers?" she asked.

I thought for a moment and then said, "Perhaps you could leave them on Oscar Wilde's grave."

She said she would.

Before I got to the gate, I sat down on one of the benches on the tree-lined path and opened the envelope. Inside was the Eiffel Tower key ring with its three keys attached, along with a hand-drawn cutaway view of 21 Rue Tonton with my aunt's apartment well marked. Whoever had done it was a very talented artist—it reminded me of Michelangelo's architectural drawings I'd once seen in an exhibit, except that it had been sketched on the back of what appeared to be a utilities bill, which, judging from the emphatically bold font, was long overdue.

I confess, in a way I was a little disappointed. I knew absolutely nothing about my aunt, how she'd lived her life, if it had been a happy life or a wasted one, who she had loved, who had loved her in return. If she would be missed by anyone at all. I'd anticipated a lugubrious funeral service eulogizing a family member who'd caused my father untold grief, pretending a sorrow I didn't feel and trying to explain myself to strangers who probably didn't even know of my existence. But it might have also shed a little light on a relative who'd been entirely disowned by our family—and given how small a family it was, her sins must have been grave indeed.

Now here I was, baffled, bemused and a little relieved, sitting on a tree-shaded park bench beneath a cloudless blue sky with my aunt and the keys to her apartment. I wasn't quite sure what I was going to do with either of them, but I was making progress.

I thought I'd have the taxi drop me off at Le Petit Verlaine since it was just down the street from the apartment. I suppose I should have left the urn at the hotel first, but I'd been too jet-lagged to eat breakfast, and now all I could think of was a basket full of warm croissants and a big café au lait. I was even having visions of tiny jars of marmalade. I hadn't expected to find Huggins there—I wouldn't have thought his wife would be out shopping this early, but there he was at the same table at the back, peering over the top of his newspaper. He looked sincerely pleased when I pulled out a chair and sat down at the table next to him.

"Hello, Henry," I said cheerily. "Or is it *Father?*"

"Good morning, my good man, and *Henry* will do just fine."

I caught the waiter's attention and ordered, then I pulled a chair around beside me and settled the urn on it.

"I see you're fond of antiques," he said. "Like my wife."

"Is it?" I asked. "An antique?"

He folded up his newspaper and peered at the urn over the rims of his spectacles.

"It certainly looks like one, but there are so many forgeries floating around. I hope you had it authenticated. That fellow down the street could do it for you."

"I didn't buy it. I guess you could say it was a gift."

He seemed to perk up at this; he peeled off his eyeglasses and leaned intently toward me.

"All the more reason to have an expert estimate. So you'd know its proper value if you should wish to sell it."

"That's very thoughtful of you, but I don't think I'll be selling it."

For some reason my response seemed to disappoint him. I couldn't help but see something of myself in him, an eagerness to be useful, to count for something or someone in the world, even if it was a total stranger. I don't think he counted much for his wife.

All the way down the street I reflected on why I had resorted to obfuscation with Huggins. Why hadn't I told him the urn contained my aunt's ashes? Maybe because the whole business would have sounded so preposterous. Or maybe because I was beginning to doubt the story I'd been told. I recalled Huggins's pointed query, *She died?* As if he had a particular interest in the incident. Maybe I'd ask him a few more questions this evening, find out what he'd heard, since he seemed to be well informed about what happened in the neighborhood. We'd already decided to meet back at the café for drinks. But first I needed to have a look around my aunt's apartment. I was more than a little suspicious—who wouldn't be after all that had gone on? Yet, I felt confident that everyone's strange behavior could be explained away as a simple failure to communicate.

This time the keys worked, all three of them, and the door opened. The entry was dark and cool, and I fumbled around feeling for a light switch. I hoped somebody had paid that bill.

CHAPTER 5

Once again my prejudices tripped me up. Being given to believe my aunt had been penniless, I expected some meager lodging where an old lady would live cramped with her errant memories; instead, the switch illuminated a large entry hall, on the other side of which were wide double doors opening onto adjoining spacious rooms. There was an immense circular table heaped with papers and books, and in the center stood a tall brass monkey wearing a collection of straw hats while holding a dish piled with keys and looking very dignified in spite of it all.

In the living room I drew back the heavy drapes at the tall double windows and silvery light rushed into the room. Everywhere I looked in any direction I saw notebooks, newspapers, journals, typewritten pages tied in bundles, along with a number of unwashed cups and wineglasses, all of it strewn across sagging couches and faded armchairs and trailing across the carpet; there were books crammed into wall shelves, piled on desks, stacked in doorways. Every surface seemed to double as both dining and workspace, as though the inhabitants had no use for formalities. Through one door I caught a glimpse of an unmade bed with a small portable typewriter propped on a stack of pillows. The bedsheets spilled onto the floor as if someone had gotten tangled up in them and dragged them across the room in a hurry to do something or other and then climbed back in. As if the bed had been lived in and slept in and lived in again.

The effect was jarring—rather like the time I was forced to sit through a Stockhausen piano concerto. The awareness of sensibilities so at odds with—and incomprehensible to—my way of life made me want to dart for the door and take the first flight back home. My mother had been a stellar housekeeper—not only because she enjoyed it, but because she appreciated the beauty of order. My thoughts rushed to my airy Florida condo with its neatly ordered spice rack and steak sauces, my dwarf cacti marshaled along my windowsill, my rows of tennis shoes in readiness at the back door. My needs are simple, but they require normality and order. I'm particularly fussy about symmetry, right angles are my favorite, which my wife thought a shade too obsessive, although I always attributed it to my thwarted passion for geometrics. But I digress.

Surely my aunt had not been living here alone. One old woman could not have possibly produced so much mess all by herself. But as I poked my head into the rooms—each one more fantastically wrecked than the other—I began to get a sense of industry operating here. Maybe this was the way the French mind worked. I thought of the French intellectuals after the war with their cigarettes dangling from their lips and their coat collars turned up against the cold, banging out existentialist manifestos on sturdy typewriters or scratching away with good old-fashioned fountain pens. Maybe their rooms had looked like this.

Odd objects caught my eye: an iron pencil-holder in the shape of a clenched fist with handcuffs dangling from the wrist, a small plaster bust of a scowling man with a very long beard. There was a dog-eared Russian–English dictionary so thick it could have served as a doorstop, and another in German. Severely academic-looking journals in languages I couldn't begin to identify. Everything seemed terribly purposeful, as if I'd wandered into a wartime communications bunker. Even the small comforts of home, a teapot painted with butterflies, seemed to have been buried under the gray monochrome debris of industry. I needed to sit down, but where? I couldn't even find a surface on which to set the urn.

In the living room I cleared some newspapers from one side of the couch and sank down onto a lumpy cushion. I didn't think it possible to disturb anything, but I was careful anyway. I set the urn on the floor between my feet and leaned back and closed my eyes. It had been a taxing morning.

I'd been so preoccupied with my aunt's business that I'd barely given a thought to my own. I imagined the anxious look on Mr. Humboldt's lined, unshaven face when I didn't show up this morning at the veterans' nursing home to help him sort out his bills. It took me less than an hour every month, sometimes more if he was in a chatty mood, but it brought him peace of mind. One time he gripped my wrist with his spidery fingers and whispered hoarsely to me, "I'll sleep better tonight, thanks, son." I'd also had to cancel a meeting with the attorney representing Mrs. Chipman, a widow whose son I'd caught stealing from her savings. I'd been able to block him from the bulk of her money, but when he couldn't get another cent out of her he vanished. I felt terribly responsible for having upset her life. I think she probably would have rather lost her savings and kept her son. Then there was the growing list of old folks who came to me for help untangling their lives from the aftermath of telephone scams. I don't know why I kept at it, perhaps because for a few weeks or a few months I felt a part of these families. I played the Don Quixote, pitting myself against the cruelties of faceless men or ruthless corporate policies or greedy relatives. But, like Whac-A-Mole, as soon as I knocked one down, another rose in its place. I felt every bit as impotent in the face of these small evils that loom so great in our individual lives as I was in the face of greater evils engulfing the world. The missiles we were scrambling to build, Chernobyl and its aftermath, the ominous threat of nuclear war.

Suddenly I heard the oddest sound, a creaking of the floorboards, a muffled thudding, the faint scraping of leather dragging on wood. Realizing I must have left the front door unlatched, I leaned forward to see who was coming. All I could see was a head of graying hair sunken into a block of shoulders swaying on its way around the table with an uneven walk. It took him a very long time to appear. When he did, the sheer theatrics of his presence were such that it was impossible to take my eyes off him. The enormous shoulders pitching forward on the mechanics of leg braces and elbow crutches brought to mind the savage physicality of a centaur; whatever his affliction, he definitely did not inspire pity.

"What a pigsty this place," he bellowed, batting a small chair out of his way with a crutch as he labored through the doorway and into the room.

His glance fell to the urn between my feet.

"Good God, is that her?"

I looked down at the vase.

"I certainly hope so."

"Where? Père Lachaise?"

I nodded.

"Oh, you can trust those people. It's her in there." He lifted his chin and twisted his neck sharply, like a sort of muscular tick, and I saw then how he was struggling to compose himself. I believe he was close to tears.

"I could use a drink. Can I make you one?" he said.

"I'll be glad to do it, if you show—" In my embarrassment I lurched to my feet, accidentally knocking over the urn, but nothing broke, and to my relief the lid remained firmly sealed.

"Sit back down," he commanded in a stentorian voice that would have been heard in the back row of a packed theater. "I'm the bartender around here."

A newspaper lay in his path, and he stabbed it with the rubber tip of his crutch and flung it into the air, a gesture he seemed to relish. Apparently he knew his way around, since he headed directly into the adjacent room, which might have been a dining room if the table hadn't been littered with fallout from a paper storm.

I could hear him taking out glasses and shifting bottles.

"Single malt scotch all right?" he called from around the corner.

It was midday, but I didn't hesitate. "Sure."

"I drink it neat. Or you can get yourself some ice from the kitchen."

"I'll take it however you make it."

He was very quick. I barely had time to clear off an armchair for him. When he appeared again he had lost the crutches and carried a glass in each hand, coming toward me with a twisted agonizing movement that caused the scotch to slosh over his hand. His effort to walk put even Billy to shame.

I started to rise again, but he ordered me to stay put. He seemed to flaunt his disability, to lend it a touch of nobility, the way a great actor might play it in a Shakespearean tragedy.

I took my glass from him and waited until he had dropped down into a deep armchair. With his stature disguised and the misshapen legs out of view, he became less intimidating, even a little dashing. He wore a blue linen jacket with a yellow silk pocket square, and his unruly salt-and-pepper hair added just the right touch of neglect.

"To Lily," he said, raising his glass to the urn.

"To Lily," I mimicked hesitantly. I had never heard her called by this name, and it instantly complicated my mental image of her. He took a drink and then let his eyes travel around the room. He looked like he was getting ready to cry again.

"Your timing is perfect," I said in a chipper tone, hoping to distract him. "I was just wondering where I might find a bottle when you appeared."

His laugh was surprisingly soft. "You don't live like she did without taking a nip of something now and then."

"This is some nip."

"Sixteen-year-old Lagavulin." He gave me a nod of approval. "If you'd gone for the ice, I would have poured you the cheap stuff."

"To Aunt Lily," I toasted again, this time with meaning.

Surely her liquor cabinet was worth a little respect.

We hadn't even introduced ourselves, and already we had fallen into an easy familiarity. I was in no rush to bombard him with questions, I was just relieved to meet someone who had known my aunt and who was willing to stick around for more than the time it took to deliver her ashes or steal her door keys. My wife thought I was always too eager to see the good in people, and then I'd be crushed when they proved to be jerks. I could see how this man's brusque manners would offend, but I suspected there was also a lot to admire. He pulled a pipe out of his jacket pocket and began to chew on it without lighting it. A smell of cold tobacco spread through the room.

"She hated winters in Paris, particularly as she grew older. At our age summer doesn't last but a heartbeat. I used to be stationed in Havana, and she liked to call me and tell me to come up and make her a rum punch. She'd come out of that door there, with a big plastic flower stuck behind her ear, walking that runway walk of hers, with Celia Cruz playing in the background. Once she had a little drink in her she'd start to rumba. How she loved to rumba." He stared morosely into his glass before knocking back the last of it. "She said I made the best rum punch in all of Cuba." He laughed that soft laugh again. "She knew how to flatter me."

Without a word, I got up and went into the other room to look for the bottle. I found the Lagavulin in a corner bar with an impressive assortment of liquor bottles. Already I was beginning to think better of my aunt. I took it back and poured us both another generous glass.

"She didn't think you'd come," he said as I fell back onto the couch.

"She talked about me?"

"We knew she had a nephew. That's all we ever got out of her."

I noted the *we*. It carried the ring of an inner circle, of loyalties.

"What is all this?" I asked with a glance around the room. I wasn't sure what to call it. I thought *pigsty* a little insulting. Even for my villainous aunt. She was still family.

He leaned forward with his elbows on his knees. "You don't know what she did?"

My ignorance seemed to amuse him.

"Stands to reason you wouldn't. She never used her own name."

"She was a writer?"

"Let's just say she was in the publishing business."

"Well, I'll need to dispose of her things. I was thinking about turning it all over to an estate agent and letting them deal with it."

"My good man, you mustn't do that, under any circumstances," he said sharply. "There are some rare manuscripts here. They would be worth something."

"What would you suggest?"

"Perhaps I can help you there. I would know what to look for. What's important."

"You worked together?"

"For many years."

I am by nature a trusting person, but I wasn't quite sure I trusted him. I didn't know what to make of his foreignness, his English accent with a trace of something not quite English, or maybe it was his eagerness to take charge.

"Had she been ill?" I asked.

"Not at all. I saw her just before noon that day. She said she'd been feeling a little weak because of the heat. She was on her way to the supermarket. I told her she should wait until it cooled down. It was too hot."

"So it was a heart attack?"

He raised his sad, tired eyes to me and said with a vehemence that took me by surprise. "She wasn't supposed to die." He took the silk from his pocket to blot his damp forehead, releasing into the air a heavy scent of cologne and with it a dull ache of pity.

"No," I said gently. "None of us are."

He lifted the glass to his lips, and I noticed his hand was trembling.

"It was sudden," he said finally.

"I'm glad for that."

When Pym, which is how he eventually introduced himself to me, rose to go, I felt the drink and companionship had done him as much good as it had me. He lived on the ground floor and invited me to drop in anytime. I told him I'd bring the bottle of Lagavulin, but he said that wouldn't be right, that we should drink it here. That he needed the memories.

I worried that he wouldn't make it to the elevator without tipping over, but I knew better than to offer assistance. I watched him make his way out as he'd made it in, slowly, with immense effort. It was a long journey to the door, and I imagined he was remembering the journeys around that bulwark of a table when he knew my aunt would be waiting on the other side, swaying to the music with a red flower in her hair. I wondered if one of those bedrooms had been his.

After he left, all I could think of was getting something to eat. Being too inebriated to get myself out the door to a restaurant, I had no choice but to brave the kitchen. To my surprise, I found a setup fit for a professional chef, with an impressive array of copper pots dangling from an overhead rack, and countertops crammed with every conceivable kitchen utensil; there were chopping boards, strainers and whisks; there were molds of every shape and knives of every size; there were mysterious items I couldn't possibly identify. Despite this testimony to the love of cooking, the kitchen yielded little more than culinary paraphernalia; the cupboards had little to offer and the fridge even less. I found an unopened bag of peanuts and took them with me to have a look around the place.

I would never make a good spy; I think you need a degree of brazenness to eavesdrop on intimate conversations or read someone's mail without their consent. Or at least a morally justifiable reason. My wife knew this about me, which was perhaps why she never bothered to hide her personal diary. She kept it in a small drawer in her bedside table, and she knew I knew it was there. I couldn't count the number of times I handled it while retrieving a tube of hand cream for her or looking for a lost earring, and not once had I opened it, not until the end when it was too late, because I already knew it was over. I still feel guilty about reading those pages, which is nonsense if you measure it against her betrayal. I felt like Superman handling kryptonite, exposing myself to a destructive, transformative substance. It was heartsickening to see how she compared all of us, our sense of humor, our lovemaking, our physical build (at least I scored high marks on that point), and all those childish exclamation marks. On those pages she sounded like a teenager who was just discovering her formidable seductive powers and was utterly delighted with her success with men. A girl who had no business being married.

I guess the truth is I don't snoop because I'm afraid of what I might find.

I decided an inspection could wait. I headed back to the couch, kicked off my shoes, and stretched out. I lay there nibbling on the peanuts and wondering how Mr. Humboldt was getting along, and if Mimi missed me even a little bit. My cacti certainly wouldn't notice my absence. As for Billy, he was undoubtedly having the time of his life between his plush bed and walks with smartly uniformed hotel clerks along streets that smelled like his old home.

I still couldn't understand my aunt's decision to leave all this to me. Perhaps it was carelessness, or some perverse sentiment that led her to entrust the family who had vilified her with not only her property but all her personal effects, the fruits of a lifetime of her labor and countless small objects that meant nothing to anyone but her. I thought of the handcuffed iron fist and wondered about its significance.

I could feel myself beginning to develop a certain sympathy for the ashes I'd left resting comfortably on the armchair where Pym had been sitting. Somewhere in my scotch-muddled consciousness I could hear the voice of my father's indignation. I was far too easily swayed, he said. Too softhearted. Too willing to give another the benefit of the doubt. Whether those were qualities or faults I suppose depends on your point of view, but one thing I knew about myself was that I was a man with a conscience. Nothing weighed you down like a conscience.

I dozed off and awoke to the gentle trill of a dove and a

warm evening breeze on my face. A window had been opened. On the coffee table was a clunky old manual typewriter that had not been there before, and rolled into the platen was a sheet of paper on which had been typed a message:

My dear boy, I'm glad to see you've made yourself comfortable. Splash some water on your face and come have a bite to eat. Jet lag is so terribly discombobulating, isn't it?

CHAPTER 6

The dining table had been cleared to make room for the key snatcher from downstairs who sat there in a bold print dress perfunctorily counting out banknotes into stacks. A whole lot of banknotes. It might have been a drug-money counting room straight out of *Scarface*, but these were not dollar bills, which are a distinctive #85bb65 green and uniform in size; these bills were different sizes and multicolored. I noticed she had no notepad, no adding machine. I watched as she paused to stare into space, silently mouthing numbers, then resumed counting the banknotes.

"Hello there," I said.

I didn't expect a response and didn't get one—running numbers in your head requires focus, and I appreciated that. At the other end of the table a place had been set with silverware, a wineglass, a white cloth napkin neatly folded. There was a large bowl of salad and a bottle of wine. Someone knew I was here. Someone even intended to feed me. But who?

I heard footsteps and turned to see a tall silver-haired woman in a butcher's apron appear in the hall and shuffle toward me with a skillet in her hand.

"Sit," she said cheerily. "*Sit, sit, sit, sit*. Did your mother ever read that book to you?"

"Someone who speaks English," I exclaimed with a surge of relief. "Thank goodness. I'm Carl Box. Lillian's nephew."

"Well, of course you are."

"And you are?"

"Dr. Seuss was never one of my favorites. Frankly, I always found him a little terrifying." She said this as she shoveled a massive omelet onto my plate. "I made it nice and runny. Omelets must never be overcooked."

"Did you know my aunt?"

"Ah, yes, we need to have a little talk about that," she said matter-of-factly.

She reached in front of me to carefully straighten the knife and fork so that they were perfectly aligned. She did the same with the dinner plate. Then she fussed with the wineglass, positioning it just above the tip of the knife.

"Now, sit down and eat before it gets cold," she said again, quite pleasantly but in a tone not to be denied.

"Why did you do that?"

"What?"

"All that. Straighten my knife and fork."

"My dear boy, even omelets deserve to be eaten in style," she said.

"My mother always used to do that very same thing."

It was an obsession with line and color that I traced back to Disney's *Sleeping Beauty*, a film that so dazzled my four-year-old brain that I persuaded my mother to take me back to see it eight times before it left town, although I don't recall her needing much persuasion. She loved to indulge me in complicit ways that defied my father, and paying to see a movie more than once (let alone eight times) was high on our list. The visual impact of that film, its colors and graphic use of vertical and horizontal lines, sparked an obsession that only grew with age. My coloring books, geometric for the most part, were rigorous studies in palettes. By the time I was eight, my breakfast routine involved identifying colors on the cereal boxes by their Hex codes. I mowed the lawn and set the table with equally fanatical precision. My father, baffled by my talents and determined to keep me out of the arts, channeled my obsession into business and put me to work in his paint store. Eventually, adolescent hormones rose to the challenge; my interests shifted to judo and model airplanes, bringing me in line with masculine expectations. The obsessions lingered, however, hidden below the surface, and after my mother's death, I never set the table without remembering how she had encouraged my oddities. But I digress.

"Did you know her?" I asked this stranger as I spread the napkin on my knees and dove into the omelet like the starving man that I was.

"Your mother? Of course I did."

She poured us both a glass of red wine from the bottle on the table and sat down beside me, watching me with a gratified smile. Fixed her look on me the way Billy did when I came home after a long day. Like she was really happy to see me.

"Are you going to tell me who you are?" I said between bites. "And who she is?" I said with a nod toward the stony-faced counting machine. "And that fellow who showed up on the motorcycle with my aunt's ashes? I gather you all know one another."

"Indeed we do," she said. "That's Eleanor," she said as she reached for the salad bowl and began tossing the salad. "Van Gogh delivered the urn with my ashes."

"*Your* ashes."

"I'm your Aunt Lillian."

"No you're not."

"I am."

"No you're not," I scoffed as she heaped salad onto my plate.

"Am too."

She was pulling my leg and clearly enjoying it. Then suddenly I recognized her, that girl in the photo with my parents, the one wearing trousers and the stylishly knotted bandanna. It was the smile that gave her away. The smile hadn't aged at all.

"But I got a letter. I went to her funeral—uh, your funeral."

"The funeral was a smoke screen. The letter was sent out by mistake. Well, it was not a mistake, just a little premature."

"What do you mean?"

"You will inherit all this, but not quite yet. I just never imagined my *notaire* would be so efficient. It usually takes them forever to act. Perhaps it was sent out by a young intern. Some overly zealous law student trying to make a good impression. You know how it is when you're young and trying to get a foot in the door."

Before I had a chance to respond, she shot up and back to the kitchen. I suppose I should have been annoyed, but I tried to see the bright side. My aunt was not dead. There was nothing to inherit—at least not yet. She seemed in perfectly good health and remarkably youthful-looking. Perhaps I could convince her to change her will. Leave it all to Pym or Eleanor.

It would be a huge comfort to know I wouldn't be put through these hijinks again.

She returned with a large bowl of fresh strawberries and set it under my nose.

"I'm glad to know you're alive and well," I said, "but was it really necessary to fly me to Paris? Couldn't these things be handled more economically, like through the mail?" I said it as nicely as I could; I didn't want to sound like I was ungrateful.

"Oh, I do hope you had a good flight."

"Very comfortable, yes, thank you. Now, about your dying—"

"I'm afraid Air France is falling off a little. But then, first-class patrons aren't what they used to be either. I do hope you behaved yourself. You didn't get drunk and disorderly, did you?—it's easy to do when they start serving you champagne as soon as you take your seat. And I hope you didn't wear one of those dreadful T-shirts and jeans that young people think so fashionable."

I reassured her that I had conducted myself properly, but I'm not sure she believed me.

By then Eleanor had finished her accounting, and the two of them had a brief exchange. I got the distinct impression they were talking about me.

"If you're involved in something illegal," I said, "I don't want to know anything about it."

"Good heavens, whatever would give you that idea?"

I bit off a strawberry and nodded to the wads of banknotes that Eleanor was now sweeping into a large plastic shopping bag.

"Oh, Eleanor has a thing about banks—she's convinced the money will disappear overnight. I have to say I don't place much trust in banks myself. Tell me, was your hotel room comfortable?"

"Very, but that's—"

"Oscar Wilde died there, you know. I wish the hotel had taken Lord Byron as their mascot, but poor Byron died—" She eyed my empty plate. "More salad?"

"No, thank you."

"But Byron died in Greece, not Paris. It was those dreadfully incompetent doctors he'd brought along with him. Who knows what he'd caught in that infested sewer of a place? Malaria probably, and those idiots bled nearly five pounds of blood from him. He must have hemorrhaged to death. Such a brilliant wit."

"Aunt Lily, if you could please just stick to the point."

So, there she was, my aunt Lily, I'd called her by name. She had surged back to life and was already living up to her reputation as a troublemaker.

"Which brings me to my point. If you could just go on as if I *were*—dead, I mean. Just play along."

"Why would I do that?"

She reached for the bottle of wine and refilled my glass.

"Because Eleanor's right. She said you'd be perfect for the job. I was to go myself, but that's out of the question now. Since I have to be dead."

"What job?"

"You're Everyman, she said. I think that's a fairly decent translation. She used a word in Wolof—"

"Wolf?"

"No, dear, Wolof—it's one of the languages spoken in Senegal—Eleanor is from Cape Verde, where they speak

Portuguese, but when her family moved to Dakar she learned Wolof and French."

She caught my blank look and added pointedly, "Dakar is in Senegal, my dear boy. Africa. Now, Eleanor is very astute and I rely heavily on her judgment, and I believe what she means to say is that you have no distinguishing features that set you apart from others. You would pass unnoticed in a crowd."

"You mean I'm ordinary-looking." I tried to catch Eleanor's eye as she trundled past, but she ignored me. Much like that café dog had ignored Billy with a sniff of dismissal. "Look, Aunt Lily, thank you for thinking of me, but if you're not dead, then I'll go back home."

"It's only temporary."

"I'm terribly sorry to disappoint you—"

"But you won't disappoint me, I'm quite sure of it."

Her smile did more than dazzle, it challenged me to rise to the occasion. Take a risk. Charge into the disorderly unknown. She made me feel like I'd be a schmuck if I didn't.

I was confounded, befuddled. Trapped. I went for another strawberry.

"What's so important back home? What is it that you do?"

"I'm a paint and varnish consultant for Disney's Epcot Center. Box Paints used to formulate Disney's paints, way back when. That was Dad's company. Disneyland was our biggest client."

"Box Paints," she said with a note of reminiscence. "I remember your father's first store. I always thought it was an odd sort of business, but he did quite well with it. Your father had a nose for a good business opportunity."

At the sound of voices at the front door, she stood to

remove her apron and pin a stray hair back in place. I remembered the picture I'd seen of her when she was just a teenager. Now the hair was silver and drawn back in what they call a French twist, but she still looked striking.

"Oh, by the way, I've taken the liberty of checking you out of your hotel and having your things delivered here. You mustn't worry, as they are very thorough and trustworthy. I can assure you they won't miss a thing."

As she was speaking, Billy was just coming through the door, and there was a terrible racket as he knocked into furniture and plowed through stacks of books on his way to find me. I winced at the thought of the destruction he was leaving in his wake.

I squatted down to greet him just as he came banging around the dining room table like a kid at the wheel of a bumper car with his tongue hanging out.

When my aunt saw him she said, "Oh my, this does complicate things."

"I beg your pardon?"

"Your dog. You came with a dog."

It seemed to me that she was the one who had complicated things. After all, she was supposed to be dead.

Billy, who knew he was the subject of conversation, dragged himself forward a few steps, contorting himself grotesquely in an attempt to wag his back side and make friends.

"*Quelle horreur*," she muttered, staring down at him.

It required no translation, for the repulsion on her face said it all. At that moment I felt my sympathies for her dry up. Instantly the old battle lines were drawn—my father, Billy and myself aligned against this heartless woman. I squared my shoulders and shot her a look of dignified indignation.

"Billy is not a horror. He is a cripple."

She ignored my protestations and continued to scrutinize Billy.

"Perhaps Van Gogh can help. He's remarkably inventive."

I wondered what Van Gogh could do, given his deceased state.

My aunt bent down and lifted a wheel off the ground to test its weight, and it suddenly occurred to me that she was referring to the contraption, not the dog. And Van Gogh was the man in motorcycle leathers who had roared up to the steps with the urn.

"Yes, I'm sure he could improve on this. It's far too cumbersome."

"I built it myself," I said a tad bit defensively. "I went through quite a few prototypes, actually."

She had locked eyes with Billy again, who was gazing up at her with unconcealed adoration. "We'll put you in something a little more stylish. What do you say, my good man? This is Paris, after all."

CHAPTER 7

It was Huggins's idea to have the taxi driver take us on a spin around the Arc de Triomphe, although he was disappointed because the driver didn't live up to his expectations of recklessness. "It's quite a thrill to see them coming straight for you," he said excitedly, pointing to the stream of cars barreling into the flow of traffic just outside his window. "Naturally the locals are accustomed to it, all this jockeying to get to the inside, and then getting back to the outside to leave the roundabout, that's another battle." He was gripping the back of the seat in front of him so tightly that his knuckles had turned white. Our driver was uncharacteristically obliging, making three tours around the grand triumphal arch at Huggins's request; I think he found the spectacle of a priest's unbridled enthusiasm for the fight vaguely amusing—and besides, it was August and the traffic was thin.

"Imagine rush hour!" Huggins exclaimed breathlessly as we peeled off the roundabout onto the Champs-Élysées and he fell back, exhausted, in his seat.

I was a little euphoric myself now that my aunt had

returned from the dead; once I had recovered from our involuntary extraction from the hotel and resettled under her roof, I found myself surprisingly at ease in her company—while nonetheless reminding myself I was being charmed by a relative who had committed some great, mysteriously foul deed. Or any number of them. Whose ungratefulness had left my father bitterly wounded. Billy, oblivious to our family feud, had no such reservations. I watched in awe as he followed her around like she was a Pied Piper, wheeling over scattered papers without drawing even a hint of reprimand. Once when he knocked over a stack of literary reviews, I thought for sure he was in for a good scolding. Instead, when her gaze fell on the heap she clapped her hands like a child and cried, "Ah! There it is!" as she swept up a review and flipped through it. "This is the one with Sartre's defense of Tarkovsky's first *long-métrage*. I've been looking for this issue for a year now." She patted Billy on the head, called him a Good Billy Boy, and waved the review at me. "Have you seen the film? *Ivan's Childhood?* Well, you must. Sartre typically over-philosophizes the whole thing. Intellectuals have a tendency to get carried away with absolutely groundless speculations. Intellectual rubbish is still just that, rubbish."

She was an odd duck, to be sure, and off-puttingly imperious, with a whiff of anarchism and a dash of flamboyance that didn't sit well with my conservative American upbringing, but if there were unpaid debts she was intending to unload on me, as my father would have had me believe, I certainly didn't see any signs of them. On the contrary, there seemed to be plenty of money floating around. My aunt had insisted on stuffing my pockets with franc notes as I walked out the door, "for expenses," she claimed. Rather than tussle with her, I let her have her way; I could quietly return it at the end of the evening, leave it in the brass monkey's paw along with the keys on the reception hall table, where she wouldn't find it until long after I'd gone.

Since I had already promised to meet Huggins for a drink, I felt I should at least stop by Le Petit Verlaine and have a quick beer before politely excusing myself. I certainly didn't think he would invite himself along.

"Harry's New York Bar? Never been there," he said.

"Thought I'd give it a try."

"Sure. Why not?" he said cheerily, as if I had asked him to join me. "Would make for a nice change of scenery."

"Are you sure? Your wife won't miss you?" I hinted, although I no longer believed in the wife-gone-shopping story.

"Naw," he drawled, in the manner of a man eager to get into the spirit of the evening.

I suppose I could have come up with an excuse to get him off my back, but I didn't have the heart to abandon him to yet another lonely evening. Besides, I enjoyed his company. I figured his presence would make my cover more believable.

My aunt, I learned, was in the business of publishing works by dissident Soviet writers—novels and poetry for the most part, but also politically sensitive accounts of trials and prison diaries that revealed the true face of the Evil Soviet Empire. Occasionally, something very special came down the pipeline, and my aunt always tried to get her hands on it before any of her competitors. That was the case here. My mission was simply to surreptitiously pass information to the author's contact, which would cement her bid on a manuscript by a very important Russian author. When all this was put to rest, she promised to explain the faked death and answer my questions.

It would have been churlish of me to refuse. As I took her French francs, bid her goodbye and tripped down the stairs, I admit I felt more alive than I'd felt in a long time. Months. Years, even. Me, Carl Box, lately CEO of Box Paints, heading off to perform some small feat of derring-do. It may have been nothing more than a bit of publishing cloak-and-dagger, but I was heading into unknown territory. I had been entrusted with a mission by an aunt who had no reason to trust me. But she did. Whatever her reasons, she seemed absolutely confident in my ability to pull it off. To my surprise, I found the challenge exhilarating.

My aunt had filled me in on the history of Harry's Bar and its popularity with famous expats like Hemingway, and I'd been a little worried about getting seats at the bar, which was where I'd been instructed to sit. But finding the place nearly empty, we got stools at the far end, where I could keep an eye on the door. At precisely a quarter past eight, I was to order a James Bond, then change my mind to a French 75, then back to a James Bond again. My contact, a Russian by the name of Petrov Zhukovsky, who would also be seated at the bar, would then excuse himself to head to the men's room—I was to do the same. In the men's room he would tell me that I should have stuck with the French 75. I'd reply that the night was still young, and he'd pass me an envelope. That was the extent of it. Then I could enjoy my evening and my aunt would be forever grateful to me. She assured me there was nothing remotely illegal in the dealings, unless you considered free speech illegal, as the

Soviet authorities did. I think it was that last bit that brought me into the camp. I would drink a James Bond on behalf of free speech anytime. My role certainly seemed innocent enough. She also said the cocktails at Harry's were the best anywhere. Bar none. And that I must absolutely try their hot dogs.

We had plenty of time before I had to order my Bond, so we decided on a pair of Irish whiskeys from the long list of spirits. A few sips gone and Huggins came clean, telling me the whole long, sad tale of how his wife had run away.

"You mean she left you?"

"She didn't just leave me, as in pack up and move across town. She's run off with a man, or perhaps several men, not all together—I don't mean to imply that—but one after the other. It's been rather difficult to keep up with her. There's one she seems to have grown very attached to. Maybe it was true love. I don't know. But she keeps going back to him. I don't think he treated her very well. Women go back to that type, don't they?

"I've had a few postcards here and there," he continued after draining his glass. "One from Brighton, then Lille, and a quite beautiful one from Florence—the Ponte Vecchio at night. We always used to talk about visiting Florence one day, and now she's gone off to see it with someone else. It's like she's taunting me. I thought, maybe she wants me to find her. So that's what I'm doing."

"Did you get a postcard from Paris?"

"Oh, I've known about Paris for a long time. That fellow—the antique dealer—that's the one she fell in love with."

He said his wife used to meet the man at Le Petit Verlaine, and Huggins was convinced if he stayed put long enough she'd pass through.

"It's a waiting game, then," I said. "You must love her very much."

I'd been so wrapped up in his story that I'd lost track of time. It was nearly a quarter past eight and time to reel off my lines, but the bartender was nowhere in sight. The only other people at the bar were a middle-aged couple in a tense tête-à-tête a few stools down. If someone was supposed to hear me, it could only be them. I decided to improvise.

"Excuse me," I said, leaning forward. "Sorry to bother you folks, but I was hoping to get a recommendation for a drink—I can't make up my mind. It's between the James Bond and the French 75. What do you think?" I flashed them my best happy drunk grin.

They didn't seem to notice I was addressing them; the woman, a tame-looking little blonde with eyeglasses that smothered her face, was whispering quietly in the guy's ear and holding his arm like you'd expect a good woman to do when a man was in a funk, which pretty much described him. He slouched low at the bar, the posture of a man burdened with worry. He'd already obliterated one half of a paper napkin and was working on the other half, tearing it into tiny strips, which he screwed up and dropped into an ashtray. It's just the sort of habit that irritates me. I was inclined to go over and offer him something else to fiddle with, something he could line up nicely, like matchsticks. Or a stick of chewing gum. Once, she lit up a cigarette and passed it to him, but he only shook his head morosely.

At that moment the bartender returned and a second later another man slid onto the barstool right next to the morose fellow worrying that napkin to shreds. The newcomer had a long pale face and moved like a man who wasn't very friendly. He didn't greet the bartender. Didn't loosen his tie. Didn't take off the cheap brown sports coat that was way too heavy for this heat. He pulled a brand-new pack of Gauloises out of his pocket and set about removing the cellophane wrapper. That's when I noticed the little finger was in a splint and taped to the fourth finger. He fumbled with the pack for a second, then put it back in his pocket. Like he'd changed his mind. Then he folded his hands on the counter in front of him and became very still in a threatening sort of way. I wasn't sure which of the two guys was my contact, but I figured I'd find out soon enough.

"Harry," I cried, loud enough for all to hear, "give me a James Bond. Wait, make that a French 75. No, make it a Bond."

My delivery was appalling. I'd just rattled it off like I was reciting a paint formula. Huggins seemed to be the only one who noticed my odd behavior. He started to caution me about mixing alcohols, but he never got to finish because the sad fellow was having a meltdown. Shrugging off his girlfriend's hand, he reached behind the bar for a bottle of vodka, gripped it by the neck and brought it down on the counter. Glass shattering and vodka flying while he bellowed something in a language I didn't recognize, and the blonde trying to calm him down and brush the glass off his shoulder. The little woman offered a hurried apology and managed to coax him off the stool and out the door. It had all happened so quickly that the rest of us just sat there in stunned silence. He hadn't been bellowing at any of us, nor at her—just the vodka bottle. I noticed how she'd carefully removed the broken bottleneck from his hand; she didn't seem afraid of him. She was afraid *for* him.

The door had barely closed behind them when the guy in

the badly cut sports jacket rose and silently followed them out.

What the hell had just happened?

Meanwhile the bartender was doing a great job cleaning up like a pro and pretending it was all in a day's work.

"I'd recommend the French 75," he said coolly as he mopped up the splinters of glass on the counter. "And my name's Phil, not Harry. Harry's long gone."

"I'll just go for another Black Bush, Phil," I said. "What about you, Huggins? Another Redbreast?"

"Don't mind if I do."

"And two hot dogs. No, make that four."

We waited in silence while Phil poured two generous glasses of whiskey.

Huggins lifted his glass to mine and said, "Looks like I'm not the only one with woman problems."

I wasn't sure he was right; the woman didn't seem to be the problem. Maybe it was my fault. I was supposed to have come alone. Maybe the Russian saw Huggins and didn't dare make contact.

I waited a few minutes, planning my next move. Just before their hasty exit, the little blonde had managed to surreptitiously slide her ashtray my way. I wasn't sure why, but it was intentional, so I'd kept it tucked right under my elbow. I figured it must have something to do with those little wads of torn-up napkin. As I was getting off the stool to head to the men's room, I accidentally-on-purpose knocked it to the floor, which gave me a chance to snatch the paper before returning the ashtray to the bar. As I expected, there was nobody in the men's room, just an empty stall and a cracked urinal.

We decided to take a walk before flagging a taxi, so we

headed down to the Rue de la Paix, which Huggins said was lined with luxury jewelry shops. He never shopped here, he said, but he and his wife used to enjoy strolling along the avenue, particularly at Christmas, when the lights were strung up and the store windows twinkled like diamonds.

There were two police cars at the corner, their blue lights flashing in the muggy night air. A squadron of police were busy cordoning off the area where a car had driven up onto the sidewalk and straight into a jewelry storefront.

There were a few gawkers hanging around, and I found one who spoke English and asked what had happened. Some Russian and his British girlfriend, he said. The Russian had even taken a swing at one of the policemen, as if he wasn't in enough trouble already. Both were handcuffed and taken off to jail.

We looked on while a crew nailed up wood panels to shore up the gaping hole in the glass display window.

No doubt the guy was my intended contact. I wasn't sure what role I'd played in the calamity, if any. Had my lines triggered his rage? Or was it the quiet guy who'd rubbed shoulders with him? I had tried to make amends at the bar—I tipped Phil handsomely on my credit card and topped it off with my aunt's French francs. Now I was stone-cold sober and wanted nothing more than to get back to the Rue Tonton and to bed.

CHAPTER 8

B illy's persistent whining and the smell of coffee brought me out of a deep sleep that had been only faintly muddled by strange dreams. I pulled on a T-shirt over my shorts and dragged myself to the dining room just as my aunt was setting a platter of roast chicken and potatoes on the table.

"There you are, sleepyhead," she said as she tugged off her oven mitts. The bird crackled and sizzled in its juices like something still alive. I wasn't quite sure I was ready for it.

"Why didn't you wake me?" I mumbled as I poured myself a cup of coffee from a pot set out for me. I figured it must be well after noon.

"I would never be so brutal," she said as she settled down in the chair at my right. She seemed to take such delight in feeding me—and she'd gone out of her way to make me feel at home. By some sleight of hand she'd cleared a back bedroom and made up the bed with freshly laundered sheets. I suppose I should have been more skeptical—my father would say she was softening me up only to exploit me, but my father viewed relationships as strictly transactional. Kindness was never to be taken at face value. If that was the case, she was fooling me good. Her flushed cheeks reminded me of my mother's after we'd stuffed ourselves silly on her famous barbecued ribs. I think my aunt would have liked having children of her own.

She must have been waiting all morning to question me about my evening at Harry's Bar, and I sensed she was making a serious effort to restrain herself from grilling me. She slipped on a pair of reading glasses and busied herself making notes on what appeared to be a manuscript, kindly leaving me to drink my coffee in peace and wait for the caffeine to clear the fog. Several minutes of silence had gone by before I noticed Billy sneaking a peek at me from her lap, his ears twitching guiltily. Only the top of his head was visible, and his crafty little eyes as they shifted from me to the chicken and back to me; when he saw I'd caught him *in flagrante* he didn't even blink.

I was getting ready to tell my aunt about the previous night's disaster when a loud knocking on the door sent Billy diving from her lap and making his way boisterously to the entry hall.

"It's probably your neighbor, Pym," I said. "He wants to help me sort through your papers."

"You'll have to put him off, I'm afraid. Poor Pym, I do so hate keeping him in the dark." She had put the pages aside and had picked up the carving knife and was tussling with a thigh. She wasn't very good at carving. I was afraid she might injure herself. "But he's so vulnerable. He translates, you know. Russian to English. Mostly very dull technical and trade-related reports, but occasionally he's asked to translate sensitive state documents. More than once they've tried to blackmail him."

"You've lost me. Who's they?"

She was bearing down on a bone with the knife, I heard a crunch and the thigh finally fell off with a plop into the juice. "Why, the KGB, dear. They prey on the secretaries and translators who work at the international and trade organizations here in Paris. Many of the women are single and lonely, and they do it for love and for the excitement."

"You mean spying?"

"Pym's had several lady friends who've been arrested. One girl even ran off to the Soviet Union. Marlene. She and Pym had been very close. They used to read poetry together."

Now she was prodding around inside the bird with the tip of the knife. I had no idea what she expected to find.

The knocking on the door grew louder, sending Billy into a frenzy of high-pitched yelps.

I took the knife out of her hand and laid it down.

"Let me do that when I come back, Aunt Lily."

Two policemen stood at the door—at least that's how they introduced themselves, the young one in uniform and the older one sweating heavily in a dove gray sports jacket that nicely matched the gray at his temples. His slicked-back hair looked as if he'd just run his head under a faucet. The young one looked like a light breeze would have taken him down, the older one not so much. I took a long time scrutinizing the badge holder he flashed at me—not that I could distinguish a fake badge from a real one, but the only police I'd ever had anything to do with were traffic cops, and I'd never met one who had the courtesy of presenting me his credentials

"Have you finished?" the older one said impatiently. I guess he thought I was taking too long with his ID card.

I handed it back to him. I wondered how he knew to

speak English.

"Yeah. Sure. What's up?"

"Can we come in?"

"No."

"We have some questions of a personal nature."

"Shoot away."

The well-dressed one shot me a startled look. "Shoot?"

"I mean, go ahead. What can I do for you?"

I suppose I sounded cocky, which is how I come off when I'm uncomfortable. I was standing there unshaven in my boxer shorts and T-shirt, and I hadn't had enough coffee to be civil to strangers.

"It concerns Madame de la Pérouse."

"You mean Aunt Lily. What about her?"

"And you are?"

"Carl Box."

"We want to open an investigation into her death."

"Why?"

"We have reason to believe she was murdered."

"Her death certificate said it was a heart attack."

"She may have been poisoned."

"Poisoned? How?"

"At the tearoom in the Mosquée de Paris. Fortunately for your aunt, she did not drink the tea, but a dog did. And the dog died."

The young one finally spoke up. "We wood leek too eekzameen ur bodee." I'd never seen anyone struggle so much to say so little. Poor fellow, he sounded like he had a mouthful of nails.

"You'd like permission to examine her body," I repeated.

He nodded stiffly.

"Just a moment, please."

I left Billy to guard the door while I went to get my aunt's ashes.

"I think it may be too late," I said when I returned, cradling the urn in an arm and doing my best to appear grieved.

"*Évidement*," the talkative one said.

Suddenly the whole thing took a turn I hadn't expected.

"You're her nephew, yes?"

"I am."

"And only hair."

"Heir. Yes, that's my understanding, although I wasn't aware of it until a few days ago. And how on earth do you know these things?"

"She was a very rich lady, your aunt."

"Was she?"

"And you will be a very rich young man." His smile wasn't what I'd call friendly.

The slight one in the uniform had leaned down to pet Billy, who let out an uncharacteristic growl.

"I hope you weren't planning on going back home soon."

"Actually, I was."

"A hasty departure would only make things look very bad for you."

"Are you saying you suspect me of murdering my aunt?"

"*Mais pas du tout!*" he exclaimed as if I had offended him. "However, I'd advise you to watch your back, Monsieur Box," he said while handing me his card. I took a look at the name. Duclos. Captain Roland Duclos.

"Our sources are very reliable, and we believe there was an attempt on your aunt's life just a few days before she died.

Your aunt had connections with some very important people."

"The good sort or the bad sort?"

"Both."

The bird looked as if she'd taken a hatchet to it.

"You handled that very nicely, Carlito. Well done," my aunt said as I sat down.

She wore the surprised look of a parent whose plodding child has just come home with a stellar report card, reminding me that she had her own preconceived notions about my character; for all her blithe cheerfulness, her opinion of me could not be very high. What kind of loyalty could she expect from a nephew who'd never once tried to break the hardened silence imposed by my father and reach out to her? And why hadn't I? I'd been my own man long enough. Or so I thought.

"They think I killed you," I said in dismay.

"But of course you didn't," she said soothingly while spooning potatoes onto my plate. "Thigh or breast?"

It was time to have a heart-to-heart with her. She'd gone from being nonexistent to dead, to alive, to my murder victim. A dizzying trajectory, by all accounts. I felt she was in some deep trouble.

"Thigh, please. Aunt Lily, did someone try to kill you? Tell me the truth. No hedging."

Billy had settled back in her lap with his eyes fixed on the chicken.

"It was the bees that tipped me off. A lady sitting down at the table next to me jostled my elbow and I spilt half the glass—"

"The bees?"

"It's the sweetened mint tea that attracts them—"

"Where was this?"

"The mosque's tearoom. I'd arranged to meet a friend on the outdoor patio. It's absolutely delightful in the summer—I always feel like I'm back in Marrakesh. We must go there after all this blows over—to the tearoom, I mean. Better yet, we'll plan a little trip to Marrakech."

"Aunt Lily, the bees."

"Yes, well, naturally a little spilt tea on the table and the bees were on it lickety-split—it's no use shooing them away. But something very odd was happening—they would light on the tea, then shoot up in this bizarre spinning motion and tumble straight to the ground. Within seconds there was a puddle of dead bees at my feet. Only me. No one else seemed to be accumulating dead bees. So I grabbed my bag and went off to look for the waiter, but I couldn't find him. He'd gone. Disappeared." She stroked Billy's head thoughtfully and said, "The lady next to me had a Chihuahua. Poor thing."

"Who do you think was behind it?"

"Oh, it could be any number of people."

"I had no idea publishing was so cutthroat," I said dryly.

"It's very competitive these days, depending on what your author is getting ready to deliver and who wants to get their hands on it."

"So, that's when you decided to fake your death."

"That's right."

"And playing dead is supposed to put them off the scent?"

"It's a matter of practicality. I have urgent business to take care of, and I can't constantly worry about being murdered."

Seeing that I had finished the thigh, she loaded the other one onto my plate.

"Now, about last night," she said.

I explained my decision to take Huggins along as "part of my cover," failing to mention how easily he had played on my sympathies. Then I launched into a blow-by-blow account of the incident at Harry's, describing the couple in excruciating detail, their appearance, dress, mannerisms, and the latecomer who had taken the barstool beside them. It's another one of my quirks, sort of like a visual spin on my symmetry obsession, recalling an incident almost like a camera recording a scene. I used to bore the hell out of my wife when I did this, but my aunt wasn't bored in the least. I told her how, just before helping her man out the door, the little blonde with the glasses had nudged the ashtray right under my elbow, where I had guarded it while the barman cleaned up the mess, then retrieved the wads of paper on my way to the men's room.

When I'd finished telling her all this, I got up and came back with the desiccated napkin.

"There's nothing on it," I said. "But if she wanted me to have it, I figured it must mean something."

I watched as my aunt flattened the napkin and examined the pieces.

"Oh my," she said in a whisper. "It does indeed mean something." She pointed to the name of a café printed on a corner.

"Café de la Paix. He wants us to know he's in danger. That's why he wanted to meet."

"Well, they took him off to jail, but he couldn't have been referring to that. He left the napkin before the car accident."

"It wasn't an accident."

I met her look. Suddenly it all made sense. "It was intentional," I said. "The bar scene, the crash."

As she sat there studying the napkin in thoughtful silence, I was struck by a sudden awareness of her fragility and aloneness, but then she turned to me and broke into a smile. It was funny, the way she changed when her gaze fell on me, as though I brightened up her life.

"How brilliant you are."

"Oh, I don't know about that."

"You had good reflexes."

I shrugged. "I practiced judo when I was a kid." I was intentionally misreading her. Those weren't the sort of reflexes she meant.

"I bet you were good at that too."

I brushed it off with a self-deprecatory chuckle, but the truth was that I felt terribly proud. It reminded me of how I used to feel when praised by a father who was equally quick with ridicule if I didn't perform according to expectations.

"I'm glad I could be of help, Aunt Lily," I said, and I meant it wholeheartedly.

"I could try to get you on a flight home this afternoon if you like."

"I won't get arrested at the airport?"

"Who would arrest you?"

"That detective. Duclos. He advised me not to leave town until they finished investigating your death."

"My dear, all they have is a rumor and a dead Chihuahua. That's hardly enough evidence to detain you."

"But you won't stay dead."

"Certainly not. You'll see, it will all be revealed as a simple miscalculation."

"That happens?"

"All the time. Morticians getting ready to embalm a body only to find it's breathing."

I had a vision of my aunt lying on a table with a mortician poised to cut her open. "Good grief, you won't let it go that far."

She reached for my hand and gave it a firm squeeze.

"I promise. You have been a great help to me, Carl. I won't forget it."

CHAPTER 9

Despite my my growing fondness for my aunt, I was honestly relieved to be going home. The incident at Harry's and the encounter with Duclos had left me thinking there might be valid reasons behind my father's decision to cut all ties with her. She was clearly involved in some risky business, and I had no doubt it extended far beyond a few literary publications by Russian dissidents. Removing myself from her orbit as quickly as possible seemed the prudent thing to do. I regretted not having a chance to say goodbye to Huggins. I thought I might write him at his hotel and wish him luck finding his wife. I might even be back one day, and perhaps we would meet again. But that would be unlikely. I had never been inclined to travel abroad, even less inclined to become a spy. I had already determined I would write Aunt Lily and kindly request her to bequeath her apartment and its contents to one of her friends or some charitable organization. I would need to word it carefully to avoid hurting her feelings. She had seemed so eager to think highly of me, and I felt a little guilty because the opinion was not entirely shared. I still bore my father's grudge toward her, whatever it was. A predisposition that had been taught to me from birth and which would be very difficult to erase.

When I emerged from my bedroom with my bag in hand, Eleanor was waiting with my flight information scrawled on a piece of paper, along with the urn, which I had been instructed to take back with me to keep up appearances. She hurried me down to the street, where a taxi was waiting, and Billy and I were unceremoniously whisked away to catch an afternoon flight to Miami. I had no idea where my aunt had disappeared to—off taking care of urgent business, no doubt—but I was hurt that she hadn't hung around to bid me goodbye. As the taxi pulled away I glanced back, hoping to catch a glimpse of her waving to me, but then I remembered she was officially dead. I had no idea how she managed it, coming and going without being seen. I didn't even know where she slept. I'd never bothered to ask. I realized how sadly uncurious I had been about her life, which must have been extraordinary.

As we crossed the Seine I looked back toward the enclave of stucco, stone and slate gray rooftops, that little corner of Paris that had thoroughly disrupted my life, a place of brief but intense encounters with the sort of people I would never normally meet. Now, as distance stretched between me and those moments, I was struck by the thought of all the lost opportunities. I thought about how little of the day I had seized.

I didn't notice the motorcycle tailing us until we were approaching the airport. The fellow, who I guessed to be the ubiquitous Van Gogh, roared up behind us, left his bike at the curb and followed me into the terminal. He hung back in the crowd, waiting while I checked in and then following me to the security screening. I wasn't sure if he'd been sent to protect me or to make sure I got on the plane.

I turned and waved to him when I reached the front of the security line, but he was too cool to wave back, standing there muscle-bound with arms crossed like a centurion, in his motorcycle leathers and shiny silver helmet.

The hang-up was with the urn. Not the contents, but the urn itself, which had caught the eye of a plainclothes customs official. I was pulled into a side room with bright fluorescent lights and grilled harshly about the urn, while Billy was allowed out of his carry-on crate and left to wheel around the room, sniffing in all the corners. Apparently dogs could do no wrong in this country. But my urn was suspect. It was Grecian, they claimed, Athenian by the looks of it, from the Greek Geometric Period, and where was my proof of sale? One official after another was brought in, statements taken, my passport examined twice, thrice, taken away, returned to me. The room had no ventilation apart from an overhead fan that didn't seem to be working. I was sweating and Billy had fallen asleep, twisted around a wheel in a position that could have been comfortable only to him. Finally, they let me go. By then my flight was long gone.

I collapsed onto a seat in the waiting area with my head between my hands. I felt gutted. Damn the urn, damn my aunt. I could have refused to carry it back. But I hadn't. I was a wuss. Eternally ready to go along with whatever you asked of me. And this was where it got me.

Some people might have seen this incident as the intervening hand of fate. But I have never been one of those who cried, "It was meant to be!" in the face of coincidence or benevolent circumstance. For if good things are meant to be, then conversely, evil things are meant to be, and even though evil may be swirling around me, I do have a hard time accepting its inevitability. We have choice, piddling and limited in scope as it may be for most of us insignificant beings. Sometimes life lays down stepping stones and we can choose to follow them or not. Or conversely, we can come up against seemingly insurmountable obstacles, and we can choose to persevere or not. That's what that damn urn was. It was either a stepping stone or an obstacle, depending on how I chose to see it.

A girl who was emptying trash cans tapped me on the shoulder and said something—by the worried look on her face I figured she was asking if I was feeling sick. I shook my head with a mumbled thanks and tried to smile to let her know I was okay. She went away and came back with a bottle of water and then went off to empty more trash cans.

I took a long drink and then poured a little water into a cup I always kept in my backpack for Billy.

"I don't know how she manages, but apparently she does, or does she?" I said to him. "I mean, she's got herself into a bit of a pickle. And her friends, well, I'm sure they're devoted to her—except for that Pym fellow—but they don't strike me as the sort to keep to the straight and narrow."

Billy lapped up the water and then looked up at me in silence. It didn't seem to bother him that water was dripping from the fur on his chin. He didn't have my hang-ups.

I voice thoughts to Billy that I would never dare voice to a human being. Mainly thoughts that reflect my less generous self. My petty self. My cowardly self. While Billy lapped away, I commented on the disorder of Aunt Lily's life, the unwashed dishes and unmade beds, the unpaid bills I'd seen lying around.

Not to mention the detectives knocking on doors, the Russians and exploding vodka bottles. The chaos and unpredictability of the last forty-eight hours.

Hard to describe the look he gave me then. It was rather like a dog's version of *Shame on you*.

He needed some persuading, so I poured more water into the cup and pointed out that my parents must have had reason to sever all ties with her. The vile Aunt Lillian. A name I had only heard uttered with scorn, or as a rebuke of some failing, so that it tainted her person like a patina built up over years. A person with no redeeming traits, for whom no allowances were to be made. A person who deserved not an ounce of grace or forgiveness. It's hard to get past that sort of judgment when it comes down from parents you love and trust.

I argued, "I don't like messes, Billy. I like my life laid out and orderly. I meet deadlines and make sure accounts balance. I need to know what I'm going to wake up to the next morning. That's the only way I can sleep at night."

He finished the last of the water, licked his lips and lifted his pleading brown eyes to me and said, *You wake up to me, a small dog. It's a big bed. There's room for more.*

It gave me something to think about as I stood in line waiting to rebook my flight. When I started to explain about the hang-up with the urn and customs, the ticketing agent wasn't the least bit interested; apparently the airline had already put me on the next flight out, departing in an hour. It would mean two flight changes, but I'd be home tonight. My bag had gone ahead and would be waiting for me in Orlando.

I stopped in a souvenir shop to buy some chewing gum but they didn't have Wrigley's, so I sat down in the terminal and fished around in my backpack, thinking I might find a stray stick, and what did I find but the green Eiffel Tower key ring with my aunt's keys. It seems I'd forgotten to return them—a small enough misstep, but not one I usually make. Surely my aunt had spares. She wouldn't need them. There was a trash bin at my elbow. I could dump them and be done with Paris.

The key ring lay there in my sweaty palm, inert, meaningless unless I chose to give it meaning. Stepping stone or obstacle. Up to me to decide.

One single thought cut through all the noise in my head: She's family—all that's left of it anyway.

I hitched my backpack over my shoulder, gathered up Billy and his wheels in a football hold, and with the confounded urn swinging from my hand I headed for the exit.

CHAPTER 10

All the way back into Paris I was regretting my decision. I kept thinking I should tell the driver to turn around and drive me back to the airport. But the meter ticked on and I just rolled along with it, feeling indecisive and stupid. What would I say when I showed up at her door? What could I do? What use would I be? Saving Billy had been the most courageous act I'd ever performed, and to be honest, I hadn't even seen the gator coming until I had the pup by the scruff, and I sure wasn't going to let go then.

In the taxi I tried to read a *Time* magazine I'd bought at the airport, but I ended up fanning myself with it and thinking how I'd spent the last several years of my life marooned in a dullness I found a little frightening. Wondering why at the age of thirty-four, once again single and considerably well off, I was having so much trouble getting on with life. Why nothing moved me to action. And then in that moment there flashed before my eyes my aunt's face when her gaze had fallen on me, the gratitude I read there and, quite inexplicably, the love. It was my mother all over again, a look that brought home how her gentle understanding had softened the fearsomeness of my father's disapproval, reminding me how much I missed her still.

I was still trying to work out what I would say while I waited for the elevator; it was taking an excruciatingly long time to descend, so I started up on foot. I was just past the first-floor landing when I heard the trample of feet coming down the stairs toward me, and looking up I was slammed by a solid mass of T-shirt-clad muscle, smashing me against the wall. He was through the door pell-mell and gone before I could catch my breath and get to my feet.

I found my aunt's door standing open and Eleanor sprawled face down on the floor. As I dropped down beside her, she rolled to her side and let out a groan. A lump the size of an egg had already formed on her forehead, and blood was oozing from her scalp and fingers where she must have tried to protect herself from the blow. She recognized me and tried to speak.

Who had done this? Where was my aunt? Was she lying unconscious in another room? I was asking and Eleanor was answering, but we were getting nowhere. I couldn't make out a word she said. In my head I was frantically running through the French expressions I'd memorized on the flight over—*How much is it? Where is the Eiffel Tower? I'd like the chicken, please.* There had been no phrase for *Who mugged you?*

Then I heard the familiar scraping of leather on wood, the thumping of crutches, and Pym came lumbering in, pitching his massive shoulders into each step and muttering. "Goddamn legs. Useless when you need to play the hero."

"Thank heavens you're here," I said. "What's she trying to tell me?"

Eleanor was muttering something while poking me in the

chest with a finger.

"Sorry, can't make it out," Pym said. He seemed more interested in looking around the apartment.

I was trying to help her sit up, but the way her eyes moved in her head I thought maybe sitting up wasn't such a good idea.

"What were they after?"

"I think I know," he said as he swung off in the direction of the hall. "Pretty bloomin' brazen of them, I'd say."

I turned back to Eleanor. Her eyes were rolling around in her head like a pinball machine, but her grip on my shirt made it clear she had her wits about her.

"You Everyman," she wheezed into my ear as I helped her up and onto a chair. "You stay."

I whispered, "Is my aunt okay?"

She nodded and threw a glance at the door.

"She's gone?"

She nodded again and gestured to the hall where Pym had disappeared. "Go."

I found Pym surveying the wreckage of a back room where I'd seen my aunt working. There wasn't a single book left on a shelf, or a drawer or file cabinet that hadn't been emptied onto the floor. Film canisters had been opened and thirty-five-millimeter film lay in tangles on the heap.

"What were they after?" I asked.

"The Pasternak files."

"The Pasternak files?"

"That's what I said."

"Okay. Fill me in here."

"Can't do that," he said as he turned away.

"I think you can," I said, landing a hand on his arm with

a firm grip. "There's a woman out there with a concussion and this is legally my property." I must have sounded pretty unconvincing—I was a terrible liar. "Well, it will be. One day."

Seeing his bloodshot eyes close-up and how miserable he looked, much worse than the day before, I released his arm. I felt sorry for the guy.

He said, "Didn't I see you get into a taxi this afternoon—with your dog and your suitcase?"

"I missed my flight."

"Looks like you scared them off."

"Or they got what they were coming for."

"Or maybe someone tipped them off that you were on your way up."

He lifted his eyes to the window—I don't know who he imagined he was seeing out there.

"So who wants these Pasternak files?"

"Could be any of them. KGB, CIA. Doubt it's the French—their intelligence service wouldn't prioritize something like this. Not unless the affair came to the attention of certain politicians. Possibly the British SIS. Although from the simpleminded brutality I'd bet on the Russkies."

"What are these papers? What's in them that's so important?"

"Suffice it to say they're extremely sensitive."

"What was my aunt doing with them?"

"She planned to barter them."

My thoughts immediately turned to theft—had she stolen them from some intelligence service? No wonder she'd gone into hiding. And here I'd been worrying about a few unpaid bills.

"In exchange for what?"

"A man's freedom."

"Who?"

"My brother," he said with asperity.

Pym was already laboring his way toward the front door, and I let him go without any more questions. The matter seemed to be a sore spot with him. He wasn't exactly oozing brotherly love.

Eleanor sat at the small kitchen table pressing an ice pack to her head while I went to look for the Lagavulin. She declined the glass I'd poured for her, at the same time indicating that I wasn't to speak. It didn't take much to figure out what she was thinking: Whoever broke in might have planted a bug while she lay unconscious on the floor.

Eleanor shoved a piece of paper at me on which she'd written a telephone number and jabbed at it with her finger. I made a gesture of dialing a phone, which prompted an energetic nod, followed by another charade instructing me to memorize the number then destroy it. I gave her a thumbs-up, then tore up the scrap of paper and flushed it down the kitchen drain. She gave me a thumbs-up in return.

"Are you gonna be okay?" I said, pointing to her head, but she just shooed me out, mouthing something like, "Go! *Vite!*"

Billy had taken to his Prussian-blue dog bed like an overwrought lady in a Victorian melodrama. He'd been in his carry-on travel crate when that guy smashed into us, and he'd taken a bit of a bruising. I left a bowl of kibble beside his bed but he ignored it; instead he burrowed into a ball, heaved a sigh and was out.

I remembered seeing a public phone inside Le Petit Verlaine, but I wanted to avoid a chance encounter with Huggins. It was well into happy hour and he was sure to be there. I could almost feel his sad eyes searching for me, waiting to pour his heart out.

I headed to the Rue de Buci and popped into the first café I came to. The bartender was drying glasses and with a mute jerk of the head sent me downstairs, where I found a wall phone next to the men's room. My hand was shaking so badly I was afraid I'd punch in the wrong number, but to my relief my aunt answered with a sober "*Allo?*"

"It's me."

There was a stunned silence. I heard the dull throbbing of some sort of engine in the background.

"Carlito! Why aren't you on that plane?" she scolded.

I told her about the urn.

"It was a very nice urn, wasn't it? One of his best forgeries, I'd say."

"Who's *he?*"

"Why, Van Gogh. I asked him to follow you to the airport. To make sure you got off safely."

"Ah, well, that he did," I said with a touch of irony, then proceeded to tell her about the break-in. She listened carefully while I gave her the whole story from start to finish, including my exchange with Pym verbatim, and how I'd left Eleanor in a chair with an ice pack.

She asked where I was.

"The Bar du Marché."

"Go to the Pont des Arts," she said. "It's a pedestrian bridge.

Meet me there."

The café terraces were filling up, mostly people around my age with glasses of beer or wine in front of them and clouds of cigarette smoke drifting over their heads, bubbling with talk and laughter. I remembered my first night walking through these crowds, my misbegotten attempt to be part of the scene and my sense of estrangement. How distant that night seemed to me. Now there was Eleanor's bloodied head and the horrifying destruction of my aunt's apartment. How serious life had become all of a sudden.

The seriousness gave way momentarily to a sense of awe as I stepped onto the uneven wooden boards of the walkway stretching across the Seine. The sun was still far from setting and yet low enough so that the light had lost harshness. I'd known California sunsets and Florida sunrises, and lodged in my head were words for every color you could imagine progressing from light to dark to light, but with all my clever vocabulary I couldn't find a color for this light, in this city, over this river, at this very hour. There wasn't one. It would need to say something about the light rippling over the gray water and the riverbanks flanked in leafy green and the stretches of milky stone facades that lay solid, pressed to the earth like something eternal.

A group of girls, a boom box at their feet, huddled near the rail to watch two of their girlfriends practice rock 'n' roll moves. The dancers spun around and giggled and tripped over each other, their friends giggling and clapping, their long hair flying about in the hot summer breeze and catching that light I couldn't name.

I felt a touch on my sleeve and then my aunt was standing

beside me. She wore sunglasses under a wide-rimmed straw hat, and fuchsia gingham pants that made her look more like a fashion icon than a spy.

"Falling in love, are you?"

She meant the city, of course—Paris. She must have caught the expression on my face as I looked out over the river, chasing a name for the light.

"Ah, they're half my age," I replied, intentionally misreading her. Why, I don't know. Pride, I guess. To think I'd be so easily seduced by a cliché.

She removed the dark glasses, allowing her gaze to rest on me for just long enough for me to know she knew I knew what she had meant. Then she turned toward the horizon, where the sun was disappearing behind a jagged range of chimney pots.

"What's all this about, Aunt Lilly? Tell me."

"Just a little hiccup," she said flatly.

"These Pasternak files. Sounds like you're in bit of a pickle."

"I never should have involved you," she said with sudden intensity. "It was very, very stupid of me. I—"

She stopped herself from finishing. Closing down her thoughts, the jaw dropping with the finality of the guillotine.

"I *am* involved."

When she didn't reply, I pressed on. "This man, Pym's brother—is he important to you?"

"Yes." The answer was curt and resolute.

"You could use my help."

"You did help, Carlito. I don't know what more you could do."

I didn't have an answer to that, other than *More of the same. Act as your stand-in.* I shrugged and added, "Straighten things up."

"My dear boy, this isn't Mr. Toad's Wild Ride."

I couldn't help but smile at her reference. "Don't tell me you've been on that ride—"

"I have indeed. When Disneyland first opened."

"That was one of my favorite rides. Remember when Mr. Toad arrives at a junction in the road and there's all these warning signs, like 'Do Not Enter,' 'Turn Back,' 'One Way'? And what does Mr. Toad do? He plows straight ahead."

"Ah, but the ride's rigged, literally. Mr. Toad doesn't have a choice. You have a choice."

"I do, and I've made it. I'm standing right here at your side."

"You don't even know whose side I'm on."

I remembered what the detective had said about my aunt being involved with both the good and the bad sorts. I wanted to press her with questions, but I suspected the answers were more complicated than a simple good or bad.

She was leaning forward, her hands resting on the railing, and I reached out and placed my hand over one of hers. The gesture surprised her, and a startling change came over her expression, a sudden softening of her features, the way someone would look when you lifted a burden they'd been carrying for miles and years.

I thought of this man, Pym's brother, and said, "It sounds to me like your heart's in it, whatever side it is."

A gust of wind came in off the river, rippling the brim of her hat, and her hand flew to her head to hold it down.

"See that classical domed structure?" she said, nodding to the Left Bank. "It was built as a college in 1670—now it's the heartbeat of everything of beauty this country stands for. And facing it—" she turned to the Right Bank "—is the Louvre Palace, built continuously for over, oh, maybe six hundred years, give or take a few. Now, take yourself back a thousand years, imagine flotillas of barbarians coming up the river, the Saxons massing in the headlands to the north, the Goths, the Franks, all hell-bent on wiping out the Romans. Well, the Romans pulled out and Rome collapsed. After that followed centuries of destruction and darkness. Then, miraculously, this emerged, and it still stands. I can't define it for you, but it's here. You're looking at it. And it matters."

She turned to scrutinize me with disconcerting directness. Like a commanding officer might size up a recruit to determine if he was fit for duty. Then she slipped on the sunglasses. The gesture was one of finality, of a decision having been made.

"I have to go away. It's imperative to protect what we already have in our possession so it doesn't fall into the wrong hands."

A tourist had stopped beside us to snap a photo, and my aunt linked her arm through mine and drew me farther down the railing, out of earshot. Seagulls swooped up from the pylons in a cacophony of cries, then glided away downriver.

"The man you saw in Harry's Bar," she said, "Zhukovsky, he's with the Soviet trade delegation here in Paris. He was one of our contacts. He had a very urgent piece of information he was trying to get to us. Something must have gone dreadfully wrong for him to bolt like that.

"I need you to find him—or the woman who was with him that night. Louise. Try to find out what's happened to him. Get in to see him if you can."

"Where would they take him?"

"Start with the commissariat for the second *arrondissement*."

She slipped something small and bulky into my hand.

"This may come in useful. And take care of Eleanor. We can't manage without her."

She pecked me on the cheek and strolled off, still holding down the hat, looking every bit the summer vacationer without a worry in the world.

I looked at what she'd left me—imagining some nifty piece of spycraft that would magically facilitate my mission.

It was a French–English pocket dictionary.

CHAPTER 11

The dictionary was helpful only if you could read the phonetic pronunciation, which I couldn't. Consequently, we lost a good half hour because my taxi driver took me to the police station for the twelfth instead of the second, the two sounding somewhat alike in French. I slipped him a five-franc note on the way back and in return got a little help with a few phrases I thought I'd need. I'd never been inside a police station, and I was expecting the teeming grittiness of the squad rooms portrayed in *Hill Street Blues* or *Miami Vice*. It was dark and gritty, all right, but not the way I imagined. There was a small waiting room with cheap contoured-plastic chairs lining the walls, many of which were littered with discarded newspapers or plastic bags, and high on the wall a photographic portrait of President Mitterrand looking sternly magisterial and very superior to grit and grime. Somebody had left an empty Coke can on the radiator. The room smelled the way cold, abandoned places smell and looked all locked up for the night. It might have been a train station in the middle of nowhere. Even crime seemed to have taken a holiday. I tapped on the desk clerk's window but no one appeared. I even got daring and tried a few doors—only to be sharply reprimanded by a blue-uniformed young officer when she opened it and found me there.

The desk clerk finally showed up and ordered me back to my chair to wait. As a last resort I pulled my pen out of my backpack, printed Zhukovsky's name in big letters on a scrap torn from a newspaper and plastered it up against the glass separation window. This, along with my best no-nonsense look, got him off his swivel chair and sent him into the back room.

The pen was a beautiful gold-plated Dupont with a hand-crafted fourteen-karat solid gold nib, my wife's wedding gift to me back when she had hopes of my maturing into something beyond a paint and varnish consultant for Box Paints. I kept it not so much out of nostalgia but because it was useful, and I never lost it. You just don't lose something like that. A few minutes later a smartly uniformed man with a lean bureaucratic face came out a side door straightening his jacket and looking every bit the interrupted diner. I couldn't help but fix on the dab of mayonnaise on his lower lip—eyes will do that whether you want them to or not. He noticed my gaze and licked it off, then scowled at me as if I'd put it there to embarrass him.

I did my best to get my story across about how Monsieur Zhukovsky had left his gold-plated pen in the bar the night before, and how I heard he'd been brought in here, and perhaps I could speak to him, or the woman with him, just to verify ownership before I left the pen with them, seeing how it must be worth a lot. I don't know how much was getting through to him, but his look said he took me for a fool as well as an extreme annoyance. When he tried to take the pen to examine it, I held on to it, causing us to engage in a swift childish tug-of-war. I was afraid he'd take it away and I was trying to explain that I needed it back. Finally he threw up his hands in exasperation and barked an equivalent of *Get lost*. That would have been the end of my mission if it hadn't been for the door again. This time it flew open and a trio of miniskirted girls tumbled out, followed by as many policemen—who watched, again with stern superiority, while the girls teetered across the hall on their stiletto heels and out the door.

"Greta," my man called out, and the tall one turned back and approached in a manner I could only describe as regal, the way I imagined Egyptian queens walked thousands of years ago. Her flaxen blond hair hung in a long braid down her back, and her makeup must have worn off during the night because her pale skin looked as bare as polished marble. Her eyelashes were pale too. And her eyes a frosted blue. I'd never seen a real live hooker before and certainly had never talked to one. Immediately I started to stammer. Heaven knows why; I wasn't expected to talk since no one had said anything to me. The officer spoke to her, and she turned to me with a wooden, unsmiling face and said in perfect English, "Would you like me to interpret for you?"

When I opened my mouth to answer, all that came out was more stammering, so I snapped it shut. The pen slipped from my sweaty hand and when I stood up again I caught the officer with a cocked eyebrow trying very hard not to smile. They both stared at me, him with the smirk, her inscrutable. Finally I got my wits about me and repeated my story, which the girl listened to unblinkingly before turning and fluently repeating it in as much detail, or so I presumed. I could tell from the way his face sobered that now the guy was taking my story seriously, or maybe it was just the way "Greta" delivered it, with authority. I never imagined a hooker could have such presence.

She explained, "He said this prisoner has been moved to another location. He can't tell you where."

"What about the woman with him? Did they hold her?"

"She was released this afternoon."

"Perhaps I could get the pen to her. They must have an address for her."

They could not release that information to me.

I played up the honest Good Samaritan. Turning over the pen in my hand, looking regretful. "It's a very expensive pen—I'm sure he'd want to have it back."

If I were to leave my name and number?

I was able to steady my hand enough to write down my name, which I gave as Mr. C. B. Pasternak, and the phone number of Oscar Wilde's hotel, which I knew I could rely upon to relay the message to me. I left it with the detective and said if they heard from her to ask her to call me.

I'd never been so eager to get out of a place as I was that police station. I stood on the sidewalk breathing the muggy night air with deep relief and thinking how ridiculous I must have appeared in there. Both of them could see right through me and my fabrications.

As I turned down the street I heard her light footsteps behind me.

"If you're looking for a taxi," she said, "it's this way. There's a stand on the boulevard."

I muttered my thanks and we walked together, neither of us speaking. I noticed how tall she was, probably five ten, just a few inches shorter than me. She'd been the only one wearing flats. And I guess if her skirt looked short, it was only because her legs were so long.

I began, "Uh, are you here often? What I mean is, the police officer we were talking to, he seemed to know you—" I made a pretense of shifting my backpack to the other shoulder to cover my awkwardness, thinking she might try to help me out and finish my sentence, but no. Not a word. I took a breath and tried again. "I mean, he looked important. Who is he?"

"He's the *commissaire*. Sort of like the equivalent of the precinct captain in the States."

"I see. You American?"

"No."

She landed that word like a full stop, and I wondered, where had she learned how to do that? To evade scrutiny with such poise? It was very disarming, to say the least.

There weren't any taxis at the stand; she said if we waited, one would come along. So we waited together.

Finally she asked, "What did you want with that prisoner?"

"I told you—to give him back his pen. If I lost something like this, I'd sure want it back." Now I sounded believable.

"That's unusually thoughtful of you, to go to so much trouble."

I shrugged. "It wasn't that much trouble. I got his name from the bartender. He was a regular. It's the sort of thing I wish someone would do for me." I paused. "I felt sorry for him. He was having a bad night." I was getting the hang of it, making up stories, dissimilation.

"He must be important."

I shrugged again. "I don't know about that."

A taxi pulled in and she walked to the driver's window to ask him a question. She shook her head, then came back to stand next to me.

"You take it," she said.

"No, go ahead."

"He uses leaded fuel."

"Okay."

"I won't ride in a car that doesn't use unleaded gas."

"I see."

"Go on, take it."

"Are you sure?"

"Positively."

I hesitated. I didn't like leaving her standing there alone. It probably wasn't dangerous; it was late but still daylight, and there were plenty of people out on the sidewalks. Nevertheless, my sense of decency intervened.

"I'm in no rush," I lied. "I'll wait with you."

"Good," she said as if she'd won a convert, and she waved the taxi away. The driver gunned it and roared off in a cloud of exhaust.

It was the same thing for the next taxi that pulled up, and once again we waited in silence.

I thought of Billy waiting to be walked, and my aunt anxiously waiting for a report. I was thinking if the next taxi didn't meet her standards I'd take it anyway, and then all of a sudden she slipped to the ground, just buckled, knees and elbows and everything jointed just seemed to turn to rubber. She had fainted.

I was trying to help her sit up when the next taxi pulled up and the driver helped me get her onto the seat. I slid in next to her and put my hand on the back of her neck.

"Put your head between your legs. That's it. Stay there."

"I haven't eaten," she muttered. "That must be it."

"Since when?"

"I don't know. Maybe yesterday morning."

I leaned forward and gave the address of Le Petit Verlaine to the driver.

Her long braid had fallen over her face, and I gently reached down and moved it aside.

"Thank you," she whispered.

CHAPTER 12

I wondered what Huggins would say when I showed up with a prostitute in tow; but then, he had struck me as pretty tolerant for a clergyman. You'd need to be, if you had a wife like his. Besides, Greta, if that was her name, looked as much like a hooker as I did a spy.

I pointed out the faded red awning of Le Petit Verlaine to the driver, and as he pulled to the curb I felt the gladdening sensation of familiarity wash over me, like pulling in the driveway to home. Huggins's table was empty, but I recognized a stooped white-haired gentleman slowly turning the pages of the evening paper, and the usual waiter was lounging in the doorway with his tray under his arm. At another table sat a young woman in dark glasses, with bright red nails, holding an unlit cigarette in one hand and a lighter in the other, as if in no hurry to smoke—or to do anything, for that matter. It was a picture of perfect quietude. The setting sun had washed the buildings in golden light and tinted the clouds a flaming flamingo pink. At last the long summer day was coming to an end. I settled Greta at the table and looked around anxiously to get the waiter's attention.

"I hope this place is okay with you. I know it and we can get pretty quick service."

"It's fine," she said weakly. She took the menu from the waiter, gave it a swift glance then ordered a vegetable entrée, a side of fries, a side of green beans and a green salad. I ordered my steak and fries and a bottle of burgundy recommended by the waiter. Greta had fresh squeezed orange juice.

I would have normally inquired how it was that she hadn't eaten in over thirty-six hours, but even the most banal efforts at conversation seemed fraught with pitfalls. Had she been too busy with back-to-back clients?

She still looked like she might faint.

I said, "I think I have some peanuts in my backpack."

"Okay."

I found the peanuts and tore open the bag and poured some into her outstretched palm.

"Tough to stick to principles on an empty stomach. By the way, my name's Carl. Carl Box."

"I thought it was Pasternak."

"Carl Box is easier to remember."

"Hello, Carl Box."

"You must find yourself walking a lot."

"Which is sort of counterproductive because I'm breathing all that pollution. Diesel is bad enough, but lead? My God, even the Romans knew that lead was poisonous."

Her juice came and she washed down a handful of peanuts, then went on.

"Back in the 1920s when the first factories started producing leaded gas, almost all the workers ended up in the hospital.

They were running around hallucinating and screaming about the insects crawling all over them, dropping like dead flies—the workers, I mean. So they gave us fifty years of breathing this stuff and now we have children with brain damage and adults with heart disease. That's not conjecture or some dark plot against corporate capitalism, it's a fact. We've had unleaded gas on the market for nearly fifteen years and yet only about ten percent of gas stations sell it."

I nodded. I could imagine all sorts of arguments to throw out, platitudes like *Change is slow. Change is costly.* But I didn't want to argue with her.

"Yeah," I said, smiling, imagining a world where everyone would stand in line waiting for the one taxi running on unleaded. "You've got a point."

Then she said, "The future is always something you have to invest in, you just have to decide if you want a future for everyone or for a few."

All of this was said without the slightest hint of agitation. Her grapefruit and avocado salad came and she fell to eating.

"Do you get locked up a lot?"

"Depends," she said easily, "on what's going on. Usually there's a group of us. We were supposed to meet in front of a jewelry store on Rue de la Paix, but everybody bailed, so I went alone. I handcuffed myself to the door."

"Let me guess—diamonds. South Africa. Apartheid."

She nodded and lit into her fries. I had almost finished my steak. Mind you, she'd made no effort to shame me for eating a slab of cow. We were just two people on two different sides of things. I had a burning desire to be on the same side, whichever it was.

"I thought you were a prostitute."

"I know."

"I mean, not that you look like one—" I buttoned it before I could get my foot any farther down my throat.

"It's not illegal here. But pimping is. And anything associated with organized crime."

"What about the other girls?"

"They'd come in to volunteer some information about a very nasty guy, that's all. What about you? Are you a spy?"

"A spy? Me?" I confess, at that moment I felt a rush of pride. It was much better than being presumed an accountant.

"Are you?"

"Do I look like a spy?"

"Spies never look like spies, except in novels."

"I haven't read many spy novels."

"They're generally burnt-out cynical old alcoholics with wives who hang like an albatross around their necks, or in some cases the wives even turn out to be the traitor. Which, being a woman, I find quite offensive."

"As you should."

"And the men are all wallowing in self-pity, which is only a mask for their grandiose egos."

"Well, that's probably true for most males, whether spies or not. Go on, what else? You seem to have given this some thought."

"I imagine real spies are ordinary people who are just very good at stealing secrets and passing them along without getting caught, which makes them rather extraordinary."

The waiter had moved a neighboring table next to ours to make room for all the food, and now Greta's empty dishes were stacked on it. Somehow she had managed to finish everything.

"So why do you want to meet this man Zhukovsky?"

"Just trying to do a good deed. Honestly."

"You're no fun." She pouted then, pulling a long lingering moue. I thought she was kidding, but then her lower lip started to tremble. And tremble. The change was shocking. You would have thought I'd backed over her kitten.

"Hey," I said, leaning forward anxiously and peering into her moist blue eyes. I wanted desperately to touch her golden braid again. Then she slid me a sideways look and a mischievous grin broke out on her face. It was her first smile and I would never forget it.

I sat back, feeling like I'd been had.

"Do you pull that often?"

"Only on my dad. I swear to God, I've never tried it on anybody else before."

"I look like a sucker, do I?"

"No, you look like a Good Samaritan."

I picked up the bottle of burgundy and poured myself a final splash. It was a Côte de Nuits. A stunning wine. I didn't need a course in wine tasting to appreciate its unique qualities. Nor did I need to meet a million women to know Greta was one in a million. I didn't want to finish the bottle. I didn't want the night to end.

She was scrutinizing me as I emptied my glass, maybe trying to figure out my secrets. I really didn't have any. Not until today.

"Hey," I said, making no effort to hide my regret about leaving her and half a bottle of wine, "I've got things to do this evening. I'm glad you got something to eat. I'm glad I met you.

But I've got to take off now."

I caught the waiter's attention and signaled for the check.

I thought I detected a hint of consternation on her brow. She waited until the waiter had brought the bill, then she lowered her voice and said, "Your friend, the Russian, I overheard them calling to get him transferred to a secure location. He was demanding to meet with the DGSE."

"What's the DGSE?"

"France's espionage agency. Like your CIA."

"So he wasn't drunk."

"Not in the slightest. Sober as a church mouse. Were you really at Harry's Bar?"

"I really was. I watched him have a very serious dispute with a bottle of vodka."

"Was the pen some sort of cipher?"

I didn't answer. I was busy fishing out my wallet and wondering where she picked up words like that. Her spy novels, probably.

"His girlfriend," she said. "What do you want with her?"

That's when I knew she knew more than she was letting on.

"Did you speak to her? Louise?" I asked.

"How do you know her name?"

"Look, I just need to talk to her. She might be in danger. So if you know anything—"

"You really aren't a spy, are you?"

She clearly had a thing about spies.

"So what makes you come to that conclusion?"

"You're nice."

"I hope so."

"I was in the same cell with her all night. I think I know

where to find her."

"Where?"

"The Hôtel Daguerre in the Rue Daguerre."

I tossed some franc bills onto the table and rose to my feet.

"You're coming with me," I said, extending my hand to her.

"Why?"

"I need a guide."

She looked at me solemnly, then at my hand. She didn't take it, but she didn't refuse.

CHAPTER 13

I'd forgotten how good it felt, the throttle sensitive to a slight roll of the wrist, the powerful rush of acceleration, leaning into the turns, the wind at my face and a girl's arms tight around my waist. At that moment I thought life couldn't get any better, cruising along Boulevard Saint Germain and onto Boulevard Saint Michel with Greta as my own private tour guide pointing out the Sorbonne on our left, then the Pantheon, the burial ground of France's great men's-only club, as she called it, and on the right the Luxembourg Gardens framed by the light of streetlamps and disappearing deep behind the spearheaded grill into a mysterious forest of shadows.

Leaving Le Petit Verlaine, I'd noticed the motorcycle parked in front of the antique store, and there was light coming from behind the metal shutter that was only half-drawn. Van Gogh had been working late, trying to get his vintage pizza oven operating; he didn't show the slightest surprise when I poked my head underneath the shutter, he just waved us inside and launched into a proud demonstration of his engineering accomplishments and the challenges of getting the chimney to properly draw, or so I suppose, since Greta didn't bother to translate. When I finally got him to listen to my request, he didn't bat an eye, just handed over the keys and helmets and said the tank was probably empty. We left him with his head inside the oven, shining a flashlight into the chimney.

The bike was a Honda, and I assured Greta that this model ran happily on unleaded.

"Who is he?" Greta asked as I strapped on her helmet for her.

"He goes by Van Gogh," I said, trying to sound mysterious.

I'd sold my own Honda when I left California, and after two years in Orlando I'd never felt the urge to buy another one. Florida just didn't seem to beg for a bike. In California I could escape into deserts and mountains; Florida had only marshland, lagoons and the ocean.

Paris was a thrill on a bike—I leaned into Paris, I hugged its macadam and sped smoothly along the flow of traffic, dodging in and out with ease. Greta didn't seem to mind that her skirt was halfway to her hips. Neither did the other drivers. Heads turned as we roared by, and I was thinking it had been a long time since I'd felt this good.

Most of the shops were shut down by the time we pulled up at the end of the Rue Daguerre; this section was pedestrian only, so we parked the bike and set off on foot. At the fish stand men wearing heavy full-length plastic aprons were hosing down the pavement, and the greengrocers were moving the last crates of produce indoors, although there were lights still on in the bakery and the wine shop was open. Market street in the daytime, at night la Rue Daguerre belonged to the café scene; the terraces were jam-packed and noisy, and the night crowd strolled easily along trying to make up their minds where to sit and play out the evening. Two white-haired old ladies—sisters, by the looks of it—wearing cardigans and cotton dresses they had probably worn in the forties, were operating some sort of antiquated accordion-like machine that made music equally antiquated. I always thought that sort of quaint folklore was for the benefit of tourists but, as Greta had mentioned, tourists didn't venture down here. These were locals.

We found the hotel not far down the street, the door sandwiched between a cheese shop and a butcher shop that specialized in horse meat, witnessed by three plaster horse heads jutting out like trophies above the awning.

Greta managed to be only marginally believable as my girlfriend—I could feel the resistance when I casually draped my arm over her shoulder, but she was perfectly convincing as Louise's friend, and devastated to know she'd missed her. The desk clerk said Louise had seemed very upset, and he'd made some calls to help her find a train for Calais so she could get an early morning ferry for Dover. I think Greta must have mesmerized the desk clerk because she even had him digging through the trash to come up with the notes he'd tossed. The train Louise was hoping to catch departed from la Gare du Nord on the other side of Paris in less than forty minutes.

It was a straight shot up tree-lined avenues and boulevards, and over the Pont Saint Michel with a glimpse of Notre Dame de Paris lit up against the night sky. I had a flash of a fantasy about returning to this very spot, at night, with Greta, and just staring at it for hours, like an indoor cat watching the world from a window, but for now I had to keep my eyes on the traffic. Greta knew the layout of the city, all we had to do was follow the directional signs like stepping stones from one hub to the next.

I don't know what made me think we could find Louise. It was like looking for a needle in a haystack. I'd never seen a train station on this scale: Fronting the street was a gigantic triumphal arch built into a facade of colossal proportions, then a main hall of equally staggering size, all of it supported by cast-iron columns soaring skyward to a glass-and-metal roof covering countless platforms that stretched into the distant night.

"There," Greta said, drawing my attention to an overhead display board with spinning flaps that made a sound like dominos falling; every few seconds it rattled clickety-clack, then paused while the hours and destinations settled into place, then rattled again. "Calais. Platform twelve."

We had fifteen minutes.

As we raced toward the platform I told her the plan I'd hatched: She would wait at the head of the platform in case Louise arrived after us, meanwhile I'd search the train. I pulled out my pen and inked a phone number into her palm.

"Tell her to leave a message at this number. Ask for Billy the Kid. Let me know where I can reach her." I left her with our gear and climbed onto the first car.

I didn't have much hope of finding her in the squeeze of last-minute boarding; I saw plenty of haggard mothers wrestling with a surplus of odd bags and children, there was a troupe of rowdy Boy Scouts shoving one another around, and quite a few older couples in bucket hats and sunburns whom I took to be English returning home from holidays, but no one who looked remotely like the woman I'd seen the night before. I hurried from wagon to wagon along the stuffy corridors, forcing my way past people smoking and hanging out the windows, poking my head into the compartments as I went.

I must have covered five or six cars when I noticed two men striding along the platform beside the train, looking into the windows. Sweating through their mud brown suit jackets and tripping over luggage trolleys, there was no doubt they were searching for someone, and from the looks of them, I'd bet my bottom dollar we were looking for the same lady. Then one of them raised a hand to point down the platform, and I saw the flash of white tape. It was the guy with the broken finger from Harry's Bar.

Just as I turned away from the window, there she was in the compartment behind me, stowing her bag overhead.

"Louise," I said, and she whirled around to face me, a square-jawed woman with soft and very frightened brown eyes behind oversized glasses. "Come with me," I said, "and keep your head down." I grabbed her by the elbow and dragged her into the corridor, away from the direction the men were moving. The toilet at the end of the car was empty, and I pulled her inside and shut the door.

It wasn't ideal for an introduction; she was paralyzed with fright, and we were sandwiched flat, face-to-face like sardines in a sweltering hot wormhole of a cubicle. I probably didn't smell all that good either.

"We got your message. The napkin. What happened?"

She had a hard time keeping her mouth steady as she spoke—I don't think I've ever seen someone so terrified. She said Zhukovsky had been suddenly recalled to Moscow, he wasn't sure why—maybe they suspected him, or maybe they'd learned about his affair with her, an Englishwoman, which was reason enough to be accused of treason, but either way it spelled trouble. Then in the bar, just after I had identified myself with the French 75 line, the other guy appeared.

"He was KGB," she said in a voice choked by fear. "Petrov told me when we left the bar."

"How did he know?"

"Petrov knows everybody at the Soviet Embassy. This guy must have been sent in from Moscow. You can always spot them. The way they dress and handle themselves. That's why Petrov made the scene he did. To get us arrested. He'll ask for asylum. But they had to let me go."

She then said he'd given her a single memorandum from the Pasternak files to pass on to us.

"He didn't say what it was, but it was really important. Someone is going to be assassinated."

"Who?"

"I don't know."

"Where's the memo?"

She had been afraid to keep it on her so she'd left it in Paris. She was telling me where to find it when there was an angry pounding on the door and voices shouting to open up.

If it was the men in the mud brown suits, the one with the broken finger would surely recognize me.

I clamped a hand over Louise's mouth to quiet her, which wasn't really necessary given how frightened she was. There was a tiny sink and a faucet that produced just a dribble of water, enough to slick back my hair, then I quickly packed some wads of toilet paper around my gums. The effect was slightly grotesque and definitely lacked symmetry, but I didn't have time to refine it. Lastly I motioned for Louise to give me her glasses.

With Louise huddled on the toilet seat behind me I opened the door partway. Sure enough, it was the brown suits. My appearance was just strange enough to startle them. I cracked a sickly smile and mumbled an apology, then started to gag. It wasn't all that hard, what with the heat and the smell of urine, and the toilet paper drying out my mouth. They backed away in horror, then turned to shove aside a couple of backpacking students and hurry into the next car.

I managed to get off the train just before the doors locked.

Greta was standing just where I'd left her. She didn't look worried or hopeful or anything like you might expect, until I got close enough to see her eyes. And a tiny wrinkle of a frown that might have been a shoe pinching.

"Blimey, what happened to you?" she asked.

"Found her," I said as I dug the toilet paper out of my mouth.

I swept up my backpack and helmet, and we turned and walked casually toward the exit. I asked her, "Did you see those two guys in the brown suits?"

"Yeah. Couldn't miss them."

"They're KGB."

"I'm not surprised."

"Oh?"

"The way they dress."

"Terrible to be stereotyped like that," I said. "I know how it feels."

"Do you think they were looking for her? Louise?"

"I do."

"What are you mixed up in?"

"I wish I knew."

CHAPTER 14

Outside, sirens were blasting in some street nearby. The sun had finally set and the city was beginning to cool down, which brought us to a parting of the ways.

Once again Greta was docile as a lamb while I strapped the helmet on her. Sure, I could have just tossed it at her, but this way my fingers would graze her skin for a split second that I'd remember for years to come. I couldn't get her to meet my gaze. She stood there staring up at a streetlamp while I fiddled with the snap.

"There you go. All suited up."

She didn't move, so I dropped the face shield for her.

"I'll take you home now."

Something odd was happening. She wasn't moving, just standing there, fixated on that streetlamp. I thought she was setting me up again. But this wasn't a tease. Her eyes were filling with tears.

In my life I've watched a few girls cry—it's not something I particularly enjoy, although I've been told I take it better than most guys. But I got the feeling that something earth-shattering was happening behind that plastic bubble. I swear I would have moved heaven and earth to stop it.

"Greta?"

I bent my head to peer into those swimming blue eyes. She was trying valiantly to hold back the tears but the tears just wouldn't cooperate.

I lifted the plastic shield.

Sirens moved through the streets again and the big arched entrance continued to spew out people and bulky suitcases. To one side were a trio of skinny dudes with a boom box performing Michael Jackson dance moves to "Thriller". It was an awfully noisy place for Greta to have a breakdown.

"The DGSE murdered my boyfriend," she said.

I waited, expecting more, but none was forthcoming. I knew better than to press her. She just needed a moment for the tears to dry up.

And they did. Not one slipped away.

"I don't want to go home."

There were any number of replies to that, so I chose my favorite.

"You want to hang with me a little while longer? Up for a little more adventure?"

She had a way of saying yes without saying yes.

Getting on the bike, I told her to direct me back to the Rue Daguerre. I didn't tell her anything else, I wanted to give her a little time with her own thoughts. I hoped a night ride on the bike would smooth out her soul the way it did mine.

We parked around a side street this time, closer to the hotel, and I told her what we needed to find, and where Louise had hidden it.

She broke into a smile.

"Yeah," I said. "Not exactly sophisticated high tech, is it?"

"I think it's rather ingenious. A man would never think of looking there, and all these thugs are men."

The desk clerk looked pleased as punch to see Greta again. This time I hung back and let her deploy her icy charm. She didn't try to explain anything, just asked if she might have her friend's room since Louise had already paid for the night. He was all set to comply, and then he remembered—upon checking out, Louise had complained that the toilet was backed up. However, he said, they had plenty of rooms and he could stretch the rules a little and give her a clean one. Seeing no reason to argue, she handed over her ID with a wide-eyed look of gratitude and asked for a room on the first floor. When he craned his neck and indicated me with a lift of the chin, she told him I wouldn't be staying.

Or at least that's the way she told me it happened.

"Are you sure you want to do this?" she said as I threw open the double-cased window and leaned out. The room he gave us was right next door to the one Louise had taken—one strike in our favor.

"The shutter's open," I said as I eyed the distance from our balcony to the next. "It's not far. I can make it. All depends on if she left the window open."

"I could go back and say she left something in the room."

"What? And walk away with a down comforter?"

What I hadn't counted on was navigating around the trio of plaster horse heads above the butcher shop. They were big suckers, life-size, projecting like mounted trophies above the storefront. There was one attached to the facade right outside the other window, and not only would I need to climb through a jungle of overhang support rods fixed to the stone wall, I'd have to avoid the neon light tubes molded around the horse's head. The tubes wouldn't be hot, but the electrodes at the ends could zap me.

I wasn't built for that sort of thing, and there was one moment when I was caught in a bizarrely contortionist squeeze that was so insane I might have laughed if I hadn't been hanging on to a grotesquely grinning horse glowing in orange-red light like something out of a horror show. From the perky angle of his ears he seemed to be trying to reassure me that he didn't have a clue as to what was coming.

Luckily the window wasn't latched; I don't think I could have made it back the way I came. So far nobody in the street had noticed me.

A few moments later I opened the door for Greta.

I showed her the comforter piled on the bed. "Found it on the top shelf of the wardrobe, just where she said it would be."

We stared at it like a thing of mystery.

"Do you think it's the same one?" I asked.

"Why wouldn't it be?"

I shrugged. "Maybe housekeeping took it away to clean."

"In August? Fat chance."

So for the next twenty minutes we sat cross-legged on the bed feeling for lumps in the comforter where Louise had worked the scraps into the feathers through tiny slits she'd cut in the fabric. We took our time. It was an odd but relaxing way to finish the crazy evening. No distractions, only the hum of voices from the cafés below and the accordion music floating up from farther down the street.

Talking came a lot more easily now, although we delicately picked our way around certain subjects, like her boyfriend and my ex-wife. I told her how I had ended up in Florida after my parents' death, that I had been an only child born late in the life of parents who thought they'd miss out on parenting. We'd been a close-knit family, but there were few of us, only a handful of my parents' cousins scattered so far afield that I knew of them only through Christmas cards received punctually every year, sometimes with an enclosed photo, strangers crushed together and smiling, but still strangers. Dad had succumbed to a heart attack at the age of seventy-five and my mother several years later from breast cancer. I'd always harbored the suspicion that the cancer had just sauntered in the door that grief had left wide open.

I'd had a happy childhood with them. I told her how, as a boy, I'd worked in my father's Santa Ana paint company. I'd always been good at numbers and I had a good memory too, and I made a game out of memorizing the Hex codes of every paint we sold. I found I had a real talent for identifying and reproducing color. I had this great collection of model fighters and bombers and I'd spend my entire weekend mixing shades of gray—I used to think if I got it just right I could make the aircraft magically disappear in the sky.

"I know it sounds geeky, but to a kid, being able to show off is a big deal. For example, for your eyes I'd start with Carolina Blue 57A0D3."

I definitely was not trying to impress her—you don't impress women with Hex codes. I think I was testing her to see how much of the real me she could swallow. It was hard to say. Nothing much got a rise out of her.

"I got my degree in industrial chemistry, but then, well, family priorities intervened. My dad brought me in to run the financial side of his business."

We expanded, I explained, developed new technology, military-grade varnishes, we built a few factories and turned out some innovative products. Maybe not as big as our competitors, but we did well. Disney was always our favored client. We'd been their first supplier.

I wondered if she was bored yet. She didn't look bored. But neither did she look interested.

"And now?" she asked.

"My best buddy, Mike, got a job as an Imagineer with Disney in Orlando. He convinced me to move out there after my parents died. It seemed like a good idea. So now I do some consulting for Disney on odd projects. It's a cushy job."

"Here," she said with typical calm. "I feel something."

Sure enough, there it was, our first find—a tightly folded up strip of paper amid the feathers. She worked it out through the slit and held it up to the dim lamplight. It looked like the sort of note an adolescent would pass around during class. She dropped it into my hand like a gold miner with his first nugget of gold.

I unfolded it. It was a section of a photocopied document in a language I couldn't read.

I let her take a look.

"It looks like Cyrillic."

"Russian?"

"Maybe. How many pieces are there?"

"Eight."

She went back to patting down her end of the duvet. I

could tell she was tired. I, on the other hand, was only midway through my jet-lagged day and was looking forward to happy hour in Florida.

"You don't have any other family?" she asked.

"My father had a sister here in Paris. But they weren't close." I hesitated, thinking how to choose my words without lying outright. "Last week I received a letter saying she'd died and left me some property. So I flew over to get things sorted out."

"There seems to be a lot to sort out."

Briefly, I portrayed my deceased Aunt Lily as an innocent editor who'd gotten her hands on an explosive manuscript that the Soviets didn't want published.

"Explosive indeed," she said, trying to subdue a yawn, which she politely shielded from view with her hand. The hand reminded me of the one Da Vinci painted in his portrait of a woman holding an ermine. Long, slender fingers that left you to imagine how light her touch would be.

"Sorry," she said.

"You sure you don't want me to take you home?"

"I don't want to go back there. I can't sleep."

She found another folded paper.

"That's two."

"Is it your boyfriend's place?" I asked.

She hesitated, then nodded.

"Do you want to tell me what happened?"

She again hesitated, longer this time; I waited. Most women I knew were loquacious quick responders, voicing the first thoughts on their mind. Greta deliberated. Her silences could be unnerving.

"It was last year," she began, "he was on the Greenpeace

flagship on their way to Tahiti to protest against nuclear testing the French were carrying out on one of the atolls. The French government wanted to make sure the ship never reached Tahiti, so the DGSE sent a team to attach mines to the bottom of the hull when they docked in a port in New Zealand. Olivier was the only one on board at the time."

"Boom," she said as she dropped a third tightly folded strip of paper onto the pile.

She went silent. So did I. I felt stupid. I had no idea how to respond to that sort of thing.

"I'm sorry, Greta," I mumbled.

Meanwhile, I fished out a fourth strip.

She continued. "I'm still very angry. I jerk them around every chance I get."

"Isn't that dangerous?"

"Not as dangerous as editing Russian manuscripts, apparently."

I fished out another. "Three to go."

"It doesn't sound like much, handcuffing myself to doors. It gets media coverage and focuses attention on the problem, which we need, but it's not enough. Not for me. One day I'll find a way to get back at them. I'll do them some real damage."

Her distilled coolheaded passion made me a little afraid for her. I wondered about the love they'd shared, and how much it had been strengthened by their commitment to a common goal. I thought how easily my marriage had dissolved, how little commitment had been there in the first place. Although the pain of losing the woman I loved had been deep and searing at the time, there had been nothing else we had been fighting for.

My thoughts turned to my aunt's motivations. Who was

the Pasternak behind the files? Was he the same man as Pym's brother? What had he meant to her? That she would put in motion all these players and fashion this intrigue to save him, but from what? I couldn't even be sure my aunt wasn't working for one of the secret services herself, although I doubted it. Pym seemed to think any one of them could have been behind the attempt on her life.

I wondered at how easily I had thrown myself into these waters, knowing so little about the dangers involved.

At that moment we heard footsteps coming down the hall. They stopped just outside our door. Both of us froze while Greta listened to an exchange between three men. I recognized one of the voices to be that of the front desk clerk.

Greta's eyes widened with alarm.

"Somebody wants to search the room," she whispered, but before she had the words out of her mouth I had already gathered up the strips of paper we'd removed and stuffed them into my pocket.

There was a swift polite knock on the door. Then a pause—more discussion.

"He brought the wrong key," she whispered to me. "He has to go back downstairs."

I glanced at the window—there was no way both of us could make it back to the other room in time.

I stood and started pulling off my shirt.

"Take something off. Anything. Your blouse."

She didn't hesitate—she quickly tugged off her shirt and we stuffed our clothes into my backpack.

Moments later when they opened the door we were underneath the duvet moaning and groaning and humping away.

When they flipped on the lights, I peered out from beneath the comforter, shielding my face and keeping Greta buried, crying, "What the fuck?" and then Greta let loose with a peel of laughter that completely took me by surprise.

The poor desk clerk couldn't make out what was going on—with an embarrassed apology, he stepped back into the hallway, then took a moment to check the room number, giving us just the break in time we needed to wrap Greta in the comforter, grab my backpack and make a shirtless dash for the door. Hand in hand we barreled right past them, Greta wearing the duvet over her head and squealing with laughter.

And so we roared off into the night on the bike, me shirtless and Greta wrapped in the duvet with its tail flying behind her like a cape. Once we were well away from la Rue Daguerre I pulled onto a quiet impasse, where we parked the bike and dug our clothes out of the bag. My heart was thumping like crazy and my hands were trembling while I tucked in my shirt. Greta was calmly buttoning up her blouse. Her hands were steady, I noticed. A wisp of hair had come loose from her braid and it fell over her face so I couldn't read her expression in the dark. The squeal of laughter still rang in my ears. I wanted to hear her laugh like that again.

"Who do you think they were?" she asked

"They weren't the same two guys I met on the train."

"These two were French."

"It wouldn't be the police," I said. "There's no reason why they'd want to get into that room. Zhukovsky must have talked to someone."

"Internal security. The DST."

This was getting messy, and I was angry at myself for

involving her.

"Damn," I said, remembering that the hotel had registered her name from her ID. "You identified yourself as Louisa's friend. They can find you."

"Not easily. It's an old address on the ID card."

"Even so, I can't take you back to your place. Do you have a friend you can stay with?" I added lamely, hoping she didn't.

"I'll sleep on your sofa."

"It's too risky. The less you know about me and my aunt, the better it is for both of us."

"So blindfold me."

"What?"

"I always wear a sleep mask anyway," she said. "Light bothers me."

Problem there was that my aunt's apartment had probably been bugged.

"You won't be able to talk either," I said.

"That's not a problem."

"This is crazy." It had all been crazy, every minute, from the moment we met.

"You make me feel safe."

"I do?" I said, trying to keep astonishment out of my voice.

She was giving me one of those wooden stares, but I think she was just determined not to cry again. She didn't strike me as the manipulative kind, but she sure was willful. Either way, the last thing I wanted was to see those blue eyes fill with tears again.

She said, "I'll fall asleep and I won't move again until you get me up. Then in the morning you can drive me home. Blindfolded."

"God, that sounds kinky."

We stuffed the duvet into the motorcycle's storage compartment. As she straddled the bike behind me and wrapped her arms around my waist, I added over my shoulder, "By the way, I have to walk my dog when I get home."

CHAPTER 15

One of the skills my mom had insisted I learn was how to iron my own shirts. It was a task I thoroughly disliked but one I'd performed with my usual meticulousness: I hated creases as much as poorly aligned tableware. Now here I was in a Paris apartment at an ironing board in one of the back bedrooms, flattening scraps of paper with a warm iron at one o'clock in the morning. I remembered seeing a portable photocopy machine lying on the floor in my aunt's office where the intruders had dumped it. It made some wounded grinding noises when I turned it on but worked well enough to make a few copies. Before heading out, I checked in on Greta. She'd gone to sleep with the top of her head wrapped in a scarf I'd dug out of the coat closet. Somehow, Billy had made it up on the bed—undoubtedly with a little bit of fumbling help from Greta, and despite the heat, the two were snuggled together as if snuggling together were old habit.

The Bar du Marché was just closing down when I asked to use their phone. My aunt answered after the first ring; she didn't sound like she'd been sleeping.

I gave her an abbreviated version of the evening's events, making sure to give Greta credit for leading me to both Louise and the memorandum Zhukovsky had wanted her to have.

"So you recruited her."

"I wouldn't go so far as to call her a recruit."

"You are quite good at getting people to trust you."

I told her how I'd brought Greta home. Although I'd taken precautions.

"My dear boy, I'm sure you did. Well-brought-up young men always seem to have those things handy when the moment arises."

"I don't mean those kind of precautions. I mean—oh, never mind." I wasn't about to tell her I'd left Greta blindfolded and alone with only Billy to defend her. "The memorandum. It's two pages, something official-looking, stamped and dated," I concluded.

"It's in Russian?"

"It's in the same script as that clunky old typewriter in your office."

"So you noticed my Cyrillic typewriter." She sounded pleased.

"Found it on the floor along with the copy machine. I haven't had time to do anything but straighten the things that got knocked over. I'll have a go at your books tomorrow. They're still scattered all over the floor. It's a real mess."

"Carlito, my dear boy, all in good time."

"It's the disorder, Aunt Lily, it makes me very uncomfortable. I'm not even sure I'll be able to sleep tonight unless I do something about it."

"Well, be very careful with my Gogol. Those editions were

gifts." There was a hesitation—was she remembering? "And I would highly recommend you set aside *Darkness at Noon* for a little late-night reading. I don't enjoy reading Koestler, I don't think anybody does, but he's important. He recognized the dangers of Communism much sooner and more clearly than others on the left, although the French could not be weaned from it—it was too important to them, a truth the Americans have never understood. It took the Hungarian uprising for them to start leaving the party, and that wasn't until 1956. I'd arrived not long after the war . . ."

She paused, and I waited. She had strayed off topic, but I was beginning to understand that this, her life, *was* the topic, and so I listened.

"Oh, Carlito, you can't imagine what Paris was like back then, such a bleak, hardscrabble place, ragtag children who didn't know how to smile, the stone buildings black from soot as if they had absorbed all the misery of resentment and humiliation, horses collapsing in the street, cats staring from the rubbish, rats staring at the cats, everyone with hacking coughs because there was no coal to heat their homes, but then you'd come upon an artist with his easel set up in the street, or a flower stall, or a crowd gathered around a pair of violinists playing a Bach concerto in the freezing cold—and you would pause and think, it's still there, that hunger for beauty that no degree of squalor or exhaustion could ever extinguish. I was young and in love . . ."

There was another hesitation. "Have you been in love? But of course you have. I wonder, does love count as a moral failing? It's certainly not on the same scale as Koestler's moral failings, which were very severe and not to be taken lightly.

The question is, how do we read him, in light of the personal dimension? People in the intelligence community often speak of the relationship between the message and the messenger. If you trust the messenger, you trust the message. Is it the same with literature and philosophy and film? Should it be? On second thought, read Gogol, but handle him carefully."

Somehow, she had found her way back to Gogol.

"Noted. Now, how can I get this to you?"

"Ah, yes, the file."

She told me to go to the night clerk at the hotel and ask them to fax it to a number she gave me.

I was to send it to the attention of Madame Margarita.

The only sound was the fan whirring softly in the bedroom next door, where Greta was sleeping. I put down my book, went to the open window and peered up at the narrow strip of night sky wedged between the rooftops; toward the east the deep blue was tinting toward a softer shade, revealing a faint contour of chimneys in the dim light of dawn. I leaned out and was met with the freshness and stillness of night's end, and right on cue there it was, the hesitant chirping of a solitary bird, the first herald of morning. I hadn't been able to sleep, not even after my aunt's books were neatly shelved. Instead, I had settled into the only armchair in the room, with a much marked-up edition of Gogol's short stories and a glass of Lagavulin and started reading.

My aunt's personal library was astonishing. There were extensive collections in French and Russian, just as many in English, and a number in Italian. I recognized some titles as classics I'd heard of but never read. We didn't have many books when I was growing up—books were expensive, and the only ones we invested in were Bibles or motivational reads that my father ranked up there with the Gospels, like Dale Carnegie's *How to Win Friends and Influence People* and Norman Vincent Peale's *The Power of Positive Thinking*. We also had a copy of Dr. Spock, who for some reason was shelved in the kitchen next to the toaster along with my mother's *Good Housekeeping Cookbook*. But the holy grail of all reads were my father's old college chemistry books that he kept in the garage he had converted into a workshop. His university education having been cut short by the war, he relied on his strong strain of autodidact to cobble together a business suited to his interests—which were chemistry, engineering and a determination to succeed. While I watched television in our large chintzy sunroom with my mom every evening after dinner, he was in his workshop in a paint-spattered jumpsuit, blowtorching his latest industrial coating to test its heat resistance, or scrubbing our new latex product to see how well it stood up to repeated washings.

At breakfast I would find him all cleaned up, mustache trimmed and collar starched, drinking coffee and flipping through *U.S. News and World Report*, or Kiplinger's *Changing Times*, and then he would be off to our paint store, or our new factory. He worked desperately hard at what he did, so much so that I feared I wouldn't be able to live up to his model of manhood.

He had an unspoken prejudice against novels and film, maybe because he associated them with liberal-leaning Hollywood just up the coast, liberals being the bane of all entrepreneurial endeavor. But perhaps it had more to do with how fiction drew the reader's gaze inward to human nature, and my father was all about surfaces. I remember coming home one night and finding him sitting on the living room sofa in his pajamas with his nose in one of my mother's romance novels, which she would borrow from the library or from friends. There was an expression of utter bafflement, almost horror on his face. Seeing me walk in, he peeled off his glasses and set the book back on the end table with a deep sigh of relief, as if my arrival had spared him further torture. I suspect they had quarreled, which was very rare, and as a last-ditch effort he had picked up one of her novels, hoping for enlightenment. I can't recall a single evening when he watched television with us, or came with us to the movies, despite my mother's urging. Valuing his approval as I did, I turned up my nose at anything remotely resembling literature. I'd been exposed to a very short list of greats in my basic lit introductory class at UC Irvine; of Salinger, Hemingway and *Gatsby*, I had read only excerpts.

Now here I was at the age of thirty-four in my aunt's Paris home, reading a story by a nineteenth-century Russian about a man who wakes up without a nose. I had no idea why my aunt had chosen to make a life so far away from her family, but I was beginning to get a glimpse of the vast gulf between her and us.

I felt like she had sprinkled a few crumbs in our conversations for me to follow, perhaps intentionally, or perhaps it was just her habit of discursive wandering as if she were setting off on an adventure. But I think she hoped I'd find the trail and follow the crumbs.

Dawn was breaking as I sat on the side of the bed in the back room, the one with the exercise bicycle and the ironing board, removing my shoes. I set the alarm for 8:00 a.m. and fell back onto the pillow, and within seconds I was sound asleep.

CHAPTER 16

The next thing I knew, someone was shaking me out of a pleasant but muddled dream. I was aware of the hot sun streaming through the window and my face buried in a sweat-sodden pillow.

There was a woman in the dream and I didn't want it to fade, so I tried to hold on to it with my mind like a child grasping at smoke rings, only to have it vanish. Then the dream became a voice, and the voice was Greta's. She was still here. I hadn't lost her.

"Come on, get up. You shouldn't sleep any longer."

I rolled over, blinking at the harsh sunlight. "What time is it?"

"It's past noon. Your friend wanted to wake you hours ago but I talked him out of it."

I swept my legs around to sit up on the side of the bed and rubbed my face briskly with both hands. I was all stubble and bad breath and wrinkled boxer shorts. I squinted up at her. "What friend?"

"The one you call Van Gogh."

"Van Gogh? He was here?"

"He was pounding on the front door. You'd blocked it with a bookcase."

"Why didn't you wake me?"

"I tried to. I had a hard time finding you until I decided to throw caution to the wind and take off my sleep mask. I got you to sit up, but then you fell back onto the bed. So I moved the bookcase myself."

I looked up at her through a sleep-addled haze. Why I'd let her talk me into staying the night was beyond me. It was stupid of me—divinely, splendidly stupid.

"What did he want?"

She held out an upturned hand; in her palm lay a tiny metal disc that must have once looked like a transistor before being smashed, probably with a hammer.

"This. It's a bug."

"How did he find it?"

"He came with a ladder and a sweep detector—I got the impression he's done this before."

"No doubt."

"They'd planted it in a lamp in the living room. So we can talk normally now. He also said to tell you the bug looks like the sort the British use rather than the KGB."

"He knows an awful lot for a man of so few words."

"Why is the British SIS bugging your aunt's apartment?"

"That's what I've been trying to find out." I wasn't thinking very quickly yet; I was trying to recall if I'd seen deodorant or a razor somewhere in one of the bathrooms. "He shouldn't be telling you all this."

"I told him I was your accomplice."

"It seems to me that too many people know too much, and yet no one knows exactly what it is we need to know."

"I think your aunt would welcome my cooperation. In fact, I'm sure of it. I feel her vibe very strongly here."

"I don't doubt it one bit." I darted a nervous glance toward the doorway, wondering if I'd find her standing there. I still hadn't figured out how she came and went so secretly.

"I took your dog out too."

I glanced over at Billy watching me from the doorway. He wagged his tail as if to say he held no grudges for being neglected.

"So much for secrecy," I said. "Can you pass me my pants, please?"

I nodded in the direction of the ironing board, where I'd neatly laid out my khakis and polo shirt the night before.

"I don't think anyone would have recognized us," she said as she tossed the pants and shirt to me. "I put on a Moroccan djellaba I found in a closet—one with a hood—and sunglasses. Then I put your dog in a shopping caddy and went down the service stairs, the ones opening onto the kitchen. You'd only blocked that door with a broomstick."

"You're a natural at this."

"I'd rather be sabotaging bulldozers in the Amazon forest, but business is slow right now."

I'd managed to get my shirt on but I couldn't bring myself to stand.

"Greta, you can't repeat any of this. Nothing you've seen or heard around here. Not to anyone."

"I won't. Even under torture."

"No one's going to torture you. I wouldn't ever let things

go that far."

"Good, that's solved. Now can you please get up and make us something to eat?"

Shortly thereafter, Greta and I were on our way to Le Petit Verlaine, her for lunch and me for breakfast. The sidewalk had been baking in the blistering hot sun all morning so I was carrying Billy in a football hold and Greta had his wheels. She didn't make a fuss over Billy like most people do, or question my decision to bring him to Paris in light of the obvious challenges; rather, she just accepted his disability as a fact of life to be accommodated, like nearsightedness or hay fever. It was like she had moved into my head and made herself comfortably at home. I wasn't sure how that would work out, but it certainly eliminated the need for explanations, which I found refreshing.

On the stairs I had started telling her about Huggins and his runaway wife.

"He's terribly resolute," I said. "I've never met a man so patient and devoted. It makes me wonder if perhaps he doesn't deserve better."

"Maybe she wasn't made for that kind of life. Being a priest's wife. Imagine all the perfectly horrible people you have to pretend to love."

Approaching us on the sidewalk at that moment was an older woman leading a small terrier that had taken a sudden and visceral dislike to Billy. The woman seemed to think his aggressiveness terribly amusing and paused to discuss the matter with the canine while he trembled and yapped furiously, oblivious to the fact that his leash was stretched across the sidewalk, making it impossible for us to pass. While I squeezed around them, Greta with a long-legged stride stepped high over the leash without so much as a glance at the pair, prompting the woman to erupt in a storm of indignation.

"You see what I mean?" Greta murmured. I said I did. We could still hear the woman railing at us as we moved on down the street.

"So your friend's wife was having an affair with Van Gogh."

"Huggins certainly thinks so. Personally, I find the idea a little far-fetched."

"Why?"

"I don't see how a woman could find him attractive."

"He seems to know what he's doing, in his own oddball manner. Women like that in a man. And I'm sure he'd clean up well."

My hackles rose. Remembering that they had spent the morning together searching the apartment for electronic bugs while I slept. My God, I was jealous. It had been years since I'd been stung by jealousy. It was an ugly feeling and I disliked it intensely. I felt much like that terrier had looked.

When we got to the café Huggins was at his habitual table at the back, completely walled in behind his newspaper. The awning had been rolled out to cover the entire terrace, lowering the temperature only slightly. Not so much as a breeze found its way to the Rue Tonton.

"Morning, Henry," I said as I pulled out a chair for Greta. "Or afternoon, rather."

He lowered his newspaper reluctantly, as though he'd been caught out. He was not flushed, like you would expect in this heat, but pale and sweating, and I wondered if he was ill. He nodded and gave me a ghostly smile, then withdrew behind his paper again.

"That's odd," I said in a low voice. "He's usually so sociable. It's probably the heat."

Greta was busy speaking to the waiter, who reappeared a moment later with a dish of cool water for Billy.

"Or maybe he's just being polite, seeing I'm with you," I continued, more to myself since Greta was now perusing the menu with her usual intensity. The waiter, newly attentive, hovered over her shoulder, waiting patiently for our order. She had that effect, the ability to wordlessly command attention without so much as a glance.

I was diving into a basket of freshly baked *viennoiseries* and Greta was starting in on her plate of raw vegetables doused in vinaigrette, when I noticed Huggins trying to sneak out. He sidled between the tables along the back and onto the street with his head down, as though he didn't want to be seen. It was a strange change in behavior—and it worried me a little. I wondered if I'd done something to offend the good man. I would have let him go without a word if it hadn't been for the waiter, who rushed onto the sidewalk calling, "Monsieur!" and waving reading glasses he'd left behind. Huggins only ignored him and hurried on down the street at a brisk pace.

Greta quickly sized up the situation, hopped up from the table, snatched the glasses from the waiter's hand and ran off after him. What happened next totally floored me. It played out very briefly, Huggins stopping in his tracks to take the glasses, smiling, offering a cheerful thanks while mopping his upper lip with a handkerchief and eyes darting in my direction. Turning to cross the street. Greta following him close on his heels until he turned again. Greta leaning in with her full height, back to me so I couldn't see her face, but angry, oh so angry. Then Huggins stiffened, looking very stern and again glancing my way. A few more words were exchanged and then he faked a smile and went on his way.

That was the first time I'd seen her flustered. Stepping over Billy and slipping back onto her chair, whipping her long blond braid around with an angry jerk of her head, then attacking her grated carrots with unsteady hands, then putting down her fork and staring off into the distance. Her eyes shaded by the dark glasses. Jaw set like stone.

"So you two know each other," I said.

"Family connection," she answered dismissively.

"Close family?"

No comment.

"Is he your dad?"

She started. "Why would you think that?"

"Your eyes, Greta. He's got those unusual Carolina Blue eyes."

Her silence was confirmation enough.

"Why didn't he come up to us? Why all the secretiveness?"

I sat there incredulous, waiting for an explanation, there was none. I was accustomed to her taciturnity, I even found it refreshing. But not in this case, not now. She was still staring at the big nothing in front of us, at the hot and clammy air thick as fog, at the vacant intersection of three empty streets, and I was staring at her.

"He fed me this story about how his wife had left him and he comes here hoping he'll run into her."

She stopped me. She lifted a hand in warning and shook her head. "No. Not a single word. I don't want to know."

"Don't tell me he's a spy too." I said it jokingly, given that my life was sort of swarming with spies at the moment, but she flinched ever so slightly, and my heart dropped. I'd hit the nail on the head. "You're kidding. No, really? What is he, British intelligence?"

She didn't bother to deny it.

Good Lord. I'd invited him to Harry's and given him a front-row seat to my aunt's smuggling operation.

"So, he's been manipulating me all along. And I just played right into his hands."

Greta removed her sunglasses, softly slipped her fingers around my neck and leaned close to my ear, whispering in a tone of tenderness I will never forget. "I'm so sorry, Carl."

She kissed me gently on the cheek, lingering just near my ear so that I could hear the sound of her breath as her lips pressed against my sweaty skin.

"Bye, Billy," she said sadly as she rose, giving him a wave. It was a little girl wave, endearingly childish and out of character for someone with the grit to stare down bulldozers or chain herself to the gates of nuclear reactor sites. Or walk away from a half-eaten raw vegetable platter, her favorite dish.

She didn't even look back.

CHAPTER 17

A summer squall was blowing in as I walked home, chasing clouds dark and ominous across the sky and rattling shutters. I secured all the windows in the apartment and headed down the stairs to Pym's door, clutching the bottle of Lagavulin the way I'd once seen my grandmother coming across the backyard of her farmhouse with a dead chicken she'd just wrung by the neck. She was wearing galoshes and an apron over a colorful homemade housedress, and she was whistling (she whistled beautifully) some snippet of a church hymn with a martial air. I watched her stride purposefully across the yard to the outdoor workbench, where she slammed that chicken down (I can still hear the thud) and started plucking its feathers with a zeal that made a lasting impression on my young mind. She knew every one of those chickens by name—and this one, Penny, an old hen past her egg-laying days, had been one of her favorites. Caught by gusts of hot wind, Penny's feathers flew through the air, swirling and spinning before settling on my grandmother's hair and her arms, and through it all my grandmother whistled. My father said she held the county record for plucking the most chickens in a given time. I loved her, but she intimidated me. Even as a boy I suspected there was a lot more going on behind that homely floral print dress than met the eye, in the way we sense what's going on in obscure ways. Just as I had intuited the truth about Huggins from a distance, at a glance.

The polished bronze plaque fixed on Pym's door read, "P. M. Bukovsky, Traducteur," followed by a trail of acronyms and his office hours. The door stood slightly open, which is how I'd often seen it, I suppose to facilitate the coming and going of students or clients and sparing him the long grinding effort of making his way to the door. Consequently the noise of his life spilled into the hallway, depriving him of privacy; my aunt said the open door alleviated his sense of isolation.

"It's his Batcave," she had said. "Down there he has at his fingertips all his powers. He's in his element."

There was an absurdly cheerful doormat in front of the door, colorful flowers with smiley faces that I thought very un-Pym-like, and inside Pym was bawling out some poor soul. The mat was crooked, and I bent down to straighten it just as the door swung open and a pale-faced adolescent with a satchel on his back rammed straight into me. Pym barked something at the kid, prompting the boy to utter an apology in French, then, after a sharp correction from Pym, in English. The boy's ears, oddly shaped protruding things that gave him a strange insect-like appearance, flushed beet red and his eyes mirrored the panic of somebody escaping a burning building. I stepped aside to let him pass and we wound up doing one of those silly dodging duets, bobbing back and forth until he made a dash for it, tripped over my foot and went sprawling face down on the tile entryway.

"Hey," I said as I bent down to help him up, "are you okay?"

Pym spoke up, dismissing the incident with a sharp staccato laugh. Sharp like a barb tipped with scorn. "He's got two good legs, hasn't he? Let him get up by himself."

Then he abruptly switched modes, like a stage actor with a gift for heightened drama. Or maybe he was trying to tone it down a bit for my sake.

"Stand up, Matthew. Stand up. Get yourself under control. Now, tell my friend here your failings. One word."

Contritely, but now standing erect as if summoned by a call to arms, he answered, "Laziness, monsieur."

"I would expect laziness in a privileged child. Are you one of the privileged class, Matthew?"

"No, monsieur. I'm the son of a machinist." The boy inched a little taller as he said it, the voice bolder.

"And a prodigy. A boy of infinite abilities that you are presently squandering. A brilliant intellectual in the making. But you must master your cruder impulses. You must discipline yourself. No one is going to give you a hand up in the world, Matthew. You will never benefit from nepotism nor from connections in high places. If you rise in this world, it will be on your own merits alone. Because you, Matthew, willed it so. Now, you will go home and finish your translation, and you will return tomorrow *prepared*. You will no longer waste my valuable time. Tomorrow you will make me proud."

"Yes, monsieur."

He scrambled away. The heavy door struggled against the wind and finally heaved shut. The boy would be drenched by the time he got home.

I held up the bottle of Lagavulin. "If this is a bad time, I can come back."

"No such thing as a bad time. Come in, come in. I'll round up some clean glasses."

I followed him inside. It was cooler down here but airless. Daylight diffused by the frosted glass of the street-level window cast a stale grayness upon the room.

"Nice doormat," I said.

"Ha! A gift from your aunt. Every time I threw the bloody thing away it would come right back. Maybe she bought a whole store of them, maybe it's the same one. I don't know."

The rain began slowly, a few hard drops pelting the street. He cocked his head to listen to it and said quietly as though to himself, "I suppose if I throw it away now, it will stay gone for good."

"You should definitely hold on to it," I counseled. What little I'd learned about my aunt had convinced me that logic was not her strong suit; she might very well replace it from the dead.

He motioned me to a table and chairs.

"Have a seat."

"Hey," I said as I set the bottle on the table, "that was a fine Saint Crispin's Day speech you gave that kid."

"*Henry V.* I would never have taken you for a student of Shakespeare."

"I've seen the movie probably a half-dozen times. Laurence Olivier was one of my mother's favorites."

"You saw the movie," he repeated, with a low tone of contempt.

I saw no reason for contempt; after all, Shakespeare was meant to be performed, and who better than Olivier? I flashed him a sunny grin. He swung away muttering under his breath. I suppose I reminded him of the Welcome mat.

A doorway opened to what I presumed to be a bedroom, and through another doorway I glimpsed a tiny kitchen where I could hear him rinsing out some glasses. A large table spread with a vinyl tablecloth held all his paraphernalia; by the looks of it he spent his day there, ate there, worked there, gave lessons there. Other than the wheelchair positioned by the table, the furniture was sparse and the floor bare. There was a pull-up bar affixed to a doorframe and a rack of dumbbells in the corner; chest-level bookshelves were crammed with reference books and dictionaries; diplomas and certifications in dusty frames crowded the walls. It bothered me that nobody thought to straighten them for him. I wondered how many years he'd spent inside these walls. Sitting with a hideous loneliness hiding just beneath the surface.

The rain fell harder, slapping the pavement and battering the window.

He eased himself down into the wheelchair, opposite me, and popped a cassette into a boom box—a Bach violin concerto. I poured him a double and waited while he packed his pipe. He seemed to need the stage set for his pleasure ritual—the tobacco pouch, the ready pipe, Bach.

He raised his glass to mine with a nod and we drank; then he leaned back in his chair, lifted his eyes to the ceiling and fell silent.

The strains of Bach took me back to a world I thought I'd lost—a Sunday morning, squeezed between my parents in a front pew, my mother reaching for my fidgety hands, the smell of my father's freshly ironed shirt, and the sound of the music.

Music was my escape. Bach gave me wings. I hovered high in the dome looking down at us, at our unified front of rectitude and righteousness. The wholeness of three.

Pym and I sat together for a long moment, listening to the rain and Bach.

"Tell me about the Pasternak files," I said finally.

"It's a long story."

"I've got plenty of time."

He tilted his head forward to meet my eye and saw a steadiness he hadn't expected.

They'd been publishing *samizdat* for years, he said, small stuff, the sort of thing big publishers weren't interested in. The major Western publishers all wanted another Solzhenitsyn, and these were inglorious men and women, faceless and nameless, writing about the absurdities of exile, paranoia and betrayal, experiences the coddled Western mind could never quite grasp.

"What's *samizdat*?"

"You want the long version or the short?"

"Let's start with the short."

"*Samizdat* refers to the clandestine reproduction and distribution of a literary work—poetry, stories, novels, memoirs, prison diaries, anything banned or censored by the Soviet authorities—it could be George Orwell or Boris Pasternak or Sigmund Freud, it could be something your neighbor wrote."

In between puffs he explained how *samizdat* functioned. It sounded to me a bit like a clandestine network of subscribers to an underground library, where most of the readers belonged to the well-educated classes. Everything was either copied by hand or secretly typed on unregistered typewriters. As he spoke I imagined Russians pounding away on typewriters in the attics of their dachas, behind locked doors, in offices after hours. Carbon copies typed on flimsy onion skin with typos, smears, folds and creases. Long hours reproducing long works. Hundreds of pages, hundreds of thousands of words. Carbon paper pounded down to the very last blurry impression.

"It didn't have to be political to qualify as *samizdat*. Whether in form or substance, any independent thought is anti-Soviet and subversive," Pym explained. "Perhaps the work was too original, too modern, too inventive, too erotic, too psychological, too religious or just too truthful, didn't matter—if it didn't promote the Soviet utopia, it was forbidden fruit. In short, *samizdat* meant freedom, it meant the West. You could get arrested and thrown in jail just for possession, let alone authorship. You hid *samizdat*, under floorboards or stuffed into old boots, and when you sat down to read it, you were engaged in a powerful clandestine activity. The very object became a symbol of an entirely separate culture operating free of censorship.

"It's hard to imagine the effect this material had on the population—okay, the majority of the working class wasn't reading poetry and prison diaries, nor were the peasants, but the people it affected were thoughtful. They were the ones who would determine the fate of their country. It brought awareness. People learned about the existence of political prisoners and the labor camps. They understood for the first time how steeped in totalitarianism their system truly was. They learned about the vast scope of repression. About resistance. *Samizdat* changed their worldview.

"We were publishing the later, more politicized works by Russian and Polish dissidents. They were like cries in the wilderness," he went on, "stories about doctors, scientists, schoolteachers, artists, sent to prison because of their anti-Soviet thinking. There were stories of men fleeing to escape arrest, disappearing into the tundra, hiding out in regions so sparsely populated that the villages have no name, losing fingers and toes to the cold, until they missed their loved ones so much that they gave up and went home and got arrested. Lily was determined to give these people a voice. Every story that made its way to us found a publisher. She never let up. She never let anyone down."

"You did the translating, is that it?"

"We did it all—translation, editing—we got the works ready for the printers. We put out the Russian editions ourselves. Those we'd smuggle back into Russia. The English translations we quietly farmed out to other small imprints who had decent distribution deals. We had to be careful though—if you scratched deep enough sometimes you'd find these groups were funded by the CIA, and Lily was adamant about steering clear of those boys. It was a sure way to lose credibility with the dissidents. It was always a dodgy business, but we did a good job. Lillian had a reputation for integrity. We got a lot in print over the years. She was devoted to the work. It was a passion. It was all she cared about.

"Then, several years ago, Lillian was contacted by an old friend—a literary connection. The guy said he had something for her. Something a lot more explosive than prison diaries."

"The Pasternak files," I said.

"I don't believe Lily knew the source's true identity. All we knew was that this so-called Pasternak had access to high-level KGB archives. For years he'd been sneaking documents out of the facility in Lubyanka. He'd take them home, make handwritten copies, and then return them to the files. At some point he decided it was time to move them out. Making contact with the Americans was too risky. Same with the British. He'd been greatly influenced by the dissenters and particularly *samizdat*, and he'd heard of Lily through friends and knew she published dissident writers. He wanted her to smuggle the material out of Russia."

"What did she plan to do with it?"

"Turn it over to a Western intelligence agency, just as Pasternak wanted. But for a price."

"Go on."

"The money would go into an account to be held for Pasternak. For when he made it out. At least that was the plan, until last year when she came across a document that mentioned Maxim's release from prison. He was alive."

"Maxim Bukovsky. Your brother."

"Half brother, to be exact." The air exploded with his laugh, punctuating his speech like a bullet. "I should have been the one to be sent away to die, not him. I was the maimed one. He was brawny and athletic, perfectly sound in body and mind. Damn him, he was even selfless. My God, you'd have thought he was the model for the New Soviet Man."

"But he didn't die."

"We hadn't heard from him in years. He'd been in and out of prison so many times we'd lost count. They'd throw him in jail, then release him and ship him off to a labor camp, then as soon as they set him free he'd be back in public campaigning and making a big stink about human rights. He knew the law, he knew the Soviet Constitution, and he tied them in knots with their mountains of bloody bureaucratic rope. And every time they shut him away, the sentence would be longer, the prison harsher, the labor camp more remote. Finally, they locked him up in a psychiatric hospital. Maxim wasn't crazy and everyone knew it. A saner more truth-seeking man never walked the earth.

"For years Lily had been searching for some proof that he was alive. She knew he'd write under a pseudonym—so every time we got a manuscript, she read it hoping to find echoes of his voice. She never quit searching for him, hoping for a clue. And then, out of the blue, there it was."

"He was alive."

"In a psychiatric hospital. Lillian knew she could leverage the files to get money for Pasternak. Now she wanted Maxim's freedom thrown into the bargain."

"Who was she going to sell the files to? The English?"

"Or the Americans. Maybe the CIA could offer more money, but SIS had a jailed Russian spy they could offer in exchange. You understand this is all conjecture on my part. I never knew details. I do know it got complicated. Then somewhere along the line there was a leak. The KGB knew something big was going down but they didn't know what. Now it's a race to get the last of the files out of Moscow and secured in the West."

"So how much paper are we talking about here?"

"It's not just a few few scattered reports, there must be suitcases full of them."

"What happened to them?"

"Lily stashed it all someplace."

The rain had stopped long ago. The room was still and airless and reeked of pipe smoke. I was sweating heavily, my damp polo shirt plastered to my back.

I thanked him for the drink, said I needed to be going.

"Is that it?" he asked.

"What do you mean?"

His words came out stiff and brittle. "Let me up there. Let me look through her papers."

"I've been through the apartment. There aren't any suitcases full of Russian archives."

"You don't know what to look for. There has to be a clue somewhere."

"And what would you do with it? You want to be the arbiter, is that it?"

There it was again, that nervous tick of his, a sudden snap of the chin and twist of the neck.

"Look, I have connections in the intelligence community," he said. "I can get them to the British or the Americans, but whatever happens, we can't let them fall into KGB hands."

"You still think the KGB had my aunt killed?"

"They have ways. Even if the victim doesn't die right away. They can make it look like a heart attack."

It didn't make sense to me. Follow her, search her home, kidnap her, sure. But assassinate her?

As I pushed back my chair and rose, I said, "Looks to me like things are better left where they are. Although I'm sorry about your brother."

"You don't know who he was, do you?" he asked.

"Who?"

"Maxim."

He leaned forward, pressing his blunt bullish face closer to mine.

"He was the reason why she joined the Party."

"What party?"

He barked another laugh and flung himself backward in his chair.

"I say, you are even more naive than I first thought. The Communist Party, you booby. Your aunt was a Red. You didn't know?"

He must have seen the shock on my face. He looked so pleased with himself. Like he'd just brought the hammer down on my already broken thumb. Suddenly I didn't like him so much anymore.

A car passed by outside slowly, the sound of tires splashing through puddles collected in the street.

I told him to keep the bottle.

The pavement was soaked from the hard rain, and water gushed along the gutters. Billy tugged at the leash and I followed his lead. I didn't care which way we went. Odd thoughts and images were thrashing around in my head trying to connect. Like the clenched-fist pencil holder on the desk in my aunt's apartment, a symbol for revolution and Communism, and the small plaster bust of the bushy-bearded man which I now realized must be Karl Marx. A name that rhymed ominously with my own. The truth had been there under my nose all along, but hearing it stated so bluntly still came as a terrible shock. His delivery certainly didn't mitigate the effects. Calling me a naive booby. That ticked me off. I had gone to Pym for enlightenment, not to be insulted and mocked. I glanced toward the Petit Verlaine, hoping to see Greta waiting for me on the corner. I remembered the way she had walked away from me, the long fair braid falling perfectly straight between her shoulder blades, not looking back.

CHAPTER 18

Not so much as a flutter of a breeze passed through the open windows. The storm had come and gone and left more of the same: stultifying heat and the stillness of a city holding its breath. That wasn't what was getting me down. Florida was ten times worse. Florida was a swamp.

On top of these unsettling revelations about Greta and my aunt, the strangeness and foreignness of the place was beginning to unnerve me. I felt keenly alone. I needed a touch of home to perk me up. It was late enough in the day to call the East Coast, so I sat in front of a fan and called Mimi at work—she didn't have but a minute, the bakery was terribly busy and they were short-staffed. I told her I was getting along fine and broadening my horizons. That Billy was happy as a clam and that we'd be home soon. She sounded distracted and distant. Her boss shouted at her and she had to hang up.

Next I called Mike, who had promised to check my phone messages and pick up my mail.

"Hey, buddy," he said, fairly shouting down the line. "How's it goin' over there?"

"No need to yell, Mike, I can hear you fine."

"You didn't tell me you were looking for a job."

"Yeah, I am, sort of. Why?"

"You already have a job."

"If you can call it that. I read a few proposals from service providers now and then and give my opinion."

I always believed deep down I was the unwanted baggage from my own successful negotiations with Disney, like a stepchild you'd never really warm to but would tolerate politely and kindly for your spouse's sake. I thought my consulting gig with Epcot in Florida would be a fresh new start, but it turned out to be a bit of a quagmire. I gave my advice to Disney Imagineering on technological advances in industrial primers and topcoats and high performance lacquers, and occasionally they called me in to get just the right shade for an architectural theme. Lord knows what they thought, or if anyone ever read the reports I wrote. My thoughts kept going back to that pivoting moment, the summer before my senior year at university when I interned at a color lab, me in a white technician's coat splattered with paint, developing just the right color to renovate the metal facade of a prominent hospital. The client had wanted something very special, a blue facade that would reflect the whole spectrum of green from the palm trees and wide sweeps of grass, and the ever-shifting blues from the ocean, a spectral color that changed with the light and angle of view. I did it, I'd formulated the color and the coatings that did just that. The director was so pleased that he kept me on part-time through the school year and promised me a job after I graduated.

But that year Dad started to show signs of decline, so I

took my degree in industrial chemistry and went off to do an MBA. I never regretted it. It brought us closer together those last years, and made him proud of me, and that was much more important than a career in a paint-splattered lab coat.

"Well, you got a message on your machine," Mike said. "They said they liked your résumé and wanted to know if you were available for an interview."

Mike read me the phone number and I jotted it down.

He asked if I was getting my aunt's business all sorted out. I said it wasn't what I'd expected, but it was keeping me busy developing new skill sets. I told him I'd be home in a few days at the most.

I made myself a cup of Nescafé and took it back to the living room and stood in front of the fan to drink it, turning Pym's words over in my head, trying to reconcile this knowledge with my image of a dignified old lady in oven mitts trotting out her roasted chicken. All the clues had been there, but the conclusion still hit me hard. I couldn't shake my notions of what I knew about Communists—mainly that they stood for everything that was wrong with the world.

And my aunt had been one of them. Perhaps she still was.

Had she spied for them? Was she spying for them still? What if she'd double-crossed them? The questions and doubts just kept piling up.

I filled a plastic bottle and went around watering her plants, the big leafy ficus, the bright red geraniums springing up at the windows, I even remembered to check the potted strawberry plant in the kitchen window. I felt like a burglar at the moment of moral reckoning. To burgle or not to burgle? Finally, I put aside my squeamishness and started searching her apartment.

I peered into the dining room buffet, poked around the silverware, the porcelain and candlesticks; I sifted through the contents of a writing desk in the living room. I felt her looking over my shoulder as I turned over maps of Berlin, Vienna, Rome, Prague, Leningrad, Milano; in her bedroom I rummaged through piles of fleece-lined mittens and earmuffs, old bathing suits and swim caps. In an armoire I came across a trove of odd objects in gift boxes with the contents undisturbed, a selection of quality teas, a piece of costume jewelry; a large oval box of chocolates tied with a ribbon and a note to deliver to Eleanor; things that seemed to speak of intentions forgotten, old intentions in turn covered by a layer of new intentions and subsequently forgotten. I found recipes for cabbage pies and beet salad, scattered lists of music with names like Gershwin, Louis Armstrong, Ella Fitzgerald. Under her bed I found boxes crammed with lecture notes from UC Berkeley and the Sorbonne written in large loopy handwriting—French, English and Russian all scrambled together—files labeled Pushkin, Tolstoy, Gogol, Somerset Maugham, Flaubert. The most curious were the boxes of brand-new paperback editions of romance novels by Melody Bly. I wondered if the author might be a friend and she'd bought up copies in demonstration of her support. It was the sort of thing I could imagine her doing.

Do spies do that sort of thing? Do spies have a good heart?

I found the letters in a large red heart-shaped box that had once held chocolates. They were all neatly folded in their envelopes and addressed to Lillian de la Pérouse at various hotel addresses—Istanbul, Rome, Alexandria, Athens. There was a heap of them. Written neatly, on the upper left-hand corner, was our home address in Santa Ana. It was my mother's handwriting.

My mother had been writing to my aunt all these years. While I'd been told she had disappeared, vanished, probably died.

A photograph fell out and I picked it up. It was me playing ball in the park, wearing the Tour de France T-shirt my mom had given me for my birthday that year. I was eight years old and I loved that T-shirt. I turned over the photo. On the back my mother had written *Carl in his favorite T-shirt. Thank you, Lily*.

Billy came dragging himself in to see what I was up to; there was a chair beside the bed where my aunt piled her clothes before going to sleep, and he trotted straight there and curled up on a long dressing gown that had spilled onto the floor. He knew the dressing gown was hers. Leave it to Billy, to a dog, to grow so attached in so short a time. Billy obviously cared naught for political sympathies. I figured even Commies had dogs that loved them.

"Do I really want to know?" I said to him, clutching a handful of letters, measuring the weight of words, maybe lies.

Usually I could read his thoughts, but his wide-eyed gaze betrayed nothing.

The phone rang and I answered it on the bedroom extension. It was a woman rattling off a stream of breathless French. I replied that I didn't speak French, only English.

She shouted back at me, perhaps thinking shouting would crack the language barrier. She sounded like she'd just run up a flight of stairs.

Votre mère, Lillian, I understood. "She's my aunt, not my mother," I corrected. "Where is she? Is she okay?"

There was a brief moment when all I heard were people

talking over one another, and then a boy's voice came on the line.

"We call from la Gare de Fontainebleau. There is a lady on the *quai*. She waits here with a suitcase. She writes this number and wants that I call you."

After a bit of back and forth I got them to convince my aunt to come to the telephone.

"Aunt Lily! What happened? Are you all right?"

"Oh, Carlito, my dear boy, why, I'm perfectly fine. How good of you to call after all these years. Are you calling from California?"

Forty-five minutes later my taxi pulled up in front of the train station of Fontainebleau. The driver waited while I hurried inside. The kind souls who had called had long since departed, but she was still there on the platform, a lonely figure seated on a bench in her wrinkled fuchsia capris, the sun hat on her knees, an old seafoam green suitcase at her feet. Gazing expectantly down the railway line.

She turned her head and caught sight of me and brightened immediately. I could see she was tired, but I discerned no confusion on her face.

"My dear boy," she said, her hat slipping to the pavement as she extended her slender hands to me. "This was quite unnecessary, traipsing all the way out here for me. And however did you get here so quickly? I thought you'd be on the next train."

I scooped up her hat and sat down next to her. "I came by taxi."

"Oh, my dear, what an extravagance. I do hope he had an

air conditioner. This heat is ghastly. No one is equipped for it."

She had the look of a wilted bloom. I sensed it was more than heat. "What happened? Do you remember?"

"Naturally I remember," she said huffily. "I'm afraid those people alarmed you unnecessarily. Although I'm sure they meant well. I'm overly tired, that's all. It's been a busy week. So many nights with so little sleep." She glanced around to see if anyone was within earshot, but the platform was nearly empty. The other passengers were waiting inside in the cool lounge. "All that tea business," she said, lowering her voice, "then arranging my death, which has been exhausting, to say the least, and your unexpected arrival—oh, don't get me wrong, Carlito, that is the one thing I don't regret, but I never expected to have the pleasure of meeting you face-to-face, you see?" She reached for my hand. "And here you are, my own flesh and blood, come to rescue me. Rescue all of us, it seems."

She gave my hand a little squeeze and then snatched hers back, as if unnerved by her sudden lapse into sentimentality.

She put on a convincing show of mental clarity, and the trouble was, I wanted to believe her. It was just possible that I had misunderstood, that the people who'd found her had mistaken her whimsical eccentricity for confusion.

Or she'd pulled it intentionally, to get me out here.

She couldn't have possibly known that I had been digging through her drawers at exactly the moment when she called. Or did she? Did guilt show on my face? Could she read my mind?

She took up the sun hat and began to fan herself. "This old suitcase is dreadfully heavy, you see," she said. "I couldn't manage it one more step on my own."

It was hardly the sort of valise that went unnoticed. My

mother had something similar back in the fifties, an entire set with a vanity case that she later donated to the Salvation Army.

"Is that them?"

"What, dear?"

"The Pasternak files."

"Goodness, no. You don't think I'd be dragging those papers around the country in plain sight." She rapped the hard top of the suitcase. "No, these are just a few things I brought back from my country hideaway. Some memories I'd buried. Thought it best to keep them out of sight. Out of sight, out of mind. Which is good to a point. Then there comes a time when you don't want to forget, and remembering becomes so important."

She cocked her head to listen to the announcement coming over the loudspeaker.

"That's us. The train to Paris."

"But the taxi's waiting," I said.

She patted me sharply on the knee. "Well, you can send him on. We're taking the train—one of the many advantages of first class is that it's always adjacent to the restaurant car. There's nothing wrong with me that an icy gin and tonic won't put right."

At this point, you might say I put my foot down.

"I honestly think you've got it rigged, Aunt Lily," I suddenly broke out, a shade petulantly.

"Rigged? Why, whatever do you mean?" She gave me a stunned look like a monarch whose divine right had just been doubted.

I didn't know where to begin. So I pushed on with my metaphor. "The ride. Mr. Toad's Ride. I'm flying along, holding on for dear life, completely clueless, while you know perfectly well what trap is waiting for me around the next bend, and yet you leave me in the dark."

An announcement chimed again, followed by another loudspeaker announcement.

"Yes, Carl, go on," she said calmly.

Is it true? Are you a Communist? The sworn enemy of my country? Or something like that, since my aunt didn't look like anybody's enemy just then, she looked like a tired and somewhat haughty old lady in rumpled capris. I'd always pictured Communists to look like Nikita Khrushchev or Ho Chi Minh, or the wildly romantic Che Guevarra type. I'd had a professor at university who was rumored to be one, but my aunt? At the same time, I knew it had nothing to do with outward appearance and everything to do with a particular mindset, a system of beliefs. I knew the Communists were hell-bent on messing with our heads, convincing us of the evils of our way of thinking and living. Scorning our comforts and pleasures while exploiting our weaknesses. Inflaming those with cause for anger and resentment, sympathizing with their perceived humiliation and misfortune, fanning hatred and rage.

Odd, I thought, how a few words, truthful or not, can alter completely our perception of another. Forever. It's like, we can't put those words back in the bottle. They sit and rot and corrode and mess with our minds.

Passengers who had been waiting inside were swarming onto the platform. This was not the moment for a showdown. I wasn't even sure I wanted to hear the truth.

I wanted to get what I knew about this business off my chest and go home.

"Aunt Lily, you should know, you're being watched."

"Go on."

"There's a man posing as an Anglican priest. He hangs out at the café on the corner. He's been there ever since I arrived." I pressed on to explain that we'd become friendly, that he'd fed me this story about his wife running off with another guy and I felt sorry for him, so I invited him along to Harry's. That he witnessed the scene with the Russian fellow at the bar.

"Does he know about the napkin?"

"No, I made sure of it."

"Would he know you're looking for the files?"

"He might. Because of Greta."

"Greta?"

"A girl I met at the police station."

"Oh, my dear. *Chercher la femme*," she whispered. I didn't ask what she meant, knowing her love of digressions, but I concluded (and rightly so, I later learned) that when there's trouble, there's usually a woman involved.

"Greta needed to eat, so I brought her back to Le Petit Verlaine. Turned out she'd spent the night in the jail cell with Louise. She helped me track her down."

"She was in jail?"

"For protesting."

Aunt Lily's eyebrows shot up. I got the impression she approved. She poked me on the chest with a sharp nail. A little too hard, I thought. "You have a good heart, Carlito. A good heart. But that can be an Achilles' heel in this line of work."

"Well, I'm afraid I involved her unnecessarily—"

"My dear, you'll need to finish this story on the train."

The train had ground to a stop in front of us and bodies were surging in a tidal wave of human flesh.

"Go, run now," she said, "send your taxi away."

"Listen, Huggins is her father."

"Huggins?"

"The priest with the runaway wife. The one who's had you under surveillance."

The perplexed look lasted only an instant while she put the pieces together. "So this girl of yours, you think she might be with British intelligence?"

"On the contrary, I think she strongly disapproves of her father's line of work."

"How did you figure out Huggins was her father?"

"It was the way they behaved when we ran into him at the café, but the clincher was the color of their eyes. It's very unusual. Carolina Blue."

Not many people appreciate my particular skill, apart from the Imagineers at Disney, but to my astonishment, she gave me a broad smile of approval—I might even say pride.

"All is not lost, Carlito, now go."

Settling with the taxi took some haggling, and when I returned she was gone.

I remembered Lily had said we were traveling first class, so I hustled down the platform toward the front of the train. A commotion behind me drew my attention. Even at a distance I recognized Duclos, the debonair inspector with the slicked-back hair who had paid me a visit the previous day. Beside him trotted an abnormally tall young man in khaki battle fatigues with a black Labrador retriever in lockstep. What on earth they wanted with me now I couldn't fathom, and the sight of the dog only added to my sense of wonderment. This distraction had caused me to run right past my aunt, who was watching for me from her compartment; she rapped fitfully on her window to get my attention.

"Carlito," she cried as she managed to lower the window. "Hurry!"

The conductor blew a final shrill whistle just as I jumped on board and the doors locked behind me.

The train was rolling out of the station as I collapsed into the seat opposite her with my heart pounding in my ears and my arms slick with sweat. The only other passenger in our compartment was a moonfaced man in a bow tie munching on a cookie while reading a book; he brushed the crumbs from his shirt and gave us a shy greeting then went back to reading.

My aunt leaned forward to whisper, "I think the police just boarded the train. They're looking for someone."

"Maybe me. The big guy is Duclos, the detective who paid us a visit a few days ago."

"I do hope you have your passport with you. They'll ask for an ID."

Good grief. She was going to be caught out. Alive rather than dead. Yet, she didn't seem the least bit apprehensive. She was pulling out her compact just as the door to the compartment rattled open and there stood Duclos to prove me right.

"Bonjour Monsieur Box," he said. "You are a hard man to keep track of."

I couldn't help but admire his use of the phrasal verb. I wondered where he had learned his English. Mimi was always complaining about the arbitrariness of our prepositions.

There was a bit of confusion as we all tried to make room for the black Lab who was behaving admirably despite suffering from the heat. Upon an order from Duclos, our fellow passenger nervously stuffed his cookie back into the package, squeezed past the policemen and fled down the corridor.

Once the seating arrangement was settled, my aunt leaned forward to me and said with a note of alarm, "Carl, are you in some kind of trouble?" Then to Duclos apologetically, "I'm his mother. You know how mothers worry." Then, back to me, "Does this have something to do with my sister's death?"

At that moment, I almost envied her. From infancy I had been taught to submit to authority. The threat of sanction would always keep me in line. But my aunt had no such fear. She thumbed her nose at authority and rules and my superior brand of morality. Her defiance felt like a rush of cool air in that stifling hot carriage.

I said, "Mother, this is Inspector Roland Duclos."

"Maggie," she said holding out her hand with a gracious but oh-so-slightly grief-stricken smile.

I was surprised by the effect that smile had on him. Charm, I was learning, was strong currency in France.

Duclos turned back to me. "I see you have a good memory for names."

"I could hardly forget the name of someone who suggested I may have had a hand in my aunt's death."

"What?" my aunt said with incredulity, right on cue. "Carl, what are you talking about?"

Duclos faced me with tired eyes. Whatever he was doing, I got the feeling he'd rather be doing something else.

"I'd like to see your passport, madame, if you please."

"The passport is at my sister's place." For safekeeping, she explained while rummaging in her handbag. "But here's my driver's license." As Duclos's gaze swung back and forth between her and the license, I watched with fascination as she brushed away a strand of silver hair and a softness crept into her gaze, a kind of youthful bashfulness, the expression of a girl on the brink of womanhood, of seduction in the guise of innocence. How she pulled it off at her age was nothing short of spectacular.

The ID, presumably Van Gogh's handiwork, passed muster. My aunt slipped it back into her handbag.

"Monsieur Box, I believe you had a suitcase with you in the station."

"The suitcase is mine, Officer," she said. "It's right up there." She gestured to the rack over her head while tucking the strand of hair behind her ear.

"Don't you need a search warrant?" I said.

"Customs inspection. Article sixty-four of the Customs Code."

The gangly customs agent pulled down the suitcase. I could tell it was heavy by the way he strained to lower it to the floor. The dog, now alert, gave it a quick cursory sniff then looked away, bored. He sank to the floor with a thud and went back to panting heavily.

"There. Satisfied?" I said crossly.

"We'd like to see inside."

"What's all this nonsense?" I said, braving an indignation I never would have attempted in Orlando if I'd been pulled to the side of the road by a traffic cop. I was discovering in myself a streak of lawlessness, and I found it to my liking. "Have you nothing better to do with your time than harass me and my family with half-baked accusations?"

"Your name keeps popping up on our radar, Monsieur Box, and given the suspicious nature of your aunt's business activities, we thought it best to act swiftly. We got to your apartment just as you were leaving. You seemed to be unusually rushed."

"I pop up on your radar," I said. "How exactly does that happen?."

Duclos leaned back and loosened his collar and tie. His slicked-back locks were beginning to spring free from whatever hair product had kept them in line, losing out to the humidity. These small imperfections in his otherwise faultless grooming gave him a touch of vincibility. I found him unusually respectful for a policeman and not entirely unsympathetic.

"We had a tip."

"A tip."

"It was vague. Could be anything. Tax evasion. Smuggling gold bars. Hidden Swiss accounts. We weren't sure what. We brought the dog along on the off chance it was currency. He's new to the team. The dog. Murphy's his name. We thought we'd take him out for a trial run."

My aunt gave Murphy an endearing smile.

"Such extraordinary creatures."

"I regret this intrusion, madame, but we have long suspected your sister was involved in some ... shall we say *unusual* activities, and your son's arrival has implicated him, unfortunately." He added, with a quizzing gaze my way, "And then there was this incident at the airport, something about an antique—"

"It was *not* an antique," I said hotly.

My aunt broke in and said, "I assure you, monsieur, my

son would never be involved in anything that even hinted of impropriety. He's an accountant. They're such sensible people. Real straight arrows."

Somehow, she made it sound less than flattering.

"Accountants know how to cook the books," Duclos replied.

She patted my knee and said, "I'm afraid he's not much of a cook either."

"Nevertheless, if you please—"

And so it happened. The customs agent wrangled the heavy suitcase onto the seat. I was as curious as they were about the contents of that seafoam green Taperlite. Whatever she was transporting had to be important, and it was possibly illegal. I wondered if Van Gogh could be counted on to bust us out of jail.

My aunt seemed admirably unflappable. She rotated the dials on the combination lock with a soft touch and a remarkably steady hand. The latch clicked open. She lifted the lid.

No wonder it was heavy. Inside were bulky sheaves of creamy paper bound in thick rubber bands. Bundles of typewritten pages crammed together. Thousands of pages.

I must have betrayed my shock because the Lab snapped his head around to give me a warning look, but the others had their eyes fixed on the papers inside.

It took me a moment to realize that the typescript was not in Russian, as I'd feared. It was English.

"My sister was a romance writer," my aunt said as she picked up a bundle and offered it to Duclos to inspect. "And a very good one; although the genre is terribly maligned, she took great pride in her work. She had legions of readers. Perhaps you've heard of her? Melody Bly—that was her pen name."

She waited, expectantly, for a reply.

Duclos, always well mannered, voiced a humble apology.

"Ah, well, you don't know what you're missing," she answered, as if he had truly disappointed her. She carefully placed the manuscript back in the suitcase, closed the lid and reset the lock. The pride on her face was genuine. "This is her very last novel."

Duclos didn't know what to make of it.

"Currency smuggling, my eye," I scoffed at Duclos, who was now looking very sheepish.

"Well, now that that's all settled," my aunt concluded with the finality of a detective who's just solved a crime, "I could use a good stiff drink."

I turned to Duclos. "You wouldn't mind if we headed down to the restaurant car, would you, now?"

He shook his head.

"Could we bring you something?" my aunt asked solicitously. "A beer? A Coke?"

The young customs agent opted for a Coke. Duclos passed.

As we stepped over Murphy my aunt said with the utmost sincerity, "I trust my sister's novel will be safe with you, Monsieur Duclos."

My aunt darted into the hallway and toward the restaurant car, hell-bent on that gin and tonic, but we were too late; the bar had already closed. Along the tracks, the brief stretches of forest had given way to unsightly suburban sprawl, and now we were in the city, crawling slowly toward the station.

As we made our way back to our compartment, I was thinking of the boxes of paperback books I'd seen under her bed, all of them by the same author: Melody Bly.

I said, "It's you. You write romance novels."

She gave a regal swing of the head and said in that high-handed tone of hers, "My dear boy, how else do you think I could afford to keep this publishing business going all these years?"

The train lurched and shuddered as we switched tracks. She paused in the corridor, gripping the rail to steady herself.

"You must keep this manuscript safe," she whispered. "If anything should happen to me, Pasternak will find you. Give it to him."

"I thought he was still in Moscow."

She shook her head impatiently, the way you would with a dim-witted child. Then, showing a weariness you would expect of someone her age, she said, "I have a great longing to sleep in my own bed tonight."

CHAPTER 19

I emerged from the shower and found a clean T-shirt laid out for me on my bed. The khakis would have to do service yet another evening.

I had left her in the kitchen chopping onions, intent on making guacamole with the avocados we'd bought from a sidewalk vendor. Now she was trying to pry open a bulb of garlic with the pointed end of a paring knife. She relinquished it to me without protest and went off to set the table in the dining room.

She had insisted on throwing together a Mexican dinner, which entailed stopping by a few corner markets she knew to carry tortilla chips and Corona, although for the sake of simplicity we settled on a some ready-to-grill beef brochettes from a butcher shop we passed on the way home.

"It's a little too small for you," she said, eyeing my T-shirt from across the table as she dipped a chip into her guacamole with the same mannered delicacy with which you'd dip a spoon into caviar.

I looked down at the front of my shirt, a colorful collage of vintage Italian cars, Fiat, Alfa Romeo, Ferrari. The sort of

T-shirt an adolescent boy would wear every day if you'd let him.

"Pretty cool," I said, and I meant it.

She looked pleased. "I picked it up—what?—must have been twenty years ago, when I was living in Rome, for a boy I thought might like cars."

"What boy doesn't?"

I wondered if she'd bought it for me, or perhaps there had been another child she'd doted on from afar.

She was wearing a pair of silver bracelets made of tiny delicate bells that jingled with every move of her arm, and gold hoop earrings, and she had freshened her makeup. My aunt always seemed to take great care with her personal appearance, and this evening was no exception. I thought of evenings of rum punch and laughter with a polio-stricken Russian émigré, and the devotion of a mysterious forger who went by the name of Van Gogh, and I was beginning to see how her gift for turning the ordinary into the extraordinary might have charmed many a man. Even Billy. Especially Billy. I couldn't see him, but I could tell by my aunt's shifty downward glances and telltale jingle that he had taken up his post at her feet. I could just imagine his black buttony eyes following her hand movements with laser-like attentiveness.

"Please don't feed him from the table, Aunt Lily."

"You're like your father. He was very strict about animals."

"One little indulgence and there goes their training, out the window. They don't forget. You can't go back to the old ways."

"And why should they?"

There was no use pressing the point; I was outnumbered. Blithely she struck down our Box family rules, toppled our Commandments from their pedestal. It was perhaps less her political affinities than her willfulness that had come between her and my father. The more I thought about it, the less inclined I was to believe she had ever been a true die-hard Communist, for I could not imagine her towing any party line that interfered with her own opinions.

"Would you have liked to have a child?" I asked.

"I would have made a very unsatisfactory mother, Carlito, dragging the poor thing this way and that. I did have a dog once, and the poor creature became terribly fearful of being left behind. Whenever I brought out a suitcase he'd lie down in it and I couldn't get him out. I resorted to all kinds of tricks. Finally I got into the habit of opening up a suitcase in one room to foil him and then packing furtively in the bathroom. Fortunately he was a smallish dog, about the same size as Billy, so I took him with me whenever I could. He was terribly miserable when we were separated."

I noticed that she had changed into the long Moroccan robe Greta had worn. When I told her how nice she looked, I must have betrayed some emotion.

"Something's troubling you."

Normally I would have denied it, but it was surprisingly easy to open up to my Red aunt, as I was beginning to think of her. I felt she wouldn't be so quick to judge me.

"I didn't know it showed."

"It's the girl, isn't it?"

I opened another beer for myself and launched into the full story of Greta's involvement, how we met and how she helped me track down Louise and the intelligence report. Telling the story, I was struck by its utter implausibility, its fantasticality, and the feeling that after one night with Greta I had turned my back on any possibility of a future sitting on a bench in Epcot contentedly surveying the Grand Lagoon.

When I got to the part about bringing Greta home, my aunt interrupted me.

"Oh, Carlito—you had a little romance, an adventure! Bravo!"

"It wasn't like that. She wanted protection, that's all. After everything I'd put her through, I didn't have the heart to say no. I was worried about what would happen if the police caught up with her and questioned her. So just to be safe, I said she shouldn't know where I lived and she'd need to be blindfolded."

"And she agreed?"

I nodded.

"You *do* have a gift for inspiring trust."

"Then I overslept, so it was all for nothing. If she saw anything incriminating—"

"There's nothing here to incriminate me except a bunch of dusty literary journals and an old woman's tired underclothes."

"It was about the only solution I could think of. I'm afraid I may have made things worse."

"Or, you've opened up a few doors."

"So you're not upset."

"On the contrary, my dear boy, it's a great comfort to have someone else do the thinking for me."

The bells tinkled as she held out her empty glass and I poured her more beer.

"Will you see her again?" she asked.

"I wouldn't know how to find her."

"Finding her isn't the problem."

I shrugged. Even if I should find her, I wouldn't know what to do. With it. With us. It would be a short romance, and Greta did not strike me as the sort of girl one shorted.

So I said, to sum up, "I wouldn't be able to make her any promises."

"It seems to me you can promise her a great deal."

"Like what?"

"A few hours after meeting you and she was racing across Paris on a motorcycle at midnight dressed in only a duvet. I doubt any of her Greenpeace protests could ever match that for excitement."

It must have been the music of her bracelets and the beer that eased me into the story of my short-lived marriage and how the few meaningful relationships I'd had hadn't, in the end, meant enough to either party.

"I've always had timely plans, you see. Quarterly reports, year-end taxes. Extension deadlines." I leaned back from the table, having consumed four beef brochettes and a good three avocados worth of guac. "When I sold Box Paints I left all that behind. Maybe what I need is a new plan."

"When I was young I was very open to influences," she said, "like Picasso, you might say I had my blue period and my rose period. With Plato I seriously considered converting to Judaism—"

"Plato?" I queried. "Wasn't he a Greek philosopher?"

"Plato von Donnersmarck, Carlito, a very old noble line of Russian-German heritage. We wanted to marry so he could remain in America. Of course now I'm glad I didn't do either of those things. I had my Catholic period as well, although that was quite independently of a man, if I recall. I could never reconcile with the church's patriarchy and the idea of giving all that authority to a man in Rome who's forgone the pleasures of making love to a woman in the name of a higher order of love. I have no doubt the pope is a fine human being, but it's such a perverse culture—all those power-hungry and vain men trying to fool you into believing they're humble. What could they possibly have in common with a penniless carpenter and his fishing buddies? Besides, I was never one for orthodoxy. What I loved most was the aesthetics of the ritual, the incense, the Latin liturgy, Bach and Handel performed on a cathedral organ at Christmas. There's nothing like a ritual of the senses to elevate the soul. And the magnificent edifices they constructed all in the name of God. When I think of all those Italians going blind painting their own artistic visions of the Madonna, why, it defies belief. I sometimes wonder what would have become of Western art if Christianity hadn't risen to power. What would have become of all those poor Florentines? What would they have painted or sculpted? Perhaps they would have just weaved and cobbled their way through the centuries, and we would end up with a world of Guccis and Ferragamos in the place of those magnificent paintings. And what of Bach and Handel, and Notre Dame! I shudder to think what beauties would have been lost to civilization without Christianity. I've grown very cynical in my old age, my boy, but religion has left a few good things in its devastating wake, and for those not insignificant contributions I'm deeply grateful."

"And Communism? Was that just a phase?"

"Rather like a journey that came to an end and left me considerably more enlightened than when I started out."

"So it's true?"

"I long ago cut all ties with the Party. As well as any affinities with their followers. My dear boy, I thought you knew."

"Not until Pym told me."

"Your parents didn't tell you? No, of course they wouldn't."

"It was a terrible shock."

"European communists played an important role before and during World War II, Carlito. They were the bulwark against fascism. It's a long and complex political history few Americans understand, nor do they wish to. If you're interested, I'll tell you about why I made the choices I did, but not this evening."

Perhaps it was the mellow music of those silver bells, or the softness of the night, or, more likely, the Corona, but I found my resistance to her ideas and her way of life crumbling. Along with it the notion that she was spying for anyone at all. She wasn't giving me advice so much as offering up her own life stories to show me that our choices aren't a matter of right and wrong, but of embracing the challenges of any path and following it with all our heart. I glimpsed in her the same curiosity that had driven my father into his garage every evening to blowtorch his varnishes, although hers was directed outward toward the vast diversity of human experience. I couldn't help but think their falling out must have been a huge loss for both of them.

Night was only just beginning to fall. Hours of wakefulness stretched before me.

"I suppose I could have read more novels growing up," I continued. I glanced through the double doors into the living room with its walls of books. I wondered what it would be like to hold all that in my head. All those stories and ideas to toss around. "I wouldn't know where to begin."

"The beginning is just that, wherever you begin."

"Like the story about the nose."

She beamed. "You read Gogol."

"Haven't had time to finish. Pretty hilarious so far."

This really pleased her. "I'm so glad." She went on. "You might also like the French realists. They were my first passion."

"Before the Russians?"

"Oh, long before the Russians. After I was done with the French, I launched into the English. I skipped Austen and went straight to George Eliot—I'd always preferred male writers, you see, with the exception of those wild Brontë girls, and I liked that she had styled herself a George. Reading *Middlemarch* after all those French philosophers was a wonderful release. Identifying with a young gentlewoman yearning for a more meaningful existence—a rather formless desire, as young women's aspirations generally are. I recall standing on a terraced mountaintop in Delphi looking out at the sweep of valleys with the vast Mediterranean beyond and yearning—just yearning, that's all. Feeling the pull of adventure, the unknown. Standing on that ancient site of the oracles, I divined nothing about my life—where it would lead me, who I would love, who I would betray, what I would find or lose, what I would embrace or leave behind. Facing that inchoate unknown so full of expectation, the last thing in the world I needed was a plan."

After my aunt had gone to bed and the air had begun to cool down a little, I took Billy out for a turn around the block. Coming back from the square I circled around to pass in front of Le Petit Verlaine. Huggins was sitting there on the terrace. He had abandoned the priest's collar, whether from the heat or because he thought his cover was blown, I couldn't be sure. He didn't see me approach, and he looked so forlorn staring into his empty glass that I couldn't bring myself to cold-shoulder him.

"Hello, Huggins," I said, "or whatever your name is."

"Carl!" he said, looking up with a start. I thought, with a face like that, the drooping eyes weighted with sorrow, he really should have been a priest. His whole person exhaled the world-weariness of one who has heard too many deceptions and lies, and stared into the eyes of too many soulless men.

"Out for an evening promenade, are we?" he said.

"Duty calls."

"It is indeed ghastly hot."

"Not still waiting on that runaway wife of yours, are you?"

He gave me a blank look that could have meant anything.

"Can I offer you a nightcap?" he asked.

I shook my head. "No thanks, not tonight."

I wished him good evening and took a step, then stopped.

"You wouldn't have a pen, would you?" I asked him.

I took the pen he offered me, moved his glass and flipped over the beer mat to scribble down my phone number.

"Here," I said, handing the mat to him. "Tell Greta to call me."

It was an existential moment. An act thrown out into the universe, perhaps to be lost in the immensity of the void or perhaps to come ricocheting back. I did not expect the latter.

It was after one in the morning and I had already finished Gogol's *The Nose* and was starting on Joseph Conrad's *Secret Agent* when the phone rang.

"Hello," she said.

"Hello back."

There was a long silence that neither of us rushed to fill. The moment was good enough just as it was.

CHAPTER 20

I maneuvered myself and the shopping bags into the cage elevator and hit the floor button with my elbow. Greta had taken me shopping that morning to replace the wardrobe that was now sitting in my suitcase in the Orlando airport waiting for me to claim it. As the elevator made its slow grind upward, I mentally played back the morning's events like a movie montage from a mall shopping spree, although it's generally men spending on women, or girls splurging on themselves, and in these flashbacks it was Greta guiding me through the crowded aisles of the Galeries Lafayette, up the escalator and through the dizzying maze of stands. Greta commanding the attention of the salesclerks. Greta just plain commanding. I find women love the idea of a makeover, they love to see themselves transformed by the wave of a magic wand, but for guys like me it's their worst nightmare. To her credit, Greta didn't attempt a makeover, rather she put me in a classier version of what I already had. The change was subtle but it still made me squirm. She had upgraded my durable industrial-strength khakis to lighter, smarter chinos and paired them with a white button-down shirt instead of a polo. I had stood in front of the mirror scowling at my image, although I couldn't tell you why I was scowling. It was just different. It was not me. Then Greta stepped up behind me and with her usual deadpan delivery said I looked like a younger Cary Grant in *To Catch a Thief*. After that, I was ready to buy a dozen of everything. We replaced my sneakers with black leather loafers. I bought a belt. Socks. I sent her off to sniff perfumes while I picked out some briefs.

I felt like a new man. I even liked my loafers. As I pulled out the key to let myself in, I could hear Billy whining behind the door. Then I heard my aunt's laughter and Pym's voice, and my bubble burst. I deposited my purchases on the entry table and mouthed a silent question to Billy. *What the . . . ? What's he doing here?*

As I walked into the living room, she twisted around to look at me over the back of the sofa. I was reminded of how my mother used to look when I'd come home from school on an afternoon when it was her turn to host bridge club, and she'd look up from the hand she was playing to greet me, her eyes sparkling with merriment and her face flushed from laughter and gossip and spiked punch, and it was as though my mother had slipped the bonds of motherhood and flown off to a land where I didn't belong and wasn't wanted. I would hurry upstairs with their chatter ringing in my ears, slam the door to my room and sit on my bed, sulking and wishing they would all go away. I had been too young to understand the many faces of jealousy.

Not that I was any less clueless this afternoon. I was and I wasn't.

"Carl, come in. Join us," she called to me. "Pym has been

ever so understanding of my little ruse, haven't you, Pym?"

I sat down on the sofa beside my aunt, keenly aware of my pulse beating with an irrational fury. Pym was all Cheshire cat smiles, as if the joke was on me.

Not only that, she'd drawn Billy up onto her lap and was stroking his back in just the way he loved to be stroked. She looked terribly imperial in her striped caftan, cradling a lap dog. As if to make the point, she reached for a carved wooden fan at her side, whipped it open and began fanning herself. From her fan there wafted a faint perfume that reminded me of Earl Gray tea.

"Oh, by the way, Van Gogh brought up the new set of wheels he designed for Billy. It's in your room."

Billy had his eyes closed. He looked as though he'd stopped breathing.

"I think Billy will be very happy with it," she said, looking down at him with motherly pride. "It's very sleek."

"I'll make sure to thank him."

"He's up on the rooftop at the moment, attacking a wasp's nest. He came up earlier to have me help him into his space suit and brought Billy's wheels at the same time."

Pym said, "That was a dead giveaway. When I see an astronaut in full gear lumbering up the stairs to your apartment, it means only one thing. You are alive and in residence."

"And voilà, the cat was out of the bag." The smile she gave Pym would have melted the State of Alaska.

"A space suit?" I said.

"Van Gogh had it in his *cave*. He claims it's from the Apollo space program."

"Another fake, no doubt," Pym scoffed, but half-heartedly,

like he knew he didn't dare tread too hard on my aunt's loyalties.

"You can never be sure with Van Gogh. It's truly an Aladdin's cave down there. Or perhaps more accurately a Cretan labyrinth. I'm afraid one day he'll get himself lost and we'll never be able to find him."

"It's awfully hot to be on the roof in a space suit," I said.

"Pym, darling, you must know I never planned to keep you in the dark for long," she went on, soothing him with a voice so musical she might have been singing a lullaby. And the fan. I've never seen a woman wield a fan with such effect. "You're far too important to our work."

"You should have trusted me. Instead you trust that meathead in a space suit."

"Because the ruse had to be complete and utterly believable."

"Well, it bloody well was," he huffed.

"Pym, dear, you're my rock. I couldn't manage without you."

He drilled me with a dark look. "What about him?"

"What about me?" I replied. I could feel my patience draining away.

"Can you trust him?"

"I'm family," I answered weightily.

"Ha!" The laugh felt like a slap in the face, or more like a punch in the gut. "That's hardly a recommendation."

"*We* were like family, weren't we, Pym? You, me, Maxim," she said, stepping up like a referee between fighters in a ring. "Remember the Balajo? Remember our Sunday afternoons? We'd go there to watch the dancers—"

"And because it was warm in the winter, and the drinks were cheap."

"Then we'd start drinking Maxim's vodka and God knows

how we we were able to get ourselves out of there. It was your place, Pym, you loved that accordion music. We went there because you loved it."

I could see it from a mile off, flattery falling like fairy dust, the curmudgeon turning cuddly as a kitten.

"Good God, the Balajo," he muttered, a smile breaking grudgingly over his face.

The fan flew to her heart as she exclaimed—a little too melodramatically, I thought, "Oh, how we loved to argue! Me playing the decadent bourgeoise and Maxim spouting Lenin ad nauseum, and you quoting George Orwell—"

"Four legs good, two legs bad!"

They both burst out in laughter.

I didn't think I could stand much more. Pleading thirst, I excused myself and rose.

"Oh, by the way," I said turning back to Pym, "you have a student waiting for you downstairs. The kid with ginger hair and big ears."

The laughter stopped abruptly. I caught a glimpse of my aunt's face as I set off for the kitchen, the smile flattened. The sparkle extinguished. In its place a fleeting look of consternation.

I found Eleanor in the kitchen with stacks of money spread out on the small kitchen table. A fan whirred from a countertop, keeping in motion a row of kitchen utensils and copper cookware dangling from an overhead rack so that they banged and clanked gently against one another in a constant percussive musicality, as though urging us to get cracking and serve up something fabulous. My aunt had seemed inordinately proud of her roast chicken and omelets, but seeing how busy she was kept smuggling and spying, I imagined she didn't have much time for gourmet cooking.

Eleanor didn't look up from her counting and I didn't disturb her. I took a big bottle of evian out of the fridge, took down a couple of glasses from the cupboard and pulled up a chair opposite her. I poured a glass of cold water for each of us and swigged mine down. Then I sat there, listening. Waiting to hear him go.

Eleanor was slapping down bills in a rapid count, her lips fluttering while her head racked up figures in some mystifying mental accounting system. There was still a big lump on her forehead. I wanted to ask how she was feeling but she seemed to be in good working order, so I just poured myself another glass of water and drank it while I waited. A moment later we heard my aunt's voice as she accompanied Pym to the door. Eleanor paused and with a thrust of her chin in the direction of their voices pronounced something that sounded like "*diable*." Devil.

"Yeah," I nodded, "I've soured on him too." I poured myself a third glass of cold water. I was already sweating through my brand-new shirt.

I don't know what came over me, pulling a fabrication like that out of thin air. Which is a nice way of saying I flat out lied. Just to get rid of him. There was nobody waiting at his door. Having been schooled in honesty, I've never been very skilled at lying, and I was rather proud of myself for coming up with something on the fly that made perfectly good sense. So what had sparked their surprise when I said the boy was waiting? Why had their laughter stopped as if I'd thrown cold water over their little party? And why that puzzled look on my aunt's face?

She came flying into the kitchen in her striped caftan and beamed when she saw us together looking very coconspiratorial.

"I'm so glad you're getting to know each other," she said as she slid into the chair between us and resumed fanning herself.

"We have a pretty good understanding, don't we?" I said to Eleanor.

Eleanor nodded right on cue.

I eyed the stacks of bills that she was now slipping into various envelopes of different sizes. "So this money is from your bestselling novels."

"They're just little entertainments, Carlito, what the publishers call 'easy beach reads.' But they've done quite well."

"Melody Bly. I think I recall my mother reading a few of her books."

"Her real name is Diane Farley, and she now lives in a big house in a Kansas City suburb, thanks to our collaboration. She does a brilliant job playing the role of a writer. She even did a few book tours for me, and she did them very well. She was very convincing. You'd have thought she wrote those novels herself. Now her reputation is such that she can make the bestseller list without all that publicity."

"You mean *you* made the bestseller list."

"It's a collaborative effort, Carlito. You must never underestimate the value of your team. Anyway, she's become a bit of a recluse now. She is perfectly content with the situation, as she makes a good deal of money and can indulge in her true passion of growing double-flowered peonies, which is quite a challenge in Kansas, I understand. They're not well suited to the climate."

"So you're your own ghostwriter."

"You might say that."

"You don't care? That you don't have the recognition?"

"My darling boy, my ego is perfectly content. What I'm trying to do is to carve out a little path of—"

She faltered. With a click she folded the fan in her hand, laid it on the table and grew still. Eleanor looked up, alerted to the sudden change in my aunt. Eleanor seemed to hear walls crumbling that I was deaf to.

"I don't know what to call it," she continued. "My words fail me. Soon they'll be gone altogether. I feel their absence, you know, they leak away, by the tens or hundreds or even thousands each year, I suppose. I don't keep count. But you feel it, nonetheless."

"A little path of what, Aunt Lily?" I said, hoping to guide her gently back on track.

"Could it be dignity? Yes, that's perhaps the heart of it, human dignity when faced with powerful forces—most often in our own heads—intent on poisoning us with hatred. I'm nothing great nor special, Carlito. When we're young we all believe we have something special, but I've outgrown that illusion. Beautiful as it may be, it fades and then you're faced with your powerlessness and the minuteness of your individual consciousness. Yes, I suppose that's it. It's making room for a conscience, wishing to live a life that rests kindly on the heart."

We were distracted by the late arrival of Billy, who came dragging himself in, lapped up some water from his bowl and then collapsed onto the cool tile floor with his sides heaving like bellows.

My aunt said something to Eleanor in French, then rose, took down three espresso cups and began grinding coffee beans. Eleanor packed her hoard of banknotes into a large worn shopping bag and got up and started puttering around the kitchen alongside my aunt. They seemed to have a quiet understanding of each other, an easy companionship.

I thought of my own mother and her quiet resilience. Her death, several years after my father's, had not come as a surprise. Without my father she had been a ship adrift at sea, stalled in a windless, becalmed forever, imperceptibly rocking with the vague swell of one day following the next. He had always guided and instructed her. By nature unassuming, she admired my father for his qualities of rectitude and intelligence, which she always believed superior to her own. His approval meant everything to us. My mother and I were alike in that respect; no one knew better than she how much a word of praise from him bolstered our confidence.

Eleanor and my aunt set our espressos on the table and settled down side by side, quietly sipping their coffee. There was only the whir of the fan and the clinking of copper, and a complicity so thick you would need one of those chef's knives to cut through it. I wondered what kind of tricks these two had up their sleeves.

I always had so many questions for my aunt, questions that arose as I was racing around Paris tracking down frightened secretaries, or evading shady-looking Russians, or finessing our way through a customs inspection. But then we would come together in a quiet moment, like now, and our conversations seemed to have a direction of their own. Or perhaps it was because I never felt comfortable forcing her hand.

It was time to seize the moment.

"Aunt Lily, is there someone else who would benefit financially from your death? What I mean is, are you rich enough to tempt someone to murder you for your money? Other than the usual suspects, I mean, the CIA or KGB."

"I don't know, my dear. It comes and it goes. Money, I mean, not attempts on my life. This is a first. However, to answer your question, you are my sole heir. No one else gets a centime."

"Just for the record, I didn't come here thinking I was inheriting anything of great value. On the contrary . . ."

I stalled here. I felt a sudden flush of warmth creep up my face that had nothing to do with the summer heat or the coffee. My aunt must have noticed.

"Please, dear, go on."

"I understood you had incurred some very important debts. That my father had bailed you out so many times that he finally cut off all contact with you. That you were ungrateful."

She suddenly looked very forlorn.

"So that's what they told you."

She set down her espresso cup with a delicate clink. The blue veins running along the backs of her thin hands made her seem unnaturally old and frail.

"I did turn to your father for help once. It was your mother, actually—I knew I could count on her."

She then said something in French, which I later understood to be Pascal's famous quote, *"Le Coeur a ses raisons que la raison ne connaît pas."*

She translated it for me as "The heart has its reasons that reason knows not" before going on to explain that Pascal had been speaking of the heart's yearning for God. "But I suppose there is as much truth in the corollary 'Hate has its reasons which reason knows not.'"

I knew then that she had named it, the shadow I'd grown up with, the underlying toxin that had sickened our family. The burden as old as time.

"But when I do truly and honestly die," she said, resuming her characteristic cheerfulness, "you will certainly not inherit any debts. Come to think of it, now might be a good time to transfer some property over to you—that is, unless you don't want it. But it's such a handy thing to have a hotel of one's own if you decide to come back to visit, which I hope you will."

"Hotel?"

"I would so like to name it after Byron, but I'm afraid the Ministry of Culture would never allow it."

"That hotel—it's yours?"

"They didn't tell you? Well, no, they wouldn't. They're very discrete."

"You bought it?"

"Oh, no, I was very young—I had no money of my own yet. This was before I met Maxim. I was working as a model for Christian Dior to pay for my studies at the Sorbonne when I met the *vicomte*. We were doing a photo shoot in the middle of the Place Vendôme when he rode by on his scooter. He told me later that he circled the *place* so many times that he started to grow dizzy, and finally he decided if he couldn't tear himself away from me, he'd have to abduct me. So he drove his scooter onto the *place* and swept me up, intending to whisk me away as he'd seen it done in the movies. Mind you, when they do it in the movies you have stunt doubles and the action is edited. Naturally, the *vicomte* hadn't any practice at abducting young ladies, and we ended up crashing into the photographer and sending all his assistants running for cover. The *vicomte* was very gallant and invited the entire production crew to lunch at the Ritz and paid for all the damages. The hotel was his wedding gift to me. Then he he went off to Indochina to produce a documentary and never returned."

"The *vicomte?*"

"De la Pérouse."

"Wedding gift?"

I was beginning to sound like a parrot.

"Why yes, Carlito. He was my very first husband, and wonderfully dear."

"First? There were more?"

Mercifully, the phone rang in the other room.

"You'll have to answer it," she said. "I'm still officially dead."

When I came back a moment later my aunt was at the sink washing out the cups.

"Who was it, dear?"

"He didn't identify himself. He said he had a message for you."

"Aha!" she said, turning to me as she dried her hands on a dish towel. There was an expectant light in her eyes.

"He said, 'The eagle has landed.'"

CHAPTER 21

So this is where you find the Parisians in August, I thought as we cruised slowly through a maze of narrow streets that webbed around the open-air Marché Saint Quentin. We were creeping along not only because it was a pedestrian street lined with busy stalls, but because Van Gogh had the window of his van rolled down with his elbow dangling out, and was making like Caesar parading triumphant through Rome. Everybody seemed to know him and hail him with a wave or a shout. We couldn't advance more than a few yards without somebody sticking their nose in the window and greeting him with the good fellow enthusiasm guys lavish on the star player of their neighborhood basketball team. Clearly, in these parts Van Gogh was a legend.

He dropped Eleanor and me at a small circular plaza where people were selling clothing and all sorts of imaginable and unimaginable wares from makeshift stands or the trunks of their cars. The place was cluttered with trash and packing crates, and the crumbling stucco buildings were splashed with colorful graffiti. It had none of the picturesque charm I'd imagined of Paris's famed flea markets. The shoppers had that predatory stalking look, the one they wear at bargain basement clearances and neighborhood garage sales. There was an indoor covered market, but Eleanor headed down the Rue d'Aligre, a pedestrian passage bordered on both sides by shaded stalls selling everything from persimmons to shimmering tunas laid out on ice.

I had been designated Eleanor's backup, but in my new aviator sunglasses and trailing a shopping caddy, I looked more like a cross between a bodyguard and a chef's assistant. To my neophyte eye, one stall looked no different from another, but Eleanor clearly had her favorites. She zigzagged purposefully back and forth, pausing here and there to check the price of tomatoes or leeks chalked on small green boards suspended from overhead wires. I was pleasantly full from my five-course lunch with Greta in the chic cafeteria on the top floor of the Galeries Lafayette with a rooftop view of Paris, but the sight of such abundance made me long for an appetite. I found my brain dazzled by the range of colors, the hues of berries and melons, of chiles and leafy greens; I marveled at nature's pairing of violet and sage green on an artichoke. Suddenly I felt the inadequacy of my system of Hex codes with which I'd painted life. I'd once been so proud of my skills. Now they felt so ridiculously inconsequential. What good were they, other than in a paint store?

Eleanor didn't waste time. Kilos of squash, turnips, carrots and apricots were weighed, priced and thrust at me to bundle into the caddy, which quickly filled up. I wondered who on earth we were feeding—surely not our little team on the Rue Tonton, as I'd rarely seen anything more than a leftover chicken wing or some lemons rolling around in the fridge.

Then, suddenly, Eleanor was gone. My first thought was that she'd been kidnapped. Then I caught sight of her squeezing between the stalls to the sidewalk and coming to stop before the shuttered shop front of a squat red stucco building. I managed to catch up with her just as the metal security door rattled up enough for us both to duck inside.

The fellow who'd admitted us gave Eleanor a nod of recognition and we followed him through a short passage into a seedy courtyard littered with a few broken-down bikes and large dumpsters filled to the brim with detritus. Two men sat on folding chairs playing backgammon on a stack of crates. They were big guys with shaved heads who looked like beating people up was their favorite leisure sport. They recognized Eleanor and rose to greet her with deference while I got the *happy to smash in your face anytime* look. Eleanor said the magic words and I followed her inside, trailing my caddy sprouting celery branches.

We followed our escort through a dark corridor that led into the back of a small warehouse crammed with rack after rack of leather coats. After thrashing through a jungle of suede we eventually arrived at a small clearing where there sat a man mouthing a cigarette while cranking away at an adding machine. I'd recognized the sound as soon as we stepped into the warehouse. That and the smell of burnt coffee reminded me of our old office at Box Paints when I was a kid and my father was just starting up the business and he'd hired a man named Norman to do his books. There was a remarkable resemblance between the man who looked up at us through the dirty lenses of his spectacles and our old bookkeeper. Norman had never been big on deodorant and neither was this guy, and the fan whirring atop the file cabinet behind him was like an olfactory loudspeaker announcing that he was at his desk. He was all earnestness and sweat, grinding out his cigarette in a tin ashtray and rising to shake Eleanor's hand. After a brief exchange he surprised me by addressing me in English, or something like it, since he turned out to be an honest-to-goodness Scot by the name of Dougal and I could only make out bits and pieces of sounds masquerading as vowels. Pointing at his adding machine, he said something to the effect that Eleanor was twice as quick as that thing and he'd never once caught her make an error calculating an exchange, even rounding to three decimal places, and that she struck a very hard bargain. For years he'd tried to lure her away from my aunt to come work for him, to no avail.

The transaction was quick: From beneath the potatoes at the bottom of the caddy I produced a manila envelope stuffed with tens of thousands of dollar bills, Dougal ran the bills through a counting machine and exchanged them for currencies concealed in leather bags hanging from a coat rack behind his desk. Rubles, French francs, Austrian schillings, German deutschmarks—all of which would, my aunt had reassured me, eventually make their way along the supply chain to the faceless men and women who wanted nothing more than to promote the freedom to read what they wanted to read, with maybe a little sedition thrown in.

"I could just as easily go to the bank, but Dougal gives me nine times the bank rate on Rubles," she had said as she hurried me out the door with a reminder to take good care of Eleanor.

We had just extricated ourselves from Dougal's malodorous den and were making our way out through the maze of racks when the door at the back burst open, followed by a lot of stentorious bellowing. I waved Eleanor behind me and sneaked a peek from behind the wide shoulders of a leopard-collared number: Dougal was being raided by the police. Clearly, they knew their man was there somewhere in the vast jungle of animal hide, but his adding machine had gone quiet and so they were forced to plow through the suffocatingly cramped rows of coats. Difficult as it was, given the density of garments, I knew it was only a matter of time before they stumbled upon us. I quickly stuffed the envelopes into Eleanor's tote bag, whispered to her to trust me, drew her arms behind her back and then thrust her forward into the light. I took advantage of all the chaos to make a lot of noise of my own, marching Eleanor ahead of me and flashing my American Express card while bellowing "FBI" at the stunned policemen. No doubt Eleanor's genuine wide-eyed look of bewilderment added to my game, and the fact that I kept barking nonsense in English, rambling on that this woman was an American who was being extradited for charges in the State of Virginia, in accordance with Interpol's agreement as ratified by the law of 1978, and so on and so forth. The whole idea was premised on Mike's theorem of "bullshit baffles brains," and I thought if I moved quickly enough, what with my aviators style statement, the dim light of the warehouse and sheer bravado, we could get away before they called my bluff.

    I felt bad about wrestling Eleanor around. She was quite a large woman and I'd never seen her take more than ten paces without pausing for a rest, and here I was forcing her into a trot with a currency-laden tote bag over her shoulder. Once out on the street I barged recklessly through the market crowd, dragging Eleanor along behind me and drawing glares and shouts from incensed shoppers.

    The effort was too much for her, and on the way home she had to lay down in the back of the van to catch her breath. She was making sharp gasping sounds that I found very alarming. It wasn't until we were circling the Bastille that I realized that Eleanor was seized with fits of laughter.

CHAPTER 22

"The eagle is Julius Hamm," my aunt had explained to me through the bathroom door while I stood under an icy shower trying to cool off. "He just flew in from Moscow. His wife's on his yacht so he's meeting his Italian girlfriend at the Plaza Athénée. That's your next stop, so don't dawdle."

She'd been very pleased with the way I'd extracted Eleanor and our money from the scene of the raid. Eleanor less so, since we'd been forced to abandon the caddy full of fresh manioc that she'd promised to cook for her friends this weekend. The tuber, a nutritious carbohydrate commonly consumed in tropical regions, needed to be prepared properly to avoid cyanide poisoning. Eleanor, along with being a math whiz, was also a trusted manioc cook.

As I stood toweling myself dry, I wondered how I could possibly keep up with this crowd. My aunt seemed to think I had potential for deception, which pleased me more than I was willing to admit. I was even thinking of asking Van Gogh to forge an FBI badge for me after my aunt explained that the FBI did indeed have an attaché office in Paris.

I found her at her desk whacking away at her IBM Selectric. Her next Melody Bly novel was due on the publisher's desk in a few weeks and all this business chasing down the Pasternak files had derailed her writing.

"It's crap, but at least it's on the page," she said as she batted the carriage return and knocked off a few more lines while I rolled up the sleeves of this, the second of my brand-new shirts. "Ya gotta start somewhere."

The momentary slip into vernacular sounded very California—a relic from a past she had packed away but could never bring herself to discard, like a summery dress she might have worn on the Santa Monica pier but would have been out of place on the streets of Paris.

"Narratives are powerful, Carlito," she said, removing her glasses and flattening her hand palm down on the pages stacked beside the typewriter, a sober gesture like that of someone swearing an oath of allegiance.

"A good tyrant like Stalin understands the power of a story, and he'll twist the truth to his own advantage. Any leader, for that matter, who is willing to rewrite history to eliminate opposition to his views can corrupt the truth. And once they get that corrupted version out there, the truth just doesn't have legs anymore. That's what the Soviets did. Literature, art, nothing can get made if it doesn't serve the fiction that they call truth. They dictate history, narrative, even characters. Novels are fabricated around Soviet-style heroes intended to rouse the people to feats of labor. Self-doubt is not tolerated in a hero, nor is desperation or human failings. So, what do they get? Very bad stories, that's what. You know what happens when you take away inner conflict and self-doubt and all those frustrating obstacles? You get nothing. Flat monotonous tedium. You get life, not literature. Tell me, Carlito, who wants sunny days in their novels? We want sunshine in our *lives*, but in our stories we want rain and gloom and humans trembling from misery or cold or fear or love."

Then she waved me into a chair and told me about the man I was about to meet. A man whose usefulness to the Soviets was soon to come to an end, if the communiqué Louise had buried in the duvet was to be believed.

Evening was approaching as the revolving doors of the Hotel Plaza Athénée propelled me inside into an oasis of splendor. I was greeted by a rush of cool air and cool marble underfoot. In the center of the palatial lobby stood a circular mahogany table so big and slick you could have skated on it, topped by a floral arrangement of sprays of summery blooms that rose halfway to the gilded ceiling. Everything was spotless and gleaming and looked very expensive and not at all wilted like everything outdoors. The front desk clerks were also spotless and gleaming. They smiled at me like I'd been gone a long time and they were really happy to see me return. I thought of what my aunt had told me about Julius Hamm's Moscow hotel project, and I wondered if the Soviets were planning to build a hotel like this. I tried to imagine the desk clerk saying something like "Welcome, comrade," but it was a stretch.

I gave Julius Hamm's name and waited while they called up to his room. I was carrying a slim paperback book he'd authored with the catchy title *The Art of Playing Dirty: How to Stick It to the Other Guy While Sticking to the Law*. My mission was to get his autograph, deliver an envelope and get out. In that order. It didn't sound complicated.

They passed me the phone, saying Monsieur Hamm would like to speak to me.

His voice was a pleasant baritone with a hint of a Texas drawl. "Where's Lily?"

"She couldn't make it. I'm her nephew."

There was a long pause. When he spoke again, he sounded guarded.

"Did you remember my shirts?"

To this, I responded, "No, but I stopped by the pharmacy."

"Good, then you get yourself up here, young man. They'll show you the way."

Julius Hamm had been wheeling and dealing with the Soviets for years, since before the mid-seventies, back when relations were warm and rosy and both sides had decided the other wasn't such a bad sort after all, but Reagan's military buildup and harsh rhetoric had changed all that, and the tide had shifted. Despite the fact that the West was looking for new markets and the Soviets were desperate for Western capital and technology, American companies shied away from doing business with them.

So Julius had moved to Paris and in no time had charmed even the most charm-immune of the Franks: the industrialists, bankers and bourgeoisie who owned prime properties and were developing vast swaths of the city. Pretty soon he was brokering deals between the Soviets and the French, and the Swedes, and the Japanese, masterminding proposals to build automobile factories, or make blue jeans, or build shopping centers. He flew back and forth to Moscow every month on a permanent visa, laying his deals at the ministry's doorstep like a cat depositing dead mice at the foot of the master.

The Soviets, hamstrung by their own lies and propaganda vilifying loathsome capitalists, and suffering from a long history of paranoia about all things foreign, took to Julius like a beloved uncle who could lead them childlike by the hand through the dark and dangerous woods of dealmaking.

The truth was that Julius had a soft spot for the country, his mother having been Russian, and the Russians felt safe in his hands. He was gregarious and good-natured, and gave decadent bourgeois pleasures a good name. Like a doting uncle, he never showed up without a gift in hand for the ministers and their families, luxuries that could not be had behind the Iron Curtain—Russian-language Bibles, Chanel lipstick, even disposable diapers, packed neatly into his oversized Louis Vuitton suitcases along with his double-breasted navy blue silk suits and white shirts starched so stiff they crackled when he shook your hand. And his eighteen-karat gold cuff links with his initials. He was a model of bravery, an American with a Russian soul who had the courage to be ridiculously, absurdly, preposterously rich and to be proud of it.

"So where does he fit in?" I had asked my aunt.

"When I approached Julius to ask for his help, he had just pulled off a huge deal. He'd persuaded his French investment banking partners to bankroll a modern luxury hotel in Moscow. What you call a turnkey project—everything from the lighting fixtures to bath soap would be 'Made in France,' which relieved the Soviets of the terrifying task of making sure the hotel opened with sheets on the beds and toilet paper in the rooms. The project was in the final stages of furnishing and equipping the interiors. It was a perfect foil for us. We use their supply chain to smuggle in Pasternak's archives."

She went on to tell me how it worked: The French supplier would ship lighting fixtures to Moscow—maybe a few would get broken, so they'd be returned. Or a batch of door handles would be defective or latches wouldn't fit.

"When this happens, we have a contact on the building site who slips a few boxes of files into the crates of defective merchandise that are shipped back to France. It's much less risky for Pasternak to meet up with an engineer in Moscow than to approach a Western embassy employee."

"What does Julius Hamm get?"

"He gets any intelligence in those files that might impact his business deals with the Russians. You could say he's spying on himself. So that's our deal. And this," she said, thrusting an envelope into my hand, "is for his eyes only. After he reads it, it needs to be destroyed. Immediately."

The meeting would be tricky, she warned; Julius had been in Moscow for the last several days and we shouldn't assume he knew that an attempt had been made on her life and that she was believed to be dead. Or that his Russian contact in the trade delegation, Zhukovsky, had defected.

But then, maybe he knew everything. If so, he'd be suspicious. Either way, there was a protocol in place in case she ever sent someone in her stead. Certain questions and replies that would identify me as the courier. Our conversation would be entirely in code.

"Do you think this business is why the Soviets want him eliminated?" I asked.

"I doubt it. But I can't be sure. I think he's been caught at his own game of greed and self-interest. Only a handful of people on this end know what are in those files, Carlito. Julius doesn't know the source or the actual nature of the documents we're moving, but he's the one who goes back and forth freely to Moscow. He's the final link in the chain that took us years to set up."

"Is he another one of your exes?" I asked, sounding more inquisitive than I would have liked.

"Ah, Julius and I had some good times together. We go way back," she said as a smile of nostalgia softened her face. "We were both young reporters—"

"What happened to the modeling?"

"Oh, that didn't last long, not after I met the *vicomte*. He was just making a name for himself as a documentary producer and I started writing movie reviews. Then *L'Humanité* hired me. Julius was working for *The Daily Worker* and they sent him to Paris from time to time, which is how we met. We were two Americans working for communist newspapers—it was terribly thrilling—although I took the work much more seriously than he did. Julius was a lousy journalist. He really didn't care about reporting. He was much better at talking up an idea and getting you to buy into it. He could be very persuasive and articulate, and he was brilliant at making deals. You can't help but admire him on some level. He's dangerously lovable and delightful company. He's also an unscrupulous liar who'll throw his best friend under the bus if it serves his purpose."

"Would he throw you under the bus?"

"No doubt about it," she said with humorous intent, but I didn't find it funny. I was still shocked by the idea that she had been a Communist, but I certainly didn't like the idea of anybody throwing her under a bus, or messing with her in any way.

"That's why you need to meet him quickly," she continued. "He has the info we need on the last delivery of the files, and it's a big haul. We need to get it safely in our possession before anything else happens."

She had sent me off like a mother sending her son off on his first prom date, patting my chest, smoothing down my hair, looking simultaneously proud and worried that I would muck it all up.

CHAPTER 23

Julius answered the door in a plush white hotel bathrobe. He was short and rotund with a boyish face and eyes that looked at me with reptilian calm through thick lenses. Even clad in a robe, he was easily pegged as a man who knew how to enjoy his wealth, the kind who have perfectly manicured nails and never do their own grocery shopping. The sort of man who didn't need a good physique to attract women. Despite the meticulous grooming, he did not look well. An impression he immediately confirmed.

"She's killing me," he said.

"I brought your dental floss," I replied, this being the phrase I was to use to identify myself.

"Oh, that," he answered with a dismissive wave of the hand. "Come on in," he said as I followed him into the suite. "Where's Lily?"

"She's having a hard time getting around just now."

He flashed me a quizzical look but didn't follow up with any more questions.

"That's too bad. I could use a woman's advice."

He crossed the suite to a closed door, which I presumed to be the bedroom, and planted himself in front of it with his hands on his hips, staring with watchful determination, the way Billy would sit under the dining table and stare at the floor waiting for food to drop. A light feminine fragrance hung in the air.

He tapped softly on the door.

"Darling, open up." He tapped again. "*Amore*, talk to me." Then he motioned me over.

"You hear that?" he whispered. He had his ear to the door.

All I heard was a soft muttering.

"She's praying," he said.

We stood with our ears pressed to the wood, like two children eavesdropping. We spoke in whispers.

"It's Latin," he said. "Do you know any Latin?"

"I had a year of it in ninth grade. I don't think that will get me very far."

My aunt had told me that as a young reporter Julius got his scoops by hiding in the toilet stalls in the State Department to eavesdrop on conversations. Now here he was, an aging man of great worldly influence trying in vain to unlock the secrets of his lover's heart. Secrets uttered in a language nobody spoke anymore. Except priests or God.

I followed him back across the suite. Room service had not yet cleared the dining table, and I noticed a dish of risotto gone cold, and a plate of small pastries that had barely been touched. Another plate rimmed with a few cold fries smothered in ketchup I presumed to be his. No sign of champagne or wine, nothing you would expect to woo a woman.

"She's praying for me. Can you believe it? Who on earth has

ever prayed for me? Other than my mother, God rest her soul."

"Mr. Hamm, sir, if you don't mind, I'll just get your autograph on your book here and be on my way."

"The girl doesn't want my money, she wants my goddam soul."

He cinched the robe tighter around his waist and thrust his hands deep into his pockets in the manner of a schoolboy who had been unfairly reprimanded.

"It's criminal, to let a woman like that walk the earth. She's killing me. I tell you, I won't survive her."

When he winced, I thought it was in response to some emotional pain inflicted by the pious girl behind the door. It took him a few seconds to recover.

"Mr. Hamm, are you okay?" I said.

He sank onto the sofa with his head thrown back and closed his eyes. His belly rose and fell in quick labored breaths. His bald head was beaded with sweat despite the air-conditioning.

"You don't look well, sir," I said.

He did that dismissive thing with his hand.

"Something I ate in Fun City East, that's all," he said.

"Fun City?"

"Moscow."

He lifted his head and cocked an ear.

"Has she stopped?"

He was distracted. I was going to have to play along. I walked over and put my ear to the door.

"It's quiet."

"Let's try some music. She loves Paolo Conte."

"Mr. Hamm—"

He wasn't listening. He had found the tape among a stack

of cassettes and slipped it into the tape deck.

"Sir, I'm in a bit of a hurry here, if you don't mind—"

"Shut up and sit down, sonny. Book signing can damn well wait. You need to hear this music. Next time you want to seduce a girl, you put on a little Paolo Conte. Everybody knows that Pavarotti fellow, but this guy is what the Italians listen to."

We sat together, one on each end of the wide, silver brocade sofa, me on the edge of my seat, Julius Hamm watching the door, waiting and listening. Paolo Conte seemed to understand. He sang in an earthy tuneless voice that took you back to something familiar and comforting. The girl had still not emerged, but neither was she praying. Julius turned to me with a nod and a wink, his mood visibly brightened.

"This will bring her out of her room."

How the heart hangs on the smallest hope, I thought, *when love has sway over us.*

I had been prepared to meet a high-powered wheeler-dealer, the sort of arrogant businessman who would keep me waiting while he carried on a conversation with someone important in New York or London.

But Julius Hamm was in no mood to get down to business. I thought it better not to rush things.

"What's her name?" I asked.

"Giulietta."

His face softened like wax in the heat of the sun when he spoke her name, dissolving the pain I'd seen earlier.

"Hell, I don't understand it. I've always argued with my wives. We shouted and slammed doors. I got a buzz out of it. But for the life of me, I can't bring myself to shout at her. I can't even raise my voice."

"That has to be a good thing."

"She's Italian. Italian women expect their men to slam doors and bellow."

"She didn't choose an Italian, sir, she chose you."

He seemed to be giving this some thought.

"Do you know what it's like for a man like me to give up control? My God, it's . . . " He paused. I got the impression that his imagination couldn't take him down that road. Yet, here he was.

"Liberating?"

He looked at me as if he were seeing me for the first time.

"Who are you again?"

"Carl. Lily's nephew."

His eyes narrowed on me from deep behind the thick lenses. I got a flash of a shrewd man accustomed to appraising the usefulness of others.

I watched while he withdrew a medicine vial from the pocket of his bathrobe and washed down some pills with a glass of water.

"I wish one of my kids had come into the business with me," he said. "A man needs his offspring to take an interest in his legacy."

"I'm not exactly in the business. I'm only helping out temporarily."

"It changes things, when they're your own flesh and blood. Not that your own kid won't screw you over. Boy, I tell you, when your kids turn against you, your life doesn't amount to much. My boys don't want to have anything to do with me—one became a rabbi and the other's a Buddhist who runs a bakery in Yonkers. They both know they'll be rich as Midas when

I die, so they can pretend that money doesn't interest them. My girls, well, that's another matter. They suck up to me like nobody's business. I can see right through them, but damn, it feels good all the same. They're masters at flattery, those two. 'Got it from Pop,' they tell me. That's how I made my way up in the world, Carl, telling people what they wanted to hear, flattering their egos. People like me are dangerous. We're slime. We're goddamned worms."

He wagged a finger at the door. "And that girl in there knows it. She knows more about my wormy side than anyone, dead or alive."

I was waiting for the charmer to make an appearance, the man whose eloquence and buoyancy could move mountains, so my aunt said, but all I saw was a man shorn of his defenses in a moment of deep doubt. I had come here with the purpose of informing him that the Russians were going to have him killed. But I couldn't bring myself to tell him, not yet. Whatever was causing those chest pains, it was something more serious than indigestion. And I'm sure he knew it.

"She thinks I'm going to die in a state of mortal sin. That's what worries her. And you know what? It's beginning to worry me too. All my wives, all my kids, all they want is my money. I've got tons of money. Enough to make them all rich for life. And you know what? They're all afraid of her. *Her.*" His eyes drifted off to the closed door while Paolo Comte strummed away. "I'd give her the moon if I could, but she doesn't want it. She wants me to believe. I can't even offer her marriage. Not unless I want to declare my other marriages null and void. How do you do that, for Chrissake? Sure, you can annul one marriage, but three? I've got four kids I'd have to disown. How the hell do you say I didn't want you to be born? Maybe I didn't, maybe I did, but damn, the twists and turns the mind has to take to come out the other end of this religion business—it beggars belief. I have advisers galore. I have attorneys and bankers who charge me if I so much as breathe on them, and not a single goddam one of them can help me here. Not one of those assholes gives a shit about his soul, not any more than I do about mine. Or did."

I was beginning to feel the fellow's despair. To be old and to feel death creeping up on you, and suddenly to find yourself faced with undoing everything you've done, renouncing a lifetime of unscrupulous controlling, scheming and intrigue, declaring it all null and void. All for an Italian girl in prayer behind a locked door. I figured she must be a real stunner, like Sophia Loren, and holding out on him. Otherwise, why all the fuss? Or maybe the girl really had some special quality of goodness that touched his crusty old heart and promised him a little peace. I found myself glancing at the door with curiosity.

Julius got up and went to open the balcony door; hot heavy air came billowing in. Even this late in the day, the sun was only now tipping to the horizon. He stepped onto the terrace, inviting me to follow. The Eiffel Tower loomed in the distance, framed by window boxes of red geraniums and a low-hanging red awning. It was just the kind of view you'd find on a picture postcard.

"You know how much that view costs me?" he asked. For a moment I thought it was his ego slithering out of its nest, seeking the warmth of admiring gazes. Then he fastened that unblinking gaze on me like tentacles. It spooked me. I got the feeling he'd brought me out here to say something that he couldn't say inside. And he wanted to make sure I knew it.

He quoted some ridiculously low nightly rate. A motorcycle roared by, drowning out his voice, and he repeated it.

"You tell Lily she can get the same rate anytime she wants. Tell her to see Jean Paul, the concierge. He's the one to talk to. You make sure to tell her that, son."

He quoted the room rate again and asked me to repeat it back to him, so I did.

Then he slapped me on the back and turned to stare moodily in the direction of the Eiffel Tower. The spooky moment passed. Perhaps he was thinking about what sort of deal he could broker with God, or at least the Catholic Church. As for me, I was imagining dinner with Greta on a terrace like this.

"Do you know anything about deathbed conversions?" he asked after a moment.

"I believe Oscar Wilde had one of those."

"You know what it involves?"

"The priest baptized him and then there was some sort of ritual of confession."

"That's all?"

"Well, sir, considering it's adapted to the dying, I would imagine they keep it short and to the point."

I sensed the schemer coming to life. I think the idea of a deathbed conversion appealed to him. It worked sort of like a VIP pass that allowed you to skip the line and head straight in.

"So I would only need a priest. I wouldn't need a lawyer."

"I don't see why you would. Lawyers tend to drag things out."

"That's what we'll do," he said, drawing me back indoors. "A deathbed conversion."

"But, sir, it seems to me you're right back where you started."

"What's that?"

"Pretending to believe something you don't to get what you want, it's a little wormlike, don't you think?"

"Not at all, sonny. It would ease her mind."

I wasn't about to argue. There was a lot of moral gray area here. More than most people, I knew the many shades of gray.

"Mr. Hamm . . ." I picked up the book I'd brought with me and held it out to him. "If you'll just give me your autograph, then I'll let you get on with your conversion."

"You're not going anywhere, sonny," he said, ignoring the book under his nose. "I'm going to play like I'm dying and I need you to play along. You're even going to call an ambulance. But you won't really make the call. The priest will get here first and my soul will be saved from a godless eternity. After a lifetime of godlessness. That's what the girl wants so that's what she'll get. Hell, I don't give a cock's damn about doctrine, but who knows, if you leave a little room for miracles, who knows?"

He didn't strike me at all as the sort of man who believed in miracles, but I believed he was sincere about wanting to be sincere. About wanting to be some better version of himself, even at this late hour, because something inexplicable had happened to him. Because *someone* had happened to him.

He asked me if I knew any priests in town.

"I'm sure the front desk could find one."

"I need one who can bend the rules."

"I'm afraid I can't help you there."

"You get me my priest, you get your signature."

"Priests aren't part of our deal." I thrust the book at him. "I need your autograph, sir."

"Get me my priest."

"I don't know any priests, and even if I did . . ."

I paused. I could see he had the upper hand. I figured I might as well make good use of a bad situation. I met his reptilian calm with a determination of my own.

"I tell you what, you throw in a suite like this for a weekend," I said, "a long weekend, three nights, all expenses and meals for two included, and you got yourself a deal."

I went downstairs and made the call from a phone booth in the lobby. Greta didn't answer. I waited a few minutes and tried again; this time I let it ring about twenty times before hanging up. Frankly, I felt more relieved than frustrated. It was a bad idea. But I didn't have any good ideas.

It was late; outdoors night was falling and the hotel chandeliers shimmered like stars. I walked around the public areas, nosed around a few boutiques and tried on some sunglasses. I found a gift shop that sold chewing gum and bought a pack of some brand I'd never heard of, having long ago given up trying to find Wrigley's. I checked out the bar, which was cool and packed with chic people who didn't seem to be worrying about nuclear war with Russia or secret KGB archives. Then I went back and tried Greta one last time, knowing that this entire operation hung on a slimmer than slim chance. This time she answered. I laid out my plan, crazy as it was. There was a long silence.

I said, "I understand if you find this difficult. It's just that, well, naturally he came to mind."

"You know how I feel about what he does."

"But your dad isn't the DGSE. He's English."

She didn't answer that. It was a flimsy bit of reasoning from someone who didn't have the faintest idea what sort of shady work these people undertook in the name of national security.

"If you don't want to get involved, I understand."

"He's the one who doesn't want me to get involved."

"You could tell him there's something in it for him. Something big. But I also want something in exchange. Equally big. And he has to be convincing. The girl will know the difference."

"I don't know if I can get him to do it."

"Sure you can. Just pull that pouty act on him, the one where your face looks like a dam ready to burst."

I thought I could hear her smiling.

"By the way, you don't have anything against luxury hotels, do you?"

"Nothing comes to mind."

"Good."

There was another pause. I was in no hurry to hang up. I loved listening to her silences.

She said, "Do you need an accomplice for anything?"

"Actually, there is something."

"Do I get to go in disguise?"

"The disguise is optional."

She hesitated.

"Greta, I don't have the faintest idea what I'm doing."

"I know."

"It doesn't bother you?"

"Actually, I find it rather attractive."

This time the silence sounded very much like a yes.

"I'm still committed to messing with them," she said finally.

"We can do a little of that too."

I didn't know how long we would have to wait for Father Henry. I figured Julius and I could listen to more Paolo Comte and maybe I could convince him to hold up his end of the bargain. It was simple—all he had to do was write a name on the dedication page—*To Patrick Dehilerin* or *To Magnus Saint Croix*. That would indicate the dead drop where we were to leave a very large payment. Once the payment had been received, the same dead drop would be used to leave the shipping forms we needed to clear the package through customs and have it delivered to a warehouse.

He'd left the door to the suite open so I walked right in. There was no sign of Julius but the door to the bedroom was closed, which led me to think Giulietta had decided to make up with him. I checked the terrace, just to make sure, but no Julius. It was quiet. No Paolo Comte, no praying, no whispers or more urgent sounds to indicate a reconciliation was happily underway. The living area was empty—or so I thought, until I stepped around the dining table and saw him lying on the floor. My first thought was that he'd gotten tired of waiting and decided to start the show without me, then he'd fallen asleep. A friend of mine had done that once, he'd crawled under an end table to plug in a lamp and fallen sound asleep—boom, just like that. I knelt down beside Julius and whispered in his ear.

"Hey, Mr. Hamm, the priest is on his way."

He was fully stretched out, his face buried in the carpet. It couldn't have been easy to breathe like that.

"Mr. Hamm?"

I shook his shoulder. Then I tried to roll him over but he

was too heavy. I squatted down and peered into his face.

"Mr. Hamm?"

The glasses were smashed and the eyes (or at least the one staring at me) were open and unblinking. A little blood trickled out of his nose, which looked smashed as well. He must have fallen straight forward and hit the floor like a felled tree crashing to the ground. He hadn't even had time to take his hands out of his bathrobe pockets.

Not a sound came from the other room. The girl must not have heard a thing. There had been nothing to hear. Except a loud thud.

A loud thud. The sound of Julius Hamm falling face-first to the ground would have made the sort of sound you can't ignore.

I didn't bother knocking on the bedroom door. I knew she wouldn't be there. I found his Louis Vuitton suitcases packed with neatly folded men's shirts and monogrammed pajamas. I checked the armoire. Nothing but his silk suits. Either she'd cleared out all her belongings or she hadn't planned to stay the night. I guessed it was the latter.

I went back into the salon. I remembered seeing his briefcase, crammed with papers and files, lying open on the writing desk. It wasn't on the desk. It wasn't anywhere. I concluded that the good Giulietta had absconded with it. I wondered how long he'd been involved with the girl, and who she was working for.

And where was that book? *The Art of Playing Dirty*. Had he signed it? When I left him, he'd had it in his hand. I looked around but couldn't find it. Maybe she had walked off with that as well.

I picked up the phone to call the front desk, then thought better of it. I can't say I was panicked, but my hands weren't all that steady either. I felt like there was a puzzle here, and I needed to solve it before alerting the authorities. I poured myself a glass of scotch from the minibar, pulled up a chair at the dining table and sat down to keep Julius company while I thought this through. All I could see was the black leather house slippers sticking out from behind the chair legs. I noticed what small feet he had, and that one of the slippers had fallen off his heel and was hanging cockeyed from his toes; that part bothered me. The clutter of dishes on the table bothered me too, particularly the silverware lying every which way. I knew better than to touch anything, but it wasn't easy. For some reason my mind flashed back to the day when my aunt had called me to the table to eat her omelet and then straightened my knife and fork. I had never asked why she'd done it; I only knew that it was important to me. I couldn't say it was an act of love, but on some level it felt like that. Death is such a perplexing thing. It happens right before our eyes and still we cannot fathom it. So I sat there drinking my scotch and trying not to align the silverware.

I don't know what pissed me off more, the fact that he'd died without turning over the information I needed, or the fact that the girl had so thoroughly deceived him. I don't know why I felt sorry for him. Julius Hamm had been a selfish bastard who'd double-dealt and prevaricated his way through life. But I think he'd been on the road to repentance. In his own twisted way, he'd been trying to worm his way into heaven. All on account of a girl who turned out to be a mole. At least he died before he found out the truth.

I wondered if she'd been the one to kill him. If they'd find traces of poison. Or if it was just his own heart giving out on him.

As I sat drinking the scotch and watching his house slippers (I half believed he'd come alive again and we could just pick up where we left off), slowly the pieces began to fall into place. His reluctance to get on with our transaction. The way he drew me onto the balcony and locked his eyes on mine. I think he suspected his room was bugged. Maybe he even suspected the girl was involved, but he didn't want to believe it. Maybe he knew more than he was letting on.

On a hunch, I went around the table and kneeled beside his body. I didn't like the idea of frisking a dead man, but I needed to see if I was right.

He was very heavy, but I managed to turn him over just enough to retrieve the book from his bathrobe pocket.

I flipped it open and relief washed over me. There it was, on the title page, the dedication I needed.

He'd left me something else as well. Tucked between the pages toward the back of the book was a magnetic key card emblazoned with the name of the hotel. Was it to his room? If so, why slip it in the book, which he was evidently planning to give to me? Then I noticed he'd struck through the page number and written 227.

I picked up the phone and called the front desk. I said that Mr. Hamm appeared to have had a heart attack and asked them to call an ambulance. I knew the concierge would be there within minutes, so I grabbed the book and made for the stairs. It didn't take long to find room 227. I swiped the card through the lock and the door clicked open. As it closed behind me, I could hear the sirens approaching.

CHAPTER 24

Huggins always wore an air of perpetual sadness; it weighed him down like drenched clothing on a man caught in a downpour. I had at first attributed it to his profession, then to heartbreak, and finally, when his cover was blown, to the world-weariness of a man whose identity was constructed of secrets and lies. Now sitting next to me in the taxi in his rumpled suit with the stiff priest's collar chafing his neck, he looked like someone who'd been forced into an uncomfortable Halloween costume against his will. I couldn't help but feel a little vindicated after being played for a fool myself. I was on edge and combative and in no mood to put up with anybody's shit.

I'd been standing in the shade of the big red awning near the front entrance of the Plaza Athénée, glancing impatiently at my watch and shifting my backpack from shoulder to shoulder, trying to look innocent as first the police cars and then an ambulance cruised by and turned onto a side street where they would access the hotel discretely from a staff entrance. I'd told the hotel director I'd wait in the lobby if they needed to speak to me, but I had no intention of hanging around. Against the odds, I'd managed to find what I came for—a manila envelope addressed to my aunt, which I'd buried at the bottom of my backpack. I didn't know the laws here, didn't know if the police would have the right to search me or not, but I needed to get out of there before they came looking for me.

When Huggins's taxi pulled up to the red-carpeted stairs, I didn't let him get so much as a foot on the tarmac. I slid onto the seat next to him and closed the door.

"Let's go," I said, tapping the driver on the shoulder.

"*Où?*"

"Anywhere. Just go. *Vamos.*"

He got the point and pulled away.

"Unless you want to take a few spins around the Arc de Triomphe," I taunted Huggins, remembering how he'd gotten such a thrill out of it. He had seemed so earnest that evening, and I'd rather liked him then. I was disappointed to think it had all been faked.

He flashed me a faintly apologetic look. I noticed the small leather case on his knees.

"What's that?"

"A stole and a little holy water."

"Straight out of your kitchen faucet, is it?"

He glanced forlornly at the case. "If it consoles the dying, it does no harm."

"It's too late, Charlie. He's already kicked the bucket."

"Oh my," he muttered, looking genuinely distressed.

"Okay, if you don't want to do the merry-go-round again, why don't you give directions to the guy behind the wheel. Take us someplace where we can talk."

The taxi dropped us off in a narrow cobbled street across

the river somewhere on the left bank. I followed Huggins into a dark and noisy bar, down a treacherously narrow and winding staircase into a basement jazz club where the musicians were just beginning to set up. It was hard to see just how big the room was or how many people were crammed down there, but from the sound level I figured it was packed; the only light came from candles fixed in the mouths of wine bottles coated with years of candlewax and positioned on a few tables here and there, or set in niches in the wall. There was enough chatter and laughter to drown out even the most private of conversations, and enough cigarette smoke to conceal the identity of anybody sitting more than a few feet away. The few faces I could make out seemed to be my age and were either stoned or inebriated. We settled at a pair of tiny tables at the back in a corner recessed into the rough stone wall.

"The building dates back to the medieval era," Huggins said pleasantly, as if he were showing me around town. "Used to be part of the townhouse next door—this was an underground stable for the horses. I only point it out because Americans always find it rather fascinating." He had removed his clerical collar in the taxi, so we could have easily passed for a father and son navigating an awkward father-and-son night out.

He pulled out a packet of Player's and offered me one.

I shook my head. "I don't smoke."

"No vices?"

I didn't bother to answer.

Lighting the cigarette from the candle on our table, he took a long drag then leaned back, exhaling long and slow. There was a deep weariness to his gesture, like that of a man shedding a pretense, relieved to have the ruse come to an end.

The rosy candlelight made him look kindly, like the man I'd once thought him to be.

I picked up the bottled candle and moved it to the table behind me.

"I'm not in the mood for love, Huggins."

He gave me that flicker of an apologetic smile again. I wasn't buying it.

"That story about your wife, it was really touching. I felt sorry for you."

"We play on people's sympathies, Mr. Box. It's the job."

His candidness took me by surprise.

"I was under the impression that your job didn't exist."

"It doesn't. Officially."

"Other nations don't seem to have a problem acknowledging they have a secret intelligence agency. Why can't you Brits fess up?"

"Because," he sighed, "we English would find it embarrassing to admit we spy on others."

"Is there any truth in it? The wife story?"

"My wife is home in Oxfordshire giving violin lessons just now."

"I'm glad to hear that. I wouldn't like to think that Greta had to deal with a runaway mother as well as a father who sits in cafés disguised as a priest befriending confused and naive Americans."

"And you, Mr. Box, only pretend to be naive. You are certainly well informed."

I was getting there, in any case. I'd spent a lot of night hours reading through material my aunt had left for me to study—books, stacks of newspapers and journals, all of them marked for certain pages or articles to read, and then there were her kitchen tutorials, which wandered far and wide over a vast range of subjects and which I was getting quite adept at following.

"Why do you have my aunt's apartment under surveillance? What did you want with the antique dealer on the ground floor?"

"I cannot discuss matters of national security with you."

"Dammit, Henry, cut the crap. The bodies are piling up. What are you after? Why did you search my aunt's apartment?"

He reached for the ashtray on the next table. It was metal and made a tinny rattle when he set it down. He tapped a bit of ash off his cigarette while he deliberated how much he could tell me.

"It wasn't us. When our man got there, the place had already been ransacked. He found the African woman unconscious on the floor."

"But you planted the bug."

"That's all we went in for. It was a rushed job. Your taxi was just pulling up in front."

"So that was your guy that ran me down on the stairs." A waiter materialized out of the fog to take our order. I waited until he had gone and then continued. "He left Eleanor bleeding and unconscious on the floor."

"He had a job to do."

I'm normally a mild-mannered guy and shaking people by their collar isn't the sort of fantasy I often toy with, but the image came waltzing in out of nowhere, totally unbidden and thoroughly tempting.

Instead, I sat back and took a few deep breaths, which probably shortened my life by several years, considering how much smoke I was inhaling.

"I'm afraid there's been a good deal of confusion," he said.

"No lie."

"What business did you have with Julius Hamm?"

"I don't see why I should share that with you now. Seeing as how our lead actor has kicked the bucket and the audience has fled."

"The audience?"

"The Italian girl."

"What Italian girl?"

"Exactly."

Given that I'd more or less abducted him, he was being surprisingly patient with me.

"Look," I said, "I was offering you an exchange. If Julius Hamm really had some confessing to do, you would have had a front-row seat. On my end, I wanted a little glasnost from you all. Openness, transparency. Unfortunately, the scene didn't play out as I'd planned. Fault of deus ex machina. Or maybe just plain Deus."

I was having a good time with my theatrical metaphors. Huggins merely looked perplexed.

"Perhaps we should start over," he said.

"Back with you bugging my aunt's apartment."

The waiter, with impeccable timing, arrived with our beers. The beer was lukewarm, which didn't help my mood. I thought the least Huggins could do was choose a place with cold beer.

He said, "It's the antique dealer we're interested in. He's a person of interest to us. That's all I can say."

"Well, I sure won't tell him. It would just go to his head. So why didn't you bug his shop instead of my aunt's apartment?"

"Have you ever been in his shop?"

"I have."

He shrugged. "So you can imagine the difficulty of planting a device there."

Indeed I did. The place always looked as if it had just been visited by a family of spiteful wraiths intent on mischief—layer after layer of stuff shuffled and shuffled again, as if it had all been picked up, spun around and deposited topsy-turvy, craftsmen's tools and mechanical parts piled in with artwork, antiques and every sort of collectible you could possibly imagine, some of it junk, some of it undoubtedly valuable. Impossible to get to a floorboard, or a piece of molding, to plant a device, and if you did, you couldn't be sure it would stay put. Stuff came in and stuff went out, lord knows where. You plant a bug there one day and you never knew where it would end up the next. Maybe in a kid's backpack, maybe in a Sotheby's auction.

"I don't believe a word of it, Huggins. On the other hand, the story about your runaway wife was really very good, very believable. A Holly Golightly sort of character. But married to a small-town English vicar instead of a Texas hick."

I could tell by his blank look that he'd never seen the movie. We clearly didn't have the same cultural references.

"Did you poison my aunt?"

He answered indignantly, "Absolutely not. Assassination is not the policy of Her Majesty's Government."

If he was acting, he was terribly good. He looked truly offended.

"Now your turn," he said. "What can you tell us about Julius Hamm?"

"I know he may have double-crossed some extremely important people. Someone very close to the Kremlin leader.

Maybe even blackmailed them. Maybe they had enough of him. Maybe he was too much trouble. Maybe his usefulness was running out."

What I didn't say was that the man had probably died of a heart attack. I took another sip of my beer; it was undrinkable.

Huggins said, "The KGB are a paranoid lot. They get their knickers in a twist for the smallest things."

The waiter was just close enough for me to catch his attention. I asked him if he could take this beer away and bring me a cold one. My request confused him until Huggins translated. Then he whisked away my glass with a huff and faded into the swirls of smoke.

"That's probably the last you'll see of him or your beer," Huggins said dryly.

"Everybody seems to think my aunt died under suspicious circumstances."

"What do you think?"

"I think the people who broke into her apartment were looking for something very specific."

"Well, it wasn't us."

Bull, I thought. The Brits knew something was afoot. Maybe they didn't know what they were looking for, but they knew something was coming, something important, something they'd like to have a look at. Huggins may have even suspected my aunt was somehow running the show from beyond the grave. He may have suspected I was brought in to wrap things up. That I was not the clueless nephew dropping in to settle his auntie's estate.

To be honest, I didn't have the faintest idea what he was thinking, but I rather liked that he might think I was part of the team.

"Julius Hamm was just bait, wasn't he? To get my attention," he said.

"Come on, Huggins. Get me a cold pint. I'm damned thirsty and I've been babysitting a dead man this evening, and it's hot."

He mumbled something about how I would need to learn to drink warm beer if I ever visited England, then he mashed out his cigarette and rose. I watched as he wormed his way through the crowd. The musicians had set up their sound equipment and the crowd was growing; all the bodies were squeezing out whatever remained of the space and air.

I recalled what my aunt had said, about how comforting it was to have somebody do the thinking for her.

I needed to chart a plan of action.

Aunt Lily's plan had been to bring the files to the negotiating table with either the CIA or British SIS. But the documents weren't yet in her possession. If the British were looking for the files, they would have no qualms about stealing them from my aunt. They would never intercept intelligence intended for an Allied nation, but Lily wasn't a friendly nation or a state—she was an outsider operating, perhaps illegally, beyond the bounds of government-mandated security; if the Brits were to steal the files, there would be no diplomatic repercussions, no damage done to cooperation between Allied intelligence agencies.

Huggins was amazingly quick. He could get things done when he wanted to.

The glass he set before me was icy cold to the touch. I took a few swigs. It put me in a better mood straightaway.

I said, "There's a Russian dissident by the name of Maxim Mikhailovich Bukovsky . . ."

CHAPTER 25

It was late when I let myself in. The house was dark and quiet and had that smell I was finding familiar, of leather books and dusty carpets and old wood. I could hear fans droning somewhere in the darkness, rotating rhythmically with a faint clicking sound. Hunger was finally catching up with me, and I found some cold chicken in the refrigerator and ate it standing up over the sink. I buttered what was left of a baguette and washed that down with a liter of milk. It was enough to fill my stomach and absorb some of the alcohol. I hadn't heard a peep out of Billy, nor did I find him in his Prussian-blue bed in my room, so I suspected he was camping out in my aunt's bed.

I stood in the dark at my bedroom window, looking down onto the street below lit by the soft white glow of the streetlamps, thinking of my freshly painted Florida condo with my khakis hanging neatly in the closet, and my nicely air-conditioned cubicle in Epcot where I used to sit reading reports on paints and varnishes. Thinking how I would love to sleep in my own bed tonight, without worrying about stumbling over piles of books in the middle of the night, or getting someone killed through my own stupidity.

A light came on in the bookstore across the street. I watched as an arm reached into the display case to rearrange some books. A few minutes later the lights went out and a long-haired girl emerged, locking the door behind her and walking away down the street. It meant nothing, and then again everything had significance. Everything needed to be questioned.

I awoke in the middle of the night from a strange dream where I found myself inserted into a manila envelope, like a sleeping bag; the flap needed to be folded over and sealed but my arm was hanging out. The effect hung in my consciousness for that moment between the dream and wakefulness, while I tried to make something of it. Then I remembered how I'd drunk all the milk, and I'd need to get up early and go out to buy some.

When I awoke again it was still dark. I could feel my aunt's eyes on me. Or maybe it was Billy's eyes. My aunt was holding him in her arms as she stood over me, whispering to him. She was saying she didn't know who that young man was sleeping in the bed, that she didn't have a nephew. That her sister-in-law had never been able to have children. But I looked so familiar to her, so I must be family. Then she took Billy and returned to bed, and I fell back asleep.

In the morning I awoke to the smell of brewing coffee. I was sweating like a trooper and the sun was cooking the drapes. I dragged myself out of bed, splashed cold water on my face and made my way blindly to the dining room table. I slid into my chair just as my aunt skated in on her house slippers from the kitchen, cradling a bowl of café au lait, which she'd made for herself but insisted on giving to me. I had just managed to coax my eyes open when she skated back in, carrying a tray with a box of cornflakes, milk, and a bowl of coffee for herself. She clearly had a reserve of milk somewhere, which relieved me considerably, although why I should worry about milk at breakfast was beyond me, given all the other stuff that was happening. I just felt like it was nice having someone take care of Billy and me, and I didn't want to be a bad houseguest.

I saw that she'd already opened the manila envelope I'd left on the table for her last night. Julius had addressed it to Lily, for her eyes only, and I hadn't broken the seal.

"Is it what we need?" I asked.

She reached into the envelope and withdrew a minicassette.

"Julius recorded it in the men's room at the airport after he landed at Charles de Gaulle," she said.

I reached out and laid a hand on her arm.

"Before you go on, I have to tell you about last night."

The expression on her face was like a storm system hovering on the horizon, all dark roiling clouds but not quite sure if it was coming or going.

"What happened?"

"Julius. It was a heart attack."

"He's dead?"

"Afraid so." I gave her arm a little squeeze.

"Oh no," she murmured. She set down her bowl of coffee, gently. Billy appeared in the doorway right on cue. I swear he had antennae aimed straight at her heart. He dragged himself into the dining room and she reached down and swept him onto her lap and stroked his long silky ears. He had stopped looking guilty long ago.

"But you saw him. You spoke to him," she said.

"Yes, and he wasn't well." I took another big swallow of coffee. "It's a long story."

"Tell me."

I gave her just the bare bones, explaining how I'd gone down to the lobby to make a call and found him dead on the floor when I got back to the room. "He'd been having chest pains earlier when I was with him."

"How did you get this?" she said, tapping the cassette.

I told her how he'd resisted autographing the book, how he'd seemed preoccupied with Giulietta and redeeming his lost soul.

"His soul? Good grief, that doesn't sound like the Julius I know," she said.

Then I told her how he'd drawn me out onto the balcony and made a point of telling me how much he paid for his suite.

She frowned into her coffee. "Julius never pays for a room. He doesn't pay for anything. That was part of his deal when he brokered the sale of the hotel. He even walked off with a Rolex once from one of the boutiques."

I went on. "There was something strange about the meeting from the beginning. But particularly on the balcony, the way he made me repeat the room rate. That's when I began to suspect he thought his room was bugged. That, and I don't think he trusted me."

"But you introduced yourself, the way I told you to."

"I did, and at first it all seemed to be working fine. I thought he just needed to be humored a little. Until the balcony thing."

I filled her in on the details: how he'd hidden the key card inside the book, and I'd found the room and let myself in.

"That envelope was inside the room safe," I said.

"He gave you the combination?"

"It was the room rate he quoted on the balcony. I played with the numbers and finally got the safe to open. I think he was planning on slipping the key card to you, but then you didn't show up."

"The combination to the safe was the room rate? You figured that out?"

I shrugged. "Yeah."

"Good grief! Why didn't he just give it to you?"

"I think he was a little paranoid."

"Oh, dear Julius," she sighed. "He so loved intrigue. He was always complicating our operation. But he was the best source we had. So why the change of heart? Why did he decide to trust you?"

"I'm not sure, but before I left the room, he asked me again about you, if you were well. I said you were just fine, and that he shouldn't believe everything he overhears in the toilet stalls."

She burst out with a hearty laugh and then, clutching Billy, she leaned across the table and gave me a big warm kiss on the forehead.

"My brilliant boy," she said, and I thought my heart would melt with joy.

She read the look on my face and said, "Why so surprised, Carlito?"

I shrugged.

"Do you doubt yourself?"

"My dad never thought I was brilliant."

"But of course he thought you were brilliant. Perhaps not brilliant in the way he wanted you to be. Although I imagine you tried very hard."

I eyed the cassette.

"So how does all this work?"

"We have a contact—a Russian engineer on the construction site in Moscow who's been getting the files to us—he sets up a meeting with Julius. Usually someplace on the construction site. This is how he lets us know to expect a shipment. He gives Julius two names—the name of the consignee and the name of the contact in their Paris office, along with the delivery due date. Julius passes that information to us."

"With the book."

"That was Julius's idea. To autograph one of his books with the names and date. He thought it was a nice touch. After that, Eleanor leaves a bundle of money in a dead drop here in Paris, and we alert the consignee that payment has been made. When they get their money, they fax us the transport documents and we pick up the freight."

"So what went wrong?"

"The engineer made the appointment with Julius, but he never showed up. When Julius asked about him, he was told the guy had met with an accident."

She reached inside the envelope and pulled out a bundle of documents.

"Then somebody dropped this off for Julius at his hotel in Moscow, right before he left for the airport. It's the bill of lading and all the transport documents. Not a hint as to where it came from."

My aunt grew suddenly alert. Before I could answer, with a gesture of her hand she silenced me and drew my attention to the sound of a man singing in the street below.

"Go look," she said in that imperious tone that had once offended me.

I put down my coffee, rose and went to the window.

"Tell me what you see."

"It's a street sweeper." I watched him scoop a can out of the gutter with a long pincher stick and drop it into his cart. "Pushing a handcart."

"Anything unusual about the cart?"

"There's a plastic rose attached to the handle."

"It's a fresh rose. Long-stemmed and always red."

I came back and sat down. She'd deposited Billy on the floor where he belonged and was spreading jam on a dry breakfast cracker.

"You'd be surprised at the number of people there are who can invest the lowliest of positions with meaning and beauty. They're rare, but they're out there."

The cracker crumbled as she bit into it. She picked up the pieces and slipped them delicately into her mouth, her little finger arched in the way I always pictured Victorian ladies lifting teacups.

"I speak to him from time to time, but Van Gogh knows him best. Raoul is his name—he has a degree in philosophy, and then for a while I think he studied at a rather famous music school. He has the most marvelous voice. He thinks of his job like a vocation, a ministry. He is living the perfect life. By that I mean he has found what he loves and attends to it, rejecting expectations and turning a deaf ear to false judgments, for there are plenty of those people in life, my dear boy. Those who will judge you falsely. He is a tender man. Like you, Carlito."

She poured cornflakes into a bowl and slid it across the

table to me. I helped myself to the milk, filling the bowl all the way to the rim and then diving in, wondering if she had bought the cornflakes for me. I felt wonderfully at ease at that moment, filling my stomach like a hungry child. Confident and ready to face the day. The cloud that had long shadowed my opinion of her had given way to a lightness and a freedom I could barely apprehend. As I munched away, I felt like a man who had ventured into a dark continent only to find enlightenment.

She cleaned her hands on her napkin and took up the transport documents again. "So, shall we trust what we have here?"

"I think we have to take the risk."

Her eyes shifted to the window. Raoul had turned the corner, taking the music and the rose with him.

"Yes, I think so too." She slid the documents across the table to me. "It arrives three days from now. Van Gogh will pick it up. I'd like you to go with him. He's perfectly reliable but he has a tendency to get carried away with theatrics, if you know what I mean."

CHAPTER 26

A breeze shook the broad-fingered leaves of a plane tree and blew up dirt from the footpath. I glanced up at the sky; the clouds didn't look like they held much rain, just heat and dust, but here in Luxembourg Gardens the grass gave off a refreshing coolness. The footpaths circled round cushy lawns of green meeting up with broad alleys lined with sycamores and chestnuts; there were massive beds of flowers packed with vibrant summer colors: oranges, reds and yellows that sent Hex codes shooting off like Fourth of July fireworks in my head.

I found the park bench, the one opposite the statue of a woman in deep décolleté laying flowers at the foot of the bust of a young man with long ringlets and a coldly indifferent gaze. As if he thought himself too good for those flowers and that pretty girl who clearly adored his poetry, or whatever he'd done to deserve her ardent admiration. I wasn't so crazy about the statue; I would have preferred the one with the drunk Bacchus falling off his donkey, but it wasn't my call. I motioned to Huggins to sit, and I got out our ham sandwiches and gave him one.

I didn't ask him if ham was okay. I figured he could just

pretend, or pick out the ham and eat the baguette. He seemed pleased enough and right away bit off a mouthful, but you never knew with Huggins. As for me, I was starved. We'd spent the last two hours darting around Paris with the purpose of eluding anyone who might get it into his head to tail us. We'd taken a sightseeing tour as far as Notre Dame, where we slipped out a back entrance and headed over the footbridge to the Ile Saint Louis, at which point we picked up a taxi to Châtelet. From there we boarded a city bus, exited after a few stops and got the same bus back in the other direction, which we took as far as Denfert-Rochereau, where Van Gogh was waiting for us with his motorcycle in a side street. He tossed a helmet to Huggins and one to me, and I tore off into traffic with Huggins on the back, praying I'd get to Luxembourg before the garden closed.

Huggins ate even faster than I did, and I pretty much swallow my food whole. It was a habit my mother had tried for years to correct, even resorting to visual aids. I recall a photograph of a giant python with a grotesquely bloated belly; it was hard to tell what the snake had swallowed, but it was big. Maybe a pig, or a dog, or a little human. Unfortunately the ploy only gave me nightmares and did nothing to curb my eating habits.

Huggins brushed the crumbs off his trousers and glanced around. Crowds were flowing toward the exits. The park chairs scattered along the edge of the grassy lawn were nearly all empty.

"The park's getting ready to close," he said.

I nodded.

"So where is your contact?"

"All in good time, my friend."

He was eyeing the figure seated on a metal park chair across the path from us, an elderly grandmother with a baby carriage parked at her elbow. She had opened a broad black umbrella to shield herself and the child from the sun's rays, but the sun had moved in the sky and now they sat quietly in the shade. Both of them were slumbering peacefully from the looks of it, the old lady obscured from the waist up by the pooled shadow of the umbrella as it rose and fell with the rhythm of her breath. She had come to the park in her plaid woolen house slippers and knee-length support hose and a sleeveless shift of muted print so colorless that a bee in the desert wouldn't give it a second glance. I wondered how often she came here and sat, contemplating the child, as grandmothers are prone to do, opposite a statue commemorating youth, beauty and dead poets.

"Is she one of yours?" I asked him.

"I was thinking she was one of yours."

"I was joking."

"I wasn't."

"I'm flattered," I said, "to know you think we're that well organized."

"You seem to do rather well." He said it without sarcasm, as if he meant it.

"I suppose everybody looks suspicious to you."

"It's an occupational hazard."

"I'm the opposite. I trust everybody. Even after they turn out to be schmucks. What's that line from *Pride and Prejudice?* 'My good opinion once lost is lost forever.' I always thought Elizabeth Bennet was way too hard on Mr. Darcy; but then, I suppose if he hadn't needed to prove himself there wouldn't have been a novel."

"I wouldn't have taken you for a fan of Jane Austen."

"Just the movie versions," I replied. "Every Sunday night

on *Masterpiece Theatre* in the sunroom with my mother. I was her steady date."

I was suddenly aware of how comfortable Huggins and I were together, chatting away much as we had done when we first met, unless you figure in all the lies and deception. There was no other person in our line of site except the grandmother, which is how we came to be watching her just as the umbrella began to tilt, and she began a slow-motion descent over the arm of the chair.

"Poor girl. I think she's going down," he said.

"I think you're right."

And so she did, the chair just toppled right over, the old lady and umbrella with it. Before she could hit the dirt, Huggins was out of his chair and across the path, with me right behind him. The shock of the fall had awakened her, but she'd gotten her hair tangled up in the wire underframe of the umbrella and it took some doing to get her upright again. Naturally, she was a little flustered and embarrassed. Huggins was uttering in French the sort of things one utters in such circumstances, but as soon as she was on her feet she brushed him off, latched on to the baby carriage and headed off. She had only taken a few steps when her knees buckled; we caught her just in time and helped her to the park bench where we'd left our bike helmets.

We stood over her, debating what to do.

"Maybe it's heat stroke," I said. "It can be fatal in old folks."

That got her attention. The withering look she gave me from beneath her gray wig and fake nose took me completely by surprise.

"Sit down," she said, "boys."

We did, without hesitation, one on each side. I had to give

it to her, the disguise was remarkably effective. Huggins was completely baffled until she gave me a little pat on the knee and with a wink said, "I see you've met my nephew."

Huggins tried to cover his shock by turning his attention to her umbrella, trying to straighten out the bent wings.

"We believed you to be dead, madame. I'm glad to see you looking so—" he paused, fumbling with the umbrella "—*so lively.*"

Aunt Lily's expression revealed nothing, but I swear I could hear her gloating.

"Your nephew has explained that you are in possession of intelligence that might be of interest to us."

"I am."

Huggins nodded thoughtfully. Then, after a reflective pause, "You know, there was a time when we suspected you of collusion with Soviet intelligence agencies."

"You were mistaken."

"But you were sympathetic to their cause."

"My old sympathies are just that, old sympathies."

"So, to set the record straight—"

"I have never cooperated with the Chekists, in any respect. I have never fed intelligence to them. I have never taken money from them, although, believe me, they've tried. The Soviet Union is a brutal, totalitarian regime. It is nothing but one huge prison incarcerating millions of people."

"And you would like us to free one of them."

"You have the means to get him out. Will you do it?"

Huggins seemed to have given up on the umbrella. He sat gazing at the wreck of plastic and metal ribs in his hands.

"Maxim Bukovsky isn't important politically. He's not a

spy, he's a civil rights activist."

"He's an important writer."

"He's not important to us. And his life isn't in danger. He's not going to be executed. He's not even British."

"Three years ago you traded out Anatoly Sharansky, also a civil rights activist."

"That happened because Ronald Regan had a personal interest in the case. I'm sorry, madame, but no one is interested in Maxim Bukovsky. He's just one of thousands of dissidents—"

"They would be interested if they knew what his release was worth in terms of intelligence."

"The story is that Bukovsky doesn't want out."

"That used to be the case. Not now."

"I take it you're in contact with him."

"He'll come."

From a corner of the park came the sound of a whistle; the park attendants were herding the last straggling visitors toward the gated exits.

"We don't have much time," Huggins said, "so I'll be brief. These files you have. We need to verify the identity of your source. As much as you can tell us. Your relationship with him. How you met him, when and where you've been in contact. We will have a long list of questions for you, after we've seen the files. If you can answer the questions to our satisfaction, if we conclude that the intelligence is credible, and you are not working for the other side, then we'll see what we can do to get Bukovsky out. If he even wants out. We can't force a man to walk across the Bridge of Spies if he doesn't want to."

"What about the monetary side of the agreement," I interjected. "The deal is the money *and* Bukovsky."

My aunt reached into a pocket and pulled out a small folded piece of paper that she slipped to Huggins.

Huggins looked at the number. Gave it back to her.

"This wouldn't be a problem. It's quite reasonable."

"Yes, I thought so," she said.

"Who approached you?" Huggins asked.

"You know I can't reveal that."

"Why did they choose you?"

"Mutual attraction."

"You should have come to us immediately. We could have made sure this intelligence gets into the right hands."

"It *is* in the right hands."

"This is what we do. We're trained in this sort of thing."

"Pasternak thought otherwise."

"Pasternak?"

"He remembers what happened in 1985. That was catastrophic for you and your cousins at Langley, wasn't it? Have you found your mole yet? Or was it a CIA mole? All those blown operations, all those arrests. How many did the KGB execute? A dozen? More? So who do you and your cousins have left? I can answer that—nobody. You have nobody on the inside. I doubt you could even get a cockroach to spy for you now. And if you did, his life expectancy would be very short."

Huggins answered with stony silence. I think he was trying to cover his shock and awe, that my aunt knew so many of their unhappy secrets.

"This 'Pasternak.' Is he in Moscow?" Huggins said.

Even disguised as a granny, Aunt Lily had a way of drawing herself up in a distinctly haughty manner.

"If you think you're going to mount an operation to locate

him, forget it. You won't find him. He's gone."

"Dead? Defected?"

"Just gone."

"Can we meet him?"

"You're meeting me."

"Madame de la Pérouse, you know how this works. We can't trust the message unless we trust the messenger."

"I am the only messenger you will ever know. You'll have to be content with that."

"Are we talking defense secrets?"

Another shrill whistle pierced the air.

"These files contain Soviet intelligence operations going back decades. Of a scope unimaginable. Informational cables from the First Directorate to the Politburo and Foreign Ministry; behind-the-scenes accounts of disinformation and deception campaigns, forgeries, political operations, assassinations, sabotage. Active measures in Afghanistan, Iran, Pakistan, India, the UK, East Germany. Everything you've always wanted to know about what they did to whom and how. All their dirty laundry aired. There are even files on JFK's assassination. Not to mention the files containing the legends and activities of Soviet sleeper agents operating in the US and all throughout the world."

Huggins showed a rare bit of genuine excitement. "Good lord."

"Analysis of these files would have a huge impact on resolving unresolved questions. The SIS plan operations based on long-held assumptions; these files would tell you if those assumptions are faulty or accurate. Whatever policy changes come down from the Kremlin, be it Perestroika or reform by another name, the KGB will not go away. Even if the Soviet Union should collapse, the KGB will only continue to grow stronger. Perhaps under another name. But it will live on."

"You've seen these documents?"

"I've seen enough."

"You believe they're authentic?"

"I would bet my life on it."

"No one has access to that much intelligence."

"I don't need to point out to you that the Soviets operate with pathological secrecy. At the same time, it's a rigorously legalistic system, and very heavy on paperwork. Everything is documented. Everything is filed away."

Huggins leaned closer, alert as a hunting dog, and whispered in my aunt's ear, "Are you saying your source has access to KGB archives?"

"What I'm saying is that this will prove to be the the most complete and extensive haul of intelligence ever received from any source coming out of the Soviet Union."

"Why didn't you offer it to the Americans?"

"I've always favored the underdog, Mr. Huggins."

"Is that what we are?"

She took the umbrella from his hands and added, "Let's just say I'm not keen on giving away such valuable intelligence to a government that branded me a pariah."

"No, I imagine not."

A whistle blew again, shriller and closer.

My aunt said, "My conditions are these: I will not answer a shopping list of questions. I will not reveal the source nor how I came to be in possession of these files. The documents will speak for themselves. For now, I can give you typed transcriptions, in Russian, of a number of highly sensitive documents. You will have the rest after Maxim Bukovsky is safe, either in the UK or Israel, or here in Paris, and living under a new identity."

A park attendant was heading for us.

Huggins shook his head. "My superiors would never agree to such extraordinary demands in exchange for intelligence from a source we cannot authenticate, and which, I confess, seems too good to be true. However, if you will allow us to examine these files . . ."

"Before I do that, I need to know you have a plan in place to get him out. And quickly."

"Show us what you have. If the intelligence is as valuable as you say it is, we'll see what we can do."

For a long moment she stared blankly into his eyes. Then, as if taking a moment to reclaim her dignity, she composed herself, hooked the umbrella over her elbow and rose from the park bench. Without so much as a parting glance she shuffled off in her summer shift and plaid house slippers, pushing the baby carriage.

"Was that a yes?" Huggins asked, following her with his eyes.

"Doesn't look like it to me."

"So, she's quite alive."

"I trust you'll keep her little secret, for the time being."

"Remarkable disguise."

"Yeah. It even fooled me."

"I am sorry, Mr. Box. If it were up to me, I'd go along with it. But I can tell you right now, the only thing that might tempt Whitehall are timely defense secrets."

"Such as?"

"Anything that would help answer the looming question: Are they or are they not going to launch their nuclear missiles in our direction, and where might these missiles land, either by purpose or error?"

"I thought Gorbachev had put that nightmare to rest."

"They're just cleaning up their image. Nobody seriously thinks they're going to abandon their old ways."

"So you want this morning's latest scoop. You want to know what the Soviet leaders had for breakfast and if they're in the mood to start World War III."

"More specifically, if they have the capability to do it. Technical documentation, specifications on missile guidance systems, laser weapons, detection systems for high-speed low-flying targets. That sort of thing. Something related to early detection of a surprise adversarial nuclear missile attack. Anything else isn't worth the effort, at least not our effort, not now. We're a small country, you know."

The park attendant gave another long shrill blow on his whistle.

"Although you must admit," he added, "'it defies belief to think any one person outside a national intelligence service could acquire such a wealth of secret Soviet documents. Unfortunately, in light of your aunt's past allegiances, I doubt she'll find anyone who would trust her."

My heart sank at these words. I had been the one to track down Huggins and spell out our intention to turn over highly sensitive documents in a deal that would involve Bukovsky's release, and I'd blown it. I recalled my aunt's moment of uncertainty and a flash of skepticism when I told her what I'd done, but she had agreed that we had no choice but to approach one of the intelligence services, as quickly as possible, and Huggins had more or less shown up on our doorstep.

Perhaps we would have had better luck if I'd just walked into the British Embassy and asked to speak to the intelligence attaché. Which would be tricky since the British government refused to acknowledge their spy agency even existed. I wondered how other spies did it. Shopped around their goods, hoping to find someone who would pay their asking price. It was not an exact business. Not the sort of business an accountant should be in. But I'd taken the job.

The park attendant walked right past us. As if we were invisible.

"He's one of yours, isn't he?" Huggins said with incredulity.

"He's just being nice."

"You're in this business long enough and you don't believe in *nice* anymore."

I reached for my motorcycle helmet and stood.

"Come on. I'll take you home."

Under different circumstances I might have offered to take him for a full-throttle spin around the Arc de Triomphe, but I wanted to get back to the Rue Tonton as soon as possible. We had to plan an operation to take delivery of the last shipment of files. Perhaps our negotiation had been a failure, but making contact with Huggins had pretty much settled one thing in my mind: It wasn't the British SIS who had tried to poison my aunt.

I was worried about her. She had seem so tired and defeated shuffling away in her plaid house slippers.

On the street just outside the tall grille enclosure, we passed an ice-cream vendor wheeling his cart along the sidewalk, and I thought of Mimi for the first time in what seemed like weeks but which had probably been only several days. I wondered if she was expecting a letter from me, and what I would say if I were to write just now.

Dear Mimi, I've been terribly busy scaling the walls of butcher shops to retrieve coded cables and rescuing English secretaries from shady Russian types on moving trains; we also had a close call during a police raid on a black-market currency exchange operation, but I managed to get our team out safely. I don't think Billy has noticed my absence. He gets plenty of attention from our extended family and now sleeps in a blue velvet bed and is fed from the table (against my wishes).

I wouldn't tell her about Greta. Not out of any deluded wish to spare her feelings—she would be happy for me. Mimi thought of me as a friend, nothing more.

What stopped me was the realization that I couldn't capture this phenomenon that was Greta in a few clever lines. I didn't want to capture Greta at all.

CHAPTER 27

I let myself in, dropped my keys into the brass monkey's paw on the entry table and called out a greeting to herald my return. Billy scooted in and planted himself at my feet, staring up at me with his tail fanning the air at high speed and his little body tensed like a rocket straining to lift off. He needed to be walked, and I needed a drink. I muttered an apology to Billy and headed straight for the liquor cart in the dining room.

I was enjoying my scotch, trying to ignore Billy, who was drilling me with a hot angry look, when I realized my aunt hadn't answered my greeting.

Glass in hand, I made a quick inspection of the apartment, going from room to room, calling her name. In the kitchen someone had deposited a large shopping bag on the table. I peeked inside. There was a baking mold, an assortment of pastry nozzles, a very serious-looking chef's knife. I couldn't imagine what they were planning on cooking. Anyway, my aunt wasn't home.

I went back to the living room and stood in the dark, wondering where she might be. She had seemed so discouraged earlier, and the incident on the train platform still bothered me—I hoped she hadn't gotten herself lost somewhere along her secret passage to wherever she was hiding.

Dusk was upon us, that moment when you suddenly notice the light has slipped away and taken the day with it. Lamplight had begun to appear in the windows across the street, and I could hear sounds of shutters opening, welcoming the cooler evening air.

How empty the Rue Tonton was without her. Not only empty, but meaningless. I thought how glad I was that she hadn't died and left me with these silent walls and a corrupted version of her life, with nothing to unravel.

I finished the scotch, picked up Billy and his wheels and headed downstairs. I thought I'd stop at Eleanor's place on the way out and see if she knew where my aunt had gone.

My aunt had explained that Eleanor's "cover" was that of a live-in caretaker for Madame Daunou, an elderly widow from an old bourgeois family with a claim to notable ancestors going way back. Madame Daunou spent her days in front of the TV—she slept particularly well to the sound of explosions and gunfire, and awoke only when you turned off the TV. Her children having settled abroad, and having outlived her husband and all her friends, she received very few visitors and rarely ventured outdoors.

Or so I'd been told.

I could hear a television in the background broadcasting a show with a lot of shouting and guns going off; I knocked, Eleanor's voice rose above the racket, the sound was turned off and the door opened.

Eleanor stood before me fanning herself with a dish towel,

an apron hanging loosely from her neck like an afterthought. I had just started to string together a few words in French when she turned her back to me and moved away down the corridor with great but unhurried purpose, apron strings dangling at her sides, like she'd left something on the stove that needed minding more than I did.

Taking this to be an invitation to come inside, I shut the door behind me and ventured into the living room. On the television in the corner a flaming helicopter was silently sheering off the top of a skyscraper. I looked around for Madame Daunou, thinking I'd find her snoozing in an armchair, or perhaps she'd been awakened by the sudden silence, but the room was empty.

The place had a stale but stately air about it, the home of a woman who clung to her habits and tastes while the world around her moved on. A woman who had reached that point in life when you just stop and let everyone carry on without you. *Like a relay race*, I thought, *you pass on the baton and then sit down to catch your breath. The race isn't up to you anymore.*

Or so I was telling myself.

Madame Daunou was nowhere in sight. I crossed to the adjoining salon and looked in. There, to my surprise, sat my aunt, studying a mass of jigsaw puzzle pieces spread out over an enormous dining table. With a pair of desk lamps casting bright beams of light onto the workspace, she reminded me of a wartime general hunched over his maps in the throes of strategic planning.

"Pull up a chair," she commanded, and I was so relieved by that imperious tone that I would have hugged her if I hadn't been clutching a dog and a set of wheels.

"I need to walk Billy."

"He's been walked. Van Gogh took him out."

"You little fibber," I said to Billy as I set him down. He waited while I unstrapped his wheels and then scooted off—frankly, I didn't know where to. He seemed familiar with the place. He was always one step ahead of me, even with half his horsepower missing.

"I was worried about you," I said.

"What on earth for?" she said without bothering to look up from the puzzle. But I could tell that something was off. A sadness had crept into her voice.

"Where's Madame Daunou?" I asked.

My aunt was busy trying to fit a piece where it wouldn't fit. I took it from her hand and, after a swift scan, slipped it neatly into its place.

"Well, look at you," she said with genuine pride.

I pulled up a chair beside her and lifted the box lid to examine the painting. An impressionistic wash of soft pastel colors. Cut into two thousand pieces.

"Isn't it lovely?" she said. "Monet's garden. The iris was one of his favorite flowers."

"Is there a clue in here?"

"No, no clue. No coded message." She paused before adding quietly, "Just a memory."

When she didn't elaborate, I prodded, "Of Maxim?"

"We met over irises. There was a flower seller who showed up from time to time on my street with a bucket of whatever she'd managed to find in the wild, or steal during the night, and that day it was irises. He came up and asked if I liked them and I said I didn't. I said I thought them an ugly flower. Then he turned to the flower seller and bought three irises and gave them to me."

"Why did he do that?"

"Because he knew I wasn't being truthful. You see, those were the only flowers she had and I was afraid he'd offer to buy them for me."

"You didn't want him to?"

"I could see from the way he was dressed that he didn't have much money. And I was right. I watched while he emptied out his pocket and gave every coin he had to the girl. He had enough for just three flowers. So I took them, and he offered me his arm, and I took that too, and we walked along the Seine, talking as if we had known each other for a long time, although we had just met."

It was the first time I'd heard her reminisce about Maxim, and there was a reverence in her voice I'd never heard before.

"I'm afraid Huggins isn't going to give us what we want," I said.

"I know."

"You must be disappointed."

"I am. Bitterly. But I can't let it get in the way."

With a flap of the hand she seemed to dismiss despair as if it were nothing more than a pesky fly. Suddenly she was back in her stoic aunt mode, dressed in her flowing caftan, her silver hair piled loosely on top of her head, the weariness gone the way of the fake nose and wig. She had even dabbed on a bit of perfume.

"Are you expecting Pym?" I asked.

"Pym and Madame Daunou are not on friendly terms. As a matter of fact, they've never met."

"He never comes up here?"

"He has never been invited. Why do you ask?"

"You're wearing perfume."

"A woman does not always wear perfume to seduce; she wears perfume out of self-respect, and respect for others."

Or maybe because it evokes a memory, like the irises, I thought. I was only now beginning to understand how important Maxim had been to her. How important he still was, although she rarely spoke of him. I reached for her long spidery fingers and raised them to my lips.

"Silly boy," she said and tugged her hand away. I thought I detected a warm blush rise to her cheeks, or maybe it was just the reflected pinks from the puzzle, and the glow of lamplight that shed an intimacy over the tired old bourgeois furnishings.

She slid a pile of pieces in my direction. Settling down to a puzzle seemed like a really good thing to do after the last forty-eight hours of murder and mayhem and disappointments. I started selecting pieces and sorting them into color groups.

"You don't like Pym, do you?" she said.

"I sense a streak of cruelty in the man."

"Pym would never betray me."

"I'm not so sure of that."

"He's very concerned for my safety. He's been strongly advising me to stop the whole operation."

"Getting the files out, you mean?"

"It's become too dangerous, he says."

"On that point I agree."

"I have committed myself to Pasternak. I won't let him down. And without those files, I have no leverage to get Maxim released."

"I have the impression that wouldn't bother Pym in the

least."

She took a while to reply, and when she did, there was a tenderness in her voice that spoke of an affection I had somehow missed. Or perhaps I hadn't missed it so much as I'd disliked it. I didn't esteem Pym worthy of her.

"It's a frightening disease, Carlito. It cripples more than just the body."

"All the more reason to be wary." I was sounding sulky again.

"He was a child, Carlito. A little boy. Polio afflicted children, which made it all the more terrifying, that and because it didn't kill so much as it maimed. It crept up the spine and you never knew where it would stop—maybe it left your child with just a paralyzed toe, but if it got up far enough it took his legs, and then it paralyzed his lungs. You're too young to remember."

"I'm not," I insisted.

I remembered my mother sitting in the sunroom bent over a copy of *Life Magazine* showing pictures of children encased in those huge cumbersome machines they called an iron lung. Not just one or two, there were vast hospital wards with rows and rows of children locked in those machines, all of them smiling bravely for the camera. The first mass vaccination program, initiated the year I was born, had been a disaster and had been quickly abandoned. In this instance, my dad, never a fan of federal regulation, admitted that the failing was due to poor oversight at the California laboratory that had produced the vaccine. It was years before my parents would agree to have me vaccinated, and by then, I was old enough to have seen all those photos, which were much more terrifying than any python with a bloated belly. I was so afraid of polio that when our local school announced they would be distributing the vaccine one Saturday morning, I stayed awake all night with my flashlight under the blanket, every few minutes shining the beam on my fingers and toes to make sure they were still in working order; I was convinced that fate would maliciously strike me down with the disease before I had a chance to get the vaccine. The next morning I dragged my mother out the door by the hand, urging her to hurry up, and then there was the long wait, the line snaking around the block. Looking out for my friends, waving to them, all of us creeping forward step by step. I was terribly afraid they'd run out of sugar cubes and I wouldn't get mine.

"But you see," my aunt was saying, "in the Soviet Union, children maimed by polio were more than a health crisis, they exposed the failings of their ideology. The Soviet state was supposed to protect its people. Everywhere you looked—the statues, posters, magazines—all you ever saw were images of robust, muscular-bodied, hardworking Soviet citizens. You didn't see pictures of little kids in wheelchairs and braces.

"You can imagine what school was like for Pym. He once told me how some kids picked him up and stuffed him in a trash barrel, then stood around and jeered and taunted him with slurs while he tried to climb out. He'd just won an essay competition—they said he didn't have any business winning awards—that he'd never be a good Soviet because a good Soviet is strong and healthy in body and mind, and superior as he was in the later category, he was definitely screwed in the former."

"Hey, we had bullies in my school too. Bullies sprout up everywhere, no matter what flag you're waving."

"My point is, Carlito, that Pym has institutionalized his

anger. He harbors great resentment toward the Communists and their glorification of the healthy proletariat. He has never been able to accept his brother's devotion to the homeland. Pym is bitterly aware of what his life would have been had he escaped the bullet of polio, and he carries with him a deep sense of having been born for greater things. He has always wanted to be a hero. In the eyes of a few, at least."

"And you're one of those."

"I must be. For his sake, I must see him as a hero."

"So are you saying he wouldn't turn on you? That you don't think he could be the reason why the KGB is circling?"

"Someone is always circling, Carlito. Many émigré publishing ventures like ours have collapsed over the years, and not only for lack of money. Usually it's because the Soviets learn that a Russian-language magazine run by an émigré in Paris is also publishing books that somehow manage to worm their way back into the Soviet Bloc. Books written by banned authors, or books that would never make it past the Soviet censors. Or testimonial accounts of events in Eastern Europe, or Russian labor camps, because the official rhetoric is nothing but lies, and these accounts give accurate information on what was going on. So the Soviet government leans on the French authorities who in turn find any number of reasons to close down the imprint. They have tried to bankrupt us with fines, thinking they could shut us down, but we have survived.

"I'm convinced the leak was on the Russian side. It was inevitable, after nearly two years, that someone in our network would get caught. Everyone in Moscow spies on everyone else, it's systemic, which is why Pasternak reached out to me instead of a Western diplomat. Soviet society is deeply infiltrated by the secret police, the Chekists—although they've got a new name now, they're all the same, and there are so many of them, and they're pervasive and all powerful. The handful of Russian nationals still spying for the West are under such constraint that it's nearly impossible to meet with them, and recruiting new ones is a lost cause. Westerners are under constant surveillance in Moscow. It's illegal to even speak to a foreigner. Spying is ubiquitous. Everyone has at least one member of their extended family who works for the KGB."

I wasn't about to doubt her assessment, but I believed her judgment was clouded where Pym was concerned, and that worried me. I sensed that Pym was driven by intellectual snobbery, a need to feel as if he knew more than the fool standing next to him on two good strong legs, that the more secrets he knew, the more his private power grew. Mix that with jealousy, and you got explosions the likes of which would send the mysterious Madame Daunou into a deep and peaceful slumber.

"By the way, what's all that stuff on your kitchen table?"

"Ah," she said with a bemused smile. "That's from our dead drop. A big kitchen supply store near Les Halles. It's a real Ali Baba cave of wonders, that place. Everything a professional could possibly need. Butchers, bakers, spies. The red Staub cast-iron cocotte is Eleanor's favorite. Downstairs at the back with the steamers. It's worked quite well for years now. Never yet had a payment go astray. The only problem is that she can't refrain from buying something when she's there. Did I tell you we're planning on doing a cooking course together one of these days?"

That explains all the copper pots and pans, I thought.

She went on, "Only we can't agree on where to begin—I'd

like to jump right in to pastries but we really should start with the basics. Sauces, that's where you begin." She found a flat edge and tried it on a border section. "That and finding the time."

I rose to move the lamp around to the other side of the table. Lighting was key to solving puzzles.

"So, is there a Madame Daunou?" I asked as I sat back down. I was getting much better at adjusting to shifting realities.

"There was a historian by the name of Daunou several centuries ago. He played a major role in consolidating France's historical records and creating the first ever government archives. Quite an interesting story."

I smiled inwardly at the mention of archives. Nothing seemed gratuitous with my aunt, everything seemed to have meaning—or again, maybe it didn't, which means you were always kept guessing.

"I trust you will keep up pretenses," she added.

"Goes without saying, Aunt Lily."

"Then you're welcome to join us for dinner. Eleanor's throwing together something simple. Rice and prawns, I believe." She added slyly, "Madame Daunou's favorite dish."

She slipped a piece of sky into place.

"It's teamwork, Carlito, like this puzzle. When it's all done, no one will remember who fit what piece where. We'll have the big picture. It will all be clear."

"So you're not taking Pym's advice."

"What do *you* think I should do?"

"I think you should stay dead and leave the dangerous pursuits to the living."

I had already worked out a small patch of mauve iris and grouped some blues that belonged together.

"Look at you," she said, admiring my puzzle skills. "Aren't you just the cat's pajamas?"

"It's the colors." I shrugged. "Not a particularly useful skill in life. Just means I'm good at mixing paint and doing jigsaw puzzles."

"You bring a fresh eye and a new perspective, Carlito. You see things differently, which is of great value." She slipped a little knob inside a hook and sat back with a smile of satisfaction. "Maxim would be very pleased to think you had a hand in his release."

"Why would that matter?"

"Because you matter to me."

CHAPTER 28

Seeing that my aunt was busy with her smuggling operation, I had taken it upon myself to find out what I could about the business with the bees and the Chihuahua in the mosque tearoom. Aunt Lily had never revealed who she was meeting that day, nor if she believed the target could have been her companion rather than herself, but she had taken the incident seriously enough to go underground. Knowing that Greta had contacts in the police, I had asked her to find out what she could about the police investigation into the incident. Now here she was, opening a picnic basket and ready to brief me.

"It wasn't the KGB," she said as she removed a bottle of burgundy along with an opener. I took both from her and went to work. Opening a bottle of burgundy for Greta felt like an act of chivalry. I could have been a courtly knight in clinking armor kneeling before her with bowed head, having just been awarded a token of her favor. A square of perfumed silk perhaps. Something that rippled in the wind and smelled of her hair. I concentrated on skewering the cork to hide the smile that was threatening to unmask my cool.

The Eiffel Tower loomed behind her. The arch framing her perfectly. As if a film director had told her precisely where to sit for maximum dramatic effect.

The checkered tablecloth, the wineglasses. The olives, the tiny cornichons. She had even bought a hard salami, just for me. She laid out a small cutting board, cloth napkins. She hadn't missed a thing. I could imagine her equipping an army for battle down to the last spare tire. Nothing would be forgotten.

The cheeses: a hockey-puck-shaped chèvre, another in a tiny sealed clay pot, then the ones she was now unwrapping from their papers, the way I imagined a girl of a certain class would unwrap a small package that hinted at something immensely valuable and shiny. Not for Greta to rip open a wrapper any which way, she picked an edge delicately with two fingers and with deliberation folded back the paper to reveal the wonder inside. First a Tomme, she said, and then a creamy Bleu d'Auvergne. Then she paused and sat back on her knees, folded her hands on her lap and looked off into the distance. Breathing in the green. It was a beautiful day.

The Champs de Mars spread around us, a long esplanade of green lawn stretching from the military school behind me to the Eiffel Tower just in front of the Seine. Historically it had been intended for the military cadets to practice their drills, but really it was just a beautiful green space where the public was invited to sprawl on their backs in the plush grass and watch the clouds drift by, which they were doing, both the clouds and the people.

I managed to pour two glasses of wine, not too full, as Mimi had taught me, and pass one to Greta while looking relatively at ease. Then I stretched out on my side propped on an elbow.

So the Eiffel Tower was just over her shoulder.

"Why no KGB? What brought you to that conclusion?"

"Their execution may be faulted but their methods are ruthlessly effective. If those bees had been poisoned by something the Russians had concocted, it would have contaminated more than just that poor little dog."

"Were they able to identify the poison?"

"Arsenic. Very old-fashioned."

"Very nasty, all the same."

Arsenic poisoning was a dreadful way to go. Guts churning in agony, gasping for breath.

"It might have been my aunt."

A sudden wave of anger rolled through my chest. I sat up, took a deep breath and flushed it out.

Everything was ready, cheeses unwrapped, bread sliced. Greta put a knife in my hand and I helped myself to the Bleu.

"Apparently the lady with the dog is taking legal action against the café. So it's not really a homicide investigation anymore, since they can't directly link your aunt's death to the poisoned tea."

"Yes, that would prove difficult."

"Actually the lady believes her dog was the intended victim all along. That it was the action of a Chihuahua hate group."

"Small dog owners can be terribly sensitive."

"Apparently she even made a statement implying your aunt was the perpetrator. Until she found out she'd died."

Biting into a slice of baguette topped with the Bleu d'Auvergne, I momentarily lapsed into the pleasures of the senses. The day was so gorgeous. The wind so soft, the moment so idyllic. The wine so good. How easy it would be to be trapped,

I thought. How love can do things to us, twist us inside out so that we don't recognize ourselves anymore. I thought of my aunt and wondered if she'd become a Communist out of love for a man, or for an ideology. Or perhaps the chemistry of the two together. How she must have changed when she had moved here after the war. How she must have seen things differently.

Greta was telling me how the police had questioned the staff who worked at the mosque tearoom that day. How they all gave the same story about a replacement worker turning up for a waiter who had called in sick.

She had a bit of Tomme poised to pop in her mouth; she hesitated and said with a note of reproof, "Carl, are you listening?"

"Yes. Why?"

"You look distracted."

"Do you trust me?"

"What an odd question."

"Not odd. It's fundamental."

She picked up the salami and jabbed it into my stomach.

"I do. I don't know why, but I do. Do you trust me?"

"Implicitly. From the very first. Or at least from the moment you fainted in my arms."

"I didn't faint in your arms."

"You would have hit the sidewalk if I hadn't been there. Now, please, continue," I said. "This replacement waiter—"

"The manager was too busy to check out his story so he just put him to work. After the incident, the guy handily disappeared. They haven't been able to track him down."

"Did they get a description?"

"He was older, but not ancient. Longish hair, some said

gray, others said ginger. Glasses. More than one witness said he looked like an intellectual."

"Is that a look?"

"In France, it is."

I began slicing thin slivers of salami.

"One more thing. His ears," she said.

"What about his ears?"

"They were large and protruding. The sort of ears you notice."

I put down the knife and stared at her.

The sort of ears you notice. Like the boy, Pym's student. The boy with ginger hair.

She said, "I know that's not much to go on."

I cleaned my hands on the napkin, slipped my fingers around the back of her neck, and with calm deliberation I pulled her to me and kissed her firmly on the mouth. A staunch kiss, unequivocal in its meaning. Her lips tasted like the cheese, salty with a slight tang. I released her and she sat back on her heels.

"I'm glad you did that before you ate your salami," she said.

She went back to eating her bread and cheese and drinking her wine, perfectly composed. "So, what's next?"

My kiss hadn't ruffled her in the slightest. As though she'd had many of my kisses before.

"Have you got a camera with a telephoto lens?"

"I have Olivier's cameras."

"Would you be willing to do a little surveillance?"

"Who?"

"This fellow Pym on the ground floor. There's a student he tutors twice a week after school."

The blue sky and green grass looked on and smiled.

CHAPTER 29

If Van Gogh was nervous, he certainly didn't show it. He was standing around the loading bay of a freight depot near the airport, waiting for our paperwork to be processed. Or rather, I was standing around; he was rooting in the back of his truck like the raccoons I'd seen at night tearing up our backyard in Santa Ana looking for grubs to eat; he would pull up a mysterious-looking object, turn it over in his hand and then toss it back onto the heap. I thought maybe he was making room for our consignment. But when I poked my head inside the van, it didn't look like he'd made much progress.

Van Gogh loved to talk, and the fact that I didn't understand a word he said didn't seem to make a whit of difference to him on our ride to the airport. I just looked interested and mirrored his facial expressions, which seemed to do the trick. He thoroughly enjoyed his own company, had a good time listening to himself and laughed a lot at his own stories. Once he laughed so hard that tears rolled down his cheeks. I couldn't help but laugh along, laughter being contagious, and so we got on just fine. Perhaps more than anyone else I'd met since I'd arrived in Paris, Van Gogh made me regret I didn't understand French. He was a generous fellow too, drove along swigging orange juice from a carton, which he vigorously pressed on me with all the goodwill of a bootlegger offering you his best moonshine. Then there was a still warm, foil-wrapped apricot tart he'd made himself just that morning, which I held in my lap and fed to him in slices while he drove, and which, I have to admit, was one of the best tarts I'd ever eaten. He seemed to have a sweet tooth, because after we'd finished off the tart he reached between us into the back and pulled out a plastic storage container filled with chocolate chip cookies, which I understood he had made as well. By that time we were nearing the freight depot and had to start paying attention to signs, which was a good thing, as I didn't think I could put anything else in my stomach that early in the morning.

We still didn't know how much, if anything, the KGB knew about our operation, or if we were being followed, but we had to assume as much. My aunt hadn't proposed any sort of contingency strategies should we be hijacked and robbed; she had calmly handed us the shipping documents and instructed us to bring back the goods. We had no weapons of any sort, notwithstanding the junk in the back of the van, of which any number of pieces might be used to defend ourselves in a pinch. Van Gogh certainly wasn't the type to give up without a fight, but if we were to run up against some seriously armed KGB thugs, we had no choice but to hand over whatever we were transporting. Our hope of success hung on the fact that no one knew what we were up to. I had left the Rue Tonton before dawn, made my way across Paris by various means, had a few coffees in a few obscure cafés, finally meeting up with

Van Gogh in a small street in front of a funeral parlor next to the Montparnasse Cemetery. He arrived just as I'd seen him that first day—on his motorcycle, looking very much like a centurion, minus the urn; I'd hopped on the back and we sped away into the early morning traffic. We headed north to the suburbs, where we switched to his van, then took off for Charles de Gaulle Airport.

Van Gogh was the restless sort and not good at waiting. After fifteen minutes of shifting stuff around in the back of his van, he started losing patience. Earlier we had enjoyed a cool breeze, but now the air was hot and still, and even in the shade of the overhang we were both sweating. Another truck was loading in a bay down the line, and Van Gogh went off to have a chat with the transporters. After a few minutes he came back and gave me a vigorous explanation, which I replied to with my usual nods and sympathetic grunts. Then he turned around and headed back out again, this time in the other direction. Trucks were rolling in and out as various transporters loaded and unloaded at the bays. Van Gogh disappeared into their midst.

Eventually, a woman came out with our paperwork and took me back inside to a counter, where she expertly flipped through one page after another of transport documents, pointing with a dagger-length nail where I was to initial and sign. We returned to the bay to find a guy waiting with a pallet jack loaded with a single plywood crate around four feet tall and wide.

There they are, I thought, *those suckers*. Reams of secrets packed in nice and tight. The last installment in a series documenting decades of the KGB's lethal and nefarious activities all around the world. Records revealing identities of thousands of Soviet "illegals" living under deep cover abroad, disguised as foreign citizens.

I think until that moment this had all been a game to me. Now with the physical evidence in my possession, I was struck with just how ridiculously dangerous a position it put us in. If the KGB knew we had this stuff, we'd for sure be meeting a very untidy death. The thought gave me the willies. I couldn't wait to get out of there and on the road.

I hopped into the back and shifted around some of the junk to make room for the crate. The dockworker gave me a hand and we hefted the crate into the back of the van and secured the doors.

I turned to the woman. "We good to go?"

She was giving our van one of those coolly disdainful looks that Frenchwomen do so well.

"That," she said, pointing to the van, "eez . . . " Then she said a word that sounded something like "free-gore-ee-fay."

"You mean refrigerated?"

"Yes. Cold."

"Why do I need a refrigerated truck?"

The cool disdain turned to Gallic horror.

"C'est du caviar, monsieur."

She took the papers from me and flipped through until she got to a single customs form detailing the contents and value of the goods. I had intended to check all this out on the drive to the airport, but I'd been put off by the bulk of documents and incomprehensibility of the language—that and Van Gogh's healthy appetite.

According to the customs form, we were taking delivery

of over two hundred thousand francs' worth of caviar.

I felt like a fool. Naturally, the papers would be falsified.

"No problem," I said with a shrug. "We'll drive fast."

The woman had just stepped back inside when I heard sirens approaching, that two-note whine distinctive to the French police and so foreign to my ears. I stepped out from the bay into the bright sunlight just as a caravan of Renaults pulled single-file into the lot and headed straight for me. My first thought was that someone had tipped them off. I didn't know where Van Gogh had gone but I was really pissed off that he'd disappeared just when I'd needed him.

To my surprise, Duclos stepped out of the first police car. He seemed equally surprised to find me.

"Morning, Duclos."

"Monsieur Box." His gaze took in the van behind me as he shook my hand. "What are you doing here?"

"Me? Well, you should know, shouldn't you?"

My use of the modal verb seemed to confuse him.

"What am I suspected of now?"

"This is your vehicle?"

"Not really. I'm riding shotgun. The driver's gone to take a leak."

"Riding shotgun?"

"I thought surely you'd know that one. Riding shotgun."

"I'm afraid I don't."

"I remembered your English as being excellent."

"Thank you. However, I don't get so much practice."

"Only with me."

"You are not my usual type of suspect, Monsieur Box. I enjoy very much speaking with you. Perhaps one day we will meet . . ."

He paused to search for the expression.

"Under different circumstances? Is that what you mean?"

"Precisely, yes. *Alors*, tell me, what is shotgun?"

"Riding shotgun. Has its origins in stagecoach travel, I imagine. Two guys on top, one had the reins and drove the horses, the other carried the shotgun."

His eyes lit up. "Interesting." He nodded. "Ah, the American Wild West. It is a fascinating heritage that you have, Monsieur Box."

Once again I couldn't help notice his sartorial chic. The cuffs of his shirt had the white crispness of the brand-new, the shoes and belt of fine supple leather. Despite the pall of weariness, he projected a man of deep professional pride—or perhaps his intention was to bring his own individual pride to the profession. Either way, he struck me as honorable. At the same time it crossed my mind that he might be an informant in the pay of the KGB, in which case he would not be honorable at all.

"You look like you need a vacation," I said.

"It's too hot for me. You, Monsieur Box, you do not bother this heat."

"No, I'm from Florida. I do not bother this heat."

"Unfortunately, criminals do not take vacation in August. It is their busy season, and so it is ours too."

"So you think I'm a criminal?"

"I hope not. I like you, Monsieur Box. But your family is involved in some shady business, I'm sure of it."

While we'd been discussing the etymology of English figures of speech, a half-dozen police officers had piled out of the three cars and were standing around in little cliques schmoozing like office workers gathered at the proverbial water fountain. They gave the impression that they were hanging out with pals rather than serving and protecting the community—not to say you couldn't do both, but there was always something a little lax and unprofessional about them. Maybe they didn't look intimidating enough.

I said to Duclos, "You need the shipping documents?"

"If you please."

I turned and started toward the van, only to be stopped by a chorus of loud shouts. I looked over my shoulder to find all six officers with their pistols trained on me. I was getting ready to drop to my knees with my hands in the air when Duclos gave a command to the troops and they holstered their weapons. I admit I was impressed by the speed of their draw. They were a lot more alert than I'd given them credit for.

I retrieved the shipping documents from the van and showed them to Duclos.

"M&M Import Export," he said.

"That's what it says."

"I understand your aunt was in the publishing business."

"Yep."

"What was she going to do with all this caviar?"

I shrugged. "Gifts, I guess. Now, your turn. What do you want with us?"

"We had a tip."

"Aha. One of those tips. What was it this time?"

"Publications."

I gave him my best puzzled frown.

"I do not know the precise nature of these papers, only

that they are the property of the Soviet Union and have been obtained illegally."

"We've got caviar, Duclos."

"We must to search your van."

"Have at it. It's not locked."

Duclos gave another order and the officers unlatched the door and climbed into the back. The men hefted the plywood box onto the ground.

Duclos said, "Please, open it."

I climbed into the back of the van and came out with wire cutters and a screwdriver, which I comically made a big deal of holding way up in the air to show I had no hostile intentions. Nobody laughed—not even a snicker.

I took my sweet time prying off the crate's lid while trying to come up with a good story to explain the contents. Turns out I didn't need one. Set inside the wood shavings and dry ice packs were Styrofoam cartons. I removed one and opened it to find a shiny black gift box, and inside this two tin jars, each lid labeled with the image of a sturgeon and the word *Caviar*. I turned to Duclos.

"See? Caviar."

Duclos was baffled. Although not nearly as much as I was.

We got into a spat. Duclos said I was free to go but he insisted on confiscating the crate. I said I was not going anywhere without my caviar, that duty had been paid, the paperwork was in order. Moreover, my caviar was spoiling in this heat.

I knew there had to be a message somewhere in the crate, and if so, I needed to get my hands on it.

With the cooperation of the warehouse manager, we moved the crate to a large refrigerated area reserved for perishables, where Duclos's men set about dismantling it and unloading the contents; they sifted through wood shavings, Styrofoam, dry ice. They removed every tin from its gift box and lined them all up on a table, where Duclos counted them. I was having a hard time resisting the urge to straighten the rows.

"There's nothing here but caviar, Duclos. There certainly aren't any so-called publications."

"Like always with you, it is—how do you say?—a dead inn?"

"Dead end. If we were in the States, I'd file a complaint for police harassment."

"Believe me, monsieur, I do not wish to arrest you."

"That's very good of you to say so."

"I hope it will not come to that."

"So do I. So do I."

"It's very strange that all these incidents lead us to you and your family, Monsieur Box. Do you not think?"

"Maybe somebody's playing with you."

"I think not."

"Where did this so-called tip come from?"

"This is an excellent grade of caviar."

"Let me guess—the Soviet Embassy."

I followed him around the table as he picked up each and every tin, turning it over, inspecting the bottom, the rim. Looking for markings, I imagined. A scratch perhaps. A broken seal.

"I'll trade you caviar for the name," I said.

"We do not need to make a deal with you. We already have the caviar."

"I tell you what, you give me my caviar and you can come to the house to pick up a few tins. My mother would be thrilled to see you."

Seeing how this little bit of flattery perked him up, I decided to press my advantage.

"Better yet, come for caviar and champagne some evening. She loves entertaining."

"Please, give her my regards," he said in his gentlemanly fashion, "but I keep the caviar."

"On what grounds?"

"The Soviet authorities need time to make a very close inspection."

"You mean you're going to let them open all these tins?"

"If necessary."

"That's crazy. You've got over thirty thousand dollars' worth of perishable goods that legally belong to me."

"The shipment is insured, Monsieur Box. You will be reimbursed. You, however, are free to go."

I gave him my best exasperated glare. "Okay, then, I'll take a few tins. To placate my mother. That's the least you can do."

He gave it some thought.

"You may take one." He gestured to the table. "Please."

He followed me around the table, hovering over my shoulder as I examined the tins just has he had done.

He said, "They're all the same. Caviar from the beluga sturgeon that swims in the pure waters of the Caspian Sea. It is the most flavorful caviar in the world."

I picked up a tin, turned it over, set it down again, went for another.

"You know, Duclos, my aunt was devoted to her publishing business. Nothing big. Nothing worthy of a Pulitzer. Just nice little literary journals, some poetry, an occasional novel or memoir by some obscure Russian scribbler banned or imprisoned in his home country. Occasionally they'd put out a labor camp exposé, or a juicy behind-the-scenes tell-all of a secret political trial. Not exactly beach reads. But stuff of great interest to a certain community of émigrés here in Paris—Russians, Poles, intellectuals who have ties with dissidents in the Soviet Bloc—they were big fans of those journals and memoirs. And sometimes, thanks to their network, those publications made it back into the Soviet Union—which upset Moscow to no end, naturally. You might say my aunt ran a sort of cross-border literary service. But then, you know all about that, don't you?"

"You are surprisingly well informed for someone so—how do you say?—new to the game."

"My mother was very close to my aunt. You mustn't confuse her cheerful openness for simplemindedness. She's every bit as sharp as her sister. She knows my aunt never broke any laws and she never had any problems until recently when the French authorities started trying to close down her publishing venture. Undoubtedly because the Soviet authorities were leaning on them."

I paused, I hovered, cursing the fluorescent lighting, praying my eyes wouldn't let me down.

"Now, my mother and I come to Paris to take care of family business, and we meet with extreme harassment. I'm sure our embassy will have something to say about that."

I rather liked that last part. Putting my own little spin on my aunt's story.

I took a deep steadying breath and selected a tin of caviar. Only to feel his hand on my arm.

"May I?"

My heart skipped a beat as he took the tin from me and held it up to the light.

He instructed me to open it.

"It'll spoil."

"Open it, Monsieur Box."

Briefly, very very briefly, I pictured myself snatching the caviar and making a run for it, sprinting across the warehouse, arms pumping as I crossed the parking lot and out the gate to an empty field and along an access road. With a patrol car cruising along behind me, the officers laughing up a storm while watching me sweat it out in the killer heat. Waiting for me to collapse on the blacktop.

I took the tin from him, broke the seal and pried off the lid. He leaned in to take a good look.

We both saw it. The glint of metal wedged into the mass of silvery gray pearls. Duclos didn't bat an eye. Didn't betray even a hint of suspicion. Just gave a perfunctory nod. I snapped the lid back on before he could change his mind.

"So, when are our Soviet friends dropping in to conduct their inspection?" I said.

"Tomorrow around noon, I am told."

"And then what?"

"I do not think they will find what they are looking for. In any case, you will hear from us." He dismissed me with a gesture. "You may go. Enjoy your caviar." Adding quietly, "You have a very good eye, Monsieur Box. Someday you must tell me how you do it."

Was there awe in his voice when he spoke? Or did I just imagine it?

I climbed into the van, found the carton of orange juice

and swigged down what was left; the juice was warm but wet and I was thirsty and jittery as hell. I needed to get out of there before the other shoe dropped—I kept looking over my shoulder waiting for Duclos, or those KGB thugs, to tap on my window and ask me to hand over the goods. I was on the verge of driving away and leaving Van Gogh behind when I saw him coming around the corner with two other guys, lugging a huge antique wardrobe.

So that's where he'd been—bargain hunting. I sat in the front, cradling that jar of caviar in my lap while they loaded the piece of furniture into the van. I was too exhausted to get mad at him. He slipped some bills to the two men, thanked them heartily, then climbed into the driver's seat.

"Eez good?" he asked.

"Eez good," I said, giving him the thumbs-up, and we pulled out.

Once we were well away from the airport, I opened the jar and fished out that shiny thing, which turned out to be a silver coin—Russian by the looks of it. I was pretty sure it concealed instructions on where to find the files.

After a bit of reflection, I concluded that Van Gogh's disappearance had been a blessing in disguise, as he did not deal well with authority figures and would have undoubtedly upset the apple cart—or rather the caviar cart.

CHAPTER 30

By the time I got back to the Rue Tonton I was near to collapsing from the heat and strain of it all. I sprawled in an armchair, clutching the tin of caviar like it was a winning lottery ticket while my aunt fussed over me, making cold compresses for my head and watching anxiously as I guzzled down an entire pitcher of ice water laced with fresh-squeezed lemon.

After I had perked up a bit, I turned the tin over to her and watched as she opened it and removed the coin.

"It was the label that gave it away," I said. "This one is a true Prussian blue. Hex code 003153. Also known as Berlin blue or Parisian blue if you're an artist. It's produced by oxidation of ferrous ferrocyanide salts. Chemical formula Fe_7CN_{18}. A paint maker by the name of Diesbach synthesized it for the first time in Berlin back in the early 1700s. Among paint chemists, it's sort of a star."

I didn't think she'd mind my digressing, knowing how her own stories so frequently wandered off; it seemed to be a family trait.

"Out of all the tins, this is the only label that was slightly off. It must have come from another batch of dye."

I was right about the coin, which Aunt Lily identified as a five-ruble silver piece commemorating the 1980 Moscow Summer Olympics. After a couple of attempts to tap it open, she took it to the kitchen and pitched it at one of her cast-iron-bottomed stew pots. The back of the coin fell right off, revealing a single frame of microfilm.

My aunt put me to work whipping up some omelets to eat with the caviar while she went off in search of a handheld microfilm reader she was sure she had somewhere, and which, after much rummaging and muttering and exasperated shouts like "Shoot!" and "Rats!" and "Confound it!" coming from closets and back bedrooms, she finally found the device in a kitchen drawer with the aluminum foil and swizzle sticks.

Only when we had settled at the dining table with an uncorked bottle of champagne and our caviar-topped omelets did we resume our discussion of the smuggling business.

"Here's to my dear boy Carlito," she said, raising her glass in a toast to me, "and to his extraordinary talent."

"Well, to be honest, it would have come to naught if Duclos hadn't given us a break."

"You're sure he saw the coin inside."

"No doubt about it."

"Ah, but it could be a trick. He could be a communist sympathizer. The French intelligence services are teaming with their lot."

"Then why didn't he confiscate the tin? He would have had the proof he needed to link us to the files and the entire smuggling operation."

The microfilm, we had learned, contained a list of dates

and flight information—along with instructions as to how we were to make contact with the couriers. If Duclos had turned it over to the Soviets, not only would they have recovered the Pasternak files, they would have been able to identify a network of individuals traveling to Paris from the Eastern Bloc countries, men and women who would have certainly risked arrest upon returning home to Soviet-controlled territory.

"So you think he was giving us a break."

"I do. Absolutely."

We lapsed into silence while enjoying the pleasures of the caviar and champagne. Having never tasted the delicacy, I approached it gingerly, but to my surprise I found I had an immediate liking for the stuff. I had to make a conscious effort to pace myself, following my aunt's lead and consuming it in little nibbles. Savoring it on my tongue, following it with a sip of champagne, going back for another nibble. When she spoke again I'd almost forgotten about the files.

"So now the KGB does their inspection and comes up empty-handed. Which creates a bit of a problem."

I topped up her glass and served us both another spoonful of caviar. "Why is it a problem?"

"It means they'll still be circling," she said.

Reluctantly, I tore my attention away from my taste buds and gave it some thought.

"I see what you mean."

She had that absent look on her face. I'd seen it before, when I'd walked into her study and found her at her typewriter in Melody Bly mode, staring at the wall.

"Unless they don't," she said.

"Come up empty-handed, you mean?"

"You said the crate is still in the warehouse?"

"Until tomorrow."

"Could you get back in there?"

I couldn't help but smile. "What did you have in mind?"

"What if, when the Russians do their inspection, they should find—" she reached for the Russian ruble beside her plate and held it up "—this."

"Go on."

"But with a different set of instructions inside."

"Leading them to . . ."

"Not exactly what they're looking for. But close enough."

"So they think they've got the goods, and we get them off our tail."

"Precisely."

"What did you have in mind?"

She beamed. "I have just the thing."

She told me her idea. It was a real doozy.

"I've been waiting for the opportunity to put all those copies to good use."

"Where are they?"

"Up in the maid's room. On the top floor. I use the place for storage. Old clothes, that sort of thing. But we'll need to move them to another location. The farther from here, the better."

"Easily done."

"Then all we need is a ruse to get back into the warehouse."

"You got any disguises up there in your maid's room?"

"Disguises. Wigs. A little theatrical makeup."

My aunt left me to toy with the last of my caviar while she went to make coffee. By the time she came back with our espressos, I had the logistics pretty well thought out.

"I'll need Van Gogh to falsify some papers. Nothing too difficult. A simple work order should do the job. And I'll need a reliable partner."

"Eleanor has an excellent network."

"I was thinking of Greta."

"Can she pull it off?"

I broke into a smile. "Can a fish swim?"

CHAPTER 31

It was two days before we heard from Duclos. This time he paid us the courtesy of telephoning first.

"He'll be here in an hour," my aunt said. She then disappeared into her bedroom and emerged a short while later wearing an oversized white shirt and jeans. She'd teased up her silver hair and tied it back at the neck with a floppy ribbon, and added chunky earrings and enormous glasses.

"What on earth did you do to yourself?" I asked.

"Remember, your mother is an American, Carlito," she said. "I need to get into the part." She wandered off into the kitchen to make some lemonade. I could hear her practicing her West Coast vowels.

Duclos looked even spiffier than usual this afternoon, and I caught a hint of Eau Sauvage as he unbuttoned his jacket and took the chair I offered him. Aunt Lily waltzed in right on cue.

"Detective, you remember my mother, Mrs. Box."

"Madame," he said, rising to greet her.

"Well, bust my buttons, would you look at that, Carl, a man who gets up when a lady enters the room. I believe they call those creatures gentlemen, but I do declare, they are an endangered species." And then she let out a peal of delicate laughter that sounded much like those tinkling silver bells on the bracelet I'd seen her wear. I swear I don't know where that laugh came from, if she'd just tailored it bespoke for the occasion or if it was one of her practiced performances.

"Madame," he repeated, taking the hand she offered him. I could have been watching a scene straight out of *Gone With the Wind*.

"Call me Maggie, please," she said, all California sunshine and warmth. "Would you like a drink, Detective? My sister kept a very good bar. Or perhaps just a cool glass of lemonade? It's freshly made."

"This is not a social visit, madame—"

"Well, then, let's make it one, shall we?" she said in her charmingly absolutist manner that made it clear she would brook no dissent. Besides, the pitcher of lemonade was already on the coffee table, which had been cleared of its usual journalistic wreckage and set nicely with goblets, tea napkins and sugar cookies. It would have been downright caddish of Duclos to refuse.

"Such unpleasantness, all this business," she said as she settled down onto the sofa and started serving the lemonade. "What on earth has happened to our caviar?"

"The good news is that your shipment has been released for delivery."

"Well, I should hope so. Such a bunch of nonsense," my aunt said. She'd suddenly adopted a habit of cocking her head to the side and gazing at the man with a canine look of adoration. A ploy straight out of Billy's playbook.

"Not entirely, madame. You see, one of the tins of caviar contained information the Soviet authorities believed would lead them to a number of highly sensitive classified documents that were the property of the KGB."

"The KGB?" my aunt said with a genuine look of horror. "Good lord!"

"In which case you could have been charged with dealing in stolen property. However, the storage locker contained only several hundred copies of—I believe you call them romance novels. An author by the name of Melody Bly."

"Melody Bly! Why, that's my sister's pen name."

"So it is. I remembered that you carried her manuscript in your suitcase."

"Why on earth would the Russians be looking for my sister's novels?"

"The books were Russian-language editions. The documents we found with the shipment indicated the order had been placed by a bookstore in Moscow."

"I don't understand. Why would someone go to such lengths to conceal the shipment of a few romance novels?"

"I was told this sort of novel does not exist in the Soviet Union. It's a typically Western genre and considered decadent anti-Soviet propaganda. It would never make it past the Soviet censors."

"Decadent?"

"Perhaps even pornographic."

"My sister did not write pornography," she said, bristling. "There are what you might call very passionate love scenes, but she certainly never wrote pornography."

"What did they do with the books?" I asked.

"I'm afraid the Soviet authorities confiscated them."

"The brutes."

"And our caviar?" I asked.

"Fortunately, the tin concealing the information was one of the first to be opened. They agreed to leave the rest of the shipment untouched until they were satisfied they had recovered what they were looking for."

"Which they have done."

"I believe so."

"Then no French laws were broken," I said.

"None whatsoever."

"So my sister is guilty of nothing more than attempting to provide a few hours of lighthearted entertainment to Russian readers."

"I would imagine," Duclos said as he held out his glass for my aunt to refill, "that the books are already in the hands of the KGB *rezident* here in Paris, who will make sure they are closely read and rigorously vetted for anti-Soviet ideas by his diplomatic staff."

"No doubt," I said.

"Perhaps even taken back to the Soviet Union and passed around to more readers for yet more intensive analysis," Aunt Lily added earnestly without a trace of irony. Irony was unnecessary since she and Duclos were speaking the same language.

Duclos eased back into his chair. His shoulders seemed to have loosened a little. He was clearly enjoying Aunt Lily's spiked lemonade.

"I will have your caviar delivered to you tomorrow, madame."

"I don't know about you, Carl, but all this business has

made me lose my taste for caviar."

"I see what you mean, Mother."

"Perhaps the detective might wish to take some of it off our hands?"

"Excellent idea, Mother."

Duclos smiled and said he thought that could be arranged, then he took another long pull on his drink.

"Excellent lemonade, madame."

"It's my sister's recipe, Detective. And if my hunch is right, you may soon be able to thank her yourself."

"I don't understand."

She took a moment to answer, studied her lemonade, then angled a hesitant look up at him from beneath her lowered eyes.

Duclos took the bait. Set down his drink, leaned forward with elbows on his knees. Urging her to speak.

"You can trust me, madame."

"Oh, I'm sure I can, Detective. It's not that."

She shot me a wary glance, then leaned forward just as Duclos had done and bravely locked eyes with him.

"I've had—well, not exactly premonitions, but something like that. You see, my sister and I were twins, and twins have this uncanny sense of each other, a very special bond." Then, in a whisper, "I don't think my sister is dead."

CHAPTER 32

To our relief, the dates and flight information recorded on the microfilm proved to be accurate. Over the next ten days the Pasternak files poured in, arriving on flights from cities like Vienna, Bonn, Helsinki and Warsaw, delivered in battered suitcases, or violin cases, or sports bags, or crammed into nondescript backpacks, carried by anonymous men and women identifiable only by a Marlboro shopping bag over their left shoulder. I would wait for them at flight arrivals and follow them outdoors to a bench where they would sit with their luggage and consult a map of Paris. I was to sit down next to them, place my 1980 edition of the red Michelin Guide on my knees, and they would ask me the cheapest way to get into Paris. I would respond that cheap wasn't always the best. They would fold up their map, take their luggage and head for the taxi stand, leaving behind a single bag for me.

I always wondered where they came from, why they felt compelled to take the risk, if they knew what they were carrying and how dangerous it would be if they were stopped crossing some border. But I had to content myself with observing them, and committing to memory every detail to report back to my aunt. I think she was hoping someone might have news of Maxim, that there might be some snippet of information about his whereabouts, or if he was still alive. I hated having to disappoint her, but most of them just walked in and walked out of our lives, leaving behind their significant contribution to historical truth.

With each pickup I became more confident in my role. I was getting better at surveillance and spotting suspicious characters who might be trailing me. I wouldn't say I was as good at tradecraft as I was at identifying Hex codes; that was some freak talent I was born with and not very useful, except once, when it made all the difference. I suppose aptitude for espionage does depend to a degree on character, but most of it is training, and I was getting a crash course in that. One thing I did learn is that most people don't notice what's going on around them; they're deep in their thoughts and preoccupations, and there's a lot you can pull right under their noses that they don't notice, and if they do, they don't care. Unless they're a real spy, and then they notice everything.

You might not call what I was doing espionage, as we weren't an intelligence agency involved in stealing secrets from an enemy, but we were definitely stealing state secrets. We had no state at all, we were just the State of Us, our little oddball family pitted against the world, and we were thick as thieves.

CHAPTER 33

Greta and I sat at a café table facing the Place de la Sorbonne, where a crowd of militant students had gathered in front of the university to listen to a young man with long hair shout into a megaphone. They carried signs reading things like, *Le Peuple A Soif de la Justice* (People are hungry for justice) and flags with the bold red PS of the Socialist Party and UNEF, the powerful students' union. Greta knew some of the students and they came over to talk to her; I admired the formality of the introductions, the way they kissed Greta on both cheeks and she introduced me to every single one by name, and they all shook my hand and fussed politely over Billy and his wheels. I shook their hands and smiled and wondered at the ease with which these well-mannered Parisians embraced something as radical as the Socialist Party.

Then they went back to join the demonstration, taking with them their noisy exuberance, and sobriety settled over us like frost on a windowpane. Billy was sprawled on the cool pavement beneath the café table and Greta had just announced that she was departing for Germany.

"Germany." I repeated. As if I hadn't heard right the first time.

"Yes. Bonn."

I nodded and finished off my gin and tonic, then swirled the ice cubes around to make a little noise to cut through the silence between us.

"That doesn't sound like much of a vacation destination." Not that I knew anything about Bonn except that it was the capital of West Germany, which I'd only learned recently thanks to sessions with my aunt and her atlas.

"It's not a vacation."

I gave the ice cubes another vigorous swirl. "Greenpeace?"

"Yes."

"Will you be gone long?"

Her sunglasses hid her eyes as she looked away from me.

"Greta?"

A tall man passed by with a small black dog straining on the leash. Billy cocked an ear and followed him with one eye until he moved out of sight and then shut the eye again. The Socialists started a chant but no one in the café seemed particularly interested. This was Paris in September: demonstrations in the street, students going back to school, people going back to their jobs after long vacations, Greta walking out of my life. Billy shifted his head from one paw to the other and let out a deep sigh.

"The *Rainbow Warrior* wasn't a spy boat," she said. She caught my baffled look and had to remind me. "The Greenpeace boat Olivier was on, the one the DGSE blew up, it wasn't on a spy mission. The French press spread those rumors and everyone believed them. But it wasn't true. Thanks to their propaganda, now no one here wants to be associated with Greenpeace. But the group's still strong in Germany."

"Greta?"

"Last year they launched a major campaign against the illegal export of toxic waste and they've asked me to join the team. I'll be doing research."

"Greta?"

"Yes?"

"You haven't answered my question. Will you be gone long?"

Her hand moved across the table and found my hand, threading her fingers through mine. Her hand was warm and silky and it made me ache with longing.

"I should have gotten out of Olivier's apartment a long time ago," she said quietly. "I just couldn't bring myself to do it until now."

"I thought we—" I wasn't sure how to finish that sentence.

"What?"

Did I glimpse a spark in her eyes? A look of expectancy on her face? But I could have been seeing it all wrong.

I talked about how we'd been a stellar team, another Nick and Nora, the way we'd handled those guys at the warehouse, convincing them we were there to take a temperature reading of the refrigerated areas, just a couple of bureaucrats making our rounds to verify that site conditions conform to regulatory standards. The way she'd busied the guard getting him to sign off on the paperwork while I slipped in and returned the tin to one of the packing boxes.

I said all this when what I really wanted to say was *I thought we were good together, you and me.*

But then, what had I done or said to show her how I felt? There had been that one kiss, planted on her unsuspecting lips, and then what? Nothing. I'd done absolutely nothing. I was still too in awe of the girl to make a move. Too timid to ruin what wonderful stuff we already had.

"Do you have to get out all the way to Germany?" I asked. "Can't you just—I don't know—move to another neighborhood?"

When she didn't answer I did the petulant thing. I took back my hand. I didn't know what to do with the hand so I shook my glass again, although the ice was melted now and there wasn't much left except a soggy lemon rind clinging to the bottom.

I felt her gaze on my face and that hurt too. I couldn't look at her so I watched the Socialists. I wanted to say something wickedly clever and political to show her I wasn't a complete *Americanus ignoramus*, but she would be able to see right through me. I wanted to be the kind of guy she would grieve for if I died. Or even if I just went back to Florida. I wanted her to pine for me like I pined for her.

She reached down for her backpack and hoisted it onto her lap with the attitude of someone getting down to business.

"I made extra copies, just in case," she said as she removed a large envelope and laid it on the table.

"They're lucky to get you," I said. "I hope they know that."

"Let's talk about it later."

"No need to. You gotta do what you gotta do," I said, trying to sound coolly detached but it came out really strained.

I opened the envelope and withdrew the photos Greta had taken over the last week when she had Pym under surveillance.

The grainy black-and-whites, which she'd developed herself in her boyfriend's darkroom, showed a burly fair-haired man holding the car door while Pym wrangled himself into the passenger seat. There were shots of the car, the license plate, a few close-ups of the driver as he got in behind the wheel. She'd tailed the car on her scooter to the Rue de Lille, where the driver deposited Pym in front of the entrance to the National Institute for the Study of Oriental Languages and Civilizations, where he taught translation. The driver accompanied Pym into the school, carrying his briefcase, then came out and drove away.

Greta parked her scooter and followed him inside. He had a small office on the ground floor of the courtyard, and she settled herself on a bench with a book and watched the door. A few hours later, the driver returned to pick up Pym. Greta followed them back to the Rue Tonton, then tailed the driver all the way to the suburbs just south of Paris, where he pulled up in front of a sports complex and waited. A few minutes later a kid came out dressed in soccer gear.

"Here's a photo of the boy."

It was Pym's student all right, Matthew, the kid with the big ears who'd slammed into me as he was leaving his lesson.

"So Pym's driver is the boy's father."

"By all appearances, yes."

"So if I were to take this photo of the father to the mosque tearoom, you think someone would identify him as the waiter who served my aunt her tea that day?"

"I did just that. The manager confirmed it. That's the man."

And we had connected him to Pym.

"What will you do?" she asked.

"I'll have to tell her."

"Will she believe you?"

"I don't know."

"She'll have to, won't she? When you show her the photos."

"People don't always believe the truth, even when it's staring them in the face. They believe what fits in with their picture of the world, the one they're comfortable with."

"But why would he do such a thing? You said he was in love with her."

"I don't think he was trying to poison my aunt. She said she had planned to meet someone there, and I think that was the intended victim."

"Who?"

"I don't know, but I'll bet you it was someone connected to Maxim and her efforts to get him out of jail."

I remembered what Pym had said the day I met him, that she wasn't supposed to die. At the time I'd misconstrued his meaning—thinking he wanted to say that it wasn't her time yet, that fate had taken her too soon. But I'd gotten the emphasis wrong: What he'd said was "*She* wasn't supposed to die."

I think he didn't want Maxim coming back and stealing my aunt's affections all over again. It was a story as old as time—a Cain-and-Abel story of sibling rivalry, but in this case the older brother had been cursed in advance for his crime. Or at least that's probably the way Pym saw it.

I thanked Greta and slipped the photos back into the envelope.

She said, "I wish I could have met her."

"So do I. She's planning to make a comeback from the dead any day now. I'm sure she'll come up with a good tale to tell the neighbors. She does look well. Happy. Well, maybe I should say lighthearted. She's been carrying a huge burden all these years. And now it's finished. Mission accomplished."

"What about Maxim?"

"She hasn't said anything. All I know is that the files are safe. How about your father? Have you heard from him?"

"Just the usual. We speak on the phone from time to time, but it's always guarded, as you can imagine. I don't tell him much about what I'm doing. It would only worry him. And he just talks as if he has a boring desk job with an insurance company."

"I'm going to miss him. Not the real him. But the priest with the runaway wife I met at the café the day I arrived. He asked to borrow my pen to do a crossword puzzle. I liked him."

"He is likable, just not when he's hunting spies."

"That time feels like the good old days when I think back on it. I remember how I looked forward to seeing him on the corner. He grounded me when everything was so crazy."

"Then it just got crazier."

"It sure did."

"He liked you too."

"Did he say that?"

"The priest with the runaway wife said it."

"My aunt said it was the owner of the bookshop across the street from her apartment who spread the rumor that Van Gogh had tried to knock her off over the pizza oven dispute. So Van Gogh went and had some words with him. Of course, Van Gogh being Van Gogh, they ended up in the shop owner's back office drinking a vintage burgundy and all was swept under the table. But she had a sly look on her face, and when she said the words 'swept under the table' she gave me a wink."

"What did she mean?"

"Heaven knows. But she's had her suspicions about that bookshop owner for a long time. She also seems to have taken a sudden liking to the girl who works there. Something about having similar tastes in sunglasses, but I couldn't make much sense out of it."

"When do you leave, Carl?"

"I was going to ask you the same question."

"My train's tomorrow."

"So you're all packed?"

"I don't have much to pack. I don't accumulate anything."

No, of course not. Only broken hearts.

I got the waiter's attention and ordered another gin and tonic for myself and another panaché for Greta. Prolonging the moment was painful, but saying goodbye would be far worse. Another gin and tonic solved the problem.

CHAPTER 34

The fact that I made it from the Sorbonne to the Rue Tonton, sloshed as I was, without losing my way or my dog, must have said something about how well I'd settled in to this part of the city. Granted, it's not a long walk, but some of those streets in the 6ème *arrondissement* are tricky for someone like me who expects ninety-degree angles when I turn a corner, instead of forty-eight degrees, or seventy-three, or—God forbid—a curve. Walking Billy around the neighborhood over the past month, more than once I'd tried venturing along a little side street, thinking I might find a shortcut to the Seine or a green square, and half a mile later later I'd figure out I'd been tooling along in the exact opposite direction.

I was relieved to find only Eleanor at home. There she was, sorting her piles of cash on the dining room table, much like when I'd first seen her, except this evening she stopped counting and looked up at me with concern in her eyes. I sat down in the chair next to her and hung my head in my hands.

"*C'est la fille*," she said after a moment.

I nodded. "Yeah. Girl troubles."

"*Tu es amoureux.*"

I got that one too. "Yeah, I suppose I am. *Amoureux.*" In love.

With that deftness of hand I so admired, she bundled up her cash and slipped it into her ratty plastic shopping bag. Then she slid back her chair and trundled away into the kitchen. While she was gone, I got my French–English pocket dictionary and brought it back to the table and started looking up words to try to piece together my story in French. Eleanor's crusty facade, I had learned, hid a magnanimous heart, and she was nothing if not patient. She wouldn't mind if I mangled a few phrases while pouring out my heart to her. I even started thinking of titles for my adventure. *Mr. Box in Paris. The Box Files. Carl and Billy Go to Paris.* Each one as dull as the next. That was me, Mr. Dullsville.

A few minutes later I could hear popcorn popping, and then Eleanor appeared with a big bowl of it and a pot of coffee.

My French lesson lasted about as long as the popcorn. By the time Van Gogh turned up, I was sober and losing badly to Eleanor in backgammon. He wanted my help moving something in his antique shop, but Eleanor had a little chat with him, which quickly evolved into a squabble. Finally, Van Gogh pulled out a chair and settled down at the table, rubbing his hands together like a man getting ready to make a killing. Eleanor put away the backgammon board and brought out a deck of cards. Then she reached into her bag of money and started doling out cash to each of us. I got the dollars, Eleanor got the French francs, and Van Gogh got the Italian lira. The lira weren't worth much, but he seemed to get a kick out of playing with large denomination bills.

It was the strangest poker game I've ever played, as we had to constantly calculate exchange rates to keep our bets equivalent. If I bet five dollars, Van Gogh would need to slap down a ten-thousand-lira note to call me. He was always trying to cheat, but Eleanor was too sharp, and when she caught him he'd laugh his head off. For Van Gogh, the game wasn't fun unless you cheated.

I don't think anything could have brought me out of my blue funk better than that poker game. I didn't understand any of the banter between the two of them, but they were immensely entertaining, and Van Gogh was always good for cobbling together a few sentences in English, so I wasn't left completely ignorant.

When my aunt came home, three big pies hot from Van Gogh's pizza oven were on the table, and I was setting out plates and cutlery. Eleanor was tossing greens in a big bowl with the enthusiasm of a kid playing with Silly Putty, while Van Gogh was opening a bottle of wine and complimenting himself on his pizza.

I'd never seen Aunt Lily beam like she did when she walked in, not even when I came home with the ruble in the caviar. You would have thought someone was throwing her a surprise birthday party. I felt it too, just briefly, the delight of inclusion, of having everyone who matters all in one spot, at a table with food and drink, being together. With or without Greta, I was—at that moment—part of something here.

We were all seated at the table, happily gorging ourselves on the pizza, putting away the slices as quickly as Van Gogh could dish them up, when my aunt said she thought we should invite Pym to join us. When she repeated it in French, Eleanor stiffened. Van Gogh piped up, seemingly liking the idea, but his enthusiasm was answered by Eleanor's cool reply, triggering a profuse and vigorous counterargument. Van Gogh, charming as he was, could be a bully, but going after Eleanor was like trying to dislodge a ten-ton boulder that had no intention of going anywhere.

My aunt was sawing away at her pizza, eyes cast down, the earlier joy dimmed to a look of dismay.

"What's going on?" I asked.

"They're having a little disagreement, that's all," she said, dismissing it with a shake of her head. "They never do see eye to eye."

"About Pym."

"They have differing opinions."

"And you cast the deciding vote."

"I do."

"So you'll welcome him back into the fold?"

"His exclusion was only temporary."

"Well, maybe you could delay his return another day."

She hesitated, a forkful of pizza midway to her mouth, and from the look on her face, I could see she knew what was coming.

"Why?"

"I thought, well, it's time for me to go home. And I rather like the idea of having this as my send-off party. Matter of fact, it's exactly the way I want to remember you all, bickering and noisy and eating Van Gogh's pizza. Like a family."

I'd been pondering the idea on my drunken walk home, but the pondering having been done while in a state of extreme inebriation, it wasn't until now that it came to me as a lucid and reasonable path ahead. I couldn't stay. I still had a sort-of job to return to. Disney had consented to extend my week vacation to a month—which spoke to how little they needed my services, but I was, after all, a professional. I needed to show up back at my office and pick up my life where I'd left off.

If Greta hadn't just walked out of my life, maybe I would have been coming up with all sorts of excuses to hang around. Heartache does that to you. Blurs the boundaries of reasonable thought. Your mind, your entire body, all of you just wants to flee to a place where you won't hurt anymore, wherever that may be, and in my case it was home. Epcot. Disney World. The place where people go to be happy.

Home. That was the word that stuck in my throat. Home. I wanted to go home.

The look on Aunt Lily's face, the expression of stunned disappointment, was like a punch in the gut. Perhaps I hadn't dared admit the truth to myself until that moment, the truth being this: I wanted to belong somewhere, and I had thought, in some deep part of my consciousness, that it might be here.

But it wasn't. This wasn't my world.

So, I would leave, and Pym would return to the fold. Lucky for him that I wasn't staying around. I would never be able to look the man in the face without bashing it in. Or knocking out a few teeth and breaking a nose.

Speaking of which.

I cleaned my hands on my napkin, pushed back my chair.

"I'll just pop down and tell the guy goodbye."

I went back to my bedroom and sat on the bed, wondering how I was going to handle Pym. Despite all the dots Greta and I had connected, I couldn't prove he was directly involved in the attempt on my aunt's life, short of getting a confession out of the boy's father, which was highly unlikely. I couldn't accuse Pym, but I could at least lead him down the path, tell him what we'd uncovered and see how many lies I could trap him in.

I was plotting along these lines when I heard a light tap on my door. Aunt Lily entered softly, closing the door behind her as she said, "Carl, I have a confession to make."

CHAPTER 35

"It was Pym who poisoned the bees," she said quietly, almost guiltily, as if she'd been in on the plot. "Well, not him personally. Someone else. Someone who owed him, he said. You were right. He admitted to everything. But I didn't want you to know."

I didn't need to ask why she'd been holding out on me. She could sense my hostility toward the guy.

"How long did it take him to come clean?"

"Right away, actually. You must have noticed that hideous doormat of his—the one with the smiley face? Pym and I have a little running joke—"

"So he told me. Go on."

"Well, while I was *dead*, he threw it away. It was too painful for him to walk past it every time he went out, he said. Eleanor retrieved it from the dumpster, and I held on to it thinking that when the time comes, I'd put it back in front of his door to let him know I was among the living. So I did—that was the day you went shopping with Greta—and within an hour he was pounding on my door. He knew if the mat was back, I wasn't dead. The poor man, he—"

"Poor man, my foot," I muttered.

"—he was so relieved, the whole story came pouring out. You see, that day I went to the tearoom, I had told Pym I was going to meet a friend of Maxim's, a Russian émigré who's been working to get Maxim out of the Soviet Union. Pym wanted us to think the KGB would come after Maxim's friends, or even me, if he defected. He knew Maxim would have taken the risk himself, but not if it endangered the lives of his friends, or me."

"So I was right. Pym didn't want his little brother to come back and steal you away."

"It was a great relief to him, to have the truth come out," she said. "He's been suffering terrible remorse."

"I should think so. He could have killed the guy. Or you."

"The dose wasn't enough to kill anyone. It would have made them sick, that's all."

"Is that any better?"

"He's deeply repentant, Carlito."

"So you forgive him."

"If Maxim ever makes it out, it will be up to him to forgive his brother. I was only a near mishap, and not even that."

"There's the Chihuahua."

"I suggested he make a generous donation to the SPCA as a restitution payment. He was more than happy to do so."

"What if it had been Billy?"

"Pym is awkward at this sort of thing."

"What? Declaring his love for you? Or plotting murder?"

"This is why I didn't tell you earlier, Carlito."

"Well, it's none of my business. He's you're friend, not mine. I'm going home."

"You'll be back, soon, I hope."

"I'll never drink another of his rum punches, that's for sure."

"Oh, but I hope you will, one day. If you can find it in your heart to forgive us."

The *us*. What did she mean by *us*?

"Why would I need to forgive *you*, Aunt Lily?"

The smile she gave me reminded me of my mother's sad smiles when I was little and she was hiding something worrisome, when she wanted to reassure me that everything would be fine.

That's when she noticed the book beside my bed.

"*The Master and Margarita*," she said with surprise.

I explained how I'd discovered it that evening after the break-in when I was reshelving her books. Its well-worn cover had made me think it was an old favorite, a book she'd kept for years and returned to with pleasure, and it was this, and the title—I recalled she'd used the code name *Margarita*—that had piqued my curiosity. Even as my American mother, she was Maggie.

"I had a little trouble getting into it," I said as I reached for it. "All the magic and supernatural. I don't read a lot of novels and this is nothing like anything I've ever read before."

"And now?"

"It's—well, it's pretty crazy, and imaginative. I'm liking it. Which sort of surprises me."

"Why?"

"It means maybe I'm not who I thought I was."

She looked at me for a long moment, a penetrating, inscrutable gaze.

"It's a very powerful love story," she said finally.

"Yeah. I liked that part. How Margarita is utterly devoted to him."

What I didn't tell her was that this book had somehow felt significant from the moment I picked it up, even before I found the photo.

"Take it with you when you go," she said.

"You might want this."

I pulled out the photo I'd found between the pages and had been using as a bookmark, a square deckle-edged black-and-white showing a much younger Aunt Lily standing beside a tall imposing fellow in some wintry snowbound place, both of them in bulky furs and very Russian-looking fur hats. He appeared to be saying something amusing to her, and she was trying her best not to laugh and was having a hard time doing it.

"Is this him?" I asked.

She took the photo from my hands and gazed at it tenderly for a moment, then handed it back, like a once hard-drinking man might gaze longingly at a bottle of whiskey and then turn away, acknowledging it as an old habit put to rest.

"He was a very witty man. He could make me laugh like no one else."

I noticed she spoke in the past tense, and it made me wonder if she'd given up hope.

I called Air France from the phone in my bedroom and booked myself a flight back to Florida. When I came out a little later, everyone had gone. Eleanor had decamped with her satchels of currency. Van Gogh had retreated to his cavern of antiques.

Aunt Lily had slipped silently away, as she often did. It was just Billy and me.

I was torn between relief and disappointment at not having my moment with Pym. But it didn't matter anymore. By tomorrow this time, Billy and I would be on a plane back home.

That evening I stood at the open window looking out over la Rue Tonton, watching a neighbor in the adjacent building watering her window box of scarlet geraniums, releasing the smell of fresh earth and blossoms. I'd always thought the red geraniums a bit of a cliché; that is, until I came to Paris and saw them in bloom in the windows, and they don't seem cliché anymore. They just belong. A ways down the street, a small group of friends had gathered on a balcony with their glasses of champagne, laughing and talking, enjoying the summer evening. The bakery at the other end of the street was closing down for the night. I recognized the metal shutter's familiar rattle as he locked up, and I recalled how the smell of freshly baked bread would greet me as I passed by in the morning. I suppose those are all clichés. But I'm okay with that.

I settled down on the sofa to finish the Bulgakov novel, but my attention kept returning to the photo of my aunt and Maxim. Was I just imagining something, or was there a greater truth hidden in that moment captured in black and white? Why was it so special? Where had it been taken? Why had she been so demonized by my father? What had been her crime? Treason? Had Maxim been KGB? Had he recruited her? I turned it over, tried once again to read the handwriting on the back. The ink had faded to a watery brown. A date I couldn't quite make out.

Whatever her allegiances had been in those days, I didn't

doubt her loyalties now. Whatever the truth, I could handle it. I put down the book. Turned to Billy.

"Time to do a little detective work, buddy. Last chance."

He was sound asleep. Not so much as a twitch.

"Okay, I'll go it alone."

I couldn't find the heart-shaped box, the one I'd been digging through when I'd gotten the phone call from the Fontainebleau train station. The one with all the letters from my mom, and the photos of me. My aunt must have moved it. Which meant she didn't want me finding it. I snooped anyway. I couldn't find the chocolate box but I found a handful of old French passports, along with a single US passport that had expired in 1956. Comparing it with the dates of the French passports, this seemed to be the very last one issued by the US. I rifled through the pages, trying to make sense of the jumble of entry and exit stamps. Some of them were French and German, a number in a script I guessed to be Russian, others in languages I couldn't recognize. Stamped at airports or border towns she crossed through by train. The only one clear enough to read, stamped on a page all its own, was an entry to New York International Airport, dated 1955, just a month before I was born. I remembered she'd once said in a very offhanded manner that she'd been present at my birth, so I could only surmise that the rift between her and my parents had occurred later.

After a while I gave up. Playing detective had lost its thrill. Maybe because I'd lost Greta, my partner, the Nora to my Nick. But my reluctance to ferret out the truth also spoke to my growing respect for my aunt. She must have had her reasons for her secrets. Perhaps to protect herself. Maybe she thought

I didn't have the humanity, or the imagination, requisite to deal with her secrets. If that was the case, I figured she was old and wise enough to make that call.

So I closed the door to her room, poured myself a last glass of Lagavulin and settled down to finish *The Master and Margarita*. Waiting up for Aunt Lily.

It was late when she returned. Billy, vigilant pup that he is, had taken up his post at the front door. I heard him scramble to his feet as she came in and fussed over him; I heard her footsteps in the hall, heading toward her bedroom.

After a few minutes I got up and went down the corridor to find her. She was in my bedroom, sitting on the foot of the bed next to the small suitcase I'd left open. I don't think she knew I was in the doorway watching her. I was all packed, what little I had, with the exception of my Dopp kit. Hesitantly, as if she didn't quite dare, she reached out a hand and gently fingered something in the bag. I couldn't tell what she was touching. But there was a tinge of sadness in the gesture.

"What will you wear?" she asked as I came in. "On the plane."

"My blue shirt."

"The one you bought with Greta."

Hearing Greta's name spoken like that, in the past tense, I was struck by the mutability of our lives, the ever-shifting realities that doom our moments of bliss.

When I murmured assent, she said, "Yes, that would look nice. Where is it?"

"Over there. On the chair."

"Is it clean?"

"Yeah."

"Give it to me. I'll iron it for you. You can't fly first class looking all rumpled."

"You don't have to iron it, Aunt Lily. I know how to iron."

"But I do. I would like to." She rose and said, "How about a last walk with Billy, shall we?"

At the small grassy square beneath a streetlamp we sat on a park bench while Billy sniffed joyously in the gutter, and she quietly told me the truth: Pym's near victim that day at the tearoom had been none other than Pasternak himself, the man whose purloined archives we had been spiriting out of Moscow this past month.

In late July, having endured a tense crossing to Finland, where he had boarded a boat to the northern shores of West Germany, he had finally arrived in Paris, where he had been living under an assumed identity. He was the mystery man Aunt Lily was to meet at the tearoom that afternoon, but he'd gotten turned around in the subway and arrived late to find my aunt nervously waiting for him on the street with the story about the dead bees. She had immediately spirited him away, and together they had decided on a plan of action: Pasternak would go into hiding and she would fake her death. She believed the poison had been intended for him, that his identity had been leaked to the KGB.

That is, until Pym confessed.

"I'm confident now that the KGB is ignorant of Pasternak's presence here in Paris."

"Good grief. Pym really did throw a monkey wrench into the business."

"But he doesn't know that. He doesn't know Pasternak is here, and I don't plan on telling him. Nobody knows, except you. Not even Eleanor. Nor Van Gogh."

That evening I learned Pasternak's history, how early in his career he had been demoted from his KGB posting in Berlin to archivist in the KGB's Lubyanka facility in Moscow, which housed intelligence records dating as far back as the early Stalinist years. Although it was a job he had trained for, he saw it as menial paper-pushing involving long days of fulfilling requests made by others; he became bitter and resentful. Over the years his disillusionment with the KGB grew. When it was decided to move the archives to another, larger facility, he was put in charge—giving him the opportunity to inspect hundreds of thousands of files. That's when he began removing documents from the facility. He'd sneak them out in his shoes and pockets, take them home to copy by hand then return them to the archives the next day. On the weekends he'd take the notes to his dacha, where he would type them up and then hide them under his mattress and the floorboards. Initially, he thought about publishing them as *samizdat* in the Soviet Union, but that was too risky, so he held on to them until he retired, by which time he had enough documents to fill a half-dozen suitcases. From his literary connections, he'd heard about my aunt's publishing venture in the West. It took months before he was able to safely get in touch with her.

"It's hard to imagine the strain the man has been living under all these years, but that's over. Now he can continue transcribing his notes, in peace and safety, so that one day all the dark secrets and nefarious deeds of the KGB will come to light for the world to see, and hopefully take to heart."

"Why did he do it, Aunt Lily? What makes someone turn against their country?"

"Usually it's money. Or a wounded ego. Men are particularly vulnerable on that point. Only rarely is the decision based on ideology. Pasternak was a little of all three, but mostly the latter. He believed in his country but not the regime that was destroying it. He saw the KGB's power to block reform as the source of the country's evils, and he was outraged by the contrast between the real freedoms of the West and the propaganda the Soviets were feeding their people to inspire loyalty. The abuses of the justice system and human rights appalled him. The real truth was there, in the archives."

A man with a fox terrier was approaching the square. We waited while he passed, the terrier straining at his leash and Billy whimpering the way he always does when a young female shows him the slightest bit of interest. But they moved quickly around the square and were gone, disappearing into the night. Mutability being a rule of life for dogs as well as humans.

When they were out of earshot, she said, "He wanted me to thank you for everything you've done. He was the one who said you would be perfect for the job."

"What do you mean?"

"He saw you. At the hotel, the day you arrived."

My surprise amused her.

"He was in the lounge."

I remembered only a few business types scattered around, looking very busy behind the odd open briefcase and newspaper.

And the hotel. Small, discrete, a little tired-looking, too quiet for the Hilton and Hyatt crowd. Privately managed. Owned by my aunt.

Suddenly, I knew. "So that's where you've been keeping the files."

She asked if, during my short stay at the hotel, I had by chance caught a glimpse of the small private salon at the back of the lounge. If so, perhaps I had noticed a glass-fronted bookcase displaying rare editions. And if I had happened to peruse these titles, I might have noted that the authors had all been reviled or censored in their day for homosexuality, some even forced to flee their country for their own safety.

"It is a truly exceptional collection," she continued, "to which I have added my own little gems through the years—Byron, of course, and Oscar Wilde, naturally. There's a first edition of E. M. Forster's *Maurice*—such a lovely novel. There is also a very rare 1933 unexpurgated German edition of Friedo Lampe's *At the Edge of Night*—one of only a handful in existence, I believe—how I acquired it is a story for another day."

What I would not have known, however, was that by triggering a hidden mechanical device, the bookcase would swing open to reveal a small vault.

"When the Nazis marched into Paris in 1940, knowing how fond the Nazis were of burning books, the owner of the hotel had the vault built into the wall to keep his collection safe. I'd learned about its existence when the hotel came into my possession. Now that the rare books are back on display, the vault has been sitting empty all these years. Until now." She turned and gave me a smile of pure delight. "Pretty nifty, huh?"

Bit by bit, as all these secrets spilled out, as truths were revealed, I got the feeling that we were both coming to the end of our own wild ride. My aunt Lily and me. A ride we had shared only because some clerk in a notary's office had sent out a letter prematurely, because I had decided to take that airline ticket and dare the unknown. If I had not acted, she would have gone it alone. Perhaps she would have succeeded, perhaps not. But I had been there. And she seemed to think that had made all the difference.

"So, who will the Pasternak files go to? Has anyone shown an interest? CIA?"

"We've decided to donate them."

"Donate?"

"To the *Bibliothèque* Mazarine."

Bibliothèque. Library. I pictured the local library in our neighborhood mall in Santa Ana, the one my mother frequented every Monday afternoon with me in tow to carry her stack of romance novels. It was a small airy space with high windows to let in the light, and long tables for reading, and display shelves lined with recent bestsellers by names like Sidney Sheldon, Salman Rushdie and Danielle Steel.

"You're giving them away to a library?" I said, sounding incredulous.

"Not just any library, Carlito. It's the oldest library in all of France. I pointed it out to you that day we met on the Pont des Arts. That magnificent structure at the end of the bridge. The one with the dome. The Mazarine Library is there, in the Institut de France.

"Normally they only house collections related to the history of France, but I managed to persuade them that precious archival material deserves to be preserved regardless of its origin."

"You told them they were stolen by a KGB archivist?"

"I may have left out that part. The important point is that only Pasternak has access to the files. Every day he shows his pass, he climbs the stairs and slips into a small cubicle reserved for him, and there he types up his notes. He's a very contented man who has a long and rewarding task ahead of him."

She rose from the bench and I rose with her. She linked her arm through mine and we turned to go home.

"So your work is done," I said.

"Oh, we'll still have our bits and pieces of *samizdat* to get out, although now that Gorbachev has relaxed censorship, it's not nearly as exciting as it used to be. You can read *The Gulag Archipelago* in public in Moscow now without being trussed up and thrown in jail. Young men are growing their hair long and wearing leather vests. Change is coming."

"What about Maxim?"

She looked at me and said, "I'll bring him home one day."

I had no doubt that she would.

She pressed closer to me as we walked, leaning on me. She was so light—I'll never forget how light she felt on my arm. We strolled slowly, comfortably, Billy rolling along at a clip, tugging at the leash. There was a bit of a moon, as I recall, and the sky was clear and starry. It was pleasant night for a stroll.

CHAPTER 36

Everyone was there the next day to see me off. Eleanor waving from her window with Madame Daunou's television blaring in the background, while my aunt stood on the sidewalk trying to explain to Van Gogh why it would be unwise to gift me a rare camel-shaped silver teapot from his shop. They were still arguing about it when we pulled away. He had wanted to drive me to the airport, but my aunt advised against it.

"He's very good-hearted, but you know how easily he gets sidetracked." She insisted on having a car from the hotel pick me up. "They'll be more reliable."

Seeing the long line of economy passengers waiting to check in at the airport, I felt a belated sense of gratitude for my aunt's extravagance. I recalled how I'd stewed about my first-class seat on the inbound trip and bemoaned her wasteful spending. How I'd anticipated settling debts and cleaning up the fallout from the poor financial decisions of an incompetent old woman. I suppose the only reason I didn't feel ashamed was because I was too perplexed as to why my parents had so deliberately distorted the truth about her character. Surely they must have known she had long ago denounced Communism and joined the fight against Soviet repression. Or perhaps they didn't. Maybe they had thrown up a wall and chosen to live in ignorance. Although my mother hadn't cut the ties, not entirely. Her correspondence with my aunt, the letters I'd discovered in the heart-shaped chocolate box, had been proof of some contact, albeit clandestine. My Tour de France T-shirt had been a gift from her. They had lied about that. How many other lies had they told? Perhaps they believed the lies themselves. How easy it is to judge another from a distance, from behind an Iron Curtain, when we can paint whatever picture we choose and declare it to be a true likeness.

Having checked my small bag, with Billy in his pet carrier in one hand and his wheels in the other, I was glancing around the hall wondering if I should pick up some souvenirs, when I saw that unmistakable figure making his way through the dense crowd of passengers. Watching people move out of his way was like watching the Red Sea part for Moses. People stepped aside not so much out of courtesy, but because of his commanding presence, the braces and crutches and powerful shoulders working together to give the impression of a machine propelled by an implacable will. Even without the gear he would have distinguished himself by the Homburg, the gray jacket and charcoal pants. And the scarlet pocket square. You could have easily taken him for a diplomat.

If I didn't walk toward him to shorten the distance between us, it was more out of uncertainty than malevolence on my part; I wasn't even sure he was heading for me. Why on earth would he want to see me, of all people?

But he did. I was still gawking when he finally pulled up

in front of me. He wasn't even out of breath.

"Glad to see I didn't miss you."

I waited.

"When does your flight leave?"

"Not for a while."

"Good. What I have to say won't take but a few minutes."

"I'm listening."

"You impressed me, Carl Box. You impressed your aunt. Neither of us are easily impressed."

The comment pissed me off. The balls on the guy. Addressing me as if I were some underling he'd put to the test. I let it pass. I said, "I thought you might be here to explain yourself."

"I didn't come to the airport to perform a public act of contrition. That's not my style."

Billy was squirming around in his pet carrier. He'd never much cared for Pym—I believe he was always expecting Pym to take a swipe at him with one of his crutches. I set down the carrier so that I was holding only the wheels. Looking ridiculous didn't bother me. What bothered me was that I couldn't punch the guy in the face. Surely he knew that. What I did was jab a finger at the air under his nose.

"I've seen your style and I'm not impressed. I don't know what kind of power you exert over that boy's family, to get his father to perform such an odious act, but he must owe you big-time. So I can only conclude that you manipulated him. And I hate it when people do that. I really do." I backed up and lowered my hand to my side. I really was afraid I'd punch him. "So let me tell you this," I said with admirable calm, "if I hear my aunt gets so much as a stomach ache, or gas pains—"

"You'll what? Break both my legs?"

It was his joke so he liked it. I didn't. It hit too close to home, having a legless little guy in the crate at my feet. It just made me hate him all the more.

Empathy doesn't serve you very well when you need to be a badass.

So, I leaned into his face and lowered my voice to a whisper. "If my aunt—or Eleanor, or anyone, even Madame Daunou—gets even a teeny bit under the weather, I'll be at your door before you can get up out of your chair. I'll expose you, Pym, you and your dirty secrets. I'll make sure they put you away. You can bet on it."

His smirk gave way to a look of bewilderment.

"You've met Madame Daunou?"

I did my best to suppress a smile. I'd thrown in the name for the sake of hyperbole, having forgotten Pym didn't know the neighbor was entirely fictitious.

"I have met her. Dear old soul."

"Then . . . you must know . . ."

I cocked my head. *Go on, finish your sentence, Pym.*

"Pretty much everything."

"Seems I do."

"How did you find out?"

"Did a little investigative work on my own."

"She never wanted you to know. She thought it would be better—for you. So, you'll play along, then, for your aunt Lily's sake."

It was a weird exchange. It wasn't exactly clear which secrets we were talking about, and I sure didn't want to ask, for fear of giving him the upper hand. Better to play like I knew *it* all, whatever it was. He must have taken my silence for acquiescence, because he added in a surprisingly gentle voice, "That's as it should be."

With a tip of the Homburg, he said, "Take good care of yourself, Carl Box." Then he gripped his crutches, turned, and made his way back through the crowd. Exiting the stage as he had entered, leaving the onlookers in awe.

Like I said, Pym was never one to inspire pity.

CHAPTER 37

It seemed at first a saner and simpler world that I had reentered: I was back home, in the late afternoon when the air conditioners roar, and you walk barefoot over cool tile, and beyond the sliding glass doors a flat blue Floridian sky dips to a flat blue Floridian horizon. Everything was reassuringly familiar. I whipped up a dish of Velveeta mac and cheese and ate it in front of TV while I watched the Dodgers squeak past the Braves. Nothing much seemed to have changed. Mr. Humboldt didn't remember that I'd been gone, and Mrs. Chipman was still pining for her profligate son. No bills were overdue, and my cacti seemed to be thriving—I suppose that's the point of keeping succulents, they don't mind neglect.

As a consultant at Epcot, I had never spent much time in my office, which consisted of a corner cubicle in Operations, situated underground below the Energy Pavilion. A few smiling faces greeted me upon my return, but most of them wouldn't have noticed my absence. The only thing of note in my inbox was one single report requesting my expert opinion on a new fluoropolymer top coat offering significantly higher UV stability than polyurethane top coats. This was the sort of stuff that used to get my juices flowing. I sat there staring at it for the longest time, got halfway through the first page, then shoved it into my briefcase and headed out the door.

Mike and I met up for lunch at Oley's Kitchen and Smokehouse. Right away I noticed that I could understand what people at the next table were saying. Something you take for granted until you've spent any length of time in a place where you can't understand diddly squat of what's being said around you. Secondly, the dishes on the menu were all familiar, and I could pronounce them. Next, glasses of water came filled with ice cubes. A laundry list of things I'd learned to live happily without.

Mike had his usual plate of ribs, and I went for the pulled pork. Mike knew a lot about robotics and a lot about a lot of other stuff as well, like the history of piracy and laser technology, but most importantly to me, he was a fun guy. We laughed a lot together.

"What's with the long hair?" he said.

"Yeah, I suppose I need to get it cut."

Naturally he noticed right away that I was not my normal self. Not that my spirits were low, but I must have come across as a little dazed. Like a man who'd lost his bearings. I diddled around with the salt and pepper shakers and the plastic squeeze bottles of barbecue sauce, lining them all up in a nice row along the side of the table, but even that didn't help.

"What is it, buddy? Did the job fall through?"

"What job?"

"The one you applied for."

"Oh, that. Can't say. I never called them back."

"Why not?"

It would be more of the same, I said. Running the financial side of an industrial coating business.

"I don't want to do that anymore."

"Why not? You're good at it. You took over a very successful small enterprise when your dad got sick, and you made it even more profitable."

"Surprising, since my heart was never in it."

"So what will you do?"

I shrugged. "Keep writing reports on varnishes and lacquers, I suppose."

I finished off a pickle and waved down the waiter for another couple of beers.

Mike insisted. "Something's worrying you."

"Nothing Oley's cheesecake won't cure."

I flashed a big grin just to reassure him.

"Bet they didn't have cheesecake over there."

"Damn, I missed my cheesecake," I said with brio.

I wasn't the least bit hungry for cheesecake, but I didn't want to admit to Mike what I was really feeling. Which is that I didn't want my days to slide by, each one just like the other, predictable. Sitting on a bench watching the lagoon, waiting for another chance to save another pup from the jaws of death.

When I got home, I called my aunt. It was nine in the evening in Paris.

"I just wanted to say goodnight and to make sure everything's okay."

"La Rue Tonton seems empty without you and Billy."

"Where's Pym?"

"Entertaining."

"Entertaining?"

"He has a new lady friend. She's quite the athletic type. Pym says she's training to swim the English channel."

"Has he made his rum punch for her?"

"She doesn't drink."

"That doesn't sound promising."

"He's become an expert on mixing nonalcoholic drinks. He's crazy about her."

I wanted to tell her I missed la Rue Tonton and the gang. That I missed Paris and her roast chickens. Maybe she knew it, because next she said, "Why don't you come home?"

"I am home."

"This is your home."

"Wouldn't I need some kind of visa?"

"We can work that out."

"A real one. Not one of Van Gogh's fakes."

"I could adopt you."

"That's a little extreme."

"Not really. We *are* blood relatives."

"I like living in a place where everyone speaks English."

"Pym could teach you French."

"No thanks. I'd rather take classes at the Alliance Française."

"That would hurt his feelings, and besides, he's already offered. He was hoping you'd come back."

We spoke for a long while. I told her I'd finally finished *The Master and Margarita*, which she'd slipped into my suitcase before I left for the airport. I pointed out that she'd forgotten to remove the picture of her and Maxim.

"I didn't forget. I wanted you to have it."

I said both of them looked very happy in the photo, all

bundled up in furs and smiling.

"We were. Very cold and very happy."

"Where was it taken?"

"Moscow. I tried to convince him to come back to Paris with me, but he wouldn't. He was arrested right after I left." There was a long silence. "That was the last time I saw him."

"When was that, Aunt Lily?"

"A very long time ago."

"What year."

I waded in to her silence and threw out a date. "Around 1955?"

"That sounds about right."

I said I'd keep the photo safe in the book.

Immediately after hanging up, I went down to the basement where I'd been storing a few boxes of odds and ends I'd kept from my parents' home. Family memories they'd been holding on to, the sort of trivia that had no meaning for anyone except us. After my mother died, I just stashed it all in the garage. When I moved to Florida, I brought it with me thinking one day I'd have the heart to revisit the past.

I switched on the overhead light, slung a box onto the workbench and slit open the packing tape with the idea of looking for anything that might hold a clue to those years and the feud with my aunt. There were a lot of photos, mostly of the three of us, an occasional one of Dad with his chemical engineers and Mom with her garden club, but mostly the three of us. Like I said, we were a tight little tribe, perhaps because we had been so small, and there had been a lot of love.

Other than the photos, all I found was a deed to an old home long since sold, some expired driver's licenses, and my father's university diplomas. There was even a note I'd written to Santa Claus as a five-year-old. But not a stitch of evidence, photo or otherwise, that hinted at the existence of Aunt Lily. I couldn't even find that old wartime photo with her and my parents I had once seen when I was a kid.

Amid the clutter, I'd come across a bundle of old Rolodex cards secured with a rubber band. As I tossed them back into the box, the rotted rubber band snapped and they tumbled to the floor.

When I bent to scoop them up, I noticed that many of them had business cards stapled to them. Cards embossed with an official government logo. One by one, under the light of a naked bulb, I examined the titles below those names: assistant secretaries, undersecretaries, generals and adjoints, directors of offices of the US Air Force and the Department of Defense. Individuals responsible for procurement. Contracts. Research and development.

One thing was obvious: These telephone numbers and addresses had been in frequent use. There were contacts with phone numbers scratched out and new ones penciled in. Business cards annotated in my father's hand.

I took the Rolodex cards upstairs and poured myself a drink. Then I got on the phone to our old law office in California and asked to speak to Dodson. He was on the way out the door to a meeting but had a few minutes to give me. I asked if he knew anything about an old DOD contract with Box Paints. He didn't.

"Me neither," I said. "It was before my time."

"Tim Baker handled your father's account back in those days. I can give him a call. Just had his ninety-fifth birthday but still sharp as a tack."

A week later a heavy manila envelope arrived in the mail. Inside were reams of correspondence, memos and proposals related to a 1952 contract between the Department of Defense and Box Paints and Industrial Coating to develop innovative protective coatings, specifically corrosion-resistant primers for military aircraft.

Then, abruptly, all the business came to a screeching halt with one very formally worded letter from the Assistant Secretary of Defense to my father, president of Box Industrial Coatings, stating that for security reasons they found it necessary to immediately cancel all contracts and announcing that our company would no longer be permitted to do any business with any branch of the United States military or government.

So, my father had once held important military contracts, undoubtedly very lucrative ones. Yet he'd never once mentioned this old business to me, and when on occasion I had suggested it was a market we might want to explore, he had shut me down without explanation.

The timing was the key. I didn't think the Orlando library would be carrying any California periodicals, but that evening I headed down to the main branch to give it a try. Luckily I happened upon one of those librarians who approach their job like a sleuth. Her eyes lit up when I asked if they had past issues of any local California newspapers.

"Santa Ana," I specified. "Or anything in Orange County."

"What years?"

"Nineteen fifty-five."

"I think we can help you with that," she said with the sort of brisk assurance you'd expect from your old local hardware merchant when you ask for an A354 grade BD quarter-inch anchor bolt.

I followed her to a card catalog where she pulled out a drawer and zipped through the cards.

"That was the year Disneyland opened in Anaheim. We get a lot of requests for people doing research papers. Kids really like the topic for school essays. Okay. Here we are," she said as she jotted down a reference for me. "Take that to the microfilm department. Basement level."

And that's how I spent the next few days, hunkered over a microfilm reader perusing every page of the area newspapers from that year, telling myself I was crazy suspicious or just plain crazy. Adrenaline kept me fueled, and coffee, until late on the second day when I finally found it. I had been so convinced my search was fruitless, that I was imagining it all, and then there it was. A very small article in the local Santa Ana newspaper about a local business having been infiltrated by Russian spies. The business was Box Industrial Coatings, a military subcontractor; the spy: Lillian de la Pérouse.

The reporter had misidentified my aunt as a Frenchwoman and had written up the piece in hyperbole with lurid declamations typical of the tabloids; additionally, he had failed to mention her blood ties to my father, the only accurate statement being that she was a card-carrying Communist, which I knew to have been true. Not a single reliable source, not even the *Los Angeles Times*, had picked up the story. It had all the earmarks of a tabloid piece based on rumor and embellished with fiction. The reporter, if you could call him that (I prefer scaremonger), had concluded with the inflammatory suggestion that California should follow the lead of Texas, which had recently proposed the death penalty for members of the Communist Party.

They also misidentified her as being an expectant mother and went on to add that such monsters should be prohibited from having children.

I say "misidentified." Naturally that was my first reaction.

Then I remembered the photo taken that year. The bulk of furs possibly concealing a pregnancy.

I can't recall which shocked me more at the moment, the horrific proposition of sterilizing women based on their politics, or the revelation that Aunt Lily had been expecting a baby. It seemed that part they'd gotten right too.

Nineteen fifty-five. The year the photo was taken.

The year of my birth.

I hightailed it home, settled Billy into the backseat of the car without a word of explanation and drove like a maniac to Epcot. I parked in the employee lot, scooped him up in a football hold and headed out to the lagoon. Night was falling and the air was cooling down, and the visitors were trailing off to the many eateries in the various pavilions. Thankfully, our bench was empty.

That park bench had always been where I'd gone to try to sort through my problems, always with Billy curled silently at my side. I just sat there with him, trying to absorb it all. I must have been in shock, but maybe the truth had been drifting there just under the surface for so long that the shock wasn't all that great. It was more like relief. That the mystery troubling me for months had been revealed.

If my parents had still been alive, perhaps my sense of anger and betrayal would have been greater. But now, with the prism of years messing with my emotions, as years have a way of doing, it was not anger I felt toward them so much as a sense of loss for what might have been; but then again, who was I to say that the "might have been" would have worked out better? From what I knew of my aunt's life, her passionate character and her—impulsive? dedicated? reckless? (all apply)—pursuit of adventures and causes, or to put it simply her passionate pursuit of life in general, she would not have handled motherhood well. At least not under those circumstances. And maybe my parents did know best in concealing the facts of my birth, given all the uncertainties that would have plagued me throughout my life. By demonizing her, they had only done what society would have done in their stead. To know I had a Commie mother off in the Old World, fraternizing with our enemies of the State, maybe even spying for them, would have royally messed with my head. Particularly growing up in conservative Orange County. Knowing everything I now knew about my aunt, it was hard to sit in judgment. I wasn't quite ready to absolve them. But I loved my parents, with a stubborn kind of love like a stain that doesn't wash out. All my parents. All three of them.

I recalled my aunt's plea to "forgive us." And Pym's mysterious advice to play along. That's the secret he was talking about. The secret of my parentage.

I had to decide.

What was I going to do with the truth about Aunt Lily? She called a few nights later.

"I haven't heard from you in a while," she said.

We had taken to dropping short lines to each other on postcards. Mine were from Epcot, hers from all sorts of landmarks around Paris. I called every Sunday. I had missed last Sunday.

"Sorry, Aunt Lily," I said a little too gruffly.

"Is Billy okay? Are you okay?"

"We're fine."

There was an awkward silence. There had never been awkward silences between us. I was afraid she would read my mind. Afraid that she might guess that I knew. I didn't want her to know that I knew. Not yet. Not like this. I fished for something to say and came up with, "Any news of Maxim?"

"I have a new plan."

"I?"

"I. Me. Nobody else. I'm hatching this one all alone."

"Could you use some help?"

The question just tumbled out. I didn't give it a second thought.

"Ah, Carlito, you know how I love it when you do the thinking."

There was another silence, less awkward. A silence of hope. Expectation.

"Oh, and a letter came for you this morning, from Germany. Looks like it's from Greta. I'll forward it to you."

I was sitting on the sofa with my bare feet propped on the coffee table, and the air conditioner humming. Billy was sprawled on the cool tile floor near the kitchen island. I turned to him for advice, but he was sound asleep.

"No," I said after a long pause. "Just hold on to it."

Change has always been hard for me, never having been much of a fly-by-the-seat-of-my-pants sort of guy. I'm very deliberate, and I like to mull around alternatives in my mind. I tell myself it's so I can make the right decisions. But therein lies the difficulty: I think deep down I'm too afraid of making wrong decisions. Before meeting my aunt Lily and the Rue Tonton gang, I always thought there was only right and wrong. I never left much room for the consideration that sometimes you can't see far enough down the road to determine what would end up to be right. Then again, what if "good" doesn't necessarily equal "right"? Maybe I was too young to understand that so much in life is beyond our control, and that the journey is more about navigating the rapids with courage and imagination than charting the smoothest course.

I met Mimi on the bench in front of the lagoon to tell her goodbye. By then I'd already met with Disney's attorneys and negotiated an end to my consulting services. I think they were only too happy to save themselves a few bucks, although they very kindly made a big fuss about my unusual skill set and declared themselves very sad to lose me. I'd also given notice to the rental management company and started getting rid of some of my furniture.

I thought Mimi might want my cacti, but she declined. She would be returning home to Orléans when her visa expired at the end of the year.

"I like your long hairs. Do not cut them."

"Thanks, Mimi. I wasn't planning on it."

I asked her if she would miss Disney and Epcot.

She brushed the last crumbs of a croissant from her hands and thought for a moment. Then she said, with merely a trace of an accent, "I'll miss all the happy people, Monsieur Box."

CHAPTER 38

TWO MONTHS LATER
THE BLACK FOREST, WEST GERMANY

I awoke to the sound of birds in the trees and with Greta in my arms. The easy, gentle rhythm of her soft breathing could have lulled me back to sleep if it weren't for the fact that I'd lost all sensation in my hand. It was impossible to try to worm out of the sleeping bag without waking her, so I just lay there trying to wiggle my fingers and get the blood circulating again. And grinning. Fortunately you can grin big and be preposterously happy without waking anyone. I guessed it to be midmorning since the sun had already warmed our pup tent. The night had been very cold, but then only truly hardy souls camp out in the Black Forest in November, and Greta was one. She'd been surprised to find I was as well. She said I'd surprised her in quite a few ways, except for one. She didn't say which one, but I was getting used to her deadpan delivery of compliments, so I felt relatively sure she was referring to my lovemaking. It was nice to think she hadn't expected me to come up short in that category, even nicer to think that I hadn't disappointed her. On the other hand, she'd been surprised to discover that I could pitch a tent in a matter of minutes, although the thing we were sleeping in didn't require much pitching, and that I could scrounge up good kindling and knew how to build a campfire.

Earlier, while looking for a campsite, we'd come across a very old beech tree. Greta had dropped her pack and marched straight to it like she was greeting an old friend; she'd pressed her palms against the mottled bark and gazed at it as if she were seeing straight into its gnarly old heart, admiring the lines, wrinkles and discoloration that testify to the beauty of its long, enduring life. She didn't say as much, but I think she was speaking to it in her own quirky and spiritual way. We found some soft leafy ground between the sprawling roots and rested for a while with our backs against the cool trunk, listening to the wind in the branches.

In the morning her hair smelled like woodsmoke.

When we got back to our lodge, there was a message from my aunt waiting for us at reception. I'd left her the phone number of Greta's Greenpeace office in Hamburg in case of an emergency, and they'd directed her to the lodge. The message was straightforward. *Call home immediately*, it said.

I returned her call while Greta was in the shower.

"My dear boy, we have just had the most wonderful news—Wilma has come into heat!" she exclaimed breathlessly. "We need to get to Berlin right away. Billy and I are booked on a flight tomorrow and I need you to follow."

There was no Wilma, naturally, although Billy would have been thrilled at the idea of hooking up with a female, champion or no. What Aunt Lily was saying was this: Maxim had made it to East Berlin, and it was time to move into action.

I could hear the excitement in her voice as she instructed us to take the train to Cologne, where we could catch a flight along the central air corridor to West Berlin, one of the few ways to get into a divided city in the midst of Soviet-controlled East Germany.

"Getting across to East Berlin does present a bit of a challenge, but Wilma is a champion show dog, and her owners are very selective. We can't let the wall get in the way. The timing is unfortunate, but you absolutely must be there for dear Billy. We'll meet you at the Hotel Kempinski. I've booked a suite for all of us. Tell Greta to bring something fashionable. West Berlin has a very chic scene."

"We've been camping, Aunt Lily. We brought jeans."

"Remember, the Hotel Kempinski. You must be there by tomorrow evening at the latest. Billy's date is for the day after."

I hung up as Greta came in towel-drying her hair.

I put a finger to my lips. She complied with a nod. A protocol we had established when in the hotel room or any setting that might be bugged.

She listened while I repeated the story my aunt had just given me over the phone. Nice and clear, in case anyone else was listening.

"I'm sorry," I concluded. "Interrupting our holiday like this. But you know how important this is to my aunt. These dog breeders can be so fanatic."

"Of course we'll go," she said, draping the towel over a chair and coming to me with her long tangled strands of wet hair draped over her shoulder like Lady Godiva caught in a rainstorm. She hooked her arms around my neck and with her lips at my ear whispered, "It will be like old times."

"How's that?"

"You racing around on a motorcycle with me on the back, trying to evade the KGB."

She kissed my neck and added very softly, "And you climbing over the horses' heads above the butcher shop to get us into the hotel room. I think that's when I started falling in love with you."

"Are you in love with me?"

She answered with a long kiss.

CHAPTER 39
WEST BERLIN

The skies had turned gray, and coming out of the airport we were met with a light misting of rain. I tried to focus on our plan, although I admit I was still in a rosy daze after Greta's confession of love. As the taxi approached the heart of the city I noted a resemblance to Los Angeles, the glassily modern buildings, the wide streets and lively shopping areas, all the girls with Farrah Fawcett hair. There were no palm trees and the weather was crappy, but other than that, we might have been cruising down Wiltshire Boulevard.

The hotel was lavishly modern, all polished wood and gleaming brass, with a top-hatted doorman who solemnly carried our single grubby bag, and a concierge with starched cuffs who personally escorted us to our suite. A "Do Not Disturb" sign hung on the doorknob. The concierge explained that my aunt had instructed him to let us into the rooms, as she would be napping.

When the door had latched behind him, I motioned to Greta to look around. Billy was gone, and my aunt never napped.

In one of the suite's two bedrooms, we found her suitcase unpacked, her clothes hung in the closet and toiletries in the bathroom. In the other bedroom she had left an envelope propped on the nightstand. Inside was a birthday card with a note saying there was a birthday gift waiting for me at Core Tex in Kreuzberg.

Kreuzberg was another world altogether. A West Berlin neighborhood boxed in on three sides by the wall, my first impression was of ramshackle old buildings, bold graffiti and wildly creative street art. Long-haired guys in jeans and John Lennon glasses lounged on the crumbling steps of abandoned houses, looking defiantly cool. Pot drifted down the street, following the strains of Depeche Mode and Bon Jovi. Small crowds congregated outside Turkish kebab shops.

It was growing dark by the time we found Core Tex, a small record shop with all the earmarks of obsessive hoarding. The place was empty except for a punk rocker behind the counter reading a comic book. The guy pretended like we didn't exist until Greta asked in German if there had recently been a customer by my aunt's description. I figured he must speak a little English, so I added that she left a gift for me. For my birthday. After a few more minutes of pretending like we didn't exist, he said, "When?"

"Today."

"When is your birthday?"

I told him. Without looking up he reached under the counter and pulled out a jewel-cased CD and slid it over the counter to me. Inside I found a note that read, *Go out the back down the alley. Left down the street to the Köfte Haus restaurant on the corner. Give this CD to the waiter.*

The CD was the Police's album *Synchronicity*.

Very appropriate, I thought as I guided Greta by the hand through the dark alley, the lyrics from Sting's hit single running through my mind:

Every breath you take,
Every move you make,
Every bond you break,
Every step you take,
I'll be watching you.

The Turkish meatball place stood at the end of a residential street with a smattering of small run-down shops. It was late afternoon and the only customers were a family with two small children who were settling their bill. When the waiter brought us the menu, I set the CD on the table in plain sight. He took one glance at it, locked the front door, hung out a *"Geschlossen"* sign and disappeared into a room behind the kitchen. A moment later another man appeared, introduced himself as Ahmet, the owner, and motioned for us to follow him.

We were shown into a dimly lit back dining room with pictures of whirling dervishes and colored lights strung along the walls. In the far corner a small black-and-white TV was broadcasting the evening news. The screen cast a flickering light across the faces of a trio of customers who sat in a huddle before the TV, drinking coffee and arguing loudly. Only when I saw Billy trying to wriggle out of her arms did I realize that one of them was my aunt.

"Oh, there you are!" my aunt said as she turned in her chair to set Billy on the floor. "Come here, you two, let me introduce you." There was Ismet, the owner's father, and Mesut, his uncle. They rose from their chairs smiling and pumping our hands.

After a brief exchange, Ahmet led us to a table where the waiter was laying out service for three.

"I've ordered a few of their specialty dishes for you. I'm sure you must be starved. Greta, my dear, how lovely you're looking. Fresh as a rose. I do apologize for spoiling your trip. How was Baden-Baden?"

"There's no need to apologize, madame. I'm glad you wanted me along."

"Well, of course I do, and do call me Lily, for heaven's sake."

At my aunt's insistence, Greta had spent a long weekend with us shortly after my return to Paris. My aunt had put on a rather shocking display of normality. There had been no sudden disappearances, no ruses, no disguises. And not a sign of forgetfulness. (I still wonder if that incident at the train station had been a trick.) My aunt rose early to write, breaking midmorning to walk to the outdoor market, where she routinely annoyed the merchants by inspecting every eggplant and every head of lettuce before making her choice; the afternoons were given to reading and cooking. Now that she had the time, she turned out some extraordinary culinary wonders. Our meals were always taken family style around a dining table laid formally with a white damask cloth and a vase of freshly cut flowers. Eleanor came for coffee and once for dinner. At the table she and my aunt talked only recipes and food. Not one mention of accounts or business. No one broke into the apartment, we had no visits from the police. Pym was away on a weekend tryst with his girlfriend, but he rarely showed his face anyway. Van Gogh came to dinner one night so clean and sharply dressed that Greta hardly recognized him. In short, we gave the appearance of a perfectly ordinary family. I think Greta had been a little disappointed.

Now my aunt placed a folder on the table, explaining that it contained everything I would need to document Billy's cover legend and get us into East Berlin. Registered with the AKC as William the Younger of Epcot, aka Billy the Kid, Billy had once been a European champion until he lost his legs, or so the story went. Worthless as a show dog and abandoned by his owner, I had adopted him. Now, at the invitation of the East German kennel club (correspondence in the file), I was bringing him to Berlin to breed with Wilma, an East German champion in her own right.

I thought it a plausible story. Since losing his legs, Billy may have lost his allure, although not his equipment, and certainly not his zest for life.

"I'm not so sure about this impeccable bloodline bit," I said, looking down at Billy camped on the floor. Although he did look fine. The best I'd ever seen him, to be honest, his ratty fur smoothed into an airy gray fluff, the long silky ears begging to be touched.

I said, "He never liked to be groomed. I don't know how you did it."

"He was no trouble at all. He knew it was important. The trouble was with his papers. Van Gogh had a terrible time authenticating them. Passports and antiques are more his line of work."

She removed a photo from the file.

"This is the man you'll be looking for."

She passed me a black-and-white of an older, less spirited Maxim. The years of prison had stolen his youth, his vigor and some of his hair but not his dimpled smile.

"I wish I could be the one to go," she said.

"Out of the question. It's too risky."

My aunt and Maxim had once been quite well known as a couple. Not exactly Bonnie and Clyde, since they had committed no atrocities, but they were indeed notorious in certain ministries.

"You're an enemy of the State," I reminded her.

"I'm an enemy of many states, the GDR is only one of them."

"How do I cross?"

"If you had diplomatic immunity, you could drive across at Checkpoint Charlie and no one would search the car. But the State Department is not involved. So you'll have to walk across, and you'll be searched."

"But not Billy."

"That's right. Rolled up very tightly in the crossbar of his wheels we've hidden a French passport with a day visa stamped with tomorrow's date, showing Maxim entered West Berlin in the morning. Maxim must exit tomorrow. The visa is good for one day only."

"Where will I find him?"

"The office of a veterinarian in Mitte. The address is in the folder. You'll be able to find a taxi after you cross to the East. You take Billy and sit in the reception area. Maxim will be there. You will take a seat next to him and start up a conversation. The script is all here in the file. When the vet comes out, you will ask Maxim to come in with you, to translate."

I took a hard look at the grainy photo. "I'm not sure I'd recognize him."

"He will recognize you, my dear."

"Well, of course he will," I said after a moment's reflection. "I'm the one with the dog on wheels."

"He would recognize you even without a dog on wheels."

She closed the folder and slipped it back into her bag. There was great relief in the sigh that escaped her.

She said, "He's made it all the way across Russia and Poland to Germany—a terribly risky journey. This is the last leg. The last few steps. If we can just get him to West Berlin. To this side of the wall."

Ahmet treated us to a banquet of Turkish dishes that evening, none of which I could pronounce but all of which will linger on in my memory as some of the tastiest dishes I have ever eaten. After dinner we took a walk along the residential backstreets that ran along the wall. It was a cold night and a dreary place for an evening stroll—broken cobblestone lanes, pavement patched with tar, potholes filled with rain-sodden leaves. I wondered about the people who lived here, who came in and out of those run-down buildings every day, opening the door onto that wall in the morning, turning the corner and heading to work in a free Berlin, an isolated island in the heart of a distinctly unfree nation, getting far enough away to forget about it, until you came home and there it was, still standing, smeared with graffiti, angry and defiant and boldly colorful. In daylight it might have been tolerable, but at this hour it was unbearably sad. Even Billy seemed spooked. I'm sure he could smell the dogs on the other side, and the fear thick as the fog that hung over that stretch of cement they called the death strip.

Maxim was over there, somewhere on the other side. Maxim, my aunt's great love. The man I was tasked to bring home.

Lily was not one for great displays of affection, but at that moment I felt she needed a gesture of reassurance as much as I did, so I put my arm around her and hugged her close. Greta stepped up to link my aunt's free arm in hers, and together the three of us walked along in heavy silence, with only the sound of cobblestones underfoot.

We came upon a narrow plank propped against the wall, with one end wedged between the cement blocks. Put there for the curious West Berliners, my aunt explained, to peer over the wall through the barbed wire to the other side.

"Go take a look," she said. "You should get a feel for it before tomorrow."

I reached the top as a crow passed overhead on its way into the glare of arc lights, trailing a burst of hoarse caws before it was swallowed up by silence in the East. On the other side, the beams from searchlights just touched the wall and penetrated no farther, lighting the sky with an unnatural glow; the streets beyond the death strip were empty, the buildings quiet with boarded-up windows and empty doorways. Over there in the darkness beyond the lights, I imagined a woman feeding soup to a child, a boy nodding off over his schoolwork, a man writing a sonnet. I tried to imagine Maxim waiting for the night to pass. Waiting for his freedom and to be reunited with his family. Waiting to meet the son he'd never seen. I wondered if he was afraid.

From the tower a border guard watched me through his binoculars.

We heard about the televised news conference when we went back to Köfte Haus to retrieve my aunt's gloves. A small crowd had already gathered in the back room of Ahmet's restaurant, and there was a lot of excitement and shouting going on; Ismet and Mesut were fighting over which television channel they should tune in to. Something momentous had just been announced, but there seemed to be a lot of confusion as to what exactly it meant.

Apparently at the very moment when I had been peering over the wall, only a few miles from me, in the direction the crow had flown, journalists were rushing out of the press conference and racing to phone booths to report that the new travel law had lifted restrictions between East and West Berlin.

But what did that mean? Was the Berlin Wall coming down?

For months tensions had been high all across East Germany, with massive demonstrations in Leipzig and East Berlin demanding freedom to travel to the West. Some Warsaw Pact countries like Hungary and Poland had welcomed Gorbachev's reforms, but the German Democratic Republic wanted nothing to do with glasnost. When Hungary started tearing down its border fortifications and sending the Soviet troops home, the GDR simply made a new law prohibiting transit to Hungary.

With Hungary no longer a travel option, the East Germans continued to flee to Czechoslovakia, tens of thousands of them, hoping either to emigrate to the West or make their way back into West Germany. For months now the Czech leaders had gone along with the East German demand to send the stragglers right back where they came from, but now the Czechs had had enough. Rumor was that the grounds of the West German Embassy in Prague had become a campground for East German refugees, and the same was going on in Hungary and Poland. So the GDR asked their Czech neighbors to shuttle the fleeing East Germans into cattle cars and send them back to an East German border town by train, where they would be processed, stripped of their nationality and property, then sent off to enjoy their new lives of freedom and statelessness in the West.

The situation was dissolving into a bureaucratic and national security nightmare.

Everybody knew something had to give. It couldn't go on like this. The GDR had to permit some sort of controlled opening with the West, a safety valve to let off pressure.

Then had come the press conference, with reporters from all over Europe and even an American TV network, all of them anticipating something newsworthy.

Greta translated while Ahmet explained what they'd just watched on television, how the press conference had gone along perfectly boringly, until a Western journalist had asked about travel.

Just then Ismet and Mesut called for quiet. Having earlier set up their VCR to tape an episode of *Star Trek*, it seemed they had inadvertently taped the press conference instead. So, for the benefit of their friends who had missed it, and to settle any arguments as to just what had been announced, they would replay it.

More arguing erupted—it seemed nobody wanted to sit through the whole boring thing again. Mesut didn't want to fast-forward it because he was afraid the tape would get tangled up, which it often did, but the mood of the crowd prevailed and he eventually found the point in the tape when the foreign reporter asked about travel.

As he hit Play, the room grew quiet. I glanced at the faces around me—my aunt, Greta, the Turks—everyone rapt and attentive in the cold white light as they listened to the announcement, and my thoughts flew back to that moment in Orlando when I had to decide if I was going to continue with my life of varnishes and Hex codes, or cross the border into my aunt's world which I had so briefly inhabited as a tourist. Now here I was, surrounded by foreignness, by languages I couldn't comprehend, witnessing a monumental event that promised to turn the old-world order on its head. I had shed my past life like an old skin. I had never felt so alive as I did at that moment.

Watching the tape, even without understanding German, I could see how flustered the East German spokesman was. With everyone shouting questions as if they expected him to know the answers. It was painful to see him fumble around, looking through his papers for the report, shuffling files on the table in front of him, growing more rattled and embarrassed by the second. Trying to calm down all those unruly Westerners bombarding him with questions.

Finally an aide slipped the report under his nose and he began reading it to the reporters, but there were so many questions being shouted at him that he gave up and began scanning it for answers.

"When? When does the new travel law go into effect?"

He flipped through the pages. "Right away," he said incredulously.

"Does the ruling apply to West Berlin?"

Running his finger down the page, "Yes," he replied. Although that seemed to surprise him as well.

"And the Berlin Wall?"

That was a loaded question. He didn't dare attempt an answer. He abruptly called an end to the press conference and made a hasty exit.

Mesut stopped the tape and the arguments around us rose again. My aunt explained that the confusion had to do with temporary travel: It was clear that passports and visas would still be required if you wanted to emigrate, but emigration was a drastic and irreversible decision. You would never be allowed to return. But what about a day trip? What if you just wanted to come over to West Berlin and have a beer with your good pal Günter, who did really cheap dental work, or get your hands on a Mr. Coffee drip coffeemaker, which were impossible to find in East Berlin?

What if you wanted to bring your father home?

One thing everyone agreed on was this: The new travel rules went into effect *immediately*.

Now, this very moment.

Mesut squeezed his way across the room to tell Ahmet he'd just had a call from a friend who ran a meatball place on the other side of town.

"There's already a crowd gathered at the Bornholmer Strasse crossing," my aunt said. "They're shouting for the guards to open the gate."

CHAPTER 40

By now the room had grown unbearably stuffy and crowded. All the men were smoking cigarettes and talking loudly, and the women, most of them veiled, were sitting around in their own tight little groups eating sunflower seeds and spitting the shells on the floor. Someone had turned on the strings of colored lights and there was Turkish music playing in the background. The atmosphere had all the earmarks of a big family celebration.

Lily seemed stunned.

I found an empty chair and urged her to sit down. She kept a tight hold on the bag on her knees, although she must have realized that the carefully prepared documents inside might now be worthless.

She looked up at me, her eyes full of concern. "The circumstances have altered considerably, Carl. It's not safe for you to go."

I tried to reassure her. "Don't you worry about me. Maxim will show up, and Billy and I will be there to deliver the passport. It's a good cover story. It will work."

"There's no telling what will happen next. The situation

may turn violent. The State could bring in tanks tomorrow. Even if they don't, trying to cross into East Berlin will be like paddling up the rapids."

"Nevertheless, we'll follow the plan."

The plan was for my aunt and Greta to wait out the day in the Café Adler just next to Checkpoint Charlie, where I would cross into East Berlin. After delivering the passport, I would meet them back at the café. We would then watch for Maxim, in possession of his French passport, to exit through Checkpoint Charlie.

The last thing we wanted was to go back to our hotel and wait for morning. So we decided to decamp to the Café Adler, where we could more easily follow unfolding events. Ahmet rounded up a cousin in the crowd who owned a taxi and agreed to drive us there.

The mythic Checkpoint Charlie turned out to be nothing more than a long metal structure dropped in the middle of the street. It looked like the temporary prefab offices you see on a construction site—the sort of thing that would be here today and gone tomorrow. The Café Adler sat on the corner right next to the checkpoint, making it an ideal place for foreign journalists to meet with East German dissidents fleeing to the West. A place to exchange contacts and addresses. A place for spies to spy on one another. "A little like American Express on the Rue Scribe used to be in Paris," my aunt said breezily as we walked in, and once again I marveled at her self-assurance, how she managed to adapt to the moment like a woman at home anywhere in the world. The café, all dark wood and mirrors, was crowded and very noisy, and only slightly less smoke-filled than the Köfte Haus. We found a table against the back wall, where my aunt and Greta squeezed in together on the green velvet banquette and I pulled up a chair.

I noted that I hadn't seen many people on the other side of the checkpoint when we arrived.

"Only foreigners and Allied military can cross here. The Berliners will be at Bornholmer Strasse." She spoke with a faint air of dejection, like a girl who'd somehow been left off the invitation list of a society ball.

Fortunately, the man at the next table turned out to be an Italian photojournalist who was more than happy to fill us in on recent events. He said that when the café owner had heard the announcement over his radio, seized by the euphoria of the moment, he and several lightly intoxicated friends had marched across the tracks with a bottle of bubbly and a tray of glasses to offer to the East German guards at the gate. They popped open the bottle and poured the glasses there on the spot, ready to toast to brotherly love and peace and openness, but the guards were nervous—fraternizing was out of the question, the enemy was still the enemy. They had gruffly refused the gesture and told them to take their bubbly back to the café. They didn't seem to think there was anything to celebrate.

Nevertheless, hope hung as thick in the air as cigarette smoke. To kill the hours until morning, my aunt ordered a bottle of French champagne. She wouldn't consider drinking anything else.

"And put aside a second bottle," she said as the waiter popped the cork. "For Maxim. When tomorrow comes."

The Italian at the next table joined us for a glass, professing to like champagne even more than prosecco, which instantly endeared him to my aunt. We soon learned that he had worked briefly as a fashion photographer in Paris during the early fifties and claimed to have heard about the incident when the famous Dior model by the name of Lily had been abducted from the Place Vendôme by a prince on a motor scooter.

"He was merely a viscount," my aunt corrected gently.

And then there was the incident in the Rue Lepic.

"Ah, yes, but that was much earlier. Maxim and I had just met—"

My aunt was a legend, the photographer said, turning to us, and he seemed genuinely awed to have met her. The fellow had all the charm of his race, flirtatiously admiring my aunt's beauty and praising her Italian, and sincerely regretted that he could not stay. He finished off his champagne, rose, took my aunt's hand and brought it tantalizingly close to his lips. Then, hefting his camera bag over his shoulder, he hurried off in search of some action, leaving a trail of softly fading *Ciao, ciao, caio*s in his wake. She watched him go with a look of regret, as if she'd had a fleeting encounter with her past, and then it had flown.

"Tell us about Paris back then," Greta said.

"Oh, goodness, not now."

"Why not? We have all night ahead of us," I interjected. "What's this story about the Rue Lepic?"

"Paris must have been quite wonderful," Greta added.

"Quite the contrary," my aunt said, settling into the story and the champagne. "Paris after the war was a dismal place and very difficult to reconcile for someone like me, coming from a country that had not suffered a foreign war on their own soil for hundreds of years. There was so much distress and hardship and shame, and at the same time there was so much money."

The classes were starkly divided, she explained. You had the wealthy French and diplomats and the international set breezing into the restaurants in their furs and jewels, and in the working class districts less than a mile away you had old people starving to death. There were electrical shortages and no coal for heating, and food was rationed unless you were rich, and then you could get whatever you wanted on the black market.

"It all came home to me one day when we were doing a photo shoot in the market in Rue Lepic. They dressed me in the back of a shop, and I came swishing out in my wide skirt—there I was, prancing around in all my haute couture glory while these impoverished vendors looked on from their makeshift stalls and their meager piles of beets and cabbages and onions, and suddenly this girl—she couldn't have been much older than me—came screeching at me and started ripping off my clothes, and before you knew it all the vendors were in an uproar. Other girls came at me—some of the vendors tried to hold them back, but most just looked on with this hard spiteful look I shall never forget. Well, within minutes we were all packed up and out of there. I had some bad scratches, and even teeth marks on my arm where one poor child launched herself at me like a cannibal after a long fast. It was terrifying. The dress was ripped to shreds. I braved it out the rest of the day, very stoic and prepossessed, although my face was too badly scratched for me to work, and I lost a week's wages. That night I told Maxim about the incident. He could have said, *That's what happens when the rich are ugly rich and the poor are ugly desperate*, but he just bathed my scratched face and kissed away my tears and restrained, for that night at least, from lecturing me on the nefarious consequences of unbridled capitalism.

"The thing was, haute couture helped put the French economy back on its feet after the war. Dior offered jobs to us. We got warm meals and beer and wine at the canteen. For some of these poor girls, it was the only meal they got. Some of them were so scrawny and underfed, and I felt bad because I felt like there was probably another girl out there who was a lot hungrier than I was. But it was a good job and the clothes—well, who would give up a chance like that? The clothes were extraordinary. I'd argue that point with Maxim, how entrepreneurial men and women created jobs and fed people—there were so many skilled workers begging for a chance to make and do, lacemakers, seamstresses, cutters, *les petites mains* who work with beading, rhinestones and sequins. We need capital investment, I'd say, but—well, capitalism was always a hard sell with Maxim.

"Our debates could get very intense, and eventually we'd rise to the most absurd claims that neither of us believed, but it was always as if we were one individual arguing with himself, and we would finally hush each other up with kisses or wine. He had a remarkable ability to laugh. How I miss that laugh of his."

Here my aunt faltered. She had enormous energy for a woman her age, but anxiety and fatigue were catching up with her. Helped along by the champagne. She glanced at the clock over the bar.

"How slowly the minutes pass when you are counting them," she sighed.

The atmosphere in the café was electric, with people constantly coming in and out to use the phone or to ask for news from the other crossings; there was a long line at the pay phone on the wall next to the bathrooms, and the phone behind the bar was ringing off the hook. The waiters were racing around delivering news while trying to keep up with their service. Apparently the crowd at Bornholmer Strasse across town had grown into the thousands, and they were chanting to open the gate. Outside the Café Adler, the crowd was beginning to grow.

"Why don't you go back to the hotel and rest," Greta said. "We can call you if anything happens."

"Oh, no," Aunt Lily said, shaking her head. "We'll stay right here. All of us, together. Tomorrow morning very early, if it's safe, Carl, you and Billy will cross into Berlin. You'll go straight to the address in Mitte, you'll deliver the passport."

My aunt glanced down, looking for Billy.

"Where are the wheels?" she said nervously.

"Right here," I said. I'd removed them earlier to make Billy more comfortable and set them on a chair beside me.

"Where's Billy?" Greta said.

"Saving up his energy for the big moment, I imagine," I said as I bent down and looked under the table.

"Where'd he go?" I asked.

"Isn't he there?"

Greta leaned down and looked.

"What? Billy's gone?"

All three of us peered under the table. No dog, just us.

"Billy?" my aunt called. "Billy!"

Billy never failed to respond to her voice.

I was on my feet now, checking around the neighboring tables.

"A dog, have you seen a dog? *Hund?*"

"He couldn't have gone far, not without his wheels," Greta said.

But he could. He was admirably swift when he wished to be.

Just then someone jumped up on a chair and made an excited announcement; they had just heard on the radio that all GDR checkpoints were open and police officers were instructed to issue visas immediately. There was another rush to the pay phone at the back.

"They're calling their friends in the East," Greta said. "To tell them that they need to get themselves to a police station."

"It won't help Maxim," my aunt said. "If he went to a police station and showed his papers they'd arrest him. He needs that passport."

It went without saying: We couldn't get the wheels across without Billy to pull them. No Billy, no wheels. Our superspy had slipped away.

I jumped up and started pulling on my coat.

"Stay here," I said to Greta. "I'll go look for Billy."

"Greta, go with him," my aunt said. "He'll need someone who speaks German."

"He couldn't have gone far."

"Ha," I said. "You don't know Billy."

"Unless someone took him."

"Why on earth would anyone steal a two-legged dog?"

I didn't bother trying to answer that one. We had to find him. No telling how long he'd been gone.

The crowd outside had grown so dense we could hardly move, and we had no idea where to look. On our side of the checkpoint the road was unobstructed, with only a crossing barrier to be lifted, but on the East side the Berlin Wall stretched across the road, with only a single entry lane for cars and a narrow pedestrian entrance.

West German guards had lined up across the road to hold back crowds from the West, and to make sure no one ventured to the East and got shot by some trigger-happy Stasi officer. They were armed with pistols and machine guns, and they had liberty to shoot, but they'd removed their military headgear and didn't seem the least bit threatening; some eager West Berliners had already moved past their line and across the transit area and were beginning to mass at the foot of the wall, shouting to the guards on the other side. Calling to their fellow Germans gathering on the other side. Behind us on Friedrichstrasse, people were standing on top of cars to see over the wall. The Checkpoint Charlie guardhouse was completely engulfed by bodies.

With a tight grip on Greta's hand I started inching my way through the crowd, hoping I wouldn't find Billy squashed underfoot. As we pushed forward, calling his name, I surveyed the grassy stretch of no-man's-land, hoping to God he wasn't nosing around out there, where he'd certainly get blown up by a mine.

About that time there was a roar from beyond the wall, a cry went up, and the first individuals trickled in through the pedestrian lane, walking cautiously toward us, a little stunned, still in disbelief. A cheer rose up as the first car came through from the East, sputtering across the transit area to the delirious delight of the crowd; it was like a parade, slow at first, then growing, and pretty soon you could see faces peering over the wall from the other side, and the chanting began, "Open the gates! Open the gates!"

Greta was in tears, and I kissed her madly, I kissed all the girls around me, I hugged a man in uniform, I think it was a West German uniform but who gave a damn, he was crying, tears streaming down his face, and he hugged me and sobbed. I've never seen a man cry so hard. Somewhere behind us somebody had set up some loudspeakers and music was blaring out over the bouncing, jubilant crowd intoxicated by the spectacle of what we were witnessing. I cursed Billy under my breath for disappearing on such a momentous occasion.

"We gotta find that damn dog," I said to Greta, and she wiped a tear from her face and said, "Lead the way."

We searched the area for over an hour, through the wildly euphoric crowd, down Friedrichstrasse, all along Zimmerstrasse, making sure to cover every patch of grass, every shop that was still open, stopping anyone with a dog to ask if they'd seen him.

"Helluva night to lose a dog," one guy replied in English.

After an hour, we headed back to the Café Adler, hoping he might have made his way back to us. Unsurprisingly, my aunt hadn't wasted time making new friends. A stranger was seated at her table with his back to me.

My aunt saw us and waved; her companion pushed back his chair and rose.

He was much taller than I had imagined him, and even more gaunt than in the photo. He smiled, and there they were, those dimples, oddly incongruous on a man his age. Dimples just like mine.

"Look, Carlito, we found him," my aunt said as she waved us over. It took a moment for me to realize she wasn't talking about Maxim but about Billy, who was sitting on her lap and looking not at all like he'd just ruined the most momentous night of my life.

"A beggar had him. Right here at the entrance to the café," my aunt explained as we pulled up chairs. "The poor man was very sad to give him up. He said Billy had been quite good for business." She gave Billy a solid pat on his head that carried just a hint of a reprimand. "Such a scene stealer, this dog. Maxim recognized him right away. After all, how many two-legged dogs would you find waiting at Checkpoint Charlie?"

"Good lord," I mumbled in disbelief.

Maxim was still standing, beaming at me with a smile that pulled me right in, and then he reached for me and held me in a viselike grip. My aunt looked on with a smile of smug contentment.

He gave Greta a hug as well, although it was a gentler squeeze.

Maxim raised an arm and the waiter hurried over. From the very first glimpse, I was awestruck. It was more than just Maxim's size that drew your attention, it was his entire presence, the way he commanded a room, you knew he wasn't an ordinary guy.

The waiter hurried off and Maxim sat down with us, still beaming.

"I have ordered champagne and whatever food they have," he said with only a trace of an accent, "although I don't think there are any oysters. Oysters and champagne always make a party, do they not, Lily?"

Aunt Lily just went right on beaming. She had freshened her makeup and tidied up her hair. She had the look of a starry-eyed teenager.

"My wife is always happy when there's a party."

"Your wife?"

"We will marry as soon as the papers can be arranged. I insisted it be a legal marriage, none of the fake stuff this Van Gogh is so good at doing."

The tone of jealousy was unmistakable, and I thought it remarkable that after all these years he could be jealous of my aunt's past.

"We will be married in the American Cathedral."

I did my best to conceal my surprise. I glanced at my aunt, but her eyes were fixed on the man at her side.

"It will be a quiet wedding, family only," Maxim continued.

I wondered if family would include Pym. I wondered what Maxim would say when he learned of his brother's perfidies. But Pym's betrayal would be dealt with later. I was taking in this myth of a man who had been such an influence on my aunt. And now on me. I looked for a resemblance to Pym and found none, to my relief. They were only half brothers, after all.

Maxim was a far cry from handsome, but he definitely had what you'd call charisma. He projected something solid, a bit like that wall that stood just across the road, but in a good way. The kind of man who wouldn't be shaken. I couldn't begin to imagine all that he'd been through as a dissident and a writer, surviving the gulag, prison and torture. But I could see how he would inspire admiration.

I noticed his jaw was whistle smooth—there was even a tiny cut on his chin where he had nicked himself shaving. He must have determined to cross as soon as he'd heard the news. And he'd taken the time to shave.

My aunt couldn't take her eyes off him.

Over champagne and oysters, he told us about his transit from Russia through Poland to Berlin, and at one point she reached up and lightly touched his hair as if she were stroking something of great value. After more than thirty years of separation, there wasn't the slightest awkward gesture, not a hint of doubt or discomfort. You looked at them and saw an old couple, content and still crazy in love. Together they struck me as terribly ill-suited for the world, yet oddly perfect for each other. Two lovers who refused to allow the ideological to crush the personal.

Maxim was saying, "Am I too old to start again? I thought so, but the closer I drew to Paris and your aunt—"

I corrected him. "My mother."

I don't know what got into me. Was it the sheer momentousness of the occasion? The jubilation pinging off the walls like a pinball machine in the hands of an adrenalated teenager? Was it seeing them together and witnessing the spectacle of a rare and timeless love? Or was it the gut-level assurance, here at last, that these two were my blood parents.

Both of them leveled the same startled gaze at me. It was surprising how in tune they were, even after so many years of separation.

"We've started the adoption process," I rushed to say to Maxim. "It's about time I get into the habit, don't you think?"

My aunt—or I should say, my mother—had not yet confided in me, but she knew that I knew, and until she was comfortable confiding what must have been a very painful story, I was content to wait. With time she would learn that I would neither judge her nor revile her for her choices. I think she already knew I loved her, and I knew she loved me.

She reached for my hand and squeezed it. "Yes, Mother will do fine."

Maxim twinkled his gray eyes at me and said, "Excellent! Excellent!"

My mother gave him another of her starry-eyed looks and said, "I'm so glad you are here. I shall be quite content with a spell of family life."

It was Greta who noticed the café was emptying out.

"They're going to the Brandenburg Gate," Maxim said. "That's where the cameras will be. You must go. You must follow the action."

It was my mother's idea to get a photo of us before we left, and while Greta was explaining to the guy at the next table how to focus her Canon SLR, I slipped onto the bench beside my mother and pulled the chair around for Greta. Maxim moved in closer on the other side, and Greta slipped in under my arm. Our photographer got off several shots, but he was pretty drunk and not too steady on his feet, so after he'd finished, Greta insisted on taking a few more, of just my mother and Maxim and me.

"So here we are," my mother said as Greta focused the lens on us. "The first family photo."

"Not the first," Maxim said.

My mother smiled coyly. "But the first he would remember."

I'm not sure if Greta overheard. I think she did. Because for a moment she lowered her camera and, taking in the three of us huddled together, a smile spread over her face. She lit up, I'd say. Like someone had just turned on a light and she could now see clearly. I didn't mention it to her as we left, there was a lot going on that night, but I was pretty sure she got the picture.

The world's best party was going on at the Brandenburg Gate. NBC had set up floodlights and Tom Brokaw was just getting ready to do a live broadcast of the event on the *Nightly News*. We braved our way to the front, and after a lot of excited shouting and a few swigs of the beer that was being passed around, Greta and I made it up on top of the wall. This section of wall had been built a whopping three meters wide—the Soviets had been convinced that the Western allies would come crashing through with their tanks—so you could move around on it like a stage; that night it became a platform for unity. There was no checkpoint crossing here, but that hadn't stopped the crowds from forming down the wide boulevard on the other side. They could see those of us on top of the wall and were waving to us, and the crowds on both sides kept growing. Even when the East German guards turned on the water cannons and tried to force us off the wall with the powerful spray, we stood our ground. I certainly had no great role to play in the grand scheme of history, but that night, deliriously happy and drunk with danger and action, dancing with Greta atop the Berlin Wall while we were being doused with freezing cold water felt nonetheless heroic. Looking around at all those crowds of Germans now extending for miles on each side of that wall, many of them separated for so long from their families, just as I had been separated from mine, we were all celebrating coming together again. A great big family reunion.

Mike told me later he'd spotted me on the *Nightly News*. He said the effect of the lights shimmering off the spray was nothing short of spectacular.

I hear there are videos circulating of that moment, with Tom Brokaw reporting and a crazy guy in the background getting drenched with a firehose. If you ever come across any, that's me, Carl Box—ex-paint and varnish consultant formerly of Orlando, Florida—dancing on the wall.

THE END

AUTHOR'S NOTE

This novel was inspired in part by the true story of Vasily Mitrokhin, a KGB archivist who, over a period of twelve years, systematically hand-copied masses of KGB archival material and concealed the scraps of paper in his shoes to get past the nightly security checks. Working from his dacha outside of Moscow, he transcribed the notes and hid them in milk containers, which he then buried in the garden or under the floorboards of his house.

After the collapse of the Soviet Union in 1991, Mitrokhin approached MI6, which unlike the CIA recognized the value of such intelligence. The British immediately spirited Mitrokhin and his wife to the UK and dispatched agents to dig up the documents, which filled six trunks.

The FBI later described Mitrokhin's contribution as "the most complete and extensive intelligence ever received from any source." In a 1999 interview with the BBC, Mitrokhin said, "I wanted to show the tremendous efforts of this machine of evil, and I wanted to demonstrate what happens when the foundations of conscience are trampled on and when moral principles are forgotten. I regarded this as my duty as a Russian patriot." In 2000, Mitrokhin died of pneumonia at age 81.

The term *samizdat* ("self-published") can be defined as the grassroots creation and distribution of censored or underground material. The Soviet Russian human rights activist and writer Vladimir Bukovsky (who served as an inspiration for Maxim in the novel) defined it thusly: "Samizdat: I write it myself, edit it myself, censor it myself, publish it myself, distribute it myself, and spend jail time for it myself." The danger arose in copying and distributing *samizdat* to others. If typewritten, the material could be traced back to the author since personal typewriters had to be registered with the state. Backup copies were occasionally made on microfilm, which was smuggled out for publication before being smuggled back in.

> For additional information, readers can consult the following article on the BBC website. Benjamin Ramm, *The writers who defied Soviet censors*, July 24, 2017 https://www.bbc.com/culture/article/20170724-the-writers-who-defied-soviet-censors

ACKNOWLEDGMENTS

I am profoundly grateful to the three readers who, over the years, I've trusted for their unbiased and constructive feedback: Debra Schwemmer, Sue Dondlinger and Joanne Applegate. Thank you, ladies, for your ongoing support, and for confirming that I can be amusing in print as well as in person.

I am also grateful to Mary Lynn Walker, Phyllis Robertson, Jackie Smith and Diane Johnson, who took the time to read a later version of the manuscript and share their insights with me. My sincere thanks to Claire Brown for her stunning cover design, to Nora Bellot for her excellent editorial notes, and last but not least, to Laura Apgar, who ushered the novel to its final version, and whose collaboration has been invaluable to me.

ABOUT THE AUTHOR

Janice Graham was raised in Kansas and obtained her M.A. in French literature at the University of Kansas before pursuing graduate film studies at USC and English literature at UCLA in Los Angeles, California. Her screenplay *Until September*, a romantic comedy situated in Paris, was picked up by MGM and made into a feature film starring Karen Allen and Thierry Lhermitte. Her first novel, *Firebird*, became a *New York Times* and international bestseller. After a series of contemporary women's fiction, she turned to historical fiction—first with *The Tailor's Daughter* and then with *Romancing Miss Brontë*, her critically acclaimed novel about Charlotte Brontë, which she penned as Juliet Gael. She has lived in Florence, Athens and Jerusalem, and now makes her home in Paris.

> Visit her at www.janicegraham.com
> or on Facebook at Janice Graham Author.

A CONVERSATION WITH JANICE GRAHAM

The book does a beautiful job of evoking Paris. Could you please tell readers about your relationship to the city?

My attachment to Paris goes way back. I first came here when I was studying for my M.A. in French literature, and I've lived here on an off over the years. With the exception of *Romancing Miss Brontë*, all my novels have a connection to Paris. When I started *Red Lily*, I had just moved back after a long absence, and I was rediscovering the city all over again. The aroma of freshly baked bread, the many florists, the dazzling lights at night, everything about the city felt new and exciting. Then came COVID lockdown, and writing the novel enabled me to take myself on imaginary tours of the city. It was a great ride.

The novel takes place throughout the summer and fall of 1989. Why did you choose this particular time period?

The novel explores the themes of discovery and reconciliation, how families—like regimes—demonize outliers, and what it takes to bring them together again. The fall of the Berlin Wall in November of 1989 was the beginning of the collapse of the Soviet Union and the end of the Cold War. This was a momentous turning point in history, a period when hard-line attitudes toward old enemies began to soften, when families separated by a divided Germany were reunited. Many younger readers are unfamiliar with these events and the hope they brought to people who had lived for generations under repressive authoritarian regimes. It's history that deserves our attention, particularly in light of the rise of authoritarianism in the world today.

There was also a good element of nostalgia involved in writing about that period; it enabled me to escape to a time when life was less fraught with the anxieties that hang over us today.

Your previous novels have been contemporary women's fiction or nineteenth-century historical fiction. *Red Lily* blends action, suspense and spies with a story about family secrets. It defies easy categorization. What drew you to these elements?

I wanted to write a story about a woman who had been unjustly maligned by her family. To reveal her through the eyes of a young relative who had been told malicious lies about her. I also enjoy espionage, in both novels and film. Graham Greene has long been one of my favorite authors, not only for his espionage titles, but also for his "entertainments" like *Travels with My Aunt* and *Our Man in Havana*.

I think my fascination with spies can be traced back to my experience working for an American entrepreneur in Paris in the 1970s. He negotiated major deals between Western corporations and Soviet ministries and got them financed by prestigious French private equity firms. If you wanted to do business with the Russians, you had to have the right connections, and my boss had those connections. He was one of the rare Americans who had a permanent visa to the Soviet Union. His secretary and I used to joke that we were working for a spy: decades later, we discovered it to be true. He died in a hotel room in Paris under mysterious circumstances. Julius Hamm's character is loosely based on him. I was very fond of him and close to his family—he was the first person who ever encouraged me to write.

All those influences made their way into *Red Lily*. I didn't set out to write in a particular genre, but to tell a good story and create entertaining characters.

The humor is also something that's new for you. What made you turn from drama to humor?

COVID was not a funny time, so I wrote characters and situations that made me laugh. I've always enjoyed making people laugh. The humor just came naturally. I think it's the most authentic voice-driven narrative I've written.

Was Lily's character drawn from anyone in particular?

As I mentioned in my notes, the Mitrokhin files inspired the plot, but the human story was inspired by an aunt of mine. She wasn't anything like Lily–she could be pretty awful at times–but she was also adventurous and fiercely independent, which was unusual for her time. I admired her. I always thought she was unfairly demonized by our family and I wanted to give her a voice.

RED LILY
READING GROUP QUESTIONS

1. When the novel begins, Carl has no interest in travel, but he soon finds himself forced to navigate dangerous situations in a foreign culture and a foreign language. Have you ever considered living abroad? Where would you go? What challenges would you expect to face?

2. How does Paris shape Carl's choices and his transformation? What about his circumstances make him open to change? Do you think people find it easier to reinvent themselves in a foreign country?

3. Carl doesn't put up much resistance to his aunt's schemes. Why do you think this is so? What does this say about his character? What about his aunt's life appeals to him? Would you take these kinds of risks under similar circumstances?

4. Carl discovers that everything he had been led to believe about his aunt was entirely false. Do you know of any situations where family or friends have been falsely misrepresented because of personal jealousies or grudges? Have you ever been forced to rethink your opinion of someone when faced with truths that contradict your beliefs?

5. There have been notable crime novels and TV series featuring amateur older female sleuths, such as Jessica Fletcher in *Murder, She Wrote* and Agatha Christie's Miss Marple. Although Lily isn't solving a murder, she is on a high-stakes

mission that takes her into the dangerous world of espionage. How does Lily's character fit into these traditional depictions of female sleuths and spies? Do her amateur status and her age allow her to be more effective or are they obstacles to her mission?

6. There are historical elements and events that play a major role in the novel, such as the impact of the polio vaccine and the fall of the Berlin Wall. How has the novel changed your appreciation of this period of history?

7. What do you think about Carl's decision to keep Lily's secret? Would you have made the same choice? Do you think Lily's silence was justified?